THERE
YOU ARE

Mathea Morais

THERE
YOU ARE

AMBERJACK
PUBLISHING

AMBERJACK
PUBLISHING

Amberjack Publishing
1472 E. Iron Eagle Drive
Eagle, ID 83616
amberjackpublishing.com

10 9 8 7 6 5 4 3 2 1

Book design by Pauline Neuwirth, Neuwirth & Associates.

Library of Congress Cataloging-in-Publication Data

Names: Morais, Mathea, author.
Title: There you are / Mathea Morais.
Description: Idaho : Amberjack Publishing, [2019]
Identifiers: LCCN 2019018596 (print) | LCCN 2019019373 (ebook) | ISBN
9781948705592 (ebook) | ISBN 9781948705585 (hardback)
Subjects: LCSH: Black lives matter movement–Fiction. | Saint Louis (Mo.)–Fiction. |
BISAC: FICTION / African American / Urban Life. | FICTION / Literary. | GSAFD:
Love stories.
Classification: LCC PS3613.O5836 (ebook) | LCC PS3613.O5836 T47 2019 (print) |
DDC 813/.6–dc23
LC record available at https://lccn.loc.gov/2019018596

ISBN 978-1-948705-585
eBook ISBN 978-1-948705-592

Portions of this book previously appeared in *Disclaimer Magazine,*
Slush Pile Magazine, and *The New Engagement Magazine.*

For Chioke

'Cause you know and I know that you know who I am

—PHIFE DAWG

2014

EACH SUMMER OCTAVIAN MUNROE considered not going back to
teach art at Winslow Academy for New Beginnings in Berringford, Maine, but every fall, like the yellowing of the trees, he
returned. And as the slow days of summer abruptly made way for
the hectic school year, he was always reminded of the ending of his
own childhood summers—not getting ready for new backpacks
and freshly sharpened pencils—but of climbing into a seat of the
ancient Screaming Eagle roller coaster at Six Flags. The sprawling
amusement park was a simple half-hour drive from where his family lived in St. Louis, but it was still a place they only went to right
before the school year began. Now, as he blasted Royce da 5'9" and
wiped the dust from the black-topped tables in his classroom, he
remembered the feeling of the safety bar being lowered across his
lap. And the cars that moved slowly down the rickety track, leaving
nothing for him to do but hold on and hope that the bolts were
sound, to scream at the top of his lungs until the ride ended.

So that year, when Andrea Applegate, with her long blonde
hair, walked into Octavian's art class on the first day wearing a

T-shirt with the handwritten words #BlackLivesMatter on the front, he knew the ride had definitely left the loading station.

Octavian never expected that, at nearly forty years old, he'd be living in a place like Berringford. He no longer heard heavy basslines out of passing cars, no longer passed out and missed his stop on late-night subway rides, and he was sure he was the one black friend everyone in Berringford claimed to have—even if their relationship was simply a nod at the Shell station. But nothing had prepared him for the way his eyes filled with tears when full moonlight illuminated the snow-covered field behind his rented cabin, and so he stayed. It wasn't only the wide silent spaces or the groves of sky-high pines that kept him there. Nor was it the Winslow kids with their broken-hearted complications that bolstered Octavian's still tender sense of peace. He also stayed because nothing about Berringford reminded him of St. Louis— where his past lurked like a stray in dark alleys, and ghosts hung out ten deep on corners.

Students at Winslow battled with an endless variation of tricks played on them by their own minds. They suffered from bipolar and borderline personality disorder and were oppressed by wild anxieties. Their minds seethed with voices and they tried to escape endless suffering via their grandfather's pills, or starvation, or other attempts at death. They were sent away to hospitals and rehabs and, finally—after no one could find a way to help them— they came to Winslow, where it was Octavian's job to teach them how to throw pots, blend hues and shades, to rub charcoal with their thumbs until it became shadow. Originally, Octavian worried that his associate's degree in arts education wouldn't qualify him to work at Winslow, but after his first year, he understood why it didn't matter. He was a body in a room full of kids no one knew what to do with anymore.

Something about the new girl in the homemade T-shirt seemed familiar and Octavian wondered whether she'd been there before. Winslow was part of the hospital/home heavy rotation for some, but Octavian was pretty sure he'd remember a name like Andrea Applegate. It reminded him of "Bonita Applebum."

"Good to meet you," he said walking over to her. "I'm Mr. Munroe." He cleared his throat. "Nice shirt."

Andrea scooted onto one of the high stools and hooked her boot heels over the bar at the bottom. She looked down at her shirt and said, "I almost had to punch a guy this morning when he said 'doncha mean all lives matter?'"

"Don't they?" Octavian said.

Andrea cocked her head to the side and narrowed her eyes at him. "They do, but that's not the point."

"What's the point?"

Behind her, other students began to come in. Some were hidden under hoods or long hair, whole selves locked tight like the curves of a scallop shell. Others entered loud and turbulent, intent on letting the world know that they never, under any circumstances, got enough attention. Andrea's eyes moved like rapid-fire around the room and Octavian was reminded that he didn't know this girl yet. Every kid in that building had a story of what got them there, and he had to be careful not to joke too much or be too stern. It was a constant act of balancing the scales—placing stones on one side to make sure the pile of sand on the other didn't spill onto the floor.

Andrea turned back to Octavian and said, "The point is that black lives have never mattered. Not to the cops, not to the people who make the laws. Saying black lives matter is actually saying that black lives should matter the same as all other lives."

"Jesus, Andrea, are you really still on that shit?" Summer had done little to ease the hateful emptiness in Josh Williams's eyes as he dropped a heavy hand on Andrea's shoulder making her jump. "See," he said. "Like I told you this morning, you need to chill out."

"Good afternoon, Mr. Williams," Octavian said. "Why don't you have a seat?" To Andrea, he extended his hand. "Welcome to art class, Ms. Applegate."

Andrea looked at Octavian's outstretched palm and said, "I apologize, but I can't."

"Can't what?" Octavian said.

"I can't shake your hand. I have, like, OCD or haphephobia, or something. I can't deal with touching people, or people touching me."

"Okay," Octavian said, concealing his offending hand in his pocket. "Like I said, nice shirt. Have a seat."

On the table in front of them, an old lamp from the school's storage space cast a rusted glow over an apple he pulled from his landlady's orchard and a sunflower, whose rugged brown face Octavian couldn't resist that weekend at the farmer's market. He often started his class this way—a simple piece of paper and a pencil with no eraser. Within moments, the gentle hum that descended over drawing children filled the room.

"Mr. M., can I listen to my music?" Andrea asked, as she pulled out her headphones.

"Nope." In the beginning, Octavian had allowed them to plug their ears with the little white earbuds. He understood the connection between music and art better than anyone, so who was he to stop them? But after a few days, he reconsidered. Even what they called hip-hop was a genetically modified hybrid that held no mark of its original funk and jazz DNA. He brought in a turntable and a stack of records and tried to use Sonny Rollins, Gregory Isaacs, War, and The Last Poets to summon the parts of themselves they didn't even know existed. The parts that perhaps could bring peace to the tumult that plagued them on a daily basis.

Of course, there had been a chorus of complaints. *Don't you have any Drake? Or Flo Rida? Can't we listen to Beyoncé?* He ignored them, and by mid-semester they were humming John Coltrane melodies in the lunch line and finding him in the halls to ask, *What's that song called, you know the one that goes . . . ?* and, *Hey, Mr. M., you think I can find that Bird record you played on iTunes?*

Andrea put her headphones back in her bag with a frown. Octavian walked behind his desk and took out Curtis Mayfield's

There's No Place Like America Today and turned on the receiver. He lowered the needle on "Billy Jack," the song that had been spinning in his head since he woke up that morning.

The speakers came to life and Andrea said, "Oh, cool. I love this song."

"Of course you do," said Josh. But by the time the horns came in, even he was tapping his feet, if only lightly, under the cover of the table.

The next class, Andrea Applegate arrived wearing a threadbare purple Jimi Hendrix T-shirt and carrying a copy of Billie Holiday's *Lady in Satin* in her backpack. She handed it to Octavian and said, "Can you play this? I love to listen to Billie when I draw at home."

Octavian took the record, making sure his fingers didn't touch Andrea's, and once the class had settled in, he put it on. Billie's fierce voice crackled through the art studio and told Octavian that he wouldn't know what love was 'til he learned the meaning of the blues. That's when he realized what was familiar about Andrea. It wasn't that she'd been there before or even that she made him think of a song by A Tribe Called Quest. It was that she reminded him of Mina Rose. She didn't have Mina's dark gray eyes, but she did have that same stormy look, and she stared into Octavian the way Mina once had. And even though he wasn't supposed to look at the shape of his students, especially the girls, he still noticed Andrea's frame. It was solid like Mina's, with the same curve to her hips. And Mina had loved Billie Holiday. Listened to her when she wrote those solitary stories she refused to share.

Octavian thought about how tenuous the balance of his own pile of sand and stones had been when he last knew Mina. Back when she used to sit in the window of his loft, the broken skyline of downtown St. Louis behind her, smoking away the things they couldn't talk about. On the record player would be Sly & Robbie, or a Prince bootleg, or Astrud Gilberto. Something that would make Octavian reach over and pull her to him.

"Tell me about Trinidad," she would say, sliding her thick, bare legs under the cornflower sheet they'd stolen from her mother.

"Again?"

"Yes, again."

And he would tell her about how, before his mother died, they had taken a family vacation to Trinidad. How every day his father, Cyrus, had taken him and his older brother, Francis, to get Bake & Shark sandwiches from the roadside stand. At the beach, Francis, who had always been a delicate swimmer, had waded bravely into the sea glass green water while Octavian's mother, Cordelia, helped him fill his bucket with bumpy lavender starfish that stuck to his palm. Finally, he told Mina the part he knew she was waiting for. The part about how they had stayed at a B&B owned by an old couple—a black man and a white woman—who had been married for over fifty years.

"In Trinidad," he would say, "it wouldn't matter that you were white. We could be together and no one would care."

It wasn't true. He knew that it mattered everywhere, and even if it didn't, it mattered to him. But it was what she wanted to hear, so he had said it. What harm would it do, he reasoned, to say it one more time?

When class ended, Octavian handed Andrea back her record and said, "Thanks for bringing this in. I haven't heard it in a long time."

"I'm so psyched," she said. "I just found this at the thrift store in town."

"You're right to be excited. That's a rare recording."

"How do you know it's rare?"

"I used to work in a record store," Octavian said. "Started when I was about your age."

"That's so cool," she said. "You must have a ton of records then. Do you have this one?"

Octavian nodded. "I do. But, like most of them, it's back in my father's closet in St. Louis, so it's been a while since I listened to it."

Andrea's clear eyes widened like soup bowls, and the girl who, only a few days before, had declared she couldn't stand human touch, seized Octavian by the arm. "You're from St. Louis?"

Octavian looked down at her pale fingers clutching his arm. She blushed and immediately released him. "Sorry," she said. "It's just that so many of my favorite musicians are from St. Louis."

"Yeah?" Octavian said. "Me too."

"And I don't mean Nelly or Chingy," she said. "Well, I like them, but I'm talking about Chuck Berry, Josephine Baker, Fontella Bass."

"Fontella Bass? Seriously?" Octavian couldn't help laughing. Mina had every Fontella Bass album.

Andrea laughed. "Are you kidding? Her album *Free* saves my life every time I listen to it. I'd do anything to go to St. Louis. Can you take me there?"

A silence opened up around them that made Octavian straighten his back. Thirteen other students had put papers on shelves, books into bags, pushed stools under tables, and Octavian hadn't noticed. "I can't take you there," he said, adding clarity to his voice.

"Why not?" she asked.

Octavian smiled. Taking no for an answer was not something Mina did well either. "Okay, Ms. Questions, now it's my turn. Is home hard for you to go back to sometimes?"

Andrea drew her lips into a thin tight line.

"Right," Octavian said. "Home is hard for me to go back to sometimes, too."

At the end of the day, Octavian was getting into his car and putting the key in the ignition when he felt the buzz of his cell phone in his pocket and saw a text from Bones.

Tave, Closing Rahsaan's. Having a party next month. Inviting everyone. Please come home.

St. Louis had been coming for him since early that morning, when every television channel forced him to look into Michael

Brown's down-turned eyes in his standard-issue graduation-day photo. Octavian had tried to look away, but like everyone else, he watched as Michael Brown's murder unfolded and told the world a story as old as St. Louis itself. Told the story of every one of Octavian's friends growing up who had some kind of run-in with St. Louis cops—even his boy Ivy, who was white. Some of them had come close to death, others were lucky only to get fucked with, and then there were those like that kid Jason in his graduating class who got locked up for unpaid parking tickets and died in jail waiting to get bailed out. The story of Michael Brown wasn't something new. It was just being televised.

It made Octavian remember things he had worked years to forget. Like his brother Francis when he was barely fourteen, his cheekbone purple and bruised, lips thick and swollen, who laughed and said, "Tave, when cops hit you, they hit so hard that shit don't even hurt." And the way his own seventeen-year-old wrists burned, the cuffs too tight, a police officer's face close enough for Octavian to see the brown edges of his teeth as he said, "You look like you *want* to go to jail tonight." And Mina. Her gray eyes pleading when she begged him to leave St. Louis, even if he didn't want to leave with her.

Octavian left, not when she asked him to, but eventually. His father still lived in the same apartment where Octavian grew up, still walked the same five blocks to his job at Washington University every day, but since Octavian moved away, he and his dad met in a different place each year under the guise of taking a vacation together. Really, it was because Octavian couldn't go back. It was too hard, with not only his mother, but his brother gone, too.

Octavian picked up his phone and looked at Bones's text again. No matter how long it had been since he'd been back, the thought that Rahsaan's Records would no longer be there made a cold sweat build in the hollows of his armpits.

Octavian knew what was coming next. He'd been having panic attacks since his mom got sick when he was ten years old. The only thing consistent about them was the unpredictability in what might bring them on. Sometimes they came when he thought he was fine and then went underground right when he expected one to take over. He'd go years without having them and believe he'd got them beat, only to be faced with a daily succession for the next three months. It was always an unfair fight, but Octavian bare-knuckle boxed with it every time. This one he'd felt coming since he met Michael Brown's televised eyes. Now it was clear his attempts at bobbing and weaving it had failed.

Octavian pried at the fist that tried to wrap around his heart and fought against his lungs' refusal to take a dedicated breath. He forgot about the breathing method he learned the one time he went to a therapist. He didn't count backwards from nine or remind himself that there was no reason for flight or fight. Instead, he curled into himself, like a child surrounded by bullies on the playground. Darkness hovered like a menace at the corners of his eyes and his mouth filled with bitter bile. He thought about how maybe this time, it actually was a heart attack and that the red edges on the periphery of his eyes were in fact his brain closing in. This time, he really was dying.

In the flashing moment between the next inhale and exhale, Octavian had a different thought, this one about his father and how he owed it to him not to have to bury both of his sons. He opened his eyes and saw his hands coiled into tight fists. His feet, in his Clarke Wallabees shoes—the same as his father's "teacher shoes," about which Francis and Octavian teased Cyrus, and yet also the favorite footwear of Wu-Tang's Raekwon—pressed into the floor. Octavian heard his heart slam a rapid bassline in his chest and he tried again to slow his breath.

Criminal Minded, you've been blinded.

It was the one thing that worked, reciting KRS-One lyrics.

Looking for a style like mine, you can't find it.

The menace at the edge of his vision turned and crept away.

They are the audience, I am the lyricist.

Octavian wondered what KRS would say if he knew how many times he had pulled Octavian back from the abyss.

Sometimes the suckers on the side, they gotta hear this.

The rush of blood in his veins began to slow. Octavian rubbed his sweat-covered palms along the legs of his teacher chinos. *I bet Raekwon never wore chinos,* he thought. He blinked away at the children's coloring book outline of his surroundings and smelled the cooling asphalt of the parking lot after the hot day. His phone buzzed again in his pocket and his hands shook as he took it out. His father was calling. Octavian pressed the ignore button and said aloud, "Jesus, I can't get two inches away from that fucking town today." Outside, the sky had begun to give way to twilight. Octavian waited a few more minutes until his breathing felt steady, and drove home.

Octavian's one-room white pine cabin sat behind a big house owned by Abigail Quincy, who was part Penobscot Indian and a descendent of the original Boston Quincys. She had told Octavian her blood had an assortment of American stories to tell, and not one of them ended happily. Abigail loved Octavian. She knit him thick, intricate sweaters in the winter and brought him baskets of vegetables from her gardens in the summer. And she was the only one in Maine who called him Tave.

Back in his cabin, Octavian checked his phone again. His father hadn't left him a message, and Octavian didn't want to call him back, not yet. Instead, he put on the *Lee Morgan Sextet* album and started to make a fire. He didn't really need one, but in Maine, August nights could get cold, and building a fire in the old wood stove in the corner calmed him. He had a whole system that started with building a tent of newspaper, kindling, and small logs. Then he set the door ajar to listen to the roar of the paper, the cracking of the dry wood.

The room was warm before Octavian picked up the phone and pressed the return call button. As it rang, Octavian saw his father as if he were in the room with him. Cyrus Munroe, PhD, in his faded orange reading chair in the corner, with his feet on the

matching ottoman. Octavian watched as he put his velvet bookmark in place before he stood up. Saw how he smoothed the ancient pleats of his pants and adjusted the cuffs of his button-down
shirt. His hair was silver and cut tight to his head, and his shoulders
slumped a little as his slippered feet walked across the living room,
to where the phone hung on the wall in the kitchen. Octavian
heard the whirring of the old refrigerator before his father spoke.

"Munroe residence. Cyrus Munroe speaking."

"Dang, man, why do you take so long to answer the phone?"
Octavian said, relieved to hear normalcy in his own voice.

"That you, Tave?"

"Yeah, it's me."

"You know I don't go running for the telephone."

"Yeah. I know. You alright over there, Pop? St. Louis is all over
the news."

"I'm alright. Went out to Ferguson yesterday, but I didn't stay
long."

"I figured you'd already been out there. I was worried you were
up in the middle of it."

"No, no," Cyrus said. His voice as calm as the dusk. "Those
young folks are taking care of business from what I saw. I think
I've had enough brutality and tear gas in my life."

Octavian added another log to the fire and watched the blue
and copper glow. "I saw I missed your call," he said.

"Dreamt about your mother last night. I didn't even see her,
just smelled her."

Octavian nodded. He hated those dreams. The ones where
he'd be walking through town and become spellbound by her
scent. He'd turn, sure to see her right behind him, but she would
vanish. "It's been a while since I had one of those."

"But listen," Cyrus said, "that's not why I called. The reason I
called is because . . . at that school where you work, there are kids
with problems, right?"

"Basically," Octavian said. "It's a therapeutic school for kids
who struggle with mental health issues. Why?"

"There's this new boy who moved in next door, and he has been yelling at his mother, calling her an array of interesting names. Yells so loud he wakes me up."

"That's impressive. He must really be yelling. You don't wake up easy."

"I haven't seen or heard a sign of anything that looks fatherly and I was wondering what I should do. Should I invite him over? Maybe he needs, I don't know, somebody to talk to."

"That's a great idea, Pop." Octavian smiled at the thought of his father still needing to be a father. "Not sure whether or not he'll do it, but it's worth a try."

"Well, I have to admit, I want to wring his little white-boy neck," Cyrus said, "but I'll think on it."

"Pop, you seen Bones lately?"

"I've been meaning to go down there, but it's been a minute. Why?"

"He texted me today. Told me he's closing Rahsaan's. Said he's throwing a party next month, inviting everyone back."

"I guess I better go down there and find out what he's talking about. Would that mean you'd come home?"

Octavian's mind moved in slow, fading circles like the ending of ripples in a pond. "I'm not sure."

"Well, you let me know."

"Why?"

"I have to get you and Francis's room ready is all."

He hadn't been home in years and Francis had been dead for more than two decades. Still, it was Francis's room as much as it was his.

"You think Mina will come?" Cyrus said.

"Mina Rose?"

"Yeah, Mina Rose, what other Mina do you know? Wouldn't you like to see her?"

"I don't know, Pop."

"Well, I know I'd like to see you."

"Alright," Octavian said. "I'll think about it. In the meantime, invite that kid over from next door. Play chess with him or something. It'll do him some good."

"Chess, that's a good idea. I figured you'd know what's best."

There was a pause and Octavian heard his father sigh. "Too bad I couldn't have played chess with Mike Brown," Cyrus said. "That cop probably could have used it, too."

"That's true, Pop," Octavian said. "That is definitely true."

>>>

THE FOLLOWING AFTERNOON, CYRUS looked out onto the empty summer Wash U quad. As long as the weather allowed for it, Cyrus walked to and from work every day, but in the late summer, he tended to wait for the sun to go down and the furious heat of the day to subside before heading home. That day, Cyrus decided to leave the office a little earlier. The sun was still out and it was still plenty hot, but not as bad as it could have been for an August evening in St. Louis.

Cyrus felt the tiredness of his bones from being awoken the night before by the yelling between the woman and her teenage son next door. And being tired made Cyrus think about death. The idea of death itself, or even dying, didn't trouble him. It was the inability, the infirmity of the old before they died that he didn't take to. Recently, when he had to write his age down on a piece of paper, or had to scroll endlessly through a website's drop-down menu to find the year he was born, he blinked solidly. Was he really seventy-six years old, for crying out loud? Wasn't his father that old? No, no, his father was dead.

It astonished Cyrus that he still missed his father. Jackson Munroe, with his diligent, calm face, had been Cyrus's hero and his haven. Jackson was a mail clerk on the Union Pacific train, and for two weeks every month he traveled across the country. Those two weeks were a time of torture for the only child. Long days when his mother, Fabiola, had Cyrus buttoned up swiftly and off to pay social calls, give teas, and volunteer at the hospital or visit his ancient grandmother.

Jackson knew this and as soon as he returned, he would take Cyrus into his study that was lined from floor to ceiling with books. There he would tell Cyrus stories of Indians and cowboys and prairie grass so high settlers were known to lose their children in it. After that, he read to Cyrus from plays, novels, and ancient poetry, and Cyrus would listen until his head grew heavy. Then Jackson would fill the pipe he bought from a trading post in Utah with his favorite Scottish tobacco, put on Duke Ellington, Sarah Vaughan, or Hoagy Carmichael, and send Cyrus off to bed. Words and melodies Cyrus didn't understand wrapped his dreams in the sweet, smoky smell of faraway lands.

Jackson died soon after Cyrus graduated from Harvard. But not before he'd carefully packed his pipe, his last remaining jar of tobacco, and his pearl-handled letter opener in the velvet-covered box and sent them to Cyrus. Cyrus wished there could be a guarantee that he would die like his father, who got into his bed and drifted peacefully into death. He decided that if he started to go the route of his mother, who after Jackson died, developed a natural flare to her nostrils as if something always stank, and began to lose her way home from the grocery store, he'd have to find a way out. *Maybe I can convince Octavian to shoot me, or poison me,* he thought. *We'll have to talk about that if he comes home.* Cyrus granted himself a minute of hope that Octavian might come home. They'd seen a lot of places in their yearly vacations together: Macedonia, Savannah, Trinidad at least six times, Mexico City, Highway One between Big Sur and Oregon. But it would mean something more if Octavian came home. It would mean he had healed. Or at least was beginning to.

Cyrus walked the extra block past his street into the Loop, where young people moved with the sense of postponed passion common to late-August nights. He felt the solitude of a familiar place that had become unfamiliar, as he passed the new organic juice bar and the frozen yogurt joint that used to be a comic book shop, the Starbucks that had once been Francis's favorite sandwich place when he was young. He walked on through the automatic swinging door of Rahsaan's Records, where everything was too bright and familiar for loneliness. The smell of the plastic, the vinyl, the gray carpeting that had never been properly cleaned, all brought Cyrus back to the days when Octavian worked there. To the days even before that, when he and Octavian and Francis would go together, the boys' pockets full of lawn-mowing money.

The music that played was never the same, but often it was something Cyrus recognized—an old Blue Note recording or a Marvin Gaye tune, perhaps Muddy Waters or the Ohio Players. After a while he even recognized some of Octavian's favorite rappers. *MCs, Pop, they're called MCs—you know, like Masters of Ceremony?* KRS-One, Rakim, Run-DMC, Guru, the godforsaken Geto Boys Octavian had insisted on playing nonstop for an entire weekend until even Francis was drawn up with worry.

"Pop, don't you think you should make him turn that off?" Francis had asked. He stood outside the door to their bedroom while angry voices reverberated around the room. Francis must have been around nineteen at the time, and sober again. Sober and urgently clean—clean hands, clean eyes, clean skin, the creases ironed tightly into his acid washed jeans. Cyrus looked in at Octavian lying on the floor, his head fiercely close to the speaker.

"I mean, it ain't good for Tave to be listening to these, these . . . um . . . hoodlums, talking about smoking dust and robbing and raping and killing over and over like that. I don't know. He might start thinking it's cool."

Cyrus smiled at him. "Why don't you tell him, then?"

Francis pushed open the door but didn't go in. "Yo, Tave," he yelled. "Me and Pop think it's bad for you to keep listening to this . . . this negativity."

Fifteen-year-old Octavian, his box cut and fade always perfect back then, his skin losing a fight with acne, rolled over and considered his brother with a look of disbelief before he rolled back and turned up the volume.

Francis marched into the bedroom with the exasperation of a child and ripped the needle off the record. "For real, Tave," he said. "I can't sit by and let you listen to this."

Octavian glanced at Cyrus standing in the hall before he stood up and strained his neck so he could get as much into Francis's face as possible. "I don't know what you worried about, Frankie. You're the one out there actually doing this shit, I'm just listening to it." Then Octavian lowered the needle back onto the record and turned it up even louder, releasing the violence back into the room. He stared at Francis as if this act of defiance had been burning a hole in his pocket and said, "You got something else you wanna say?"

Francis waited for Cyrus to back him up, but Cyrus held up his hands in surrender.

"Nah, man," Francis said. "I ain't got shit else to say."

"That you, Professor?"

Cyrus looked up to see Bones walking toward him. Bones wore what he always wore: a Rahsaan's Records T-shirt, some washed-out blue jeans, and a Cardinals cap pulled low over his blue eyes. His light brown hair, now thick with grays, was tied in a ponytail.

There was much about the large white man that made Cyrus chuckle, but mostly it was Bones's tendency to speak in black St. Louis slang that used to bring him, Francis, and Octavian to tears. They would spend hours trying to outdo each other with the best Bones imitation. Francis almost always won with something like, "I'se funsta go to the sto', get me a grape soda."

"My man," Bones said with a wide grin. He pulled Cyrus into a hug of Old Spice aftershave and Cyrus let his body dissolve a bit into his old friend's embrace.

"It's good to see you, Jimmy." Cyrus could never bring himself to call him that ridiculous nickname.

"Not as good as it is to see you, baby."

"You got some coffee?"

"Is a pig's pussy pork?"

Cyrus chuckled. "I guess it is, Jimmy."

"Well, then, I got your coffee." Bones laughed his deep, blues-man laugh and Cyrus followed him toward the back of the store.

Tall Fred Bosh, the one they used to call Dr. Long, and the only employee left from the old days, came out from the back carrying a box of T-shirts. Fred was at least six-foot-five and thin in every direction. He had brown skin that always looked a bit sickly, which Cyrus attributed to the fact that Fred never seemed to leave the store. He smiled when he saw Cyrus and said, "Hey there, Professor. How you been?"

"Doing alright, Fred. Doing alright."

From the next aisle over, someone called out, "Hey, Fred, can I go on break?"

Cyrus stopped. He knew that voice, would know it in a crowded room scattered with voices. It was the one that woke him in the night screaming at his mother, calling her all types of names. Cyrus readied himself to finally give the young man a talking-to. He had seen him and his mother before. Both of them small and unassuming. Cyrus remembered that the boy wore a yarmulke, deep blue velvet with silver stitching, and had shaggy brown hair falling out from underneath. His skin was pasty with gray circles around his eyes. So it took Cyrus a few beats to realize that the voice he was so sure he knew now came from a person who was wearing generous lines of black makeup around his eyes and shiny lip gloss. On closer look, Cyrus saw that it was, in fact, the same person. Except that now his shaggy hair was slicked back into a tiny ponytail and he'd traded in his nondescript trousers for some tight black leather pants. There was no sign of any yarmulke, deep blue or otherwise, but sure enough, there was the pale white skin, and the ash-colored circles under his eyes. He had a Rahsaan's Records name tag pinned on his T-shirt. Cyrus squinted. *Adam*, it said.

Cyrus opened his mouth, even brought a hand up to get the young man's attention, but in the brief moment that Adam met

Cyrus's eyes, Cyrus saw a whole lot he didn't understand. He forgot what it was that Octavian had suggested he do about the boy and so he quickly dropped his hand and turned to where Bones stood waiting for him at the back of the store.

The walls of Bones's office were decorated with tacked-up aging record covers—Art Blakey & the Jazz Messengers' *Free for All*, Lonnie Smith's *Turning Point, De La Soul Is Dead.* And around the room were autographed pictures of Bones and Chuck Berry, Bones and the Beastie Boys, Bones and Johnny Cash, The Staples Singers, Willie Nelson, the Clash, Miles Davis.

Cyrus sat down in a torn leather chair across from Bones's desk, which was scattered with papers, most of them looking like bills. Bones held up Stevie Wonder's *Songs in the Key of Life* CD and said, "You cool with this?"

"I'm always cool with Stevie," Cyrus said.

"I know that's right." Bones put the CD on and Stevie sang about love being in need of love today. He handed Cyrus a ceramic mug warm with coffee.

Cyrus turned the mug around in his hands. The outside was glazed a deep cerulean, the inside soft cream. Cyrus knew by the arc of the handle that the mug had been made by Octavian. "Tave send you this?"

Bones took a sip of his coffee and nodded. "Your boy's stuff is right on time."

Cyrus felt pride fill his chest as he held the cup and thought of Octavian making and selling his pottery, of teaching children how to find reprieve in colors and clay. Even if he did have to be far off in some Maine woods to do it, Cyrus hoped Octavian had found a bit of his own relief. He thought again about his son's healing, about his coming home. He studied Bones and decided not to ask about closing the store yet. He took a sip of the coffee. "You going to make it Irish or what?"

"Hell to the yeah." Bones pulled a bottle of Bushmills from the bottom desk drawer and poured some into both of their cups.

"Cheers," he said. Cyrus raised his mug, took a short sip, and felt the fierceness of the whiskey in his throat.

"You been over to Ferguson?" Bones said.

"I have," Cyrus said. "Have you?"

"Nah." Bones poked at a coffee-stained invoice. "I should though."

"You should."

"Things bad as they say?"

Cyrus shrugged and took another sip of coffee; this time the end went down smooth. "You know how they always tell one half of both sides to the story," he said. "Some things are worse than they say, and some aren't so bad. I haven't seen any news coverage of the kids who are guarding the businesses from being looted, or the ones making sure the old folks are getting to church, but everyone in the country knows about the twenty or so knuckle-heads—most of whom aren't even from Ferguson—burning up the QuikTrip."

"You think it's going to spread out?"

Cyrus laughed. He'd been friends with Bones going on twenty-five years now, but he forgot sometimes that Bones was from a different generation. "Don't worry, I think you're safe."

"Shit," Bones said. "You got me confused, Professor. I want 'em up in here. I'm proud of 'em. Cops forever been killing kids, but now errybody in the hood got an iPhone and you best believe they filming that shit, sharing it on Facebook or whatever. Bet you that cat in the turtleneck from Apple and that ugly Facebook kid never thought they was making tools for the revolution. Please. I want them over here. Let them burn Rahsaan's down. It would be a much more honorable death than the one it's currently dying."

Cyrus laughed. "Jimmy, man, you are always so damn dramatic. Is this why you're telling Octavian you're going to close the store?"

Bones took a sip of his coffee. "Nah," he said. "It ain't cause of Ferguson or the fact that they killed that poor boy. Though that would be a better reason than the real one."

"Why then?"

Bones picked up the CD case and shook it at Cyrus like an accusing finger. "You know, for a second, these looked like they was fixin' to be the death of me? I mean, after that, didn't no one want to buy no vinyl and those dang Strawberry stores or Peaches, or whatever the fuck they was called, you remember those, started opening up in malls and shit?" Bones leaned across his desk toward Cyrus. "I tell you, things started lookin' real bad for your boy Bones. But back then I was young, I was adaptable, you know what I'm sayin'? I just reconfigured, started buyin' up used CDs for next to nothing and sellin' them shits for a whole lot cheaper than anybody and made my way through."

Bones tossed the CD case on the desk and picked up his smartphone. "But these motherfuckers?" he said, turning it over in his hands. "These are my goddamn demise. And that's my word."

"You were singing Steve Jobs's praise a second ago," Cyrus said.

"I know," Bones said. "I'm conflicted." His eyes pleaded with Cyrus. "But it don't matter how I feel. I can't make it work. Not even for another year."

"Have you gone to city hall? Seen about getting a grant or some kind of loan?"

"It's more than the bread. I don't have what it takes anymore. Things have changed too much. Back in the day, I had all them kids—from the neighborhood, shit from alla St. Louis up in here. Had them white kids from out in Ladue coming in looking for Coltrane, and black kids from the North Side wanting to get their hands on some Steely Dan. People were here . . . just to be here, you know? This was the place to be. It's not like that no more."

Cyrus nodded.

"Shit, " Bones said. "When I opened this place in '78, black folks and white folks in U. City were trying to come together, trying to figure it out. But you seen what it looks like out there now. U. City don't care about keeping Rahsaan's open. Seems like these days people be doing whatever they can to make money and get as far apart from each other as possible."

"You forget, Bones, that 1978 was only ten years after King was killed. We were still hopeful then."

"And now?"

Cyrus didn't answer.

"See?" Bones shook his head. "Tell you what though, it wasn't cause those kids were looking to break down racial barriers or some shit that they was up in here. It was because of the music. And *that's* how shit got broken down. Nowadays, I don't know." Bones stopped and looked at Cyrus. "I used to have my finger on their pulse, on every single one of those kids—Octavian and Mina, Brendon, Evan, Ivy—even Francis. I knew what they needed to hear, knew what song would heal whatever wound they were nursing. And then, when they started talking to each other—sharing songs, trading albums? That was God's work right there. But today? Nah." Bones shook his head. "All they need is one of these damn phones and a thumb. And, I tell you what, the thought of them, up in they rooms listening to music alone and shit, it nearly kills me."

Cyrus took a sip of the whiskey and coffee out of the mug his son had made and nodded. He settled a little deeper into his chair, thinking about the memories of his children stashed about the store. Stuck between the LPs and hiding in the back room. Memories of Octavian and, like Bones said, Octavian's friends, too: Evan, who showed how much he loved Octavian by getting him in trouble; and militant Brendon, hung up hard on putting it to the man. And Francis's best friend, Ivy, and Mina with her solemn face as she watched Octavian recede into the distance. Even Francis, the good part of Francis, the part that loved Octavian enough to let Rahsaan's be Octavian's alone. All of that was here. The thought of it disappearing, of this place becoming a Banana Republic or some overpriced gourmet grocery store, pulled down on Cyrus's heart. "You sure you thought this through, Jimmy?"

"Believe me, I done thought it through." He let his voice trail off. "I usta think music could save St. Louis's soul, could save the country's soul, but looks like it's put me in the poorhouse instead.

So Ima throw a big-ass party and it's a wrap. The days of Rahsaan's Records are over."

"That's too bad. It is the end of an era."

"I gots to do it. Even thinkin' a goin' back down South or something. Didn't used to need anyone before, store's always been my girl. But in the words of the great Al Green, I'm so tired of being alone."

Cyrus glanced at the closed office door that led back into the store, and at the coming night, where his apartment sat shrouded and empty. "Seems like loneliness is the disease old folks are the most prone to."

"I heard that."

Cyrus thought of Adam. And his angry adolescent voice as it blew through the walls. And the shiny lip gloss. Chess. That's what he had forgotten. "You know that boy you got out there, Adam?"

"You mean the one with all that sugar in his pants?"

Cyrus chuckled and shook his head at Bones. "He's my next-door neighbor."

"For real?"

"You know he doesn't look like that at home."

"Oh, I know it. His ass comes up in here erry dang day, even if he ain't working, and changes his clothes. Spends damn near an hour in my bathroom, comes out made up, his hair slicked back and shit. Leaves out of here with his slacks and his yarmulke in a plastic bag."

"Octavian thinks I should invite him over to play chess."

"Yeah, well, I don't think his mama knows he looks like that, just so you know."

Cyrus nodded and finished his coffee. He tucked the empty mug under his arm. "I'm keeping this," he said.

"Take it, my friend. Just get that son of yours home for my party."

There were a few customers. Cyrus scanned the store and saw Adam standing by the cash register next to a dark-skinned boy with wire-rimmed glasses. Cyrus started in his direction, but then the boy leaned over and planted a quick, delicate kiss on Adam's cheek and Adam's face burst into a sloping smile. Cyrus forgot again about the chess and walked directly out the automatic door that swung open into the night.

Cyrus walked home and wondered what the Loop would look like busted open and burning down, the way the streets of Ferguson were when he'd gone there the other day. He'd seen the crowds that gathered in Michael Brown's name, felt their collective human pulse, like some giant animal. It sped up, slowed down, and pushed against the barricades of officers who stood like Roman soldiers with their shields in front of them.

They were different from those he'd seen at the March on Washington in '63, or the Nuclear Freeze Rally in Central Park in '82, or the Million Man March in '95. These officers were like those he'd encountered during his time as a Freedom Rider. Too angry and too afraid. One look at their stony faces took away Cyrus's nostalgic desire to join in. This was not a place for an old man with bones you could feel through the skin, he thought. Instead, he turned and walked into a nearby church, whose unwilling aging felt akin to his own.

Inside, small children sat in hushed groups on stiff wooden benches. The tops of their heads were lit softly by cracked crystal sconces set into painted pillars decades ago, and they looked more like angels than the figures watching from the faded stained glass above.

Evelyn Morris, the plump woman who met Cyrus at the door, introduced herself and nodded toward the children. "Their schools have been shut down to protect them from the unrest," she said, adjusting the sparkling scarf, which Cyrus imagined she'd put on that morning to lift the children's spirits. "But no one's paying their parents to stay home from work and watch them, so here they are, sequestered in the church. More of them over in the library."

Circling around were young teachers with blouses tucked in and ties tied. They shared a look of redoubled fear in their eyes as they attempted to teach long division, the arc of plot, and why the letters P and H made the same sound as F. A child, who couldn't have been much older than five, moved carefully and quietly to where a young white man with a dark-brown ponytail sat in the corner reading *Curious George* to a semicircle of children.

"Are all of these folks teachers?"

"Some," said Evelyn. "Others are"—she cleared her throat—"volunteers. Most of them have never once traveled this far into Ferguson, even when they missed the exit to the airport." She smiled at Cyrus. Cyrus knew volunteers was code for white folks. He had seen them outside. Their hearts beating with the rest, spit flying from their mouths as they shouted at the cops, as they were dragged by handcuffed wrists into waiting paddy wagons.

"I sure hope some good comes of this," Evelyn said, and Cyrus saw the heavy rise and fall of her large bosom as she sighed.

"Me too." Cyrus didn't say he'd seen it before, or that there had been *volunteers* back then too, and some of those had even died. But it had made no difference. If it had, Cyrus thought, he and this nice lady wouldn't be standing there, and another innocent child wouldn't be dead.

As Cyrus rounded the corner toward home, there at the front door was Adam's mother, with her hands full of grocery bags. Cyrus was far enough away that if he slowed down, there would be no obligation for him to hold the door for her, to help her inside, but instead, he sped up and reached her as she began to search for her keys. "I've got that for you." He unlocked the door and held it open for her.

She startled a little and Cyrus smiled. "I'm Cyrus Munroe," he said. "I live next door to you, in apartment five."

"Oh yes," she said. "Thank you." She met Cyrus's eyes only briefly before she let her gaze rest on his chin. "Marcia Cohen," she said, and she tucked her keys in her pocket so she could extend her hand.

Cyrus shook it. It was small and dry. The door closed behind them and they stood alone in the lobby. "Let me help you."

Marcia Cohen looked as if she wanted to object, but she also looked tired. She shrugged and let him take a handful of the plastic bags. Cyrus felt the white woman's fear walking next to him on the wide marble staircase. At this point in his life, he was accustomed to it. Regardless of how courteous, how lovely, how intelligent, how many degrees he might have, women like Marcia Cohen would always choose to stay bolted up on the inside of their fear, never doing more than peeking out at him through a crack in the curtains.

"You've got a boy, yes?" Cyrus said as they reached their floor.

"Yes," she smiled. "Adam." In front of her door, she put her bags down and offered Cyrus her hand again, her gaze still resting on his chin. "Thank you, Mr. . . . ."

"Dr. Munroe," he said. "But please call me Cyrus."

"You're a doctor?"

"Well, a professor. I teach philosophy at Wash U."

"Really?" Now she met Cyrus's eyes. "Adam loves philosophy. He's brilliant, that kid is, though you wouldn't know it from his grades these days."

"Does he play chess?"

"He does," she said. "He's actually quite good."

"Well tell him to stop by sometime. We can play chess and discuss philosophy."

Marcia Cohen nodded unconvincingly. "I'll tell him."

Cyrus started to walk down the hall toward his door and then turned back. "Please also tell your son to stop screaming at you in the middle of the night," he said. "I'm an old man and it really doesn't do for me to be woken up in such a way. I'm sure it's not good for you either."

Marcia Cohen's mouth fell open and Cyrus wished he were wearing a hat so that he might tip it in her direction. Instead, he turned on his heel and walked the ten feet down the hall to his own door without looking back.

> > >

MINA ROSE WORKED FOR a small children's publishing company in Boston. She'd been hired ten years before as a temp secretary, and slowly worked her way toward her own desk in the corner of the editorial department. On that particular bright August morning, she was unable to read a word of the manuscript she was supposed to finish by the afternoon. Instead, she obsessively refreshed the CNN website and prayed for a different image of St. Louis to emerge.

Her coworker John Robert jumped when she cursed at the screen. "I don't know why you're so upset about shit going on in a place you haven't lived in since you were eighteen," he said. Mina muttered something about him not being able to understand, but John Robert ignored her and watched over her shoulder as she refreshed a photo of protesters who'd been blinded by tear gas. "Looks to me like it's a good thing you left."

By noon, Michael Brown's graduation photo had drifted midway down the page and Mina decided she needed to leave the office. A walk would turn her right side out, she thought, but out on Huntington Avenue the wet heat of August met her intention with a laugh. Determined, she put on her sunglasses and thought of the days to come where the same street would greet her with slanting snowfalls and cold that crawled inside her bones.

At the end of her marriage to Rubio, Boston had seemed like a good idea. A sort of neutral, effortless place. Not St. Louis and not New York either. She'd arrived rattled and lost, her daughter Riley almost five and Chloe just three. They moved into their dark apartment with windows only on one side, and which smelled of whatever the neighbors had cooked the night before. But it was in walking distance to a small park, an Irish pub, and one of the finest public schools in Boston. And since Riley had been reading since she was three and had already mastered addition, Mina chose to bury her single mother anxieties under the task of her starting school. She hadn't known that Boston wasn't like St. Louis. That living by a school didn't mean you got to go to that school. A well-meaning neighbor who she met in the park informed her that she should have put her name on the list the year before, when she put Riley in preschool. However, she told Mina, there was a group of families who were coming together to try to "change" another nearby school and offered to put Mina in touch with them.

Mina went to the next meeting. Five sets of parents introduced themselves. They were all white and, except for one couple of two moms, a perfect mom and dad set. The kids weren't invited, which Mina thought was a strange way to start, but she'd went with it, leaving her girls with their neighbor Mama Nora. The other parents were at least ten years older than Mina and worked at places like Northeastern University and the Boston Public Health Commission. But they had sons and daughters the same age as Riley and lived within walking distance of each other. This is what Mina had wanted when she left New York. A neighborhood where her girls could run down the street to the park and walk home from school with their friends.

Richard and Margot Weinberg, the couple who owned the apartment, invited everyone into their living room that was nothing like Mina's living room, constantly scattered with toys. The Weinberg living room had bookshelves lining the walls and soft little lamps. A fern hung quietly in the window and the hardwood floor was covered in an ornate Oriental rug. The parents took their generous cups of tea and sat down around a rosewood coffee table that displayed books of Robert Mapplethorpe photographs and Basquiat prints.

Richard outlined the plan. They would each put down the school to be "changed" as their first choice, and since it was not currently considered one of the more desirable schools, this would ensure that their children would enter kindergarten together. "And," Richard announced, "that way we know they will at least have a cohort of well-adjusted, intelligent peers in their class."

Mina glanced around the room. "Who would be in their class otherwise?"

The parents' happy nodding faces pinched into frowns and the two moms looked down into their teacups. "Most of the kids at the school now come from . . . broken homes," Richard said.

"And they're mostly inner-city kids," Margot added.

"That is one thing I'm concerned about," said Brian. He sat on the floor across from Margot. He and his wife, Hannah, had a daughter named Juliet. "I don't know how Juju will feel being one of the only white students in the whole school. Not to be racist, but I don't know if she'll be scared."

Richard gave him an understanding nod. "That's why it's so important that we go in together."

Mina's throat felt like it might close. She looked toward the door. Her kids were from the Bronx and their home was certainly broken. And while Chloe could probably pass for Juju's cousin, Riley's brown skin might make Brian and Hannah's Juliet feel *uncomfortable.* She knew these people. They were the ones who did a double take when they heard Riley call Mina mom in the store, the ones who looked concerned when they saw Rubio walking down the street with Chloe in his arms. She stood up so quickly that she spilled her tea. "I forgot," she said, "I told my husband I'd be back to take the girls to ballet class." It was a string of bad lies, but she didn't care. She was out the door before Margot could finish inquiring about what dance school the girls went to.

Mina went back to the other well-meaning neighbor, whose daughter went to a private school she described as having a healthy scholarship program. Mina applied and breathed a heavy sigh of relief when Riley was given a diversity scholarship. But Mina's acquired Bronx toughness had no place in a private school on Beacon Hill, and her midwestern good manners were just as suspicious. The black mothers glanced at her with indifference when she tried to start a conversation, or they gave her advice on how to comb Riley's hair. And the white mothers regarded Mina with wary eyes when she told them that, even though Riley's skin was the color of strong coffee with cream, and Chloe's was more like a vanilla latte, they weren't half sisters. Their father, Mina explained, lived far away and, no, he wouldn't be able to make it to open house or the holiday concert.

The teachers seemed to question her, too. "Your children are so different, Ms. Figueroa," they said. Mina had kept her married name only to prove her point. Mina told herself they were referring to the fact that, while Riley continued her effortless sprint to the head of her class, Chloe couldn't read until the second grade. And she pretended not to notice how the other students kept a polite distance from Riley and forgot to invite her to birthday parties while Chloe never wanted for friends.

As Mina walked away from her office, she remembered that she'd left her lunch on the kitchen counter and cursed. She had sworn she would do better at bringing her lunch from home, and that morning she'd even remembered to pack one—leftover chicken and green beans from the night before. Now she walked toward Symphony and turned into Whole Foods, where the temperature-controlled air made her shiver and rub her hands against her pale, bare shoulders.

Mina decided to make herself feel better by looking around the store for sales, hoping to find something cheap to make for dinner. As adolescence had descended on their two-bedroom apartment, Mina struggled less with making sure her girls got to bed on time and more with recognizing them as they walked out of their room in the morning. Forcing them to eat dinner together was one of the ways she'd tried to keep her daughters from slipping through her fingers.

However, many nights it was dinner that showed the weakness of the binding holding them together. Discussions around the table became the premise for arguments that could lead to fights lasting weeks. The night before, Mina tried to make conversation by telling them about an article she'd read on St. Louis that called Delmar Boulevard one of the most racially divisive streets in America. Chloe, who was thirteen, wasn't listening, but she never listened when Mina talked. But fifteen-year-old Riley pushed at the glasses that always slid down her nose and said, "Wait, isn't Delmar the street where you took me where there were stores and stuff?"

Mina nodded. "Yeah, Delmar actually runs all the way into downtown St. Louis, but the part we went to is called the Loop. I took you to the record store where I used to work. You remember Rahsaan's, right?"

They'd only gone to St. Louis once, and that was because Mina's mother, Kanta, had insisted on taking them. Riley was ten and Chloe was eight, and while Kanta took Chloe to the Magic House, Mina had taken Riley to Rahsaan's. Riley got a kick out of Bones, who called her "honey child" and cried when he first saw her. Mina tried to convince Riley to buy something other than an Usher CD, but Bones shut her down, told Riley he loved Usher. Told her, "Girl, you should have seen the type of stuff your mama used to buy from me when she was your age."

"Those protests that are happening in St. Louis, are they by that record store?" Riley asked.

Mina caught her breath and looked at her daughter. "I didn't realize you'd been following that story."

Riley rolled her eyes. "Why wouldn't I be?"

Chloe looked up from her cell phone. She listened when her sister talked. "What protests?"

Riley nudged a green bean back and forth across her plate and said, "You don't know anything, do you?"

"You think you know everything, don't you?" Chloe shot back.

"You wouldn't care anyway, Chloe. This is about black people."

"News flash, Riley, you're not black."

"No, Chloe," Riley said, holding her brown-skinned hand up to the ivory of her sister's face. "*You're* not black."

"Jesus, Riley. Does Mom look black to you?"

"What about Rubio? You think he's white, too?" Recently, Riley had been referring to their estranged father by his first name or even just his initials.

Now it was Chloe's turn to roll her eyes. "Dad isn't black, Riley, he's Puerto Rican."

Riley's face folded into a furious scowl and her fork slammed on her plate. "Right. Not white. And if you knew anything, you'd know that Puerto Rican people have as much West African blood in them as European—"

Chloe turned from her sister. "Oh my God. Mom, can you tell Riley to stop lecturing me?"

Mina pressed her fingertips into her closed eyes. "How about you both stop? You're both mixed. You're white, you're black, you're Puerto Rican. You're lucky—you get to be everything."

"You would think that." Riley stood up from the table and gathered her napkin. Her knife fell on the floor, and as she bent down to pick it up, Mina saw the enormous tears pooled in the lenses of her glasses.

"Ri," she said.

Riley shook her head.

"I'd love to talk to you about Michael Brown and about home, I mean, about St. Louis."

But Riley turned her back. The moment was gone, vanished into the air around the dinner table like the feathered smoke from a blown-out candle.

Mina picked up a bag of rice that was a dollar off and wondered if Chloe was still adamant about being grain free that week. Her phone vibrated in her hand and Bones's name flashed on her screen.

Mina girl. Closing the store. Having a party. Inviting everyone. Don't let me down. Please come home.

Mina took the rice and got in the express checkout line. She texted Bones back,

What the hell are you talking about, closing the store?

She started to text Clarissa, the only person besides Bones who she kept in touch with from St. Louis, when her phone buzzed again.

Can't explain it now, Mina girl, Bones wrote. I'll call you later. Just plan to come on home. You hear?

Mina girl. Only Bones still called her that, she thought. But once Octavian had, too. Mina seldom let herself think about him. She couldn't stand the taste of regret that filled her mouth when she did. But she wondered if Bones meant Octavian when he said he was inviting everyone home. The last time she saw Octavian, he had come to New York City to find her, and she'd pushed him away. After that, whenever Bones or Clarissa tried to talk to her about him, she told them she didn't want to know.

She had only been eighteen, three years older than Riley was now, when she and Octavian had actually been together. And though she'd been through a marriage, the birth of two children and a divorce, the Mina from St. Louis, the Mina in love with Octavian, was somehow more real to her. The Mina she'd become felt like a distant someone, a character on a television show with too many seasons. She never got far in finding an answer to why she felt this way. Maybe because then she would have had to feel it—and with so many chores to finish before bedtime, there was no time left for feeling.

Maybe he'll be there, she thought. *Maybe I should go.* Something turned in her stomach, something that had been dormant for twenty years. It jumped up and fluttered about like one of those tiny jewelry-box ballerinas, finally released from its spring.

the '80s:

A MIX TAPE

DOWN TO ZERO—JOAN ARMATRADING

CACTUS TREE—JONI MITCHELL

SOMEONE TO WATCH OVER ME—ELLA FITZGERALD

PLANET ROCK—AFRIKA BAMBAATAA

LITTLE RED CORVETTE—PRINCE

STOLEN MOMENTS—OLIVER NELSON

ONCE IN A WHILE—RAHSAAN ROLAND KIRK

FOR THE GOOD TIMES—AL GREEN

BEAST OF BURDEN—THE ROLLING STONES

A LOVE BIZARRE—SHEILA E

TENDER LOVE—FORCE MDs

Down to Zero

CORDELIA MUNROE GREW UP in an oceanside town in North Carolina. Living in St. Louis meant she suffered occasionally from a sadness brought on by a longing for the sea. When this happened, Cyrus took the family on trips to the beach—Maryland, Jamaica, Orlando, Cape Cod. In the spring of 1984, when Octavian was almost ten and Francis was fourteen, they went to Trinidad. There, Cordelia showed Octavian how to find joy in the delicate peach of a conch shell and taught him and Francis to lie on their backs and watch the night sky for shooting stars. "You have to be willing to wait," she explained. "It's hard, but eventually, you will be rewarded."

Francis could never wait. He chose to skip stones across the flat darkness of the night ocean instead. The rocks jumping five, six, eight times.

The day before they were to leave, as she was gathering up the green plastic shovel and pail that Octavian had left by the shore, Cordelia collapsed, folded in on herself and fell onto the sand, the waves lapping around her feet. At the hospital the doctor said it was heat stroke, but on the way home, Francis wouldn't talk to anyone. He didn't even fight with Octavian over who got to listen to the Walkman while the plane took off.

They had been home a month, long enough for the humid heat of the St. Louis summer to rear its ugly head, when Cyrus sat Octavian on one side and Francis on the other of the kitchen table. He had planned it like a seminar, even jotted down a few notes, and he was able to stick to his script when he looked at Francis's carved and already angry eyes, but when he looked into Octavian's bread-dough face, he faltered and only managed to say, "Your mother is dying."

"That's impossible," Octavian said. "Mama's only thirty-four."

Francis stood up and walked out of the room.

Cordelia was becoming a published, venerated poet by the time she began to die. Her book *The White Man Talk* earned her nominations on a few prestigious award lists, and invitations to read were coming in from as far away as San Francisco. She taught classes at St. Louis University to inspired young writers, who adored her. And on Tuesday afternoons, she met with prisoners who wept when she read to them, and who composed pieces that made her weep in turn. When she found out she had less than a year to live, she did what she always did. She cracked herself open and wrote about what she discovered inside—her children, her scars, her rotting breasts, her disintegrating mind. And as always, she wrote love poems to Cyrus, her now-iron-haired husband who cried into her back while he thought she slept.

Octavian didn't how to take care of a dying woman, but he learned. When fifth grade started in the fall, he knew how to make chamomile tea without burning his hand on the kettle. He knew how to lift his mother gently and help her sit up, to take the pillows from behind her and plump them, and carefully help her sit back. After school, instead of going over to friends' houses to watch *Scooby Doo* or playing baseball at Heman Park, Octavian went directly home, where Cyrus would pat Octavian gratefully on the shoulder and disappear into his study, locking the door behind him.

Octavian took out his homework from his Spider-Man backpack and spread himself on the floor while Cordelia watched *The Jeffersons* and *One Day at a Time*. When he was finished, she helped him practice long division, and he read to her from the *A Wrinkle in Time* series until she fell asleep. Sometimes Cordelia asked him to play her favorite songs. Octavian would get her albums: Roberta Flack, Joan Armatrading, Joan Baez. Then she told him stories that she said she wanted him to remember for her—often the one about the day he was born. "They put you in my arms, and I put my nose in your little plum mouth and breathed in the sweet newness of the world," she said. Her voice was sleepy, her throat full of gravel.

Sometimes she told him things Octavian thought she wouldn't have if she hadn't been dying, like the story about the time in college when she smoked pot with a white girl at a party and they kissed in the hallway.

On good days she read to Octavian: Gwendolyn Brooks, Garcia Marquez, Audre Lorde, Faulkner, James Baldwin—*The Fire Next Time*. Octavian noticed that Cyrus never asked where Francis was, but Cordelia always did. "Where's Francis?" she'd say. "Where's your brother?" No matter what, she eventually said, "Go and find him. Bring him home to me."

Octavian could stand the wincing noises his mother made when she rolled over in her sleep, and the way she left her sentences suspended in the air when her morphine pill kicked in. He could even stand the sharp smell of her yellow-brown urine in the toilet that she forgot to flush. But he hated having to go and look for Francis.

Before Cordelia got sick, there were only two places Francis would be. Sitting in his room listening to records and looking at baseball cards with his best friend, Michael Ivy, or over at Brendon Graves's house playing Atari. But after she got sick, Francis was in neither of those places.

If Octavian hadn't been so worried about his mother, he might have let himself worry about what was happening to Francis. He still told his mother that Francis was at the library. But really, Francis was over in Eastgate, a neighborhood on the other side of Delmar where Cordelia had forbidden them to go.

The St. Louis suburb of University City where they lived was divided down the middle by Delmar Boulevard. On the south side sat Washington University and the gated communities with grand homes and elegant apartment buildings where professors like Octavian's parents lived. On the north side, middle-income housing quickly gave way to low-income neighborhoods lined with identical one-story houses that reminded Octavian of sideways Cracker Jack boxes. Eastgate was a place where angry voices tumbled out of apartment windows, where the streetlights never worked, and dogs, on unreliable chains, barked from behind broken fences when Octavian walked by.

Sometimes Francis was in the park that ran down the middle of Enright Avenue with his new friends, Chris Dumar and Dante Nickerson, and sometimes Francis was there alone, hidden except for the orange glow at the end of his cigarette. Those nights it was easy to get him to come home. But most of the time he was over at Chris's big cousin's house over on Clemens, and then getting him home was more complicated.

Chris's cousin, known as City Ass Cedric, was much older than Francis and his friends. Cedric was big, big like a football player, with square shoulders and no neck. He had green eyes, a gold tooth, and skin the color of cold butter. He was always the one to open the door when Octavian knocked.

Usually, by the time he got there, Octavian had psyched himself up to be mad. What was Francis thinking, being over there in Eastgate, getting high and drunk with City Ass Cedric while their mother was dying? Octavian would promise himself he was going to threaten to tell their father when they got home, but then Cedric would open the door a crack and Octavian would look through the cover of weed smoke, beyond where Cedric stood guard, and see a handgun on the table or a pipe in an ashtray and feel afraid. He'd swallow and look up at Cedric. "Francis needs to come home," he'd say. "My mama's sick, you know?"

"Aight, lil man, aight, chill," Cedric always said. "Frankie'll be right out."

Sometimes Francis did come right away, but most of the time Octavian sat on the hard, heavy steps of the hallway and waited. He ran his index finger up and down the grooves of dirty grout between the broken tiles on the hallway floor and listened to the sounds of the neighbor's television that echoed through the building.

One night, he fell asleep waiting, his body curled onto the landing. Francis woke him, shaking him by the shoulder. The hallway was quiet, and Francis had creases on his face like he'd been asleep.

"C'mon," Francis said. Octavian got up and followed him as he pushed open the heavy front door of the building and let it slam back on Octavian.

"What the hell, Francis?" Octavian said.

Francis, who was already many steps ahead of him, turned back, palmed Octavian's face, and mushed him to the ground. Then he turned and walked away.

It was the first cold night of fall, and Octavian sat on the frigid sidewalk. Around him, Eastgate was nearly silent and Octavian realized it must be extra late. Like late enough that they both might get in trouble.

Octavian's mind filled with static. This was not the Francis Octavian knew. Octavian's brother, Francis, wasn't always nice, but he was always his friend. The one who always split his candy bar in half, who showed Octavian how to throw a strike and how to organize his baseball cards. Francis took Octavian with him to the comic book store and the record store and, if Francis had money, he always bought something for Octavian. It wasn't that he couldn't be cruel. Francis never missed a chance to tease Octavian about how he wasn't nearly as cool or cute as Francis was, but Francis would never let anything bad happen to him.

Octavian sat on the sidewalk and waited for Francis to come back the way he always did when he'd been too mean. But Francis didn't turn around. He just kept walking away. Octavian scampered to his feet and began to run toward the yellow-and-white stripes of Francis's Polo rugby. He had almost caught up when the lights on Delmar changed, and Octavian heard his mother's warning voice to wait for the walk sign before he crossed the wide boulevard. He was grateful to be only three blocks from home.

He turned the corner onto their street and saw the blue, the red, the white lights of the police car before he saw Francis. A cop had him. Francis's long, thin arms were pressed behind his back and his face was smashed up against the window of the car. "What the hell are you doing over here, boy?" the cop said.

Octavian stood transfixed on the corner. He was only twenty feet away but enough in the shadows that neither Francis nor the cop saw him. The lights of the cop car burned his eyes and his breath was taut in his throat.

"I live right there," Francis said. "6616 Washington."

"I just got a call from an extremely worried woman," the cop said. "She said there's been some suspicious characters in this neighborhood, especially late at night. I'm thinking she musta been talking about you."

"I told you," Francis said. "I live here."

The officer let go of Francis's arms and got close to his face and sniffed. "You been drinking, haven't you?" he said. "What else you been doing? Smokin' a little reefer? Been shooting dope?"

In his head, Octavian heard what their father told them every time they passed someone getting pulled over, *Boys, if you ever find yourself in an encounter with the police, be polite, don't talk back. Say "I'm sorry." Say "I'm sorry, sir."* Francis turned away from the officer and, at that moment, his eyes met Octavian's.

Francis turned back to the cop and stood up straighter and said, "Yeah. I been drinking, smoking too. But I ain't been shootin' dope. At least not today."

There was a cadence to Francis's voice that made the hair on the back of Octavian's neck stand up. The cop must have heard it, too, because he grabbed ahold of Francis's arm with one hand,

and with the other, he wound up and swung long and hard across Francis's face. Octavian gasped as the spit and blood flew out of his brother's mouth and splattered across the hood of the cop car.

Octavian whispered, "Cut it out, Frankie. Cut it out *right now.* Stop being crazy, he's going to kill you." But Francis didn't hear him. He wobbled and swayed. Then he hauled off and smiled, his teeth soaked with blood.

What happened next was as bitter as coal on the tongue, as sand under the fingernails. A black boot struck, a club smashed. Francis's handsome face twisted as his slender body rolled across the sidewalk under the impact. And Octavian was only able to stand in the haze of the flashing lights and watch. Inside his head the screaming was so loud he wished he could hold his hands over his ears, but outside he was silent until he saw his brother's golden eyes close and he was sure he was dead. Then Octavian ran, ran right for the cop who had the club up over his head, ready to bring it down hard, again.

"Please, please, Mr. Officer. Sir," Octavian said as he grabbed hold of the suspended arm. "That's my brother, please stop. We live right here. Like he said. I promise you. Please stop. I can go inside right now and get my father. Please, my mother is sick, she's dying. I was supposed to bring him home. Please."

The cop looked down at Octavian and said, "Who the fuck are you?"

Octavian looked up at him. The skin on his face was thick and marked with angry black stubble. "I'm his brother, sir," he said. "My name is Octavian. Octavian Munroe. That's Francis."

"Where'd you come from?" the cop said, and shook Octavian off his arm.

"I was right there," Octavian said and pointed to the corner. "I was bringing him home, like I said. My mother is sick. She wants him home with her."

The cop looked down the empty street before he lowered his body so he could be eye-to-eye with Octavian. "You didn't see nothing, you understand me?" he said. "Your fucking brother, he fell down and that's what happened. If I find out that some uppity parents have reported their son got pushed around by a cop, I'm coming for you. Not your brother. You. You understand?"

Octavian nodded.

Francis was laid out on the sidewalk and still. Still and silent. The cop stood up and gave him a shove with the toe of his boot. "Remember," he said to Octavian, "I know where you live."

Octavian waited until the car, lights still going, turned the corner before he fell to the ground in a frightened ball. In his chest, he felt his heart seize and then began to slam up against his ribs while his lungs grasped at threads of air. He lay on the sidewalk and wondered if he was going to die, die right there next to his wounded brother with the light from their living room window glowing down on the both of them. He felt nothing but his heart and the squeezing of his lungs until Francis's fingers, long and scraped, reached over and intertwined with his.

Octavian tried to focus on the soft rhythm with which Frankie's thumb ran across the back of his hand and willed his heart to match that beat instead. They lay there holding hands until Octavian's breath came easier and until Francis could push himself to sit up.

Octavian felt as fragile as the lavender tissue paper that lined his grandmother's drawers. Francis's lip was split wide and his angled cheeks were swollen, crusted over with dark brown blood. He looked young in a way he rarely did. So young that Octavian hesitated before he said, "What do we do now, Frankie?"

Francis stood up and pulled Octavian to his feet. He hunched a bit to the side where the cop had hit him the hardest and looked up at the second floor. "We wait for Pop to go to sleep," he said.

"And then?"

"What do you mean, 'And then?'" The youth that had been in Francis's face for that brief, kind moment was gone. "And then you take your ass to sleep and don't say shit. That's what."

"What are you going to tell Pop about those bruises?"

Francis looked away and shrugged. "I don't know. That I got in a fight or something. He doesn't pay any attention to anything but Mama now anyway."

"You're not going to tell him that it was a cop? You wasn't doin' nothing wrong, Frankie, he shouldn't a done that to you."

"Don't be stupid, Tave," Francis said, looking Octavian in the eye for the first time that night. "What's Pop going to do anyway? You know he told us we don't have any rights when it comes to the cops. Plus, you heard the motherfucker, didn't you? He knows where we live. Believe me, he will come find my ass and yours too. Just like he said he would. So do me a favor and keep your big fucking mouth shut."

Octavian felt his heart start to beat fast again and he swallowed the breath that tried to catch. "Okay, Frankie," he said.

"I'm not playing, Tave."

"I said okay."

After the night with the cop, Octavian thought of little else other than when his heart would seize up again. During class, as long as he could focus on the concrete, definitive answers of long division, the pattern of diagramming sentences, he was able to keep the attacks away, but the playground was another story. He no longer saw the point of kickball or playing hopscotch with the girls. Instead, he concealed himself inside one of the big cement climbing tunnels on the far end of the playground and listened for his tormented heartbeat.

It reminded him of a time, back before his grandmother Fabiola died, when he and Francis used to spend tortuously long Sunday afternoons after church at her house. One vicious hot day, a bird flew in through the open back door and, unable to understand Francis and Octavian's desperate movements to get it to fly back out, the bird flung itself again and again toward the blue sky on the other side of the living room window, until finally, it landed in a clump on the floor.

With tender hands, Francis had picked up the bird and cradled it in his palm. The bird's neck was bent like a wilted flower. The two brothers sat beside each other on the plastic-covered orange couch and Octavian ran his forefinger along the dappled brown breast. The bird's body began to stiffen and Fabiola came in and told them to "dispose of the damn thing, would you please?"

Inside the climbing tunnel on the playground, Octavian's heart bashed against the window of his rib cage and he wondered if his heart would also wilt, stiffening into hardened stone. Sometimes he sang songs to himself. One of Frankie's favorites like "Cool It Now" by New Edition, or one of his mother's like "Ain't Nobody" by Chaka Khan. But that also made him sad. So he searched the black expanse of asphalt of the playground and the unsympathetic brown bricks of the school, until he found some point of color—the flash of a pink coat on a girl playing tag, or the red hat on a second-grader crossing the monkey bars hand over hand—and followed it with his eyes until his heart begin to slow. Sometimes afterwards he was so exhausted he fell into a short, deep sleep—only to jerk awake to buoyant children running relays on the other side of the tunnel's wide cold opening, the boy in the red hat far in the lead.

Cactus Tree

MINA ROSE UNDERSTOOD AT an early age that nothing she had mattered. She didn't have a father, or own a pair of Jordache jeans, and there was no way her mother would get her jelly sandals. Instead, she had crooked teeth, sprout sandwiches in her lunch box, and her mother, Kanta Rose, who never wore makeup and refused to shave any part of her body. Mina gathered from thinly veiled whispers that this equation left Mina with a lonely fate, and she gave up on anything else making sense.

While Mina would argue otherwise, Kanta couldn't really be charged with malicious neglect. Kanta was a divorce attorney who refused to represent men. She believed she and her daughter were two women of equal merit. In her mind, her hands-off mothering of Mina was a huge improvement over the extreme, anxiety-ridden devotion of the New Jersey conservative Jewish childhood she had endured.

Mina, on the other hand, was fairly certain she had been switched at birth. She believed that, somewhere out there, her real mother longed for her. That she was waiting for the day she could make her a Jiffy peanut butter and Welch's grape jelly sandwich with the crusts cut off. If not, then her father would return someday and rescue her—a dream that, when Mina shared it, made Kanta laugh out loud and say, "That should be interesting, seeing how I was impregnated by the stars. And Joni Mitchell."

This, of course, was a lie. The real story was one that Kanta would never tell a soul, not even Mina. This was partially because the only thing she would have been able to tell Mina about her father was that he was a man named Rob who sold peyote and lived somewhere in New Mexico. But also, on the night Kanta got pregnant with Mina in the summer of '73, she heard Joni Mitchell sing for the first time, and lay in a field as meteors rushed toward earth, lighting up the sky with an explosion of shooting stars. And this was a much better story.

Back then Kanta had run from her oppressive, conservative Jewish childhood and wound up on Willow Farm—500 acres of Missouri woods and dry river hollers, with clear creeks and algae-covered rocks that made your feet slip. Willow Farm was owned by Marianne Hendricks, who opened it in 1962, proclaiming any wayward girl, discarded woman, or runaway was welcome. The word spread in whispers behind barns and under the stalls of girls' bathrooms. From the lips of one girl to another they told each other: *There's this place you can go. A place far away from everything, where you don't have to get married, where you could be in love with another woman, where your dad, your mom, your stepfather with the belt, can't find you.*

If they arrived pregnant, they had choices. For those who didn't want their babies, Marianne knew how to work the magic of teas and berries. And if they did want their children, they weren't left to the mercy of bitter doctors with blue plastic gloves and high forceps. Their babies arrived like Mina did, on soft patches of green moss atop a pile of handmade quilts, lovingly coaxed into the world by Marianne's soft hands. It never concerned Kanta to inform Rob, and a year after Mina was born, Kanta was long gone from Willow Farm. The story she told herself about her child being created by the stars and Joni's sweet voice was already the only story she knew.

Mina secretly wished that Kanta was more like her third-grade teacher, Ms. Fitzgerald. Ms. Fitzgerald was the most beautiful woman Mina had ever seen. She had deep brown skin and eye-lashes that reached up and touched her eyebrows. She wore her hair tied in a bun and had a neck that curved like a swan's. When Ms. Fitzgerald leaned over to help Mina with a math problem, Mina would inhale long, slow breaths of rosewater and bleach. More than once, Mina invented a bad headache so that she could sit with Ms. Fitzgerald during recess and suck on the round pep-permint candies she kept in her purse.

When Kanta showed up for Third Grade Parent Night wearing a threadbare tank top, Mina gasped as she watched her embrace Ms. Fitzgerald in an unexpected hug. She saw Kanta's thick black armpit hair cascade across Ms. Fitzgerald's immaculate silk blouse with the cloth-covered buttons like tiny pillows. On the car ride home, Mina continued to see the uncomfortable smile Ms. Fitz-gerald gave them when they left, and she unleashed on Kanta a fury of tears and sobs.

"Who cares about my hairy armpits?" Kanta wanted to know. She was sure, she told Mina, that Ms. Fitzgerald didn't shave her armpits. "Have you ever seen her armpits?" Kanta asked.

"Of course I haven't seen her armpits," Mina said. "But I'm sure if I did, they would not be overflowing with hair like yours."

Kanta scoffed. "You think you know everything. Most black women don't shave their armpits."

Mina looked out the window at the tall stone lions guarding the entrance to the Loop and felt overwhelmed by the conviction that her mother would never understand her. It was not the first time or the last she would feel this way. A few months later, Kanta an-nounced to her friend Hermine at dinner one night that Mina could speak jive. Hermine, who dressed in unfortunate shades of purple, had thin, mottled skin covered with rusty freckles and bright red hair. She opened her eyes wide.

"You *can*? That is so cool! I wish I could speak jive. Speak jive, Mina. Go ahead."

Mina flipped the bland fava beans over on her plate and felt her face grow bitter hot. "No," she said. That day at recess, her best friend, Makeba, had told her, "You ain't never gonna be black, Mina." It was after she'd tried and failed again to jump Double Dutch without the ropes winding around her neck, her ankle, or catching on her arm. And the turners, Patrice and Sheryl, had groaned, "Come *on!*"

Makeba was nearly a foot taller than everyone else in third grade and rail thin. She had dark brown skin and wore her hair in thin broken cornrows. Makeba was the closest thing Mina had to a best friend. Makeba also didn't have a father. But Makeba didn't have a mother either. Just an angry auntie who'd never let Makeba go over to Mina's house to play. And sometimes, like that afternoon at recess, Makeba had bruises on her face or scratches on her arms. Like Mina, Makeba's pants were always too short and she wore threadbare T-shirts in the winter, but even though Mina was often accused of flooding, nobody ever teased Makeba. She'd been known to wait for girls or boys after school who talked about her during the day and give them bruises worse than her own. She was the fastest runner in the whole school and definitely the best Double Dutch jumper in the third grade—and probably the fourth grade, too.

"It's alright," Makeba said, handing Mina a green apple Jolly Rancher. "I ain't never gonna be white."

Kanta got up and began stacking the plates on top of the pile of dirty dishes that clambered up out of the sink and spilled onto the counter. "Oh, come on," she said. "I heard you talking jive the other day when you were playing with your dolls. And back in February, when you recited that poem by, by—what was the poet's name?"

"Langston Hughes?"

"Right, Langston Hughes," Kanta said. "You spoke jive when you read that poem, remember? The one about the crystal stair?"

"I don't remember how that goes anymore," Mina said.

"So just speak jive." Kanta gave Mina a frustrated look.

"I thought you said I should never feel forced to do something I don't want to do."

Hermine laughed her rough smoker's laugh and said, "Told you you were creating a monster."

Kanta sat back down and changed her tone. "Please, Mina Min," she said. "I think it's so cool that you can speak jive. I wish I could."

"I can't just *speak jive*," Mina said. "I need something to talk about, someone to talk to."

"I know, you can read a book." Kanta jumped up again and grabbed the copy of *Grimm's Fairy Tales* that had been left on the counter by the phone years before and never moved. She put it down hard on the table in front of Mina. "Read something from this." The book was covered in a sticky layer of oil, pollen, and dust and Mina saw it held Kanta's fingerprints from where she'd picked it up. "Read *Little Red Riding Hood* in jive!" Kanta's eyes were full of bright anticipation. She was ready to be entertained.

Mina stared long and hard at the woman whom she'd never called "Mama" or "Mom" or even "Mother." She was Kanta. A word that balled up in Mina's throat as she took her plate to the sink. "Kiss my ass, Kanta," she said, and walked out of the kitchen.

Behind her she heard Hermine say, "I think that was jive, wasn't it?" And they burst into laughter.

Someone to Watch Over Me

BY THE FIFTH GRADE, Mina had given into her life with Kanta and no longer thought about the mother she wished she had. There were moments, Mina was pretty sure, that Kanta loved her. One was the day, while waiting for Kanta to buy Ivory soap at Williams Pharmacy, Mina absentmindedly picked up a copy of *The Mighty Avengers: The Wraiths Walk Among Us* off the comic book stand and asked Kanta to buy it for her. In untrue form, Kanta nodded, handed the comic book to the blue-haired lady behind the counter, and paid the extra fifty cents.

After that, Mina didn't need jellies, or jeans that fit. She didn't dream of her long-lost father. Her powers were endless. She could freeze the world around her and skate over the frozen shapes of children with fingers pointed, mouths open in laughter. She became bigger than the buildings, her muscles stretching out her skin—which turned blue or green, and was instantly cloaked in armor, in invisibility. Mina was no longer sad that Makeba had moved away, or as rumor had it, was sent to a foster home, and instead played games where she used her powers to go rescue her and they flew off together to save the world. At home, she played alone on the rusting swing set in the backyard until the chill of darkness overcame her. At school, she spent recess sitting in a climbing tunnel perfect for hiding and reading.

The first time Mina saw Octavian in the tunnel with his eyes closed, she cursed. Her one escape from the terrifying stew that was the playground had been taken and she was left with dismal alternatives. She resolved to take cover in the last stall of the girls' bathroom, surrounded by angry pink metal walls spotted with the names of classmates and excrement wiped from errant fingers. She didn't care, really. The stall worked as well as the tunnel, was less distracting even, and she was happy until the day the thick brown shoes of Mrs. Korchoran, the playground monitor, appeared under the stall door and Mina was forced back outside.

Mina circled the climbing tunnel for a week until she came to the reluctant conclusion that Octavian wasn't going anywhere. No matter how fast she got outside, he was always huddled there, his face hidden between his knees, or leaned back, eyes closed— sometimes looking like he'd fallen asleep. She gave up hoping that he would leave and did her best to join the fray, but after one particularly long recess, in which she was somehow convinced to join an unfortunate game of dodge ball, she determined she had no other choice, and scooted in next to him.

Right away she knew something was wrong. When he looked at her, his eyes showed too much white, his irises black dots of terror. His breath came in and out of his open mouth in dry, short bursts and he grabbed hold of her hand when she tried to get up and go.

"Don't," he said, his voice pitched high with fear.

"I'm going to get help," she said. "You need help."

Octavian closed his eyes and swallowed so hard Mina saw the skin of his neck fold in and out around his throat.

"Wait," he said. "It goes away."

"What does?" Mina asked and turned her hand around in his so that he was no longer hurting her fingers, but so she still held his hand.

"My heart," he said. Now his voice was barely audible.

"Your heart doesn't go away," she said.

"The beating does," he said. "I just got to hold on."

Mina waited a few minutes. "Should I read my comic to you while we wait?" Mina said. She was still holding his hand. Octavian shrugged.

Mina pulled the rolled-up comic out of her coat pocket, spread it across her thin knees, and started to read aloud. Over the banging in his chest, Octavian listened. There was something hushed and warm in her voice that made his heart slow down enough that it felt safe to look at her. He had seen her before. There had once been a lot of white kids at Delmar Harvard, but most of them had moved away, so he recognized the ones who were left. Mina was the one in his grade with the long hair and holes in her sneakers. Her pants were always flooding. Octavian remembered she used to hang out with Makeba before Makeba got sent to a foster home. Her hand in his was dry and cold.

"Who's your favorite?" he managed to say. "I mean, of the characters."

She was relieved to hear his voice sound more normal. "I like the X-Men," she said. "And Daredevil is one of my favorites, and the Amazing Spider-Man. Oh, and I like Power Man and Iron Fist and Fire Star." She also loved Rogue and Wonder Woman but, she said, "Superman is stupid."

Octavian nodded. "I can't stand Superman either."

Now recess meant Octavian and Mina sitting side by side in the tunnel with their feet up on one wall, their backs against the other, and comics open across their laps. Neither said much to the other, but when Octavian's heart began to act up, he would reach over and grip Mina's hand and she would start reading aloud from wherever she was.

On a day when winter finally began to carry the smell of spring, Mina brought a new *X-Men* comic with Wolverine on the cover. Octavian examined the beast's angry face, his razor claws, the torment in his eyes, and said, "I could draw that."

Mina moved her hair aside to get a closer look and said, "Probably." She motioned for him to trade her for his copy of *Fantastic Four*.

The next day, Octavian brought a pencil, a piece of paper, and a hardcover book to lean on and carefully copied the picture of Wolverine. When the bell rang, he showed it to Mina. She studied it and smiled big enough that Octavian saw her crooked bottom teeth for the first time.

"It looks just like him," she said, and handed it back. "You should sign it, like a real artist."

Wolverine's pointed fangs were honed and sharp, and the menacing saliva on his lips dripped down into a puddle at the bottom of the page. Octavian turned the paper over and wrote, *For Mina Rose From Octavian Munroe*. He handed her the drawing and abruptly tucked the book under his arm, the pencil behind his ear, and scrambled out of the tunnel. He walked fast toward the building without looking back.

That night, Octavian went home and drew the Hulk saving the Scarlett Witch from an alien who had legs like a praying mantis, a mouth like a great white shark, and a long serpent's tail. He was especially pleased with the alien because he hadn't copied him, but had made it up himself. Octavian took the drawing in to show his mother.

Cordelia sat up a little on her pillows when he walked in and handed her the drawing. "Did you do this?" she asked, her glassy eyes brightening. Octavian noticed how her wedding ring slid down and caught on the dark knot of her knuckle when she held up the drawing. Octavian nodded and sat down on the bed. She pointed at the alien and said, "I like him the best."

"I got the idea from a *Doctor Who* episode I watched last week."

"Is your father still letting you watch that show? Doesn't it come on at midnight on Sunday or something?"

"Not midnight, Mama. It comes on at ten. Pop said it's okay since I don't want to watch nothing else."

"Anything else. You don't want to watch anything else."

"Right. Sorry, Mama."

Cordelia pointed to the Scarlett Witch. "I thought there were black girls in comic books," she said.

"There are."

"Then why'd you draw her?" Her voice sounded crisp with anger. Octavian shrugged.

"You know what Malcolm X said about white women?" Octavian shook his head.

"He said they were the black man's poison." She widened her eyes and Octavian saw that the yellow went way back behind her eyelids.

"Yes, Mama," he said. He felt the bird fluttering in his chest.

"Don't hate who you are, Octavian," she said.

"I don't, Mama," he said.

"Ever," she said and handed him the drawing.

"I won't. I promise." He stood up and brushed his lips against the fine gauze of her cheek.

"Is your brother home?" she asked.

"No, Mama, I think he's with Ivy at the library, but he'll be home soon," Octavian said. He worried she would know he was lying, but her eyes were already getting heavy and he closed the door quietly behind him.

In the living room, his father sat reading in his orange chair and listening to Ella Fitzgerald. He looked up when Octavian walked in. "Hey, Son," he said.

"Hey, Pop."

"You alright?"

Octavian nodded.

"What you got there?" Cyrus asked and pointed to the drawing Octavian forgot he held in his hand. Octavian walked over and handed it to him.

Cyrus pushed his reading glasses back up and said, "This is really cool. You got an eye for this, Octavian. I didn't know that. Did you show your mother?"

"I showed her."

Cyrus looked at him over his glasses. "What she'd say?"

"That Malcolm X said white women were poison."

Cyrus moved his slippered feet off the ottoman and motioned for Octavian to sit down. He reached into his pocket for one of his soft white handkerchiefs and cleaned his lenses. "Life hasn't been easy for your mother," he said.

"I know."

"Death isn't going to be any easier."

Octavian felt the thick promise of tears that would come if he looked at his father, so he stared instead at the knotty ochre of the ottoman.

"You know, Tave," Cyrus said trying to reach his son's eyes, "your mother was, is, one of the most loving and accepting people you'll ever meet. But she spent most of her life working hard not to hate, working hard to find love and compassion, many times for people who never once thought to give it to her. Trying to continue doing *that*? When you're *dying*? It's a tall order for any of us." Cyrus stopped and waited for Octavian to look up, but he didn't. "Seems to me," Cyrus said, "that a lot of the things she didn't want to think, didn't want to say, because she was working so hard not to be hateful, are coming out now. Do you understand?"

"I think so."

"She's just worried about the decisions you're going to make since she's not going to be here to help you make them."

Octavian nodded. He hated when his father talked about his mother's furiously approaching death like it was real.

Cyrus reached over and rubbed the back of Octavian's neck. He handed him the drawing and said, "It's really good, Son, really. Keep it up."

Planet Rock

WITH THE END OF winter came the day when school photo packages were distributed. Few days conveyed the disparity of fifth-grade families' available finances as profoundly. You could quickly measure wealth by how much of a child's face showed from under the cellophane square of the white envelopes placed on each desk. The middle portion of that child's face meant their parents had enough funds to purchase the biggest package, the one that included the eight-by-ten—maybe even with the additional silhouette in the corner. Those with cellophane squares that showed the full face of the simple five-by-seven—or worse still, the sad solitary sheet of wallet photos—were quick to flip their envelopes over. And the kids who only had the free class photo that was given to every child never seemed to care.

At recess, Octavian met Mina in the tunnel and worked hard on a picture of Lt. Monica Rambeau. He brought along a dark brown pencil for her skin, blue for her giant afro, and silver for her body-tight suit. The wind had begun to blow, and it was colder in the afternoon than it had been in the morning, but his face got hot as he sat next to Mina and tried to draw Monica Rambeau's long, curvy legs, her cleavage, her hips, and he was relieved when the bell rang and he could shove the drawing inside his hardcover book without showing it to Mina.

Mina called to him as he hurried toward the building.

He stopped and turned around.

"I have to say goodbye."

"What do you mean?"

"We're moving. I have to go to a school in Clayton. My mom got a new house."

Octavian didn't know what to say, so he said, "My mom is dying."

"Right now?"

"She has cancer. She's been dying since last summer. The doctor says she's going to die soon."

Mina's eyes filled with tears, and Octavian wished he hadn't told her.

"I didn't mean to make you cry," he said.

Mina wiped her eyes. "How can I not cry? That's the saddest thing I've ever heard."

Octavian was about to tell her how he wanted to cry all the time, but that, even when he tried, really tried, it was like his tears had dried up or something, but Mrs. Korchoran screamed at them from the door to get their butts inside.

"I guess this is goodbye, then," he said.

"Goodbye, Octavian," she said. He saw that her eyes still shimmered with tears and he felt her shove something into his hand as she quickly kissed him on the cheek. Her hair against his ear was soft, not like straw the way he imagined it would be. She turned and ran and Octavian watched her skinny legs in too-short jeans dash across the playground and through the double blue doors of the building.

He looked down. In his palm was one of Mina's wallet-sized photos, her knotty hair hastily tucked behind her ears. She was smiling, but not enough to reveal those crooked bottom teeth. He wondered why no one had bothered to brush her hair—at least for picture day. Cordelia exhausted him on picture day—washing behind his ears and smoothing down his eyebrows. He wondered whether she would still be there next picture day and, if not, whether Cyrus would know to slick his eyebrows down with spit or if he'd have to do it himself. The late bell rang, and Octavian shoved the picture in his coat pocket and ran inside.

After school, Octavian looked for Mina thinking he could give her one of his pictures, but instead he found Francis with his friends Michael Ivy and Brendon Graves. Sometimes they took the bus from the high school to Delmar Harvard, to buy candy at U. City Grille and wait for Octavian.

As they walked toward home, a car drove by blasting Afrika Bambaataa, and Ivy started popping until Brendon flicked him on the ear. It was getting colder, and Octavian took his gloves out of his pocket. Mina's picture fell out and onto the ground and Francis snatched it with a crooked grin before Octavian could pick it up.

"Aw shit, look at this," he said, his eyes taunting and alive. "Tave got hisself a girrllfriend."

"Ooooh, for real?" said Ivy. He gave Francis a high five. Ivy had been Francis's best friend since the first day of kindergarten when they got in a fistfight. No one ever called him Michael or Mike anymore. For a while, he was White Mike or White Mikey, but these days he was just Ivy. Ivy lived down the street from Octavian and Francis, but Ivy spent more time at the Munroes' than he did at home—mostly because his mother was the kind of crazy that went for months without doing the laundry or cooking any type of food, but bought Ivy hundred-dollar pairs of sneakers. Ivy was small and clever and hopped around Francis and Brendon in his shell-toe Adidas like a fugitive Jack Russell Terrier.

Brendon, also known as Big Brendon or B-Boogie or just plain B, was dark skinned and massive. He wore thick glasses that were often foggy or smudged and he had a habit of licking his lips. Brendon had at least two inches and fifty pounds on Francis and he grabbed the photo out of Francis's hand. He held it up high over his head as Octavian jumped about frantically trying to get to the photograph.

"Oh, look," Brendon said, "she wrote on it."

Octavian stopped jumping. "She did?"

"Give it here," Francis said, snatching it back. "'To Octavian the artist,'" Francis read. "'Love Mina.' Ooohh," he said, slanting his eyes toward Octavian. "Love."

"Frankie," Octavian said, "can I have it back, please?"

Francis ignored him and studied the photograph carefully, moving from side to side when Octavian tried to take it. "I can't believe it," he said. "Tave got him a white girl."

Octavian kicked a rock down the street with a curse.

"She's white?" Ivy asked.

Francis held up the picture and said, "Yeah, but she's wullaford. Anyone can get a white girl like this here. It's motherfuckas like me that get the pretty ones."

"Don't say motherfucker," Octavian said under his breath.

"Since when you mess with white girls?" Brendon said.

"I been messed with them," Francis said, ignoring Octavian. "Especially the ones at the pool in Clayton in the summertime. They say, 'Ooh, Frankie, you got such pretty brown skin and such pretty light eyes,' and then they let me put my tongue in they mouths, let me feel on their little pink titties."

Octavian watched his feet. *Don't step on the crack or you'll break your mama's back,* he said to himself.

"You ain't never gonna get the kind of white girls I get, Tave," Francis said. "You're too dark and your nose is as wide as all out-side." Ivy laughed and gave Francis another high five.

They had reached the corner of Waterman where Ivy lived. Brendon turned to Francis and said, "What're you up to, Frankie?"

Francis shrugged. "Prolly going over to see Dante and them," he said. "You want to come?"

Octavian saw a shadow cross over Brendon's face. "Nah," he said. "I think Ima go play Galaga with this white boy. Why don't you come?"

"Maybe," Francis said. "Gonna take Tave home first."

Brendon smiled at Octavian and laid a massive hand on Octavian's shoulder. "You okay, Tave? How's your mom doing?"

Octavian shrugged and looked away from Brendon. He didn't feel like hearing Francis's mouth if he started to cry.

Brendon tried to snatch the photo of Mina out of Francis's hand, but Francis was too quick. "Don't worry," Brendon said. "Ain't nothing special about white girls. Your brother is just color-struck. It happens to light-skinned cats sometimes."

"Whatever, B," Francis said. They gave each other pounds and Ivy and Brendon walked up the steps to Ivy's apartment building.

When they were down the block, Francis turned to Octavian and said, "Mama's going to be mad, you know?"

"About what?"

"You know what Malcolm X said about white women?" he said, imitating Cordelia's voice. "She's gonna give you a whoopin' for sure."

Octavian knew his mother wasn't going to whoop him, she could barely stand up, but still, he didn't want Francis to upset her. And this was the new Francis. The mean one who left Octavian alone in Eastgate, the one who talked back to the cops and maybe even the one who would tell on him to his mother, even if she was sick. "Okay, Frankie," he said. "What do I have to do so that you won't tell Mama?"

Francis stopped walking. "I won't say nothing if, from now on, when Mama sends you out to find me, you don't. You hear?"

Octavian pictured his mother, her pillows wilting behind her head as she waited for Francis to come home. He thought his heart might start up, but it was quiet.

"I'm waiting," Francis said.

The dirty white sky made Octavian tighten the collar of his blue-and-black lumberjack coat against the gathering wind. He looked at Francis's refined face, his sharp cheekbones, his full lips. It would be easy to draw Francis. "Okay, Frankie," he said.

Francis smiled his lazy, handsome smile and started to walk away throwing the picture of Mina over his shoulder. It caught the wind and flew into the air. Mina's sad smile, her stringy hair, fluttered about like a butterfly lost and left over to find its way in the cold. The picture landed facedown on the sidewalk and Octavian picked it up, saw her neat, clear handwriting. *To Octavian the artist.*

The artist, it said.

Down the block, Francis's shoulders were broad inside his Raiders starter jacket. Octavian thought about the day they had bought their coats. It hadn't even gotten cold yet and Cordelia was already sick, but she took them coat shopping every year, and this year wasn't going to be any different. Frankie had been nice that day. Octavian remembered he'd even grabbed a hold of Octavian's hand in the Venture, said he didn't want him to get lost. Octavian had been grateful for Francis's strong hand around his. Their mother, who had never been a thin woman, now seemed to disappear inside her sweater, and she walked so slowly through the store that it made Octavian afraid. He'd wondered if Frankie knew he was scared. Maybe he was, too.

Octavian pulled his own coat tighter around himself and followed his brother. At the corner, there was a wide opening in the sidewalk that led down to the sewer system and Octavian crumpled the photo in his fist and threw it in, sending Mina down to the Mississippi.

At home, Octavian quietly put the envelope of photos on Cordelia's bedside table. The section of the eight-by-ten that was visible showed Octavian's wide smile, and the nose Francis called wide as all outside. Cordelia opened her heavy eyes. "Hey, baby," she said and reached out for his hand.

Octavian wanted to fall into her long arms, to have her scratch the hollering out of his head with her crescent moon fingernails. But her eyelids began to droop again and he knew there was no space left in his mother for him to curl up in anymore. He let his small hand drop into her thin, shaking palm. "Got our school pictures back today," he said.

Cordelia opened her eyes again and pushed herself up. "Let me see," she said.

Octavian handed her the envelope and she pulled out the eight-by-ten and smiled, showing her bottom teeth that, unlike Mina's, were perfect and straight. Cordelia traced the side of Octavian's face in the photograph. There were tears in her eyes, but she was smiling.

"You are the most beautiful boy," she said, and pulled Octavian into her arms.

He tried not to think about how different it felt from how he wanted it to.

"I love you," she said.

"I love you too," he said into the paper skin of her neck.

She sat back on the pillows and Octavian stood up. "You got homework to do?"

"Nah, I finished it already."

"What are you going to do?"

"I was thinking about drawing a picture of Francis."

"Now that's a good idea," she said, and put the photograph back into the envelope.

Octavian began to walk out of the room. "Hey, Tave," she said, and Octavian turned around.

"You want any of these wallet-sized ones to give to your friends?" She was still elegant. Even though she seemed to be getting dimmer and dimmer every day.

"No thanks, Mama," he said.

"You sure?"

"I'm sure."

Little Red Corvette

AFTER KANTA SOLD THEIR house in U. City, they stayed in Hermine's house down the street from their old house while their new house in Clayton was fixed up. "I don't understand why we had to move or why you took me out of Delmar Harvard in the first place," Mina said.

"I like our new house," Kanta said. "It's in a good neighborhood."

But this made no sense to Mina, as she'd heard Kanta tell Hermine the other day how much she loved their old neighborhood. She and Hermine were arguing because Hermine had been trying to get Kanta to help her revamp the Freedom of Residence Committee of the 1960s to further integrate their neighborhood.

"Do you realize, Kanta, that there is only one black family in the whole Parkview neighborhood?" Hermine said.

"And Jews still can't buy real estate in Webster Groves," Kanta said.

"That's not true anymore," Hermine said, and pushed the petition she'd been circulating across the table to Kanta. "I've only been able to get three signatures on this thing. I never thought everyone around me could still be a racist."

"Don't bother, Hermine," Kanta said, pushing the petition back. "What with the white people moving out of the school district, it is just a matter of time."

Mina sat on Hermine's toilet and wondered, a matter of time before what? Mina stared at one of the many dark brown freckles on her legs. Try as she might, she couldn't will one to grow bigger and wider, to spread across her pink mottled body until she was all that same dark brown. Still, she stared and waited. Nothing happened. She stood up and looked at her stringy hair in her reflection. "Makeba was right," she said aloud. "You ain't never gonna be black."

It was no longer because of Double Dutch or Ms. Fitzgerald that Mina wished she could make herself black. It was because Mina Rose, descendent of Menachem Rosencrantz—who came to America to escape the Russian pogroms and promptly changed his name to Michael Rose—wished more than anything she could be Thelma Evans. The afroed older sister on *Good Times* was everything that Mina was not. Thelma was beautiful, wise, strong-willed, and cool-cool. If Mina were Thelma, she would definitely be able to jump Double Dutch—and it wouldn't even matter if she couldn't.

Mina stuck her tongue out at her reflection and walked into Hermine's study. On her desk was an open pack of Winston Lights and a pile of dollar bills. Mina picked them up. There were fifteen of them. What would it matter if she took four? Hermine would still have eleven whole dollars. With four dollars, she could buy a lot of candy *and* soda. Or she could get two comics and at least one Milky Way bar, and maybe still have enough for a Pepsi. Mina looked out the window at Limits Walk, the path that divided U. City and St. Louis City, and ran into the Loop. Mina remembered hearing the boys who hung out in front of Delmar Harvard talking about a record store in the Loop that had all the jams. Mina wondered if four dollars was enough to buy a record. Mina was sure she had to be better at dancing than she was at Double Dutch, and even if she wasn't, she could still listen to cool music the way

Thelma did. Plus, she thought, Octavian lived in U. City, maybe she'd run into him.

Mina folded the money and put it in the back pocket of her jeans and felt bold. She picked up the pack of cigarettes and shook one out and grabbed the lighter, too. These she put carefully in her other pocket.

She smoked the cigarette as she walked and, at first, she coughed so hard she thought she was going to throw up. But then she slowed down, took shorter drags, and stopped coughing. When she reached the Loop, she put it out. She felt light headed. Light headed and cool. Mina passed a bookshop and a pizza place. There was a store that advertised used instruments for U. City High jazz band students. From another shop, where the front window was filled with pipes and boxes of cigars, a sweet smell spread out from the open door. The marquis at the Tivoli movie theater announced Hitchcock's *Rope* Monday through Friday, and *Rocky Horror Picture Show* on Saturday at midnight.

Out on the sun-drenched boulevard, Mina's sense of coolness began to fade, as she became aware of the dirt on her sweatshirt, the tape at the end of her frayed shoelaces. She passed nodding junkies leaning on the side of a graffiti-covered building, and skinheads sitting on a brick wall by the parking lot. *I am the only ten-year-old girl walking alone here*, she thought. Even though she was intimate with her own loneliness, this was the first time she'd seen it out on display for the rest of the world.

She was about to turn around and head back, when the sound of a screeching guitar made her stop. Above the door was a sign that said "Rahsaan's Records" and next to it was a drawing of a man playing three saxophones at once. In the window, David Bowie's pensive eyes burned deep from the cover of *Young Americans* into her own.

She walked in as the music changed to a smooth trumpet and a piano. Mina blinked to adjust to the smoky, dust-filled room. She saw a maze of record shelves and two customers—a black man wearing glasses and a brown leather hat, and a white girl with heavy blue eyelids and dark hair chopped short. From the ceiling hung signs handwritten in graffiti to mark different sections: Funk, Reggae, Rock, R&B, Classical, Jazz, Pop. On the walls were more posters: Aerosmith live at Kiel Auditorium, Aretha Franklin's *Lady Soul*, Johnny Cash's *At Folsom Prison*, John Coltrane's *Blue Train*.

"Hey there, girl," a voice said. "You lost?" A big white man with pale, puffy skin stood behind a high counter. He wore a Cardinals baseball cap pulled down low.

Mina swallowed. "No," she said.

"Well, perhaps I can help you," he said.

"Is four dollars enough to buy a record?" she asked.

"That depends on what kind of record you be wantin'," the man said.

Mina shrugged her thin shoulders. She thought again of the hole in her sneaker, the snarls in her hair. "I don't know," she said.

"How old are you, chile?" he asked.

"Ten," she said.

"Your mama know where you at? And your daddy?"

"My mom, she knows. I don't have a father."

"Mhmm-hmmm," he said. "What's your name?"

"I'm Mina Rose," she said. "Who are you?"

He held a hand to his heart in mock disbelief. "Baby girl, you mean to tell me you don't know who I am?"

Mina shook her head seriously.

He laughed. "My given name's Jimmy, baby, but my friends call me Bones, so you call me Bones, aight? This your first time here at Rahsaan's?"

Mina nodded.

Bones looked around proudly and said, "Well, welcome. And now that we friends, you gonna tell me what kind of record is you lookin' for?"

Mina swallowed. "You wouldn't happen to know what kind of music Thelma Evans listens to, would you?" she asked.

Bones slapped the counter with his fleshy palms. "Thelma? From *Good Times?*"

Mina looked him right in the eye and said, "She's cool-cool."

Bones nodded. "Cool-cool is right. And finer than frog hair."

"So do you know what kind of music she listens to?"

"Let me think on that now," Bones said. "Hey, Freddy," he yelled to a tall man in the corner who was hanging up a Tito Puente poster.

"What's up, Bones?" he said.

"You got any idea what kinda music Thelma from *Good Times* might listen to?"

Fred scratched his head. "I know it was Blinky Williams and Jim Gilstrap that did the theme song. But I've never thought about it otherwise." Fred looked at Mina and gave her a gentle wave. She waved back.

"I've got an idea," Bones said. He took the jazz record off the player that was behind the counter and eased the needle down on a different record. A slow synthesized beat came out of the speakers.

"I know this song," Mina said. "It's about a car."

Bones laughed again. "This is Prince. What you know about Prince, girl?"

"I like this song. Do you think Thelma likes Prince?"

"You God damn right," Bones said, his eyes twinkling down at her.

"Can I buy this record, the one with this song on it, for four dollars?"

Bones pointed Mina toward the section under the FUNK sign and said, "The Prince records are over there. Look for the one called *1999*." Mina wound her way through the record shelves to the Funk section. Her hands flipped slowly through the records until she found *1999* with its purple cover. She turned it over and read the names of the songs. "'Little Red Corvette.' That's this song, right?" Mina asked over her shoulder.

"Right," Bones said, and stuck a cigarette between his lips.

"The price tag says \$6.99," Mina said, walking back to him. "I told you, I only have four dollars."

Bones took the record from her and put it into a brown bag. "Listen here," he said. "Ima give it to you for fo' dollars, but you got to make me a deal."

Mina looked at him with her sharp gray eyes and waited.

"You gotta promise me you won't just listen to 'Little Red Corvette' over and over and then cut the record off. You gotta listen to the whole thing from beginning to end. Matter of fact, there's two records in there. If you gotta stop, then you start again right where you left off. You hear?"

"Why?"

"Because that's how Prince meant for it to be listened to," Bones said. "And . . . because that's what Thelma Evans would do. Okay?"

Mina considered this. "I can do that," she said.

"Then it's yours."

Mina took the folded bills out of her back pocket and pushed them across the counter. Bones picked them up and slowly smoothed them before putting them into the cash register. "Thank you, madam," he said. "You come on back whenever you want, you hear?"

Mina shrugged and said, "Can't."

"Now why's that?"

"We don't live in the neighborhood anymore. My mother said it was only a matter of time. We're moving to Clayton."

"Hmmmm . . . she let you ride the Bi-State?"

"Probably. She pretty much lets me do whatever I want."

"The number seventy-three from Clayton brings you right there," he said and pointed to the bus stop in front of the store.

Mina smiled at him, showing her row of crooked teeth on the bottom. "Alright," she said. "The number seventy-three?"

Bones nodded. "Cost you a quarter," he said.

She started to turn away and then turned back. "Thank you, Mr. Bones," she said.

"Mmmm-hmmm. I'll be seeing you."

"See you," Mina said.

When she got to the door, Bones called out, "Hey, Mina girl."

She stopped and turned around.

"You cool-cool, just like Thelma Evans. Don't never want to be nobody but you, you hear?"

Mina nodded and walked out the door. The sun was going down on Delmar Boulevard, but Mina was no longer afraid. She skip-walked back to Hermine's, unaware of anything other than the record that she held tight to her chest. When she got to the house, Kanta and Hermine were still out and Mina opened the back door with the key Kanta had tied to a piece of twine and put around Mina's neck.

Mina took the record from the bag and pulled out the sleeve. It had a photo of a barely covered Prince lying on a purple expanse, with an untouched set of watercolors in front of him. The center of the record was filled with a darkly lined eye and Mina put it on Hermine's record player and lowered the needle. She lay down on her stomach on the rug with her feet in the air and listened.

From the beginning, Prince told her in a computerized, God-like voice not to worry, that he wouldn't hurt her, that he only wanted her to have some fun. Mina kept her promise to Bones and listened to both albums from start to finish and, as the sun went down and one song blended into the next, Mina dissolved into a funk-induced trance. For a second time that day, she saw herself in a new way. This time through Prince's eyes: black and white, boy and girl, and cool-cool, Double Dutching so fast, she couldn't even see her own feet.

Stolen Moments

ON A LATE SUMMER night in 1972, over a decade before Mina walked in Rahsaan's Records, Bones heard his first jazz recording. He was sitting in his uncle's car parked in the red-light district of Memphis, and ever since, he'd dedicated his life to chasing the feeling he got that night. It was like the door to his soul came unbolted and the hollow and angry spaces got filled up with the closest thing he would ever know to God. From that moment forward, the only thing he cared about was finding a way to make sure the lock stayed broken forever.

Back then, Bones was seventeen and wasn't called Bones yet. He was still Little Jimmy. Even though the only thing that was little about him was what he knew. Otherwise, Little Jimmy was big— big head, big calves, big wrists, big red pimples across his big wide face. His only friend was his uncle Floyd. Floyd was ten years older than Jimmy, but he was what back then was called slow, and that made him more like a cousin than an uncle. Floyd had recently won a personal injury claim against the local plastics company where he worked, so he had more money than anyone in the family, but he didn't have a job. One Saturday, Floyd came over still drunk from the night before, and told Jimmy to come with him to get some pussy. Jimmy had no intention of getting anything, but he didn't want Floyd to drive. He'd busted up his car too many times that year as it was.

In the twilight of the late-summer evening on a reckless street on the other side of town, Jimmy watched as Floyd walked up the block and took hold of a prostitute's hand with something sort of kin to tenderness. She wore a red feather in her ragged wig and Jimmy watched the backs of her dark-brown legs, thin and worn down, as she followed Floyd into one of the many crumbling buildings.

Jimmy sank down in the seat so as not to be seen, turned on the car, and pressed in the lighter. He checked to be sure the doors were locked and that the windows were rolled up and thought about how his mother would kill Floyd if she knew he'd left her son alone in the car over on the black side of town. Jimmy jumped when the lighter popped and he scolded himself as he pressed the hot orange circle to the end of his cigarette. He switched on the radio, thinking a little music might calm him down, but he couldn't get reception on the stations he knew.

Down the block, a storefront was lit from within and the sign in the window read *WKWK 1080AM*. Jimmy turned the dial and the car filled with sounds Jimmy had never heard before. There were proud horns, thick stand-up bass lines, rolling drumbeats, and a gentle hi-hat. He was mesmerized and turned up the volume, no longer afraid of what was happening outside the locked car door.

The song ended and a man's honeyed voice came through the speakers. "That, my friends, was The Oliver Nelson Sextet featuring none other than Bill Evans, Roy Haynes, Eric Dolphy, Paul Chambers, *and* Freddie Hubbard, from one of my favorite albums, *The Blues and the Abstract Truth*. And if that record ain't truth, I don't know what is."

Jimmy fumbled around his uncle's car for a pen, a scrap of paper, anything to write down the words the man said, but he found only pennies and cigarette butts buried deep in the burgundy upholstery. Jimmy turned the names over and over in his mind. What was it he said? Paul Chambers, Eric something, Freddie what? The only thing he could remember was the name of the album and he repeated it to himself like a broken record until Floyd came back, his hair disheveled and a blank look in his eyes.

"Have you ever heard of an album called *Blues and the—*"

But Floyd told him to shut the fuck up and switched off the radio. As he drove away, he kept one eye fixed on the woman in his rearview mirror, who looked in the other direction and exhaled a long stream of smoke like a lonely cloud.

Jimmy had no more luck getting reception of WKWK 1080 AM in his bedroom than he did finding a copy of *Blues and the Abstract Truth* alongside the Beach Boys, the Beatles, and Elvis in the record rack at the Franklin Five & Dime around the corner.

And when Jimmy asked Uncle Floyd when he might be going back over there, Floyd cut him a look and said, "Never. I ain't never going back there again." Floyd opened a can of Coors Light and sat down next to him and said, "I told her I loved her, after so many years of going there, pretending I was just there for some trim. I told her everything I'd been thinking about for months, I told her I'd take her out of there, bring her home with me, make her honest. And do you know what she did, Jim?"

Jimmy shook his head.

"She laughed. Threw that black whore head of hers back and laughed. Told me there was no way I was going to take her out of there. 'What you going to do, Floyd?' she said. 'Going to move me into your white mama's house? You think she's going to let me live there, let me shit in her toilet?'"

"And I told her yeah, I don't care, I'll get us our own house. But it didn't matter. She kept right on laughing. She wouldn't even give me a freebie that night." Floyd paused, took a long sip of his beer, and said, "So no, I ain't going back there never."

While this made Jimmy feel sorrier than ever for his uncle, it did nothing to help him get ahold of that album or get him back over to where he could hear WKWK 1080 AM again. He'd known people who got hooked on drugs, and his own grandfather had died from alcoholism, but Jimmy had never felt like he needed anything before this music. It was different, was nothing like what they played at the school dance, or what his older sister listened to, and he needed it, he imagined, like a junkie needed a fix. Needed it so bad that, after a few days, he got on a crosstown bus and went back.

Without the night shadows and flickering streetlights, Jimmy could see the flowers in the window at Isola's Beauty Salon and the sidewalk swept clean in front of the Shoe and Boot Repair and Shine Shop. From the speaker outside the door of WKWK 1080 AM, a song ended and the same sweet voice came across the airwaves. "That there, my friends, was Peaches & Herb's, 'Let's Fall in Love.' If any of y'all out there have anyone you want to fall in love with, give me a call and tell me about it; maybe I can help you out. 329-0055. Here's a new one from Brenda and the Tabulations, 'Don't Make Me Over'—don't you do it, now."

Jimmy pushed open the door.

Ulysses Wolfe wore thick bifocal glasses with brown plastic frames and styled his hair in a short salt-and-peppered natural. When he smiled, you could see his gold tooth on the front left. But he had never been generous with his smiles, and he certainly didn't smile when Jimmy lumbered through the door.

"You a little early, ain't you?" Ulysses said.

"Early?" Jimmy said. "I don't know, I thought you played jazz all day."

Ulysses took in the boy, with his dusty hair and striking blue eyes. He noticed how Jimmy had rolled the front of his shirt up in a ball with his hands. "Aren't you looking for the whores?" he asked.

"No," Jimmy said, "I'm looking for the Abstract Truth."

Ulysses didn't have time for Jimmy, but Jimmy came around anyway. One thing Ulysses would give him was that he sure wasn't short on persistence. Jimmy hit him with question after question—mostly about music, and it didn't matter that Ulysses grunted answers at him, that he made fun of him over the airwaves, or that he was often downright cruel. Jimmy kept showing up. And once school started, Jimmy left each morning like he was getting on the school bus and instead made his way across town.

It was Ulysses who gave Jimmy his nickname. He liked to tell his audience about how, even though Jimmy was so fat, you'd think he was starving, the way he asked questions. "You'd think he was skin 'n bones," he said one night. After that, Ulysses would announce over the airwaves, "Hey, y'all, Mr. Skin 'n Bones is up in here again. Doin' what he do best, askin' questions and gettin' on my last nerve. Didn't even know I had any nerves left for him to get on, but here he is, wreckin' the very last one I got. Mr. Wolfe, can you play this? Mr. Wolfe, who's that singing on that? Mr. Wolfe, can you put on James Brown 'Sex Machine' one more time? Like he some kind of sex machine or something. So here it is for y'all, the Godfather of Soul, care of the seductive Mr. Skin 'n Bones."

Jimmy looked up from the pile of records Ulysses had given him to put back on the shelves and said, "But, Mr. Wolfe, I didn't ask you to play 'Sex Machine.'"

"So? What you care for?"

"Well, it isn't good to lie."

"You white, ain't you? That's what y'all do. No use in stopping now."

By Thanksgiving, Ulysses had taken to simply calling him Bones, and by Christmas folks were calling in and asking after him. Jimmy liked being Bones. It put a swagger in his walk, lit cigarettes for him, and splashed aftershave on his neck. As soon as Jimmy walked out of his house in the morning, Jimmy's new identity wrapped onto him like a scuba suit. Only thing left of Little Jimmy were his eyes peeking out, blue and still afraid.

When his parents got the note that he failed the year and wouldn't be graduating, his father stripped Jimmy of his nickname and his newfound armor, stripped him down to the shirt off his back and hit him with a switch from the tree in the yard, with a belt he pulled from his waist, but when he went for a chair from the dining room table, his mother pulled her own mountain of a body off of the sagging sofa and stood between them.

"Jimmy baby," she said. "Go on, now, get. This ain't going to end in nothing but blood and mayhem. I'll let you know when it's safe to come back."

And Jimmy left.

Ulysses endured Bones's blubbering, his constant going to the mirror to look at the marks across his expansive back for a while. Ulysses even let himself get a little kick out of it. "Umm-hmm," he said. "Don't feel good, do it? It's what your people been doing to my people for hundreds of years and you up in here snotting everywhere after one little whooping. I don't know what you so worried for—you white *and* a man, this whole world is set up for you. Can't nobody tell you not to do nothing."

Bones stopped crying. "What should I do, Mr. Wolfe?" he said. "'Cause, I ain't going home."

"Well, you gonna have to go away from around here. This ain't no refugee camp."

"That's the thing, Mr. Wolfe," Bones said. "I don't got nowhere else I can go. I'll go anywhere, anywhere but home."

Ulysses leaned back in his chair and scratched his chin, then he wrote down the words *Jimmy's Records* on a piece of paper with an address and handed it to Bones.

"This is in St. Louis," Bones said.

"Yeah. That's my man Jimmy Wallace. I know, I know, his name is Jimmy too. He's an old friend of mine. He's got a record store up there in St. Louis. I ain't heard from him in a minute, but he said if I—or anyone I know—ever wanted to get out of Memphis, he'd give 'em a job."

Bones stood up and walked around the room. "A record store?" he said. "That's even better than a radio station." He stopped and looked at Ulysses. "No offense, Mr. Wolfe. I just don't have the knack for it, you know?"

"Shit, you ain't gotta tell me."

"How do you know he'll give me a job?"

"I don't."

"How do you know I won't get up there and find it was a waste of time?"

Ulysses shrugged and said, "I don't. But don't say I ain't never done nothing for you."

Once in a While

DOWNTOWN ST. LOUIS IN 1973 was majestic—with closely packed buildings, boasting wide stone steps and thick, heavy columns—but it was damn near abandoned other than the cars that sped past on the broad avenues. Bones pressed his face against the filthy windows of Jimmy's Records and saw sad rows of empty shelves covered in a thick shroud of dust. Along the walls were what looked like crates and crates of records. A menacing chain padlocked the door.

On the entire 1400 block of Washington Avenue, the only store that looked open was the one with a huge white sign that said *Levine Hat Co.* Bones huffed up the hill and through the door. The walls were lined with photos of presidents in hats, movie stars in hats, old war photographs of soldiers in hats. And everywhere Bones looked there were hats. Straw hats with wide brims, felt hats with satin ribbons, black rubber police hats, bowlers in every color. There were top hats under glass, wool caps and berets stacked high like colorful pancakes. And behind the counter stood an old woman so short that Bones didn't see her until she came out and ordered him into an upholstered chair and proceeded to try to put a clear plastic helmet on his head.

"Excuse me," Bones said, hoping to interrupt, to let her know that he didn't, in fact, want to buy a hat.

"Name's Ethel," she told him. "Ethel Levine. And I'm sorry about the plastic helmet, but I have to," she said. "Keeps the lice off the hats, you know. Lousy people, they try on the hats, then you try on the hat, and before you know it—" she stopped and held up both hands—"an epidemic."

"Ma'am," Bones said, the plastic helmet now fixed over his head, pressing his eyebrows down into his eyes. "I'm not looking to buy a hat."

Ethel blinked at him and said, "You don't want a hat?"

"No, ma'am."

"What are you here for then? You selling something? Because I can't buy nothing. You'll have to come back when my son is here. He's the boss now. It's because of him that you have to wear that stupid helmet and you'll have to come back Monday. We close tomorrow, for the Sabbath. Are you Jewish?"

"No," Bones said. "I'm not."

"Didn't think so. You don't look it, but these days you can't tell with the mixing and matching that's going on. Not that I object, I mean love is love, right? And not love is not love. My husband was as Jewish as they came, but I wish he hadn't taken so long to die. Then maybe I could have had some fun in my life. Now he's finally gone, but you know what? His son is even worse than his father." She stopped talking and said to Bones, "You can take that thing off your head if you want. What did you say you were doing here, again?"

Bones removed the plastic helmet. "Do you know anything about that record store down the block, Jimmy's?"

"I know it. Been closed for near six months now. Jimmy got sick and went home, never came back. I went to check on his wife, Millie, a month or so ago, she said Jimmy died. Just went to sleep and didn't wake up. That's the way every one of us hopes we'll go and good for him, he deserved it."

"I'd like to talk to her," Bones said. "Do you know how I can find her?"

Ethel snatched the plastic helmet from Bones's hands. "I know who you are," she said. "You're some kind of tax collector or a debt collector. Come after those good people to take everything they got. Why don't people like you leave people like them alone? Maybe you think because they're colored that I'll help you, well you got that part wrong, fat man. I know good people when I see them and good don't have a color, you understand me?"

For a moment, Bones thought she might hit him with the helmet now that she had him backed to the door. He held up his hands as if he were at gunpoint and said, "No, no, no. Please, you don't understand, I want to buy the store." The words came out with way more confidence than anything Bones had ever said in his life and certainly more confidence than he felt.

"You want to what?" Ethel said.

"Buy the store."

"You're nothing but a kid. Do you have money like that?"

"I've got an uncle. My uncle Floyd. He's got a bunch of money, said he would help me out," Bones said. Now that he had said it, he felt as if he were looking at Ethel through the lens of a camera that only just came into focus. He saw the gray hairs that sprouted out of a mole on her cheek, the faded brown and white flowers of her dress, its fabric so thin it might rip if he hugged her too tight, and so he rested a hand on her angular shoulder and smiled.

Ethel drew her face to a point and squinted at Bones. "I guess we better go see Millie then."

Bones didn't know whether to be more terrified of Ethel crashing the car, since she barely saw over the dashboard, or of actually buying a record store. He balled up his shirt and looked out the window at North St. Louis where the buildings, lives, and cars sat scattered in various states of despair. It reminded him a bit of the neighborhood around WKWK and he kept his eyes out for a store-front radio station.

Ethel parked the car in front of a squat, one-story house that looked exactly like every other house on the block. "You sure she's home?" Bones said.

"Don't know where else she'd be," Ethel said.

The paint around the windows had fallen off in chunks onto a patch of faded plastic flowers behind a small, bent-up fence. In the distance, Bones heard the bark of a small dog; otherwise it was strikingly silent. Ethel walked up the two short front steps and rang the ancient doorbell. After a few moments, she knocked loudly on the screen door.

"Millie, it's me, Ethel," she yelled. "Brought someone round to see you. You in there?"

Bones tried futilely to straighten out the creases he'd made in his shirt.

A woman, even smaller than Ethel, opened the door. She wore a long, faded housedress. Her white afro made a soft halo around her face.

"Who's there?" she said, squinting through the dirty screen door.

"It's Ethel, for heaven's sakes. I told you to let me take you to the eye doctor, you've gone damn near blind now, haven't you?"

"You here to take me to the eye doctor, Ethel?"

"No, no. I'm here to bring you this, this Jimmy, here. Says he wants to buy your Jimmy's store."

Millie clicked the lock on the screen door and opened it. "C'mon then," she said.

The hot, stagnant air of the home smelled of years of spilled whiskey, cigarette ashes, and loss. Bones wondered why she didn't open the windows, but as he sat down on the plush, burgundy, stiff-backed sofa under a painting of black Jesus, he thought that maybe Millie Wallace would crumble without the smells there to hold her up.

81

"His name was Jimmy, too," Millie said, and smiled at Bones as he drank the tea she'd handed to him in a chipped china cup with a matching saucer.

"That's right," Bones said. "Mr. Wolfe told me that."

"Humph, Ulysses," Millie said. "He made a whole host of promises to help my Jimmy out and never came through."

"Maybe that's why he sent me here."

Millie gave a short laugh. "I doubt that." She swirled the tea around in her delicate cup and said, "Tell me something, what makes you think you're going to do better than my Jimmy did?"

Bones balled up his shirt again. "I don't know that I'm going to do better, Ms. Wallace. But I think I want to try."

"Well, don't try it here, I'll give you that much advice," Millie said.

Bones nodded and wondered if it would be rude to ask if he could smoke.

"St. Louis wasn't always like this," Millie said. "Believe it or not, this used to be a nice part of town. Businesses did well here, schools too. People were happy, kept to themselves. Then you people had to desegregate everything and messed it up."

Bones looked up, a little shocked. "What do you mean desegregation messed it up?"

"Took everything away from folks. Used to be that white people didn't know and didn't care what went on on the North Side. As long as they didn't have to see or think about the coloreds, they were happy. Then desegregation happened, and next thing you know, white people find out colored people are making money, are living happy, successful lives and there's not a white person in sight making a single dollar off of it? Heavens. It's been downhill ever since.

"The Italians, they came in with their drugs. Then the Jews— your people, Ethel," Millie said, pointing her teacup in Ethel's direction, "they came in, opening banks and businesses, buying up the houses only to tear 'em down. Pretty soon everything was taken away—especially the dignity of folks; stole off with that, first thing."

Bones looked over at Ethel, who was nodding. "She's telling the truth, Jimmy, so listen up," Ethel said. "This town isn't what it could have been."

"Well, maybe it can be," Bones said. Both ladies looked at each other and laughed.

"You're a young one, Young Jimmy," Millie said. "And I can't sell you the store. Bank's already took that, but if you think you can do something with those records, well, you go on down there and look it through. Come back and make me an offer I won't refuse."

The following morning, Bones called Floyd and asked him to loan him enough to buy the records, pay a few months' rent, and maybe even pay himself a few dollars too. Floyd told him he'd send the money up Western Union the following day if Bones promised to let him know whether there were pretty girls in St. Louis.

Millie accompanied Bones back to the store, and while he loaded the crates of records into a rented van, she sat on a stool in the corner and tapped her fingers on her tan polyester pants to Freda Payne singing "Band of Gold." When what remained were the empty, dusty shelves and the broken light fixtures, Bones went to her and took her hand.

"This was our child," Millie said. "Our only baby. He loved it so, my Jimmy did. Going to have to start calling him Old Jimmy now." She smiled. "What's next for you, Young Jimmy? You taking these records back to Memphis?"

Bones imagined riding the sweaty bus across town and walking back through the doors of WKWK 1080 AM. He imagined the face Ulysses would make when he did. He thought about Floyd searching for love in the whorehouse and his father, with his belt, the switch, the wrench in his hand. His father who had not loved him the way Old Jimmy had loved his record store. Bones's throat felt like he'd swallowed a jagged stone.

"No," he said and shook his head at Millie. "No. I ain't going back to Memphis."

"Well, don't open up downtown," Millie said and pointed out the dirty plate glass windows toward the deserted street. "Maybe go on up there where Ethel's nephew opened that store selling saxophones and whatnot. In that area they call the Loop. Old Jimmy used to say that he'd a done better up there."

"The Loop?"

"Yeah, you'll like it there, Young Jimmy," Millie said. "All sorts of weirdos in the Loop." She leaned her soft, haloed head against his shoulder and laughed.

The new store hadn't been open two hours before Fred Bosch walked in. He looked about thirty years old, with light-brown skin and a rough, full beard. He entered the store like a turtle, eyes first, long neck following behind, and when he stood up straight, he was a half a foot taller than Bones. Bones decided, based on the green sweater with the worn-out sleeves, he was either a bum or a professor. Bones had seen plenty of both in his few weeks setting up the store in the Loop. Either way, it didn't matter, this was his first customer. Bones went over immediately and introduced himself.

Fred nodded at him briefly, his fingers rapidly flipping through a nearby stack of records. "You a dominoes player?" Fred asked.

"No, sir."

"What you call yourself Bones for, then?"

"Just a nickname."

"What do you call this place? Bones's Records?" Fred asked and chuckled a little.

Bones smiled. "Nah, I reckon as soon as someone buys a record, I'm going to call it whatever that record is."

Fred stopped flipping and looked square at Bones. "So if I buy a Chopin record, you'd call the place what? Chopin's Records?"

"I guess I'd have to, but I ain't never heard of no Chopin."

"He was a composer from Warsaw, Poland," Fred said. "Favored solo piano concertos. Where'd you come upon these records, Bones?"

"I bought 'em from Jimmy's Records that done closed downtown."

Fred's face opened up into a full smile. "These are Jimmy's records?" he asked.

"Shol is," said Bones. "Bought 'em off his wife, Millie, few months back."

Fred looked around frantically. "Where's the jazz?"

"Over there," Bones said pointing to the corner.

Fred damn near pushed Bones out of the way and rushed across the store. "Oh, I'm good now," he said. "I am good."

Bones walked back behind the counter and watched him, waiting. When Fred came up to the register with only three records in his hands, Bones said, "That's all you want? You been up in here for hours."

Fred held up a copy of *Triple Threat* and said, "This here, this is Roland Kirk's first record and it's worth a hell of a lot more than two dollars."

"It is?" Bones said.

"Listen," Fred said. "First thing you might want to do is get to removing as many of these stickers as you can before someone else walks in. Jimmy, as much as he knew about music, and as much as he was one of the best men I ever knew, never did charge enough for his vinyl."

"How am I supposed to know how much to charge?" Bones asked.

"Damn, what did you do, wake up one day and decide to open a record store?"

"Something like that," Bones said.

"How old are you, if you don't mind my asking?"

"Twenty. How old are you?"

"Older than twenty," Fred said. "Listen, I got a couple of collectors books at home. I could bring 'em by. They'd at least help you know which ones of these you got that are worth real money."

"Are you a collector?"

"I guess you could say that," Fred said. "Got about three thousand records in my collection. It's not much, I know, but I like to think I got three thousand of the good ones."

"Three thousand? Jesus H. Christ," Bones said. "You wouldn't want a job, would you? I mean taking the stickers off the records and helping me out? I can't pay you much, but you can have first dibs on the records and I'll sell 'em to you at cost."

Fred, who only ever spent his money on records, had been on his way over to Blueberry Hill to see about a job as a dishwasher. He looked at Bones to see if he was serious. "Hell yeah, I want a job."

"My man," Bones said.

"In the meantime," Fred said, "you're going to sell me this record for two dollars and you got yourself a name for your store."

"What's that," Bones said, "Roland's Records?"

Fred shook his head. "I'm going to do you one better," he said. "I'm going to make you look like you are a whole lot cooler than you actually are, okay?"

Bones nodded.

Fred held up the record. "This brilliant man, this genius of a musician, he had a dream, see? And in the dream, he was told to change his name, so now he isn't Roland Kirk anymore, he's Rahsaan Roland Kirk."

"Ima call the store Rahsaan's Records?"

"You're going to call the store Rahsaan's Records," Fred said.

"Now that is cool," Bones said. "Sounds like the name of a black person's record store."

Fred looked at Bones sideways and said, "Whatever you say, but I don't think you're fooling anyone, white-boy-named-Bones."

For the Good Times

CORDELIA DIED ON THE morning of May 22, 1985. Cyrus had gone out to buy bread, and when he got home, there was a magnified silence to the apartment that made him drop the bread on the floor and run to the bedroom. It was too late. She was already gone; only the shell of her was left, the sheets pulled up to her chin. She died before Cyrus could ask her the one thing that needed to be asked. So many times he had started to, but then he looked into her sunken, ancient eyes, and thought, *Not now, Cyrus. It can wait.* But death didn't wait. It arrived and he hadn't asked her how or when they were going to tell Francis and Octavian the truth. He and Cordelia both needed be there when the boys learned that Cyrus wasn't Francis's real father.

Cyrus was left holding their secret like a bag of stolen goods. He didn't know whether to lay it down or bury it with her. He wasn't sure that he would be able to do alone what they'd always said they would one day do together.

He walked into the living room and flipped on the receiver. He lowered the needle on the song Cordelia had asked him to play the night before. Nina Simone's husky voice rang through the apartment and chased death from the corners where it was trying to hide. As Nina asked the blackbird why it wanted to fly, Cyrus felt his wife's spirit lift up from the places where it still lay.

Cyrus eyes filled with hot, heavy tears. "Fly, baby girl," he whispered. "Just don't fly too far from me."

When Cyrus met Cordelia in 1972, Francis was the most troublesome barely three-year-old boy he'd ever laid eyes on. Back then they didn't have terms like ADHD or PTSD. Kids like Francis were simply bad, or wild if you were being polite. From where he sat, it seemed that something drove the child, told him to do exactly what he wasn't supposed to do, things that didn't even make sense—like sitting his little butt down in the middle of Hanley Road and flat refusing to move, or trying to eat the Ajax from under the sink. Most mothers he knew would have beat the child, but not Cordelia. She refused to even spank him. Said no one who loved another ever needed to hit them. And Cordelia was so beautiful as she looked at her son with exhausted eyes, lips drawn down into a dark curve. And who was he to tell her anything? He was merely an associate professor in the Philosophy Department, the ink still wet on his PhD.

Why she finally decided to spank Francis, in the Ladue Library no less, he couldn't remember. No matter the reason, it had been a bad choice. Ladue was the richest, most conservative and white place in the entirety of St. Louis County and Cyrus imagined every white woman in the library that day had been raised by a black nanny, or had a black woman at home raising their own children. Yet Cordelia, a young black mother whacking her son's backside with a copy of *Make Way for Ducklings*, meant a call to social services. It meant Brenda Brooks, with her home perm, pockmarked skin, and vodka breath covered by Doublemint gum at Cordelia's front door, asking to come in.

She inspected the house, opened Cordelia's refrigerator, drummed her Lee Press-on-Nails on top of the pages of Cordelia's manuscript, and eyed the reckless pile of dirty laundry behind the bathroom door. She scribbled things on a yellow legal pad and told Cordelia she'd be hearing from her.

The next day, Cordelia burst into Cyrus's office unannounced. Since his course was over, and it wouldn't be looked on with suspicion, he and Cordelia had begun officially seeing each other, and things were tenuous. Cyrus was surprised to see her there and tried not to be distracted by her flowered sundress or the way the Ethiopian cross she wore rested in the open oval of her collarbones. How her bracelets rang like delicate church bells as her hands flew around while she spoke.

Brenda Brooks, she told Cyrus, said to think about sending Francis to her relatives in North Carolina or consider that he might wind up in foster care.

"They can't do that, can they?" Cyrus said.

"I think they can do whatever they want to do."

"I have a friend who is a wonderful attorney," Cyrus said. "This isn't his field, but how about we start by—"

Cordelia shook her head. "I don't need you to call your friend," she said. "What I need is for you to tell her we're going to get married." The pain in her face was as wide as the ocean, and Cyrus wondered if making that pain go away would be as simple as telling a lie he wished were true.

"You think that's all it's going to take?"

Cordelia sat down heavily in the wingback chair on the other side of the desk. She wiped away the thin line of perspiration from her forehead and looked directly at him. "And that you're his father," she said.

All Cyrus could think of was that she was beautiful. That the worry on her brow, the sweat on her shoulders, the curve of her mouth gave him not a single reason to say no. And the next day, Cyrus sat down in Brenda Brooks's office wearing his best suit and his best silk tie, even though it was damn near ninety-five degrees outside.

He refused her slack offer of a glass of water. "Can we get started?" he said. "I've got a course to prepare for."

"Tell me about your history with Ms. Dixon," Brenda said.

Cyrus adjusted the cuffs of his shirt, crossed one leg over the other, and began to spin a tale of romance and memories. He filled it so fully that Brenda Brooks stopped chewing on her ballpoint pen and sat back in her chair and listened. When Cyrus got to the enchanting details of Francis's birth, Brenda Brooks held up her hands. "Enough," she said and stamped *Dismissed* on the file.

Cyrus walked out of her office dabbing his face with his handkerchief and believing every single word he'd just said. He rushed, bewildered, downtown and stumbled into Levi's Jewelry like a drunken man. Levi was the only jeweler Cyrus's father ever trusted to repair his pocket watch, and Levi rejoiced as he helped Cyrus pick out a ring. "Platinum," Cyrus insisted, "because she's better than gold."

When Cordelia opened her front door, Cyrus heard Al Green coming from the stereo, and he kneeled right there on the porch, pushed the ring into her hands. She looked down at Cyrus. "Are you doing this because you love me," she said, "or because you want to save me?"

She was wearing a long, printed orange skirt and a thin white T-shirt with no bra underneath. And for a moment, Cyrus let himself imagine what it would feel like to run his tongue across one of her nipples. He knew right then that he would be happy for the rest of his life if he could spend every moment learning everything there was to know about Cordelia. He grabbed her softly around the ankles and lowered his head. "Both," he said. It was the most truthful thing he ever uttered in his life.

Francis had been so young. He had never laid eyes on his real father, and Cyrus and Cordelia mulled over what words would help a little boy who couldn't sit still for two minutes understand the difference between biological and adopted parentage. And as every day of living together as a family passed, that difference seemed more cloud-filled and complicated to explain. So they waited. They were going to tell him, they told each other, one day.

Beast of Burden

OCTAVIAN'S MOTHER'S BODY WAS gone before he got home, but as soon as he walked in the apartment, he knew. He saw the way his father's skin was drawn so tight against his face that Octavian could see the gray shape of his skull, and he knew. Death had already come and gone. Octavian wondered if his mom died when he was in music class singing "Wade in the Water" or if she died during science hour while he was building a terrarium. Maybe she died at lunch recess when he sat alone in the tunnel still trying his damnedest to draw that picture of Francis.

Cyrus lifted his eyes from the table. "Can you tell me where Frankie is, so I can go get him?" he asked.

Octavian had an empty and sharp feeling as he imagined his father coming face-to-face with City Ass Cedric. "No," he said. "I'll get him. I need to walk."

Octavian had kept his promise and it had been months since he had been to Cedric's apartment. He passed the stores in the Loop, crossed the streets at the crosswalk, and with every step, he waited for the tears to come, waited for his heart to thrash, to break. But somehow, his feet kept moving—as if the sidewalk moved underneath him. And the thought that he would never see his mother again did not fill him with despair, or unbearable pain. Instead Octavian felt the heavy burden of relief that he would no longer have to see her try to smile at him and only be able to wince, would never again have to smell her dying flesh.

When Cedric opened the door, Octavian tried to push past, but Cedric planted his feet. "I thought I told your brother to tell you to stop comin' around here?"

Octavian took a deep breath. "Francis needs to come home," he said.

City Ass Cedric must have seen something different in the way Octavian looked deep into his weed-glazed eyes, because he opened the door and said, "Frank's in there."

The bare floor was strewn with pieces of unopened mail, newspapers, and empty Chinese food containers. A broken yellow chair stood in the corner beside a folding table littered with Styrofoam cups and beer cans overflowing with cigarette butts and ashes. Francis lay asleep on a green-and-brown plaid couch with a missing cushion. He was shirtless, with one long arm thrown over his head and the other hand shoved deep into his favorite pair of faded jeans with the frayed knees. He had turned fifteen in March, and sleeping there like that, he looked older and younger at the same time. Octavian pressed the soft brown flesh of his brother's bare arm, but Francis didn't move.

"Watch out," Cedric said and pushed Octavian aside. He shook Francis hard and yelled, "Yo, Frankie! Wake up!"

Francis opened his heavy eyes and said, "What the fuck, man?"

Cedric pushed Octavian forward.

Francis tried to focus on his face. "Tave," he said, "what did I tell you about coming here?" The words came out thick and stuck together.

Octavian held his hand out and said, "It's time to go home, Frankie."

Francis withdrew from Octavian's hand like he might burn at his touch.

"I said, come on. Mama's dead."

With his mother gone, Octavian thought Francis would disappear into Eastgate and never return. But instead, Francis stopped hanging out there altogether. He said he only wanted to be around Octavian. It was like old times again, sitting on the floor of their bedroom listening to music. But Cordelia was gone and now Francis couldn't listen to soul like he used to.

"It reminds me too much of Mama," he explained. He became obsessed with classic rock and made Octavian listen to the Rolling Stones, Neil Young, and his favorite, Pink Floyd.

Francis got up early and made his bed. He went to school every day and tried to be better. But by summer, Francis's bed was never made right, he couldn't get the corners tight enough and he'd spend an hour making and unmaking it until his hands started to shake and Octavian would push him aside and do it for him. Octavian's clumsy result was somehow satisfactory. And it was more than the bed. Francis was afraid. He whispered his fears to Octavian in the darkness of their bedroom. What if Cyrus died? What if Octavian died? What about nuclear war and hurricanes, tsunamis?

"We live in the middle of the country, Frankie," Octavian told him. "I don't think we need to worry about tsunamis."

Octavian escaped his brother's fears by falling into books. He read the *Lord of the Rings* trilogy, devoured Octavia Butler's Patternist series, and read everything and anything Marvel. In July, when Octavian turned eleven, Cyrus bought him a new color television, a VCR, and all three of the *Star Wars* movies on big, thick black tapes.

Octavian discovered that it was the details of things that made life without his mother bearable. He spent hours making model trains, lost himself in the little towns, the general store, the schoolhouse, the railroad station. He abandoned his drawing of Francis and returned to drawing comic book characters and forgot to change his socks. As long as he focused on the gears of the model train, the characteristics of his D&D figures, the arc of Black Panther's claws, he could make it from the beginning of the day to the end.

A dark space grew between himself and Francis that summer, and so Francis turned his worries to Octavian.

"You're going to middle school at the end of the summer, Tave," Francis said. "And Brittany ain't no place for punks. Do you even have any friends?"

Octavian told him to leave him alone. He had two friends—Dan Conley, a thin white kid with pimples and glasses who lived in the next apartment building, and Phil Johnson, who was the only other black kid that Octavian knew who liked *Star Trek*. Phil's parents worked for NBC and they lived in a mansion with stained-glass windows and a separate stairway that was once used by servants. Dan, Phil, and Octavian hung out at Phil's house sometimes and played Dungeons and Dragons or traded baseball cards. They watched *Land of the Lost* and didn't ask each other questions.

Francis went to Cyrus. "You can't send Octavian off to Brittany like this."

"Like what?" Cyrus asked.

"Tave is about to become one of those weird black kids none of the other black kids want to talk to. And since he's black he's never going to have a real white friend either."

"And you think I should do what?" Cyrus asked.

"I think you need to take him to see someone."

"Like who?"

"I don't know. A shrink, a priest, a rabbi? Someone to remind him where he comes from. If Mama knew he was dorked out with smelly socks on, she'd flip."

"He's eleven years old, Francis, he'll be fine. Besides, your mother would be proud he was reading Octavia Butler."

Francis shook his head at Cyrus. "You'll see," he said. "Just wait. Cats at Brittany do not care what he's reading."

Francis had been right. Octavian's newfound love of fantasy and sci-fi did not combine well with starting sixth grade at Brittany

Woods Middle School. The giant building was a long maze of green sterile hallways lit by florescent lights that hung from broken drop ceilings. At Brittany, cockroaches as big as your hand could be seen flying near the cafeteria and the eighth-grade boys—their voices deep and their bodies long and thin, or thick and hard—loomed large over everyone. Midway through the year, Dan Conley's family moved out to Brentwood, and Phil's parents put him into private school.

Francis sucked his teeth and decided to take matters into his own hands. One frigid night in December, he told Octavian to get in bed with his clothes on and not ask questions.

When the lights were out and they heard Cyrus brush his teeth and go into his room, Francis threw off his covers and said, "Get up, we're going to see Prince."

Octavian's brain went directly to some medieval place in middle earth with a court of lords and elfin ladies, but then he stopped himself, remembered his brother was Francis Munroe, and said, "We're going where?"

"To see Prince. He's playing tonight at the Arena."

Octavian turned on the lamp on his bedside table. "Do you know how much trouble I'll get in, that we'll get in, if we do that?"

Francis let out a long, exasperated sigh. "Tave, sometimes you have to do things even if you know you'll get in trouble, even if you know you're not supposed to."

Octavian gave him a look.

"Listen, man, I'm not talking about taking you with me to get fucked up. I'm talking about a once-in-a-lifetime experience. Think of it as a trip to another dimension."

Octavian scoffed. "What do you know about other dimensions?"

"Believe me, I know more than I want to know, okay? And I promise you, you won't regret one second of this."

Octavian had never been to a place like the St. Louis Arena. Around him were thousands of people. Different kinds of people. White people, black people, people who could have been girls, could have been boys, but it just didn't matter—and aside from the expanse of the arena and the crowds, the noise, the lights, and the smells, up there on the stage was Prince: tiny, beautiful, masculine, feminine, rugged, and light, singing from a bathtub in a rain shower of purple balloons.

For two hours he sang directly into Octavian's bolstered heart, told him to be glad that he was free, reminded him to be careful of the beautiful ones. At the end of the night, Octavian wrapped his arms around his brother, buried his face in Francis's smooth neck the way he used to when he was younger and afraid. He inhaled Francis's smell—which was also his mother's, and fought back the tears that filled his eyes.

"Thank you," he said. "Thank you, Frankie."

After Francis tucked Octavian into the soft cotton of his sheets, and what was left of the night rang in his ears, Octavian slept heavily and didn't dream. But while he slept, those things that he'd held deep down, the neatly packaged pains tied up in white paper and twine, unraveled and Octavian woke at dawn to the sound of his own sobbing.

For the next two days, Octavian couldn't eat and, aside from moments of pure exhaustion that lasted less than an hour, he didn't sleep. The only thing he could do was cry. It was as if a weight descended into him and pushed up the desire, the grief, the dark loneliness and hard, broken anger, until it spilled out in chest-wracking chokes and sobs. It made him wish for the familiar manic fluttering of his heart that now was too heavy to beat fast.

Cyrus sat beside Octavian and rubbed his back in big round circles. And when Francis asked him if he thought Octavian was going to be okay, Cyrus looked at him with ice behind his eyes and said, "What were you thinking, sneaking him out like that, taking him to that concert?"

Francis didn't answer. He closed the door and sat on the floor outside their bedroom and waited for Cyrus to come out, but he didn't. The next morning, Francis left without being noticed and got drunk for the first time since their mother died.

At the end of the second day, Octavian woke from a fitful dream about pulling Francis out of a deep blue pond. Octavian's eyes felt like they had sand underneath the lids and no longer any water to unleash. His heavy heart bobbed like a buoy in his chest and his brain felt clear and whole. He took a long drink from the glass of water his father left on his bedside table and got out from under the covers. The floor beneath him felt steady and warm and he walked out of his bedroom to find his father and brother disheveled and waiting.

"I think I'm alright now," he said.

Cyrus stood and, with shaking arms, pulled Octavian to him. Francis, who had just come home, was grateful that the sobbing had finally stopped, but he felt the dividing line between him and the rest of the world expand even further. He walked over and wrapped his long arms carefully around them both. None of them realized that it was Christmas Eve.

A Love Bizarre

THE SUBURB OF CLAYTON, parallel on the map to University City, was on the opposite side of Delmar and therefore had no neighborhood equivalent to Eastgate. There were no poor parts of Clayton. In Clayton, the apartment buildings were for young professionals, not families. In Clayton, families lived in three- and four-story mansions with wide manicured lawns that made the biggest houses in U. City look rough and tumble. Kanta's new house was giant and drafty, with unnecessary bedrooms and bathrooms on every floor.

A few weeks before school started, Mina told Kanta that if she was going to force her to go to this new school, she needed to at least get her some clothes.

"It was bad enough wearing boys' jeans at Delmar Harvard," Mina told her. "There's no way I'm going to Wydown in thrift-store clothes."

Kanta shrugged and said, "Well, they did make me partner at the firm, so I guess I can stop thinking we can't afford things."

Mina looked at her in disbelief. "Then I'm buying school lunch every day," she said. "Because you can't tell me we can't afford that either."

Wydown Middle School was less than four miles from Brittany Woods, but it could have been in another galaxy. The halls shone and there were murals on the walls. The library had floor-to-ceiling windows and there was a state-of-the-art science lab in the basement. On the first day, Mina wore her brand-new Jordache acid-washed jeans with a boat-neck unicorn shirt over a neon green tank top. She put her hair into a high ponytail and sprayed her bangs hard with Aqua Net. She was met at the door by the guidance counselor and a girl named Lisa Norris who was assigned to take Mina around and introduce her to people. Lisa also had a high ponytail, but hers was smooth and blonde, with no need for any hairspray. She wore meticulous Guess Jeans and a monogrammed sweater vest. She had dark-green eyes and delicate peach-and-cream fingernails, and Mina felt immediately clumsy as she followed two steps behind her.

At lunch Mina sat happily down at the table in the cafeteria and began to eat the pasta and peas dropped onto her tray by the lunch lady with the puffy face and the blue hairnet. The food was overly soft and salty, but she didn't care. At least she wasn't eating sprouted bread with sunflower butter. Around the table sat Lisa, Sarah, Jessica, Katie, and Rebecca—who shared a seat with Jessica to make room for Mina. Lisa was obviously the leader of the group and the other girls at the table waited for her before they sat down in their chairs, needing to ascertain who Lisa wanted to sit next to first.

Katie gave Mina's lunch tray a look and asked, "Did you eat the school lunch at your school in U. City?"

That's when Mina noticed the series of crisp, brand-new lunch boxes on the table. Katie pulled an American cheese sandwich on white bread out of hers. And Sarah, who was a little bit heavier than the other girls, apologized for the smell of her tuna fish as she wrenched it out of the can with a plastic spork and talked about being at fat camp that summer. Lisa and Rebecca had matching lunch boxes and also matching salads with bright asparagus spears, deep red cherry tomatoes, and slices of cold chicken sitting next to little green bottles of Perrier.

Mina felt the mushy pasta rapidly turn to paste in her mouth and she forced a swallow, opened the carton of 2 percent milk, and drank before she said, "Sometimes."

Lisa carefully cut a piece of chicken and said in an amused whisper, "I heard girls have sex with boys in the bathroom at schools in U. City."

Mina was glad she had swallowed her bite of spaghetti or else she might have spat it across the table at Lisa or choked on it, she laughed so hard. But when she stopped laughing and looked around, they were still waiting for an answer. "You're serious?"

Lisa nodded her thick blonde ponytailed head and the other ponytails nodded too.

"That's not true at all," Mina said. "I don't know anyone who's ever had sex, let alone had sex in a bathroom at school."

Sarah, with her mouth full of tuna fish, said, "We keep getting new members at my synagogue from U. City. My mom said lots of families are moving away because there are too many black people there now."

At this, the ponytailed heads turned toward the table on the other side of the cafeteria where the four black students in the sixth grade sat. Mina looked, too, and noticed they had lunch trays of pasta and peas.

"So you liked it there?" Lisa said as the heads turned back to Mina.

Mina felt the flesh on the back of her neck prickle. Lisa said it like she had something in her mouth that tasted bad. And Mina felt protective of the playground and the climbing tunnels and Octavian and Makeba and the other girls playing Double Dutch. She sat up straighter and looked Lisa in her pretty blonde face.

"Yeah," she said. "I loved it there."

The next day, when Mina exited the lunch line, none of the girls, not even Lisa, looked up, and Mina could tell that no one was sharing a chair to make room for her to sit down. The lunch tray in Mina's hands felt as if it were laden down with much more than a gray beef patty in a bland, greasy bun and bright yellow corn swimming in a butter-flavored puddle.

Across the cafeteria, at the table where only four students sat, Mina saw a vacant chair. As she walked over, she felt the pressure of Lisa's poison gaze, followed by the other gazes as she passed. Mina set her lunch tray down at the table across from Mercy, who was in her French class, and said, "Hey, I'm Mina. Can I sit here?"

Charles, Mercy, Clarissa, and Latif looked at each other and then at Mina. They nodded but said nothing else. Mina took a bite of her burger, which broke apart like sawdust in her mouth.

The only good thing about their new house in Clayton was Mina's cozy attic room that had sloping beams and creaky floors. Mina had taken to regularly stealing cigarettes from Hermine and smoking them out of her open window. Now that Kanta was a partner, she had to put in longer hours at work and was never home. From down the street, Mina heard kids playing, but she had no interest in joining them. Instead, she left her bike with the banana seat to rust in the garage and changed out of her Jordache and put on what she liked to think of as her Prince clothes—black-and-white splatter-paint T-shirts over cut-up jeans she'd tapered tight with safety pins, and leather booties spray-painted silver.

At the bottom of her hill she boarded the Seventy-Three Bi-State bus and spent her afternoons behind the counter at Rahsaan's playing with the price guns and bagging records for Bones. On the weekends, Kanta dragged Mina with her to dinners where she told everyone that Mina still had not succeeded in making a single friend at her new school.

"You don't got no friends?" Bones said after Mina lamented to him about her mother.

"That's not the point," Mina said. "The point is that she shouldn't be telling everyone that, and even though I ask her not to, she does it anyway."

"How come you ain't got no friends?" Bones asked and put on the new Sheila E record that Mina loved.

Mina didn't answer right away. She still sat at the table with Charles, Mercy, Clarissa, and Latif at lunch, but she wouldn't say they were her friends. "'Cause I'm weird," she said finally.

"The best of us are, baby. Ain't that right, Freddy?"

Fred Bosch looked up from where he was replacing the paper in the register and said, "Sure haven't been called anything else in my life." He winked at Mina and walked over to talk to Mr. Nance hovering in the jazz section.

"Come to think of it," said Bones, "I didn't have no friends when I was your age neither."

"But you have a whole bunch of friends now."

"That's 'cause I'm a music-man, girl. Music makes the world go 'round. When I learned that, I had a whole slew of friends from any number of places. Everybody loves music. Tell me, who do you want to be friends with?"

"I want to be friends with Clarissa. She's cool."

"Cool-cool like Thelma Evans?" Bones said and smiled at her.

"She is kinda like Thelma," Mina said. "Except she's real super tall."

"What kind of music does she listen to?"

Mina shrugged. "I never asked."

"Now that there's your problem, Mina girl," Bones said. "That oughta be the first question come out your mouth."

The door swung open, and Mina immediately dropped down behind the counter. She didn't need to look again. Octavian had just walked in. Bones saw her hiding and raised his eyebrows.

"I know him," she whispered.

"Who? Octavian? I know him too. Comes in here a lot with his brother and his dad."

"I don't want him to see me."

"Why not? Maybe y'all could be friends."

"No, Bones, no. Not now."

Bones gave her a look, and Mina heard Octavian's voice say, "Frankie, this is that song I told you I liked."

She heard the deeper voice of his brother say, "Pop, Ima go," and she peered over the edge of the counter.

The father stopped and said, "Where are you going?"

Octavian's brother didn't look that much like Octavian. He had a box cut and wore a Polo sweater and what looked like new Jordans. Mina bet he had a lot of girlfriends. Octavian also wore new Jordans, but he was shorter and thicker than his brother, and his box cut was not nearly so neat. Mina could see that his brother was clenching his fists. "I gotta meet some friends," he said.

Octavian's father's face pulled tight as he watched Francis walk out of the store. Octavian stood there, looking like he didn't know which way to go. Mina was reminded about his funny heart and wondered if it was going to start doing that beating fast thing it did. She remembered that she hadn't been lonely when Octavian was her friend.

Bones shuffled down from the counter and over to where they stood. "Afternoon, gentlemen," he said.

Octavian's father extended his hand to Bones with amusement in his eyes. "How are you, Jimmy?"

"Doing great, Professor, how about you?"

"We're muddling through," he said.

"Well, can I help y'all find something today?"

"Not sure yet. Octavian is looking to start his own record collection." Octavian's father looked like Octavian, Mina thought, but older, and he looked tired. Bones put a hand on the man's shoulder and they turned and walked away from her. Mina could no longer hear what they were saying.

Octavian walked into the Classic Rock section and pulled out a record. His eyes lit up. "Yes," he said loud enough that Mina could hear him clearly. "This has got 'Maybelline' *and* 'My Ding-A-Ling' on it! C'mon Pop. Let's go."

"Hold on, Son," his father said and walked toward the jazz section. Octavian followed close behind his father, holding his record, while Bones went to help a customer carry a box of old records over to the table for Fred to assess their worth.

When Bones came back to the counter, Mina quickly crouched back down to the floor. "Don't worry," he said. "I'm not gonna blow your cover." He replenished the bumper sticker display next to the cash register and gave Mina a playful kick.

When they got to the register, Octavian picked up a bumper sticker. "Can I have one?" he asked Bones.

Mina shrunk closer to the floor and held her breath.

"Take as many as you like," Bones said and put the Chuck Berry record in a bag. He held up the other. "This is a classic."

"It's for the boy," Octavian's father said.

"I thought I was getting Chuck Berry," Octavian said.

"You are. But I'm also getting you Miles Davis's *+19*. Got to start you off right."

"I heard that," Bones said.

"See you soon, Jimmy," the father said.

"See you, Bones," Octavian said.

"Have a wonderful day, *my friends*," Bones said and gave Mina another shove. Mina shoved him back. She heard the door open and close and stood up. Bones gave her the once-over. "You *are* weird," he said.

Mina picked up one of the bumper stickers and put it in her pocket. "He used to be my friend."

"Not no more?"

"We don't go to the same school."

"Well, that's too bad," Bones said. "Only cool-cool kids like Chuck Berry."

The next day Mina wore her tapered jeans, a Prince concert T-shirt she'd convinced Bones to give her, and the silver-painted boots. At lunch she sat down next to Clarissa and said, "What kind of music do you like?"

It was as if Mina had pulled the long cord for the light in a dark closet. Clarissa's smile spread wide. "Me? What kind of music do I like?"

"Oh no," Charles said. "Don't ask her *that* question."

The list was long and Mina lost track a few minutes in, but Clarissa kept talking and then the whole table was talking because Latif didn't think that Janet Jackson was better than Michael Jackson like Mercy did and Charles started singing "Pop Pop Pop Goes My Mind" after Clarissa told him he was a damn fool for thinking Luther Vandross was a member of Levertt.

Mina was almost forgotten until she said, "Well, I think Prince is better than all of them."

Mercy shook her head and said, "No way, he's too nasty for me."

Charles closed his eyes and swayed back and forth and started to sing "Purple Rain."

Clarissa reached over and put an arm around Mina. "I like Prince too," she said. "I knew you were alright, Mina Rose."

A week later, Kanta was gripping the steering wheel as she drove through North St. Louis. "I thought you said your friend Clarissa went to Wydown."

"She does," Mina said. "She rides the bus to school."

They passed houses with boarded doors and graffiti scrawled across the sides. Behind broken fences, vacant lots sat scattered with abandoned shopping carts, washing machines, and chunks of burned cars. Still, Mina saw that in some of those lots, vines of meandering morning glory ran wild, their indigo blooms perpetually happy, even when wound around such sadness.

"Are you sure this is where she lives?" Kanta asked again, and locked the already locked car door.

"I think so. We've been following the directions she gave me." On the corner of Dr. Martin Luther King Drive, Mina said, "Turn right at the Harlem Tap Room and it should be at the end of this block."

At the corner they passed a group of boys dressed in blue with bandanas hanging from their back pockets.

"There it is," Mina said, pointing. "See, there's the pot of orange chrysanthemums on the steps like she said." Mina dashed out and slammed the door behind her, leaving Kanta to drive away with words she didn't know how to say stuck in her throat.

Mina followed Clarissa through the door and into the softly lit parlor, which had feathery alabaster wallpaper, past the younger twin brothers lying on the sofa playing Atari, and into the dining room, where papers covered a shiny black table.

"My mom just went back to college," Clarissa said. "That's her homework. Can you believe how much there is?"

They kept walking and Mina was about to say something about their history teacher, Ms. Osborne, and how she gave too much homework, when Clarissa pushed through a heavy swinging door. Mina stopped short.

"What's this?" Mina said.

"A kitchen?" Clarissa said. "Don't you have one?"

"Not one like this," said Mina.

The warm room smelled of boiled milk and butter. There was a wooden table in the middle with four chairs and an old porcelain sink in front of a window that looked out onto a tidy backyard. The refrigerator hummed in the corner and boasted photos, school announcements, and lunch menus. The floor of octagonal black-and-white tile was chipped but clean.

Next to where Mina stood was the stove and on it a heavy, dark green pot. Without thinking or asking, Mina lifted the lid and looked inside. It was full of spaghetti in thick meat sauce. For a brief, beguiling moment, Mina forgot where she was and, unable to help herself, she put her face over the pot and started taking in deep, slow breaths of the hearty food, her lifetime of sprouted wheat and tofu vanishing with every inhale.

Clarissa's mother, Tracy, walked into her kitchen and found the young, skinny white girl standing over her stove with her face in the pot of spaghetti and said, "What in the world?"

Clarissa, dumbfounded at her bizarre new friend, shrugged and smiled at her mother. "Mama," she said, "this is Mina."

Tender Love

BY THE TIME MINA and Clarissa were in eighth grade, they were spending every weekend together. Usually they stayed at Clarissa's house, but sometimes they had sleepovers at Mina's where Mina taught Clarissa how to smoke cigarettes and they listened to her Prince records.

Every other weekend Clarissa went to her dad's and Mina often went too. Douglas Moore lived down in Soulard on the South Side under the cover of the sour, hoppy fumes emitted night and day from nearby Anheuser Busch. Douglas spent most nights playing gigs with his Hendrix cover band in downtown bars, so he slept late on Saturdays. When Douglas woke up, he went to Soulard Market and came home with crusty loaves of bread, soft smelly cheeses, thick white jars of French orange marmalade, marinated artichokes, and spicy peppers and olives.

Douglas hipped Mina and Clarissa to Led Zeppelin, Santana, Brazil 66, and of course Jimi Hendrix, but by the time they were thirteen, all Clarissa and Mina really wanted to listen to were slow jams. Every night they called each other at nine o'clock so they could turn on Majic 108 FM in time for the Quiet Storm. The show always started with the Smokey Robinson song of the same name and would be followed by Patti LaBelle, Rose Royce, Atlantic Star, Sade, Ready for the World, and Force MDs.

Mina brought Clarissa to Rahsaan's and introduced her to Bones before asking where they could find the Teddy Pendergrass tapes. Bones rolled his eyes and sucked his teeth. "You sure you want Teddy Pendergrass?"

They nodded.

"Do you girls know how many babies been made listenin' to Teddy Pendergrass?"

Clarissa muffled a giggle behind her hand, but Mina gave him a hard glare. "Dang, Bones," she said. "All this time you know I've been listening to Prince and now you want to be worried about Teddy Pendergrass?"

Bones gave her a long look that let her know he was worried no matter what she was listening to. He didn't need to be. Except for the one time with Paul Glazer, Mina wasn't doing any of the things that would even get her close to making a baby.

Paul Glazer and DeAndre Price lived around the corner from Clarissa and went to McKinley Middle. Close to the end of eighth grade, Clarissa and DeAndre started talking. One night, when Clarissa's mom was in class and the twins were asleep, there was a quiet knock on the door. Clarissa jumped up and went to the window.

"What are you doing?" Mina asked.

"DeAndre's here," Clarissa said and let out a muted squeal. She put her eye against the peephole and turned around. "He's with Paul," she said, and clutched Mina's hand.

The boys walked in slowly, as if even they were unsure of what was going on. They both wore Polo jeans and mock necks. Paul's was white and DeAndre's a dark green. Over his, Paul wore a thin gold herringbone chain.

The next thing Mina knew, she was sitting awkwardly on Clarissa's living room floor watching *Warriors* while Clarissa and DeAndre sat on the couch and gave each other hushed, wet kisses.

"You got a blanket or something?" Paul said. It was the most he'd said since he walked in, and Mina went clumsily to Clarissa's room to grab the afghan off her bed. On the way back, in the blinking light of the television, Mina saw that one of DeAndre's hands was up Clarissa's shirt. That her jeans were unbuttoned *and* unzipped.

Paul spread the afghan across his legs and then lifted it with a gentlemanly manner and motioned for Mina to get under. Mina, who had said even less than Paul, slid up against his warm body. He smelled like Bounce fabric softener and his legs stretched out beyond the blanket, revealing his bright white socks. Every few minutes he took out a wooden-handled brush and smoothed down his waves.

Paul's hand started on top of Mina's knee. She shivered and moved herself closer to him as if she were suddenly cold instead of racingly hot. He moved his hand up her thigh and then down between her legs, rubbing her through the tough seam of her jeans. He turned and kissed Mina without saying a word, and his soft tongue tasted like peppermint taffy in her mouth.

Paul moved his hand up under her shirt. When he lifted her bra and ran his long fingers across the skin of her breasts that had only ever been touched by her own hands, she hoped he didn't feel her tremble. When he went to unbutton and unzip Mina's jeans, Mina glanced at Clarissa and DeAndre on the couch who were definitely not spending any time worrying about what Mina and Paul were doing. Still, Mina was grateful that the afghan covered them, especially when Paul took Mina's now sweaty hand and pushed it into his unzipped jeans.

Mina held his heavy weight in her palm with no idea what to do. He was hot and hard, the skin smooth and loose, but before she could figure out what came next, they all heard the sound of a key turning in the lock of the front door. Furiously they scrambled to straighten their shirts, zip up pants, and wipe mouths. But it didn't matter. Tracy walked in, took one look at them all, and said, "Oh hell no."

108

She put the boys out and told them she would be calling their mothers in the morning. She yanked Clarissa's phone from the wall and removed the cable box from the living room TV. Then, even though it was after ten, Tracy cleared the dining room table, ordered the girls to sit down, and told them they would write *I will not be a fast, nasty girl* until their eyes burned worse than their cheeks. Finally, she sent them to bed.

As she walked to Clarissa's room, her hand aching, Mina saw Paul's wooden brush lying half hidden under the couch and grabbed it. She and Clarissa lay in the dark and took turns pressing the bristles of the brush to their faces, smelling the masculine scent of Dax Wave and Groom. They talked about how strange, how strange and how good, it felt to have a boy's fingers inside them.

2014

IN THE REARVIEW MIRROR, Riley's head was bent abstractly over her phone. Her dark-brown hair fell in thick curls around her face and Mina noticed the deeply bitten fingernail of her thumb that expertly swiped across the screen. They spent Tuesday afternoons this way, parked outside a monotonous West Roxbury strip mall, waiting for Chloe to get out of dance class while Mina attempted and failed to start conversation.

The parking lot always reminded her of the one in South County, St. Louis, where she and Clarissa used to meet up with their pot dealer, James, who looked like Nick Nolte and drove a Chrysler LeBaron. For a minute, Mina wondered if maybe Riley would have something to say if she told her about him.

But that felt too much like something Kanta would have said to her when Mina was fifteen, so instead she said, "Find anything good on there, Ri?"

"Well, if by good you mean like how fucking racist the city that you come from is, then I guess."

Mina turned to tell her to watch her mouth, but stopped when she saw Riley's accusing face. "You're right," she said.

"How'd you even come from there?" Riley asked.

"Pull up a map and I'll show you," Mina said.

Riley handed Mina the slim black phone with a map of St. Louis on the screen. Mina zoomed in until she saw street names she knew: Big Bend, Skinker, Clayton Road, Hanley, Washington Street, Olive, Delmar Boulevard. Looking at the familiar way the streets crossed and intersected, she again felt the longing she hadn't been able to shake since Bones's text a week before. Mina caught Riley's waiting look in the review mirror. "Come up here," she said.

"It's Chloe's week to sit in the front. You know how she'll act if she comes out and I'm in her seat."

Riley and Chloe fought about everything. About who had to do the dishes, about who got to choose the television show, but they fought most about who got to ride in the front seat. Mina, finally sick of listening to it, decreed that they'd have to rotate each week. This stopped the fighting but didn't end the grumbling.

From the beginning, Mina found that her role as parent was basically reduced to referee. She couldn't call herself a peace-maker, because there was never any actual peace, only neutral corners. She was most surprised at how much she had to check her own feelings, how she found herself siding with Riley more often than with Chloe. Riley looked nothing like Mina, with her deep-beige skin, her dark brown eyes, and her curly hair, but Riley made more sense to Mina. She liked to read novels and watch episodes of *The Twilight Zone* and listened to the college radio station. And though Chloe's face matched Mina's like a reflection, with the same gray eyes, the same thin, straight hair and skin nearly as pale as Mina's, Chloe confused Mina. She wanted Abercrombie & Fitch sweatshirts and UGG boots and, paining Mina, insisted on listening to Taylor Swift.

"Come up here," Mina said. "Don't worry about Chloe." Riley climbed over the seat and sat down, pushed up her glasses.

Mina wanted to wrap her arms around her daughter the way she used to when Riley was younger: back in the days when her father started forgetting to come up for his weekends, and stopped calling when he said he would, leaving Riley by the phone for a whole afternoon, missing playdates for nothing. Recently, Riley had stopped speaking to him altogether but, at the same time, she began to push her mother's arm off her shoulders, to stand up the minute Mina sat down.

Mina looked down at where Riley had drawn all over her new Chuck Taylors. "You know when I was a kid I went through a phase where I was so into ska that I drew checkerboards all over my Converse?"

"Yeah, Mom. You've told me a hundred times," Riley said, her eyes on her cell phone, which was now in Mina's lap.

Mina picked up the phone. "This is U. City," she said. "We lived here until I was about ten." Mina zoomed in on the Parkview neighborhood and showed Riley the map.

"Why'd you move?"

"Well, Kanta said it was for my education, but it was really because most of the white people were moving out of U. City and she thought I wouldn't get a good enough education if all the white kids were gone."

"I can see Kanta doing something like that," Riley said. Even as a grandmother, she was still Kanta. The girls would never think of calling her Grandma.

"It didn't matter though," Mina said. "I still hung out in U. City every day."

"Did Auntie Clarissa live in U. City?"

"No, she lived over here," Mina said, scooting the map to the North Side. "She was bussed into Clayton for school. But she hung out in U. City, too."

Riley nodded.

Mina zoomed in on Delmar. "There's Rahsaan's," she said, pointing to the little icon. "And right here, around the block, was where my boyfriend Octavian lived."

"Your boyfriend? As many times as you've told me about your stupid Converse, you never told me about any boyfriend."

"Yeah, Ri," Mina said and smiled. "Your mom had boyfriends once. You would have liked Octavian. He loved the X-Men almost as much as you do."

"Was he black?"

"Yeah."

"Figures," Riley said.

"Why do you say that?" Mina asked

"You're one of those girls."

"What do you mean I'm one of those girls?"

"Don't be offended. It's just who you are."

Riley was good at pulling Mina up short. Like the time when she was in seventh grade and she'd been accepted to a gifted and talented camp at Boston College. They'd gotten to the dorm before Riley's roommate, but when Mina saw the girl's name, Debbie Chang, on the door next to Riley's name, she'd breathed a sigh of relief.

"Good," she said, "at least you're not rooming with a white girl."

Riley put her bag down on the bed and said, "Mom, why do you say things like that?"

"What? It's true."

"But you're white," Riley said.

"That's why I know," said Mina.

"So? What if I got a roommate like you?"

Mina looked at Riley now, still studying the streets of her hometown. It had been almost thirty years since third grade with Makeba, and here was her own brown-skinned daughter offering the same assessment.

"I know I'm not black, Riley," she said.

Without looking up, Riley said, "Yeah, but sometimes you don't think you're white either. Why did you all hang out in U. City?"

"St. Louis has always been segregated," Mina said, relieved that Riley decided to change the subject. "Divided right down the middle. Here, it's mostly black." Mina swooped up north and then east on the map. "And over here," she said, "to the south and west, mostly everyone is white. But in the Loop, which is right in the middle, people from these different places hung out, because it was the one place where it didn't matter where you came from. Most people eventually ended up in Rahsaan's. Music is cool like that."

"That's true," Riley said.

"You asked how I came from here," Mina said, "but really, here, in this little pocket, were people who, like me, didn't want to fit into the molds St. Louis had to offer."

"You were lucky," Riley said.

Mina thought about this. "Well, just because there was that pocket didn't mean the giant circle of other stuff went away," she said. "It was always strong, still is, as you're finding out."

"Did you ever know anyone who got killed by the cops?"

"That happened, certainly, while I was there, it's always happened, but not to anyone I knew. But I did know people who got harassed a lot."

"Your boyfriend?"

"Him, his brother, my friend Brendon."

Mina felt Riley trying to picture her mother as a teenager whose boyfriend got harassed by the cops. "I still think you were lucky," Riley said.

Mina knew what she meant. In Riley's high-achieving high school, she had failed at making friends. Mina often wished that there was a Rahsaan's where Riley could hang out. Mina took a chance and put her hand on Riley's knee. Riley didn't push her away.

"I guess you're right," Mina said. "We were lucky. Especially because it's basically gone now."

"What do you mean gone? The Loop's still there, isn't it?"

"Well, it's become more of a place for wealthy college kids than what it used to be. Some of it has managed to survive."

"Like Rahsaan's?" Riley said. "That's still there. And that guy Bones, right?"

Mina was about to tell Riley that, actually, Rahsaan's would soon be gone, too, when there was a loud rapping at the window.

Chloe stood with her hands on her hips, her head with her dancer's bun cocked to the side.

"Been nice knowin' ya, Mom," Riley said and climbed into the back seat while Chloe hugged the other bun-headed girls and promised to text them later. Mina looked down at Riley's phone, still in her hand. She traced the map to 6616 Washington where, as far as she knew, Cyrus still lived. Her breath caught with a need to see Cyrus. To sit on the nubuck sofa while he sat in his armchair in the corner and told her stories. To hear his deep, gruff laugh, watch his hand pour her a cup of tea, smell the fennel in the sausage dish his Italian landlady in Cambridge taught him how to make.

She handed Riley back her phone and took her own out of her bag. She looked at Octavian's number that Bones had sent her, and that she had stored in her contacts. She pressed the message icon. There, in the text box, was the message she'd begun the day she got the number. She'd rewritten it seven times. How was she supposed to fit everything that happened since she last saw Octavian into a text message? There was no way. Her last attempt simply said, HI. IT'S MINA.

"We going or what?" Chloe asked, switching the radio station.

Before she could think about it any longer, Mina pressed send and jammed her phone back in her bag.

> > >

OCTAVIAN SAT DOWN IN the back of the Winslow faculty meeting as the director, Dan Martin, asked for any announcements. Phyllis the nurse raised her hand and said, "Andrea Applegate drank a cup of bleach last night. So, I'm not sure when she'll be coming back to us."

A gasp went around the room like a collection plate. Octavian learned early on that becoming familiar with this kind of story was part of the job of teaching at Winslow. Sometimes they lived, other times they were tragically successful. But Octavian had not yet heard about Andrea and he immediately began to squeeze his hands together to keep them from trembling. He searched his memory to see if there was any way he could have known yesterday in his art class that she was going to do something like this, but she had been full of smiles and questions like always. They had listened to Miles Davis's '*Round About Midnight* while she worked on her portrait of St. Louis musicians—blending acrylics and scraps of album reviews, photocopies of record covers. It was actually becoming a powerful piece of art, and she was proud of it.

"She was taken to the hospital late last night," Phyllis said.

Octavian strained to hear what others were saying about Andrea, but the rush in his ears was like a freight train coming. Octavian knew he should raise his hand, discuss the work she was doing in his class, but now his heart was slamming away and he knew there was no other choice but to focus on getting out of the room.

Cocaine business controls America, he sang inside his head.

In the background, Phyllis said something about liver failure.

Ganja business controls America

Dan Martin asked to be kept posted, and Octavian knew this was his moment. He stood up, excused himself to somebody, and walked straight through the dark gray that was closing in around him toward the door.

KRS-One come to start some hysteria

Out in the hallway, he pressed his cheek against the cold tile of the wall and closed his eyes.

Illegal business controls America

"You okay, Octavian?" He opened his eyes to see Phyllis standing there.

"I'm okay," he said, clearing his throat. "Just fighting a little flu or something."

"Come with me," she said as she walked down the hall toward her office. "If you're getting that bug that's going around, you'll need some zinc, and pronto."

Phyllis was one of those post-hippie-era remnants who had settled thickly around Berringford. They'd come of age when the
Civil Rights Movement, Vietnam War, and the sexual revolution
were over, but they still clung to the idea of having something to
fight for. They practiced the Waldorf method, lived in quasi-
communes, sewed their own clothes and birthed their own babies.
When she wasn't keeping track of the dizzying number of meds
the kids were on, Phyllis was teaching them Tai Chi and rubbing
essential oils on their pressure points.

In her office, Octavian allowed her to take his temperature, but
when she took out her stethoscope, he put up his hand. "I'm fine,
Phyllis, I promise," he said.

"Octavian, do you realize that when you left the meeting you
knocked over two chairs and nearly fell on top of Teresa?"

Octavian blinked and cocked his head, unsure of what to say.
She pressed the stethoscope to his chest. "That's what I figured,"
she said. "You were having an anxiety attack. I promise you, I've
seen enough of them so don't try to argue." She rested the stethoscope on his chest a second time. "Still going pretty strong. How
about we take some deep breaths together?"

Octavian stood and moved out of her reach and said, "Really,
I'm okay."

"Andrea was a sweet child. It makes sense that you'd be shaken
up by this, especially if you suffer from anxiety."

"Who says I suffer from anxiety?"

Phyllis narrowed her blue eyes at him. "Are you going to tell me
you don't?"

Octavian pulled at the cuff of his sleeve.

"How long?" she asked.

Outside, in the sleepy field that surrounded the school, the
bluestem grass had begun its dusky turn to gray. It bent in the
slight breeze that came through the open window. One thing Octavian knew about Phyllis was that she could out-wait anyone, and
so without taking his eyes from the field, he said, "Since before my
mom died. Since I was nine, maybe ten."

118

"You ever seen anyone about it?"

"I went to a doctor once, when I was younger. He thought it was asthma. And back when I lived in Chicago, I saw another doctor. He told me to get some therapy, to exercise more, not drink so much, and that he could prescribe me something if I wanted."

"Did you do any of that?" Phyllis asked, winding up her stethoscope.

Octavian smiled a bit sheepishly and took a full inhale. "I stopped drinking so much," he said. "And I moved out here."

Phyllis snorted out a laugh. "You came to work at a therapeutic school to help your anxiety? Now that's one I've never heard."

It felt good to laugh a little. "To be honest, it's helped," he said. "You know, thinking about other people, focusing on their problems instead of my own."

Phyllis nodded. "Yes, but by now you must know that it's not sustainable. Eventually, if you don't do at least one of those things—therapy, meds, exercise—sometimes even if you do all three, the anxiety will rear its ugly head."

"I'm starting to figure that out," Octavian said. "It's always come and gone and it's been a while since it's been bad, but it's acting up a lot now."

"Do you want me to recommend a therapist?"

Octavian shook his head. "I tried therapy once. All it did was make me want to strangle the therapist."

"Is there anyone else you can talk to?" Phyllis asked. "Sometimes we just have to say things out loud so they don't hold us captive anymore."

Without meaning to, Octavian's mind went right to Mina. She would be someone he could have talked to once. Someone who would have understood the things he could never explain.

"Actually," Octavian said, "I'm thinking about going home for a few days. See my father, some folks from before, see if I can't come to terms with a few things I never settled." He hadn't said it aloud yet, even in his own thoughts, but there it was, out in the universe. What he needed to do was go home and close up some of those holes that still ran through him.

Phyllis smiled. "Sounds like as good a place to start as any. Where's home?"

"St. Louis."

"Ah, where that young man was just killed by the police officer. A lot of stuff going on there now. No wonder you're having a hard time. Did you know him?"

In his mind Octavian said, *We don't all know each other,* but out loud he said, "No, I didn't, but the story isn't that unique. Race relations in St. Louis have never been great."

"Actually, I know that," Phyllis said. "I took a course in African American History a few summers ago at Harvard Extension. We studied the East St. Louis massacres, learned how some two hundred people were killed, though they like to say it was only forty or something, and never talk about the six thousand or however many were burned out of their homes. Not an easy place, St. Louis," she said. "At least according to what I learned in books."

Octavian smiled at Phyllis. "No, not easy," he said. "But different, too, from what you see in books and on the news. I haven't been back in a long time."

Phyllis put her stethoscope away and said, "You can go around the world, Octavian, and that anxiety will be right there with you. You're not going to outrun it, no matter how fast you go. As they say: No matter where you go, there you are."

"You quoting Confucius or Naughty by Nature?"

"What?" Phyllis said.

"Nothing, just making a bad joke."

Phyllis reached over and patted his knee. "Go on home," she said. "But don't stay away too long. We need you here."

Octavian swallowed and nodded. "Thanks, Phyllis."

"Anytime, sweetheart."

Octavian went back to his classroom and took Andrea's piece from the shelf where she'd placed it just the day before. He felt his heart begin to shake. Phyllis saw the anxiety, called it by its name. Therapy, meds, exercise, she'd said. Maybe even all three. Talking to someone. Octavian took his phone out of his pocket. The last number he'd dialed was Cyrus's. He pressed the name again.

"You decide whether or not you're coming home?" his father said when he picked up.

"Hey to you, too, Pop. How are you?"

Cyrus laughed on the other end. "I'm good. Upright, breathing. How about you? You sound like something is bothering you."

Octavian wondered how his father could always tell. "One of my students," he said. "She tried to commit suicide last night. Thankfully, she failed."

"I'm sorry to hear that," Cyrus said. "But glad to hear she survived."

Andrea had taken the lyrics to Ike & Tina's "I Idolize You" and made them into stripes on Tina Turner's dress. Octavian hoped he would have the chance to tell Andrea how much he loved her piece.

"Pop," he said, "I know we still don't talk about him much, or ever, but I got to ask you something about Frankie."

"You can always ask me about Francis."

Octavian traced his fingers along the cut-up pieces of the cover of Julius Lester's *Departures* that Andrea had incorporated and thought about how, when they listened to "See How the Rain Falls," Andrea had said, "This song always makes me so sad." But when Octavian offered to change it, she told him not to. Just like Mina, she also loved the sad songs.

"Do you think Francis wanted to die?" he asked Cyrus. "I mean, like it wasn't an overdose, but a suicide?"

There was silence on the other end and Octavian wondered if maybe he shouldn't have asked, but then Cyrus said, "I want to believe that he made a mistake, that he took too much, but I'm not going to say I haven't thought about it."

"I think he meant to do it," Octavian said quickly. "Maybe not consciously, but sometimes I think he wanted to die. Not just when he did, but all the time. You know, when we were kids, he used to lie in the bed and sob because he was so afraid?"

"What of?"

"Everything. Nothing. I think he was always in pain. That he suffered. For so long I wrote it off as Frankie's failing, his inability to just stop using. And after he died, I was convinced it was my fault, that I failed. I was supposed to be the one to save him and I didn't. And now, this little girl, my student who tried, she really tried, planned it out and none of us even saw it coming. She did not want to be alive and I wonder if really Francis wasn't just the same way. Only he made it."

"Made it? You think he's better off?"

"Sometimes. Don't get me wrong, Pop, there's not a day I don't want him back, but then I don't. I really don't. I don't want him here, still trying, still hurting, still failing." A sob broke in Octavian's chest and cracked through his throat. He swallowed and looked out the classroom window. The sun was setting, leaving dark blue and yellow streaks across the sky.

"It's alright, Tave," his father said.

"Is it? I mean, I've been trying to figure out which is harder—living with Francis alive, or living with Francis dead. And every time I miss him, I think about what my life would be like if he were still here, if I was still underneath the coming and going of his pain. And then, I don't know, I feel grateful that he's gone, but that's worse. Because how can I feel that way about someone I loved, love, more than anyone in the world?" Octavian stopped to catch his breath. Cyrus was silent on the other end.

"You remember how I used to have those attacks sometimes, where I couldn't breathe? You thought it was asthma and took me to the doctor and all?"

"I remember," Cyrus said. "They couldn't figure out what was going on. Your lungs were fine."

"It wasn't asthma. It was anxiety. I was having anxiety attacks. I've been having them since the fifth grade. I still have them." Octavian could almost feel his father's guilt seeping through the phone. "It's not your fault, Pop. You didn't know. Shit, the doctors didn't know."

"I don't know what to say, Tave. I'm really sorry."

"You don't have to be sorry. I talked to the school nurse about it today and it just got me thinking is all. I mean, they know a lot more about mental health than they used to. And maybe Frankie had anxiety attacks, too, or maybe his anxiety was worse, maybe that's why he was always so afraid, why he needed to escape. They say it's hereditary. So, I was wondering if there was ever any history of mental health problems in your family."

There was silence again before Cyrus said, "Tave, there's something I need to tell you, and I need to see your face when I do. Do you think you might be able to come home?"

The blue of the sky had gone deep indigo, the yellow turned to a heightened gray. Octavian looked down again at Andrea's piece. She had just begun painting Josephine Baker's eyes and she was getting them right.

"I'll come home," Octavian said. "I'll go to Bones's damn party and you and me'll talk, that sound alright?"

"That sounds real good, Tave."

Octavian felt a sudden weightlessness. Maybe Phyllis was right. You just had to get things out sometimes. "You know, I never did finish that drawing of Francis I started. I bet it's still somewhere in your house. Probably in a box I hoped you'd throw out but knew you never would."

Cyrus laughed. "I don't dare open that closet, I'd get crushed by what's shoved in there. We'll take care of that, too, when you come home."

"Okay, Pop. Thank you."

"Just come home," his father said.

"I'm coming."

Octavian sat and watched the rest of the sunset and thought about Andrea. In his car he queued up Billie Holiday and as he drove home, he said a silent prayer for her and let himself cry for a second time that day. When he got back to his cabin, he wiped

his eyes and said, "Enough." He took his phone out of his coat
pocket and saw he had a text message.

HI. IT'S MINA.

He put the phone in his pocket and waited until he was inside
to take it out again. He stared at the text. He wasn't sure what he
waited for—maybe for another text to come, or maybe for Mina
to appear, right out of the phone like Princess Leia. He put it
down and rubbed his forehead. "Dinner," he said out loud to the
cabin. "Dinner and a drink first."

He walked over to the record player and lowered the needle on
the Apollo Brown album he'd just got in the mail. These days his
records came from websites, since there definitely wasn't a record
store in Berringford—especially not one that would sell Apollo
Brown. He took a bunch of spinach that his landlady, Abigail, had
left on the counter for him and washed it before throwing it in a
hot skillet. For the first time since he left, Octavian felt like he
needed St. Louis. He needed to walk the Loop and play darts at
Blueberry Hill. He needed to eat a slinger at Eat-Rite at three in
the morning after drinking for hours. He needed to laugh at
Bones and talk with Brendon. He needed to reminisce about
Francis with Ivy and sit in the kitchen while Cyrus cooked dinner.
He watched as the spinach wilted and thought about Mina. He
couldn't lie. Not to himself, standing alone in his cabin in Maine.
He needed to see Mina, too. He couldn't write back. Not right
away. Anything he might say after the day he'd had would be yet
another mistake and, he thought, he'd made a lot of mistakes with
this girl. Girl. He laughed at himself. She was damn near forty
years old, but still she was a girl. His girl, even.

the '90s:

A MIX TAPE

YA SLIPPIN'—BOOGIE DOWN PRODUCTIONS

JAZZ (WE'VE GOT)—A TRIBE CALLED QUEST

FOLLOW THE LEADER—ERIC B. & RAKIM

LITTLE GIRL BLUE—JANIS JOPLIN

JOY IN REPETITION—PRINCE

YOU MUST LEARN—BOOGIE DOWN PRODUCTIONS

REBEL WITHOUT A PAUSE—PUBLIC ENEMY

IF NOT NOW . . .—TRACY CHAPMAN

SELF-PORTRAIT IN THREE COLORS—CHARLES MINGUS

FOR THE LOVE OF YOU (PART I & 2)—THE ISLEY BROTHERS

CAUTION—BOB MARLEY

HOW I COULD JUST KILL A MAN—CYPRESS HILL

CAN YOU STAND THE RAIN—NEW EDITION

SLOW DOWN—BRAND NUBIAN

HOME IS WHERE THE HATRED IS—GIL SCOTT-HERON

INNER CITY BLUES (MAKE ME WANNA HOLLER)—MARVIN GAYE

LILAC WINE—NINA SIMONE

TONIGHT'S DA NIGHT—REDMAN

BEFORE I LET GO—MAZE (FEATURING FRANKIE BEVERLY)

THIS BROKEN HEART—FUNKADELIC

Ya Slippin'

THE SUMMER OF 1990, Eric B. & Rakim released *Let the Rhythm Hit 'Em* and Compton's Most Wanted dropped their first album. It was also the summer that Octavian turned sixteen and Francis, who was twenty, seemed to have finally left the hard stuff alone, sticking to vodka and weed and the occasional line of coke. This meant that he was back to being the old Francis, the one that liked having Octavian around. And Francis had decided that, now that Octavian was sixteen, he was old enough to come out with him.

"But," Francis said, "you're still my little brother. I still gotta look after you."

That meant that there were rules to be followed, and not just by Octavian, but by everyone. Octavian could only take two hits off the joint and he was only allowed two beers or one drink. And that drink could not be vodka.

"'Cause vodka," Francis would say as he rattled the ice cubes in his own glass of Stoli on the rocks, "is the devil's work."

Most importantly, if a fight broke out—which it almost always did—it was everyone's job to get Octavian the fuck out of there, before he got hurt.

Everyone followed Francis's rules—except Ivy and Brendon. They always passed Octavian the joint a third or fourth time or got him another shot of whiskey. But Octavian didn't really care whether or not he had anything to drink or smoke. He just wanted to ride around in their cars listening to *Edutainment* and *AmeriKK-Ka's Most Wanted.*

Close to the end of that summer, Francis stopped coming out as much. When he did, sometimes he was happy to see Octavian, and sometimes he was pissed, asking him what the fuck he thought he was doing there. More than one time, Octavian found himself at a party where Brendon and Ivy had to push Octavian out the door because coke came out, or guns, or Big Chris came looking for Francis because he owed him money for both. Octavian was glad when school started again.

By Christmas, both Brendon and Ivy were working full-time at Rahsaan's. Francis, however, was usually nowhere to be found. Brendon and Ivy still let Octavian hang out though, and without Francis around, they took their big brother roles more seriously. Ivy always made sure Octavian was safe and Brendon made sure to talk shit about Octavian whatever chance he got.

Octavian didn't mind that Brendon made fun of him for trying to look like Lenny Kravitz, or how Ivy would tell him that he couldn't have another forty-ounce, as long as he didn't have to stay at home where Cyrus sat alone at the table worrying about Francis. Most of the time, Octavian just wanted to hang out in Rahsaan's. His attacks, which he thought had gone away, began to act up once Francis started disappearing again. But they lessened when he was at Rahsaan's bargaining with Bones for used vinyl or asking Brendon to put things aside for him until he saved up enough.

"Save up enough how? You ain't got a job," Brendon said one night while he, Ivy, and Bones closed up. Brendon wore a wooden fist on a long cord around his neck and it banged against his belly as he moved around the counter.

"I start work next week over at Pier One in Olivette," Octavian said.

"What the hell you working way out there for? You good at selling bamboo candles or some shit?"

"This girl I know got me the job."

Brendon laughed. "Yo, Bones," he said, "bet you didn't know it, but my man Tave over here looking like Sly Stone and shit, got some serious game."

"Shut up, B," Octavian said, sifting through his pile of records on the hold shelf. "You know you're the player."

"You goddamn right, I'm a playa," Brendon said. "Got girls calling me Heavy D and shit, asking me if I'm the real overweight lover."

From the front of the store they heard a loud banging on the door.

"What the . . . ?" Brendon said. "Don't motherfuckers know we closed?"

There was another loud series of bangs and Bones looked out from the back room. "Brendon," he said, "go see who's out there acting a fool and tell them to go on home."

"Yes, massa," Brendon said.

"Don't start on that massa shit again," Bones said. "I ain't giving you another raise."

Brendon maneuvered himself over to the front door. Octavian heard it open and looked up from his pile of records to see Brendon holding onto Francis, whose long limbs were draped around him. Francis stumbled and nearly fell.

"C'mon man," Brendon said, walking him past Octavian and toward the back of the store. "It's alright. I got you."

Octavian started to say something, but Brendon held up his hand and stopped him. Francis's clothes were torn and Octavian could see the dark sweat stains under his arms. His lips were swollen and crusted. Tears and snot streamed down his face.

"Don't tell my brother, B," Francis slurred over and over. "You better not tell him. Promise me."

"I won't, Frankie," Brendon said, glancing back at Octavian. "I promise. I won't say a thing."

Octavian stood alone for a minute and then followed quickly behind. In the back of the store, Ivy and Brendon tried to hold onto Francis, his knees buckling underneath him while Bones tried to get him to open his eyes.

"What's going on?" Octavian asked, his voice barely audible.

"Francis is just having a little trouble, baby," Bones said.

"He's fucking ODing, that's what's going on," Ivy said. Octavian could tell Ivy was pissed. His jaw was clenched and his face was red, his forehead covered with sweat.

Bones and Brendon both stopped and stared at Ivy.

"What? It's true," Ivy said. "Tave needs to know and Frankie needs to get his shit straight. I'm tired of this."

Bones looked at Octavian and then back at Ivy. "He's not ODing," Bones said. "He's just had too damn much and he's dehydrated as hell. Get his ass to the hospital so they can get some fluids in him."

"I'll take him," Ivy said as they pulled Francis out the back door.

"And call Cyrus as soon as you can," Bones yelled.

Before Bones could say anything more, Octavian walked back into the empty store and over to his stack of records. He tried to look through them, but when he got to Pink Floyd's *Wish You Were Here* and then Too Short's *Born to Mack,* he knew he wasn't going to make it. He slid down onto the floor and pressed his back into the shelf. The ringing in his ears sounded like sirens and he wondered if an ambulance had come to take Francis away. He wanted to get up and tell Brendon that, if he hadn't already, he should call one, but he couldn't gather his legs up underneath him enough to stand. Instead, he dropped his head down in between his knees. From somewhere far above him, Bones shook him by the shoulder and he heard Brendon's voice say,

"You alright, Tave? You look like you might need a doctor too." Octavian could see the dirt in the fibers of the gray carpet, the scuff on the toe of his motorcycle boots. "I'm okay," he managed to say.

Brendon lowered his big body down next to Octavian's.

Octavian kept his head lowered. He tried holding his breath in order to make his heart stop thrashing about.

From across the store he heard Bones turn on the stereo system. "Hey, Tave," Bones yelled over to him, "I just heard that your boy KRS sampled Deep Purple on one of his songs. I figured you'd know which song I'm talkin' about."

"Bones, you need to get a late pass," Brendon yelled. "That shit came out in '88, man." He nudged Octavian. "What track is it again, Tave?"

Octavian swallowed hard. He knew they were trying to act normal just for him. "It's 'Ya Slippin'," he said and cleared his throat. "Second song on the first side."

"Side A, Bones," Brendon said. "Track two."

Bones lowered the needle on the record and the static split across the room before the sampled line blasted through the speakers.

Octavian's heart wasn't slowing down. He kept thinking about Francis's face. How it looked so yellow. And why was Frankie, who was always so fresh and clean, torn up and dirty like that?

Now what you just heard, people, was a little kickin'.

Octavian focused on KRS-One's voice, and on Brendon next to him, whose head bobbed to the beat. The beat that was just a little bit slower than his heart's.

But let me tell you this while the clock is still tickin'—

Brendon began rapping along and Octavian searched deep in his chest to find his voice.

"This is the warning, known as the caution," Brendon rapped.

Octavian replied, "Do not attempt to dis, 'cause you'll soften."

With the words in his mouth, he felt better and he let himself fall into the song, leaning a bit on Brendon in case he began to slide too far.

"Just like a pillow, or better yet a mattress," Brendon went on.

"You can't match this style or attack this," Octavian said.

They kept rapping until song finished. Brendon gave him a pound. "My man," he said.

Bones lowered the needle again. This time on the original "Smoke on the Water."

"You would go and fuck it up with this white boy shit," Brendon said pressing his hands on the floor and standing up. He held out a hand to Octavian, who took it and let Brendon pull him up.

Bones walked over. "You aight, Tave?" he asked. Octavian could tell Bones wanted him to look him in the eyes, but Octavian wasn't ready for all that yet.

"Yeah," Octavian said.

"Your brother," Bones said, "he's going to be—"

"My brother is going to be my brother," Octavian said before Bones could finish. "But don't tell me he's going to be alright."

Bones took off his Cardinals cap and rubbed his head. "Maybe you're right. Maybe he won't, but this time he is, okay?" Bones looked at Brendon and Octavian could tell they were both worried.

Octavian didn't want them to worry. Everyone had worried enough about Francis. "I should probably go home," he said. "In case Ivy's called my dad by now."

"I'll go with you," Brendon said, and they walked toward the door.

Bones called after them, "Hey, Tave."

"What's up?"

"I hear you say you was working out in Olivette?"

"Yeah, starting next week. Gotta make some money to pay you for these damn records."

"How 'bout you come work for me?" Bones said.

"For real?"

"Seeing as how you always up in here anyway, I might as well hire you."

"Do I get the employee discount and everything?" Octavian asked.

"Of course."

Octavian blinked back the hot tears that filled his eyes.

"Word," Brendon said.

Octavian smiled. "When do I start?"

"What time you out of school tomorrow?" Bones asked.

"Tomorrow's Sunday, Bones."

"Right. Good. Be here at ten."

Jazz
(We've Got)

IF FRANCIS HAD BEEN scarce the year before, he almost didn't exist during Octavian's senior year. Cyrus no longer sat at the table waiting for him to come home. When Francis was there, neither Octavian nor his dad could tell whether Francis was high or not, whether he was sick or not. He never met their eyes and he didn't stay long. Long enough for a meal usually. Sometimes a shower, sometimes a good night's sleep. His visits always ended in a fight with Cyrus who, despite helpful intentions, only managed to chase Francis back out the door.

Octavian missed his brother. Even though life was more peaceful when Francis wasn't home, he wanted him there. He wanted to tell him about Ivy and the new girl he had been kicking it to. He wanted to play him the songs he'd learned about from working at Rahsaan's that he knew Frankie would like. But Francis never wanted to listen to music anymore.

"Turn that shit off," he'd say to Octavian when he tried, and would mumble something about Ivy being a punk ass white boy.

Octavian spent most of the school day in the art room with Mr. Pearson, the aging art teacher with early-stage emphysema. He gave Octavian his own key to the art supply closet and taught him how to throw pots. Octavian fell in love with the feeling of wet clay spinning under his hands, taking on forms, becoming beautiful, useful things. After school, he went straight to Rahsaan's, where Brendon was now a manager.

That summer Brendon had read all of Frantz Fanon and Stokely Carmichael, and by fall, he was planning for an inevitable race war. He stockpiled canned goods and bomb-making materials from *The Anarchist Cookbook* in his mom's basement. He stopped wearing Adidas and dressed in dashikis and beads or black turtlenecks and berets. One night, when Octavian was over at the apartment Brendon and Ivy now shared in Eastgate, Octavian heard noises coming from the kitchen. He walked in to find Brendon drunk and at the stove, sticking the tines of his pick into the flame and then touching the hot metal to his arm.

"Yo, B, what the fuck are you doing?" Octavian asked.

Brendon's glasses were so foggy that Octavian couldn't see his eyes. "What do you think?" he said. "I'm preparing for the revolution."

Brendon's first hire was a mixed kid named Evan who Octavian liked right away. Evan went to Hazelwood Central and drove his mom's banged-up Ford Escort to Rahsaan's every day. He wore baggy jeans and peace medallions and had a fade and dreadlocks. He looked like he could have been a member of De La Soul, but what Evan was really into was '80s British punk, ska, and new wave.

"You're hired," Brendon said. "'Cause there is no way I'm taking the time outta my life to learn about that shit."

Ivy had failed out of school, but Bones soon learned he had a head for business. He and Fred Bosch were always scheming some way to make the store more money. Other people came and went. Ivy's cousin Matty worked there for a little while. Dave Sherman, who was a straight fiend for hip hop, had to quit when his wife found out he'd spent his whole paycheck on records. And that September, on the day that A Tribe Called Quest dropped *The Low End Theory*, Mina Rose walked back into Rahsaan's.

Octavian was moving the Bob Seger CDs out of the Credence Clearwater Revival section and cursing Evan, who had put them there, when he heard Bones's big, heavy laugh and glanced up. He felt a momentary sense of confusion when he saw the girl Bones was talking to. There was something about her face that he knew, but he didn't know how.

St. Louis had never been a fashionable town, and the girls Octavian saw were no exception. Black girls permed their hair straight and white girls permed their hair curly and both thought they looked cute in their turtleneck sweaters and add-a-bead necklaces. He was still searching for the Lisa Bonet to his Lenny Kravitz but was convinced by then she wasn't going to walk into Rahsaan's anytime soon. But this wide-hipped white girl, who Bones was acting like was some long-lost relative, did not look like a St. Louis girl. She had chin-length reddish brown hair and wore baggy jeans, a burgundy leather jacket, and big hoop earrings. Her wrists and fingers were covered in chunky pieces of silver and turquoise. If Octavian hadn't felt like he knew her from somewhere, he would have sworn she was from out of town.

Bones walked her through the store and introduced her to Brendon. Ivy knew her and gave her a big hug, said something that made her laugh. It was the laugh that made Octavian remember. He put the CDs down and stared. Across the speakers, Q-Tip rapped about strictly butter, baby, and Octavian thought, could it be her?

They walked over to where he stood and Bones said, "Mina girl, this is the one, the only, Octavian Munroe. Octavian, meet Mina Rose."

She looked at Bones to make sure she heard him right and back at Octavian. "Holy shit," she said. "Octavian?"

"Hey, Mina," he said. A smile took over his face. "It's been a long time." Without warning she hugged him fiercely, urgently, and he lifted a nervous hand to her back.

A look of sentimental confusion crossed over Bones's face before he said, "Oh, that's right, y'all know each other, don't you?"

Mina released Octavian and blushed deeply. "Yeah, I know this guy," she said to Bones. "We were friends in fifth grade." She turned to Octavian. "I can't believe it's really you. I haven't seen you in so long. I thought you moved away or something."

Octavian felt the tips of his fingers get hot and he looked at Bones. "This girl is the reason I started drawing," he said.

"Is that right?" Bones said. "I seem to remember something about a Chuck Berry record." He smiled sideways at Mina and walked away toward the cash register.

Mina and Octavian stood silently for a moment in the Classic Rock section feeling like the children they were nearly seven years before. "Seems like you and Bones are old friends," Octavian said. "Have you known him a long time?"

"Yeah," she said, spinning one of the rings on her finger. "I met him around the time we moved out of U. City. I've been wanting to work here ever since."

"Wait, you're going to work here?" Octavian said.

She smiled. "Today's my first day."

For the first few weeks, Bones scheduled them to work the same shifts, and even though Mina smiled at Octavian as soon as he walked in the door, Octavian found himself folding up whenever she came near. He preferred to watch her from a distance. It wasn't so much that Mina was pretty—which she was—but what made her different was something else. It was how she dressed in Doc Martens and a suede coat with long fringe that swished as she walked, or a short dress with cowboy boots and an army jacket. And it was the way she snapped her fingers when a song she liked came on, how she laughed when she sat in the back talking shit with Ivy. It was those things, but that wasn't all. She didn't seem to care who other people expected her to be and, at least from what Octavian could tell, she had no intention of being anyone else. Just like when they were kids, he thought, she was still free.

Octavian wished that when she turned her gray eyes on just him, that his mouth wouldn't get dry and he wouldn't forget the things he wanted to say to her. But usually he wound up turning quickly to some mundane task he pretended was much more important. He saw that this confused her because when everyone else was around, he had plenty of things to say. He cracked jokes with her, teased her, even made a point of letting her know he respected what she knew about music, but when they were alone, he always walked away.

On a fall day when the wind was blowing so hard they had to wedge the front door of Rahsaan's so that it wouldn't keep slamming open and closed, Bones sent Octavian and Mina to the back to unload a shipment of CDs. Octavian pretended to focus on the CDs and was still trying to think of something to say when she asked, "So, do you still draw?"

A sandy feeling coated his mouth and he scolded himself and swallowed. "I do," he said. "But I've been doing more painting these days than drawing. And doing some pottery."

"That's really cool," she said. "Think I could see your work sometime?"

Octavian imagined that they were not alone, that the room was full of his friends. "Maybe," he said. "When I get to know you better."

She laughed. "Shit, Tave, I'd like to think I've changed a lot since the fifth grade, but other than wearing jeans that fit, I think I'm pretty much the same." She slid a CD out of the box. "You know it's because of you that I found Rahsaan's?"

"It was?"

She nodded. "I came down to the Loop not long after I left Delmar Harvard. I was trying to find you, but I found Bones instead. That was the day he sold me my first Prince record."

"That's crazy," Octavian said. "It was around that time Frankie took me to see Prince live at the Arena."

"You got to go to that show? God, I wanted to go so bad." She was quiet for a minute. "Funny how things work out. I was all about lace and clowns and drawing teardrops on my face after that."

139

Thinking about the way she'd been in her high-water jeans made Octavian less nervous. "I would have done anything to see that."

"Why? So you could have teased me?"

He remembered that back then she was the one who could make him feel better whenever he felt bad. The fact that she had gone to look for him made him feel brave. "Nah, Mina girl," he said. "We could have hung out, listened to 'Controversy' or something."

"I guess we were more alike than we thought," she said.

"We still are," Octavian said without looking at her.

The next day she came in to Rahsaan's even though she wasn't on the schedule and handed Octavian a cassette.

"What's this?"

Mina blushed a little. "I belong to this mail-order Prince fan-club thing that's run out of Minneapolis," she said. "They send me tapes of local radio station interviews and bootleg live recordings, some unreleased songs. I put a few of my favorites on here."

Octavian turned the tape over in his hands, saw where she'd handwritten the names of all the songs. Goddamn, he thought. She'd made him a present, a Prince mix tape. Used a Maxell XLII-S 90 and everything.

"Thanks," he said.

She did that thing where she looked into his eyes and made everything else disappear. But this time, he didn't look away. He saw the edges of her cheeks turn pink. "Let me know if you like it," she said and cleared her throat. "I got a whole lot more where that came from."

Follow the
Leader

MINA HAD ONLY BEEN working at Rahsaan's for a month before she convinced Bones to hire Clarissa. After that, Bones liked to say that he didn't need to come to work anymore. He was right. The collective knowledge of his staff was more than he could ever hope to know himself. Ivy knew everything about hip hop from the Fat Boyz to Scarface, and Brendon was a soul music genius who also had a hidden passion for women folk singers— something he and Mina talked about whenever they weren't discussing books. Clarissa knew about R&B and a whole host of obscure bands from hanging out with her dad. Mina knew what she knew about folk music, but what she loved most was funk and any band with a powerful drummer.

And then there was Octavian. Coming from Cordelia, who was a gospel, soul-loving poet, and Cyrus, who'd been born with a jazz record playing in his ear, and having an older brother like Francis, who went to sleep for a year straight listening to "Shine on You Crazy Diamond," meant that, as much as everyone else knew, Octavian knew more. Octavian had a selective taste that no one could mess with. He knew what songs were going to be the biggest hits and which were the ones people slept on. Secretly, everyone who worked in Rahsaan's waited for Octavian before they decided whether or not to really like a song. They went to him to find out what hip hop album to buy next, or what jazz song to put on to impress a date. And they deferred to him in the ongoing debate about who was the better MC—Rakim or KRS-One—to which he always said, "You know, Rakim's a dope lyricist, but can't no one fuck with Kris Parker."

They became a crew, going out weekends to play darts at Blueberry Hill or getting slingers at Eat-Rite Diner. They piled into Mina's mother's ancient Volvo station wagon, the floor of the back seat littered with cassettes, and went downtown, to Forest Park, to parties out in Kirkwood. Octavian always called shotgun and DJ'd, his insides getting tied up in knots when Mina rapped along with every word of "Sucker MCs."

Most nights they ended up in the back room at Rahsaan's playing cards, listening to music with weed smoke hanging low in the air. That was how Octavian wound up across the table from Mina, forced to meet those dark gray eyes he'd managed to avoid looking too deeply into since she gave him the Prince tape. They were playing spades against Brendon and Ivy, and since they were on the same team, Octavian couldn't look away as she tried to let him know, without saying a word, that she had a good hand.

He nodded. "Let's go blind six," he said.

Evan always lost at cards, so he sat behind the turntable with both a bong and a forty in his lap. He played the I Threes and Elvis Costello and DJ Quick and when he put on Bronski Beat, Brendon bobbed his head and said, "This shit is dope. What is this, E?"

Octavian laughed. "I love you, Brendon man," he said and threw the three of hearts.

"Why's that?" Brendon asked, throwing the queen.

"Because you're the most militant motherfucker I know, over there in your beret, looking like a big-ass Professor Griff from Public Enemy and shit, and then here you are getting your groove on to some very white British pop."

"Hey, I don't discriminate," Brendon said. "Plus, I can't be that militant now that I live with this cracker motherfucker," he said, pointing his hand of cards at Ivy.

Evan changed the song to Slick Rick and Mina threw the ace of hearts. Ivy shrugged and threw the king. Brendon let out an exasperated sigh. He didn't like losing at spades and he kicked Ivy under the table.

"What?" Ivy said. "It's the only heart I've got."

"Great," Brendon said, "good thing they know that now."

"You better not have just messed up my Nikes, B," Ivy said and he examined his latest pair of shoes. He turned to Octavian. "Yo, Tave," he said. "You shoulda seen this girl I was talking to last night at the bowling alley. Fat booty and light skinned. Cute as hell."

Brendon shook his head and licked his lips. "You seen Frankie lately, Tave?" he asked.

"Don't try to be slick, y'all," Octavian said. "You think you can distract me from beating your asses by talking about fat booties and Francis, but you can't."

"Ain't nobody trying to distract you. Brother can't ask about his boy?"

"You can ask," Octavian said. "But you better watch yourself. You know Francis is like the candy man. Say his name three times and the motherfucker will appear."

Octavian dropped the two of spades on the last hand and Brendon cursed, pushed himself away from the table. "You got a cigarette, Ivy?"

Ivy nodded and they went outside. Bones didn't care too much about them smoking weed or drinking in the back, but recently, he'd decided that smoking cigarettes was forbidden. Mina and Octavian sat alone at the table. Mina took a sip of her drink and said, "I have to tell you something."

"What? You cheat at spades?"

She laughed and said, "No, I don't cheat at spades."

"Okay, what?"

"You know, that day a long time ago when you came into Rahsaan's and bought that Chuck Berry record, with your dad and your brother?"

Octavian nodded slowly. "I remember."

"I was here."

"What do you mean you were here? In Rahsaan's? Did I see you?"

Mina shook her head. "I hid behind the counter. I didn't want you to see me."

Octavian could only stare at her.

"You remember how I told you that I used to look for you sometimes, how I thought that maybe I'd find you here?"

Octavian nodded.

"Well, when you did finally walk in, I was so petrified, I hid. Bones thought I was crazy." She stopped talking and smiled. "I remember it was the first time I ever heard of Miles Davis. I bought myself the same record your dad bought a few weeks later."

Octavian's stomach flipped a little. "*+19?*"

"*+19.*"

Mina swallowed and looked away. "I don't know why I just told you that."

It was the first time Octavian ever saw her look uncomfortable, and he was about to tell her it was cool when Brendon called his name from across the room. Octavian turned from Mina. "What's up?"

Brendon jerked his head toward the back door where Evan stood talking to Crazy Opal and Clarissa. He shot a worried look at Octavian. A look Octavian knew meant only one thing. Francis. He ignored them and turned back to Mina. "Is Crazy Opal officially crazy?"

"I don't know," Mina said. "Sometimes she walks past me like I'm a stranger. Other times she hits on me, tells me how much she loves white girls."

Octavian tried to laugh. Clarissa walked over and leaned her hip against Mina's chair. "Hey, girl," she said.

Mina reached up to hold Clarissa's hand. "Hey, Riss," she said. Clarissa looked at Octavian. "I hate to do this to you, Tave," she said. "But your brother's over at Cicero's starting all types of shit. He flipped on Opal and got her shook. Y'all probably need to go see what's up."

Evan lifted the needle off the Digital Underground's "Freaks of the Industry" and the room filled with massive silence. Everyone looked at Octavian, who looked at Ivy.

"Let's go," Ivy said.

Cicero's Restaurant was across the street from Rahsaan's. It specialized in cold pitchers of beer, St. Louis–style pizza, and lasagna baked in individual blue and red pans. There was a dining room with a long bar and a basement that featured local rock and reggae bands. Upstairs was a jukebox that hadn't been updated since the early '80s.

When they walked in, Johnny, who worked the takeout booth, said, "It's about fucking time."

"Where is he?" Octavian asked.

Johnny nodded toward the bar. Francis sat, long arms folded on the shining Formica. His head hung deep between his shoulders and he moved to a beat much slower than the Hall & Oates song coming from the speakers. The rest of the customers had given him a wide berth.

Clarissa said something about calling her mom and walked over to the pay phone. Mina gave Octavian a smile. "I'm going to get cigarettes," she said.

Octavian watched her walk to the back, where she dropped quarters into the cigarette machine and pulled the lever. He heard Francis call his name and he turned to see him gesturing wildly for Octavian to sit down. Octavian shook his head and smiled, and went to join Francis at the bar.

Evan, Brendon, and Ivy were still talking to Johnny, but Mina walked over to where they were sitting. Francis gave her a crooked smile. "Hey, Mina," he said, swaying a bit on his stool. "Wanna go do some blow with me in the men's room?"

Before Mina could answer, Octavian said, "Fuck off, Francis."

Francis turned from Mina to Octavian and back again. "Aww, shit, this your girl now, Tave? That's cool. I don't know though, she might be too cute for your ugly ass. I been trying to tap that for a minute. Haven't I, Mina?"

"What are you talking about?" Mina said.

"Oh, that's right, it wasn't you. It was your friend, the big girl, Clarissa. Now, she's cute, Tave. Where she at? She was just in here with that bitch, Opal." Francis turned toward the bartender. "Hey, Doug, lemme get another Stoli."

Doug glanced at Octavian and put a highball of ice on the bar, but he filled it with water, not vodka. "It's been a long night, Francis," he said. "Think it's time to go home."

Francis stared hard at the glass of water for a second. "Oh, so my bitch-ass little brother comes up in here and now you wanna cut me off?" he said to Doug, but he was looking at Octavian.

"Chill, Frankie," Octavian said.

Francis stood and pressed his body up against Octavian. "What, you up in here with this, this bitch, who everyone knows gives the best damn head in St. Louis, and now you better than me or something?"

Mina took a step back, and from the other side of the room, she saw Evan, Brendon, and Ivy pushing toward them, but not before Octavian swung wide and caught Francis across the chin. Francis fell backward, and as he fell, he threw the glass of water at Octavian, catching him hard on the face. The room vibrated like a deep bass line and Francis went down, taking tables and chairs with him.

It was silent until Doug hollered, "Get the fuck out. Get out, get out!"

Brendon offered Francis a hand, but Francis slapped it away and scrambled to his feet. He didn't look at any of them, just pushed his way out the door.

Octavian picked up a fallen chair, and Ivy and Evan righted the table. An angry cut opened up underneath Octavian's left eye, and he touched the tip of his fingers to the thin line of dark-red blood.

"Tell your brother he's not coming in here no more, okay?" Doug said handing Octavian a napkin. "No more fucking chances."

Octavian held the napkin to his face and nodded as he walked toward the door. Mina grabbed onto Clarissa's hand and they all followed Octavian silently outside where the early October wind had picked up. They hugged themselves inside their jackets and looked down Delmar to where Francis's tall frame, head down, hands in his pockets, was walking fast.

"You think he's gonna be alright?" Evan asked.

"Someone should prolly go make sure," Ivy said. "Want to come with me?"

Evan shrugged. "Not really."

"Fuck him," Octavian said. The streetlights of passing cars blurred. Francis was already in front of the Tivoli.

"Well, I know it's not my turn to look after Frankie's ass," Brendon said and gave Ivy a look. "I was with him three nights ago."

Ivy shook his head. "Y'all suck," he said and started jogging in Francis's direction.

"Yo, Ivy," Octavian called.

Ivy turned around.

"Hit me up later. Let me know what's up."

"Roger Dodger," Ivy said.

They watched until Ivy caught up and wrapped a thin arm around Francis's back.

"You need a ride home, Clarissa?" Brendon said.

Clarissa looked at Mina. "You good?"

"I'm good."

"You should put a Band-Aid or some shit on that cut, Tave," Evan said.

"It's not that bad," Octavian said.

"Bones has a first-aid kit in his office," Mina said.

Octavian turned to Brendon. "Can I borrow your keys?"

Brendon looked hard at Octavian and then at Mina. He looked at Octavian again. "For real?" he said. Octavian nodded and Mina lit a cigarette.

Brendon dug in his pants and pulled out his keys. "You know what you're doing, Tave?"

"Yeah. I'm going to get a fucking Band-Aid, Brendon," Octavian said and took the keys.

"I guess I'll go help out Ivy," Evan said giving a round of pounds and turning his shoulders into the wind.

"Let's go, Riss," Brendon said.

Clarissa gave Mina a quick kiss on the cheek and ran after Brendon, who walked away without saying goodbye.

Mina was unlocking the back door of Rahsaan's when Octavian felt the fingers of cold sweat on his back. "Hold up," he said. He pulled a crumpled pack of Craven A's out of his pocket with shaking hands. He felt his breath start to come in short bursts, and when he tried to light his cigarette, he dropped the lighter. He bent to pick it up, but he knew he might as well just surrender right there and sat down on the mottled sidewalk. "Just a second," he managed to say. He put his head between his knees and squeezed his eyes shut.

Mina knelt down next to him and wrapped her hand around his. "You still doing this, huh, Tave?" she said.

"What do you mean?"

"I remember back at Delmar Harvard when this would happen. You'd squeeze my hand so hard I'd think you were going to break my fingers, and I'd sit there and read to you from whatever comic until your breathing would slow down, like it's doing now."

Octavian hadn't thought she would remember.

"Does it still happen a lot?" she asked.

"Not as much as it did back then," he said. He lifted his head and brushed the sharp pieces of gravel from his palms. There was something about not having to explain his attacks to her, about not having to explain what they were like when he was little, that made his heart begin to unfurl. Made it easy for Octavian to open his eyes and look at her. "Now, they usually happen when I drink too much." He paused to light the cigarette with steadier hands. "And when Francis is tripping."

"Makes sense it would happen now."

"Yeah, but it's not supposed to happen when I'm trying to impress a girl," he said and pushed himself to stand up.

"You can't fool me, Octavian Munroe," she said standing up to face him. "I know you're not as cool as you think you are."

"What are you talking about?" he said. "I'm the coolest." He reached out and took a slow hold of her front pocket and pulled her toward him. Mina's stone-gray eyes danced in the streetlight and, without letting himself think on it long, Octavian bent his head and kissed her.

Beneath the alcohol, the cigarettes, and weed, the soap she used on her face, the detergent to wash her clothes, he remembered her smell from back then. He saw himself put his own little-boy hands to his face after they'd said goodbye to see if he smelled like her. Could that be real? He wasn't sure. Now it made him far drunker than the whiskey and weed. He stopped to catch his still-fragile breath and kept his forehead pressed against hers.

"I've been wanting to do that for the longest time," he said.

Mina's generous smile showed those same crooked teeth, and Octavian was glad she never had them fixed. "You got a lot of game," she said.

He laughed. "I'm not running game on you."

"C'mon now. You ain't been wantin' to kiss me for no long time," she said and began to walk into the store.

He followed her. "When'd you get so city, Mina girl?" Octavian said. "Don't forget, I knew you back then, too. You're not any cooler than me. You were one freckled-faced, stringy-haired white girl. *You ain't been wantin' to kiss me for no long time*," he mocked her.

She turned and walked backwards so she faced him. He smiled and backed her up into a shelf in the Metal section and kissed her again.

"The records," she murmured.

"Fuck those records. No one listens to that shit anyway."

He didn't rush this time. This time, he inhaled her smell so deeply he wanted to name it. They were twisted arms and legs, tongues deep within each other's mouths, lips soft, deep, and full. His hands were under her shirt, her leg wrapped around his waist, eyes closed, then opened, watching, being watched. He reached down to unbutton her pants but she stopped him.

"Hold up," she said.

Octavian took two steps back and Mina carefully climbed off the records. "You know that shit your brother said about me, it's not true," she said.

"I know," Octavian said. Octavian had asked around enough to know that Mina wasn't like that. The only thing anyone ever had to say about her was that she dressed kinda weird and only hung around black people.

Mina checked to see if there was any damage to the records. "Bones is going to kill us," she said, and held up a crumpled Quiet Riot record.

"I doubt that," Octavian said. "I mean, he probably would care a little about the record, but I bet he wouldn't be that mad 'cause it's you and me. You know he loves us best of all."

Octavian walked over and switched on the stereo system, dropped a record on the turntable, and lowered the needle. A high falsetto harmony filled the store.

"I love this song," Mina said.

"You don't know nothing about The Congos."

"Please," she said. "You didn't know me in the seventh grade when I went through my crazy roots reggae phase. I was worse than Evan. I started making these mix tapes for anyone who would listen. My mom still has one, she was playing it the other day. I'm pretty sure this song is on it."

Octavian shook his head and sat down in a chair next to where she leaned against the wall. "This shit is pretty wild," he said.

"What is?"

"I'm sure I made a mix tape with this song on it," he said. "I know I did."

"Seriously?"

Octavian nodded. "Where the hell have you been all this time?"

"I don't know. Alone in my room making mix tapes for my mom." Mina laughed.

"What's your mom like? Is she cool?"

"She's alright, but she's weird. She thinks I should be my own person, so I don't have any curfew, she doesn't really care how I do in school, I couldn't get in trouble if I tried. It's kinda like she cares about me, but she doesn't care."

Octavian nodded. "What about your father?"

Mina shrugged and lit a cigarette, ignoring the no-smoking-in-the-store rule. "Don't know," she said. "I never met him. Kanta said the stars got her pregnant."

"Oh boy," Octavian said. "Do you call her by her first name?"

"Yeah, always have. Like I said, she's weird."

"My mom passed away," Octavian said and took the cigarette from Mina.

"I was wondering about that," Mina said.

"You were?"

"Yeah, the day I left Delmar Harvard you told me she was dying. I remember I'd never met anyone whose mom was dying or who had died. Back then, the idea of your mom dying really flipped me out, because if my mom died, if she was even sick enough to die, I wouldn't have anyone." Mina remembered the way his scared eyes looked that day. She took the cigarette back from him. "Tell me about your dad. He's cool, right? I mean, he was that day I saw him. Miles Davis and all that."

Octavian smiled thinking about how to describe his father to Mina. "He's like Furious Styles from *Boyz n the Hood* with a PhD."

"I've never seen that movie."

"What? City-ass Mina hasn't seen *Boyz n the Hood*? I don't know, girl, you may have your I'm-down-with-black-folks pass revoked."

"There's a pass?" She smiled at him.

Octavian put out the cigarette and took ahold of her hips with both hands. He pressed his face into her soft abdomen and didn't even recognize himself. He was never bold with girls. He couldn't talk fast enough, couldn't lie on the spot and make it sound like the God's-honest truth the way Frankie did. And as far as he could tell, that's what they wanted, to be lied to. But he didn't have to lie to Mina—he couldn't. She'd known him when he was a snot-crusted, terrified ten-year-old. And still, she was here. He met her dark eyes. "Want to take me home?" he said.

Little Girl Blue

MINA'S HOUSE IN CLAYTON had a wild front lawn and a short, crumbling brick porch. Inside, it was warm and dusty and smelled like Nag Champa incense. On the walls, African masks, Chinese Buddhas, and oil paintings of white men in wigs followed Octavian up the three flights of stairs to Mina's bedroom, where different, familiar eyes greeted him. Miles Davis's wild eyes, and the sad eyes of Billie Holiday. Prince with his eyes curved and lined in charcoal, and Mick Jagger, his eyes closed.

"You like the Rolling Stones?" Octavian asked.

She blushed. "I love the Rolling Stones."

"Frankie used to love them, too," Octavian said, looking at her bookshelf. "Francis used to be a real classic rock head."

"He's not anymore?"

"Nah, Frankie stopped listening to music a long time ago." Octavian walked slowly around the attic room. Mina could tell he was taking it in, saw it with his eyes—the candles on the windowsill, the bowl of dried flowers on her desk, the moth-eaten quilt on her four poster bed. She knew what he was looking for.

"Where are they?" he asked.

Mina pointed to the corner. "Over there."

Octavian walked over and sat down at the desk that was right next to her bed. "Mina Rose's personal record collection," he said and smiled at her. "Watch out."

It would have been easier for Mina to stand in front of him naked than to watch his hands—strong and slender, with clear nails and a long scar on his left hand in the shape of a V—flip through her records. Octavian pulled out Kanta's battered copy of *I Got Dem Ol' Kozmic Blues Again Mama!* and smiled his wide Octavian smile.

"This is an original," he said.

"It was Kanta's," Mina said.

"Where's she at?"

"Kanta? She's asleep, or out, I don't know."

"She won't care that I'm here?"

"Like I said, she doesn't care about anything."

Octavian blew on the end of the needle, and gently lowered it onto the record. The static crackled and he leaned back and closed his eyes. Janis sang into the room. Sang to Mina. Told her she was never going to be able to count on anything but the raindrops. Mina swallowed the feeling that it might be dangerous that Octavian could see into the barren place where she was still the little girl whose lunch fell apart in her backpack because the bread was so hard it broke. She wondered if maybe she should tell him to go home. But she told herself, she could see into that part of him too—where he was still a little boy, his hands dry and cold, his heart confused.

"I just realized something," Mina said. Octavian looked up. From under her bed, she dragged a brown metal box and began looking through it. She pulled out yellowed pieces of paper, a string of pearls, some broken sea shells, and a small stack of birthday cards held together with a rubber band.

A ticket stub fell on the floor and Octavian picked it up. "This is from the Bobby Brown, New Edition, Salt-N-Pepa show. I went to that show. Did you go to the Rock Box concert?"

"No. I wanted to, but Kanta wouldn't let me."

"So she does care about some things," Octavian said.

"I guess," Mina said, still looking through the box. "Here it is." She handed Octavian a thin, folded piece of paper.

"What is this?"

"Open it," she said. She smiled and her dark eyes shimmered.

Octavian took it and unfolded the creases carefully until his first drawing of Wolverine stared back at him. The fangs still dripping. He swallowed. "I can't believe you kept this," he said. He turned it over. On the other side of the drawing, Octavian saw his ragged handwriting, the handwriting of a child whose mother was still alive.

The song ended and he quickly folded the drawing back up and handed it to Mina. He started to look through the records again. He held up Love's *Forever Changes*. "I've never heard of them," he said.

"Jesus, you and Kanta should hang out," Mina said. "That's another one of hers."

"Not often there's a band I've never even heard of."

"Imagine that," Mina said. "I've educated the one and only Octavian Munroe."

He laughed and put the record on. A soft guitar blended with voices, and then trumpets entered the room. "I like this."

"It's one of my favorites," she said and smiled at him.

"Just so you know, Mina girl," Octavian said and looked directly into Mina's eyes, "I can sit here all night and play records and be fine."

"Is that what you want to do?"

Octavian reached over and ran his thumb across one of her thick eyebrows. "No," he said. "But just because I'm here doesn't mean it has to be that kind of night."

She nodded and smiled. "For a quiet kid, you sure do got some game, Octavian."

Octavian got up and went to sit next to Mina on the soft quilt. "I told you," he said. "I'm not running game." She leaned into him and he kissed her, carefully pushing away the upended memories still spread across the bed. She helped him pull off her T-shirt, and unhooked her bra. Octavian had only seen two girls naked in real life. One had large breasts the color of mahogany, the other had copper skin and barely any breasts at all. He had wondered whether there would be something strange about seeing the bare white skin of Mina's naked body, but as he wrapped her in his arms, he felt a gathering of pieces of himself that had scattered since the time when he hadn't known pain so intimately. He pressed them together into his own box of memories and closed the lid. It frightened him, but it didn't stop him, and he lowered himself into her lifting hips.

When it was over, he fell onto those same breasts and willed his racing heart to slow the hell down.

Mina put her hand on his back and asked, "Are you okay?"

He could only nod.

"Do you think your dad is wondering where you are?" she asked.

He swallowed and found his voice. "Probably. Why, do you want me to leave?"

In the darkness he saw Mina shake her head. He didn't want to leave, but he couldn't say so. Even with her soft legs wrapped around his, he couldn't. Instead he cleared his throat and said, "You got cable?"

She made a face at the small, dark TV at the end of her bed. "No," she said, "and I only get like three channels."

"Which ones?"

"Nine, eleven, and sometimes thirty."

"Shit, you don't need anything else," he said. Octavian got out of bed and turned the dial through the black-and-gray static until a picture appeared. He knew that his naked silhouette was backlit by the television, but he stood there and didn't worry about his broad shoulders, his high waist, and his long legs. He liked the way it felt to be naked and in the dark of Mina's room, like he was worlds away from anything that would harm him.

A young, long-haired Arnold Schwarzenegger clad in wolf pelts and massive steroid glory galloped across the clearing static on the screen. "*Conan the Barbarian,*" Mina said. "I love this movie."

"See," he said. "I knew you were cool, Mina girl. This is one of my favorite movies."

He lay back down and Mina picked up his scarred hand. "How'd you get this?"

"Francis," Octavian said.

"He cut you like that?"

"No. Got it trying to stop him from cutting up some other dude with a broken bottle."

"Shit," she said quietly.

Octavian felt the invisible and pervasive presence of Francis. Able to reach him even in Mina's attic bedroom.

"You think he's alright?" Mina asked.

Octavian shrugged. "Francis is always alright," he said.

They stayed up until nearly sunrise watching *Conan the Barbarian* and then *Octopussy,* and fell asleep naked, legs and fingers intertwined.

Joy in
Repetition

A **WEEK AFTER OCTAVIAN SLEPT** over at Mina's house, Mina stood looking up at Octavian's apartment building, which sat at the top of a long stone stairway. She pulled the oversize sweatshirt she wore over her cold hands and started up the long stairs. With every step, she questioned whether being there was a good idea. It wasn't that she'd never skipped school before. She and Clarissa spent more time skipping classes and smoking cigarettes in the outside "smoking lounge" at Clayton than she did in class, but she had never skipped school to go to a boy's house before. Since that night, she'd seen Octavian twice at work and they'd stayed up talking on the phone until they fell asleep to the sound of each other's breathing, but neither had acknowledged being together again until Octavian asked Mina if she wanted to come over the next day.

At the top, she blew on her fingers and pressed the buzzer for apartment five. Octavian came down to open the door wearing faded flannel pajama bottoms and a torn Rahsaan's Records staff T-shirt from 1990. When Mina saw him, she was no longer nervous. Mina had always struggled with feeling self-conscious around guys she liked—trying to figure out what they wanted and whether or not she knew how to be that girl. But not Octavian. With him there was no way she could pretend to be someone she wasn't. And the fact that he still wanted her there made her stomach flutter.

Mina followed him to his room, where it was her turn to take in the giant Kenmore speakers, the worn wooden desk with silver handles, the unfinished painting of Hendrix, and the framed photograph of a dark-skinned woman with a high forehead and eyes that were like Octavian's, wide and smiling.

Along the whole left wall were crates of records. Mina touched them tenderly because they belonged to him. The Cure's *Disintegration*, Funkadelic's *Cosmic Slop*, Sam Rivers' *Contours*, Blue Mitchell's *Bantu Village*, Freddie Hubbard's *Breaking Point*, EPMD's *Strictly Business*, Joe Henderson's *Page One*, Curtis Mayfield's *Roots*, Just Ice's *Kool & Deadly*, David Bowie's *Hunky Dory*, Ohio Players' *Observations in Time*, Del Tha Funky Homosapien's *I Wish My Brother George Was Here*, Joni Mitchell's *Court and Spark*, The Heptones' *On the Run*, a 45 of LL Cool J's "Going Back to Cali," with "Jack the Ripper" on the B-side.

They smoked a joint and, to Mina's surprise, quiet Octavian, man of little words Octavian, began to talk. For every song he played, he had a story to tell. About the time he and Francis got caught sneaking in to Mississippi Nights to see Yellowman, or the first time he heard Billie Holliday at his grandmother's house. He put on song after song, never letting one finish before he put on another. Mina loved them all, leaned her head back onto his tightly made bed and listened, watched the circles of smoke dance in the sunlight coming through the slats of the wooden blinds.

When the shadows outside began to shift, Mina said, "Will you put on some Prince?"

Octavian lowered his eyes as he lowered the needle and Mina reached over and pulled him next to her on the bed.

"You wrong, Mina girl," Octavian said. "Coming over to my house and making me put on Prince so you can seduce me." But as he spoke, Octavian lay Mina down onto the bed.

In the background, Prince sang about rescuing a woman from where she was trapped onstage, and the ache between Mina's legs caught her by surprise. It expanded down into her knees and up and out the top of her head. She tasted the long angle of Octavian's neck. It had never been like this before, she thought. Before, she was more aware of what her actions looked like than how they felt—as if she were watching herself pretending to make love. But as Octavian pulled her jeans off her feet and knelt over her, he smiled and she didn't worry about whether she was doing what she was supposed to do.

Octavian's fingertips traced her body. He ran them from her mouth, across her breasts, over her abdomen and in and around her thighs before he undressed himself and lay down, the length of his body covering hers. The room faded around her, and she let her new, pulsing, and electric self disappear inside him.

Later, when Mina stood in the bathroom wearing nothing but Octavian's T-shirt, she touched her face like it belonged to someone else. Sex had always left her unfulfilled and wondering, but now she smiled thinking about the way she trembled, how her toes curled, how she'd called out his name and dug her nails into his back. She opened the door of the bathroom, her vision clouded by her love-filled daze, and nearly walked squarely into a man, who was not Octavian, standing in the hallway.

"Oh shit," she said softly.

"Hello," he said and hesitated.

"Hi," Mina said. Mina knew it was Octavian's father. He was older, but she recognized him from the record store. Silently she thanked God that the length of Octavian's T-shirt covered her upper thighs, but she was afraid to move in case moving revealed more. The door to Octavian's room opened and Octavian stood there, fully clothed, making Mina's state of undress even more odd.

"Pop," he said. "You're home early."

"Son," Cyrus said looking at his wristwatch. "No earlier than usual."

Octavian opened his mouth to protest, but Cyrus stopped him. "How about you let this young lady get dressed so we can be introduced properly?"

Mina hoped not to look too grateful, and ducked into Octavian's room. She listened as their footsteps disappeared and quickly pulled on her clothes. She was lacing up her Chuck Taylors when Octavian opened the door. His face broke into a crooked smile.

"Dang, girl," he said. "It's not that bad."

"That's not funny," she said. "Your father basically saw me naked and you're telling me I should chill?"

"He could have come home sooner and heard you hollering like you were."

"I was not hollering."

"Okay," he said and motioned her toward the door. "C'mon, he wants to meet you."

Cyrus Munroe sat in an orange chair in the corner of the front room, a book open on his lap, glasses at the end of his nose. Mina walked in, and he slowly placed the bookmark on the open pages and closed the book. He placed it on the table next to him and removed his glasses. He did it so slowly that Mina was sure it was his way of letting her know he didn't tolerate this kind of behavior in his house. *He's a philosopher,* Octavian would later explain. *He thinks about everything before he does it.*

If the man had eyes any less gentle, Mina would have run, but as it was, she stood mute, smiling weakly at Cyrus. Octavian started to laugh and Mina felt like turning around and punching him, but then Cyrus let out a low chuckle.

"I imagine this is about as terrible as it can get," he said.

Mina nodded, even though he was wrong. If she started crying it would be worse.

"Mina, this is my father, Dr. Munroe," Octavian said. "Pop, this is Mina."

"It's nice to meet you, Dr.—"

"Please call me Cyrus," he said. "Mina. Like the poet, Mina Loy?"

The cinderblocks fell from Mina's shoulders. "Yes," she said. "I was named after her."

"You're named after a poet?" Octavian asked.

Mina nodded, glad to have a reason to turn her head and look at Octavian. "She's my mother's favorite. Some kind of crazy, bohemian French woman."

"Very ahead of her time politically," Cyrus said. "A radical really."

Mina turned back to Cyrus. "You're the first person that's ever recognized her name when I introduce myself," she said.

"Octavian's mother was a poet," Cyrus said. "She liked Mina Loy, too. I must still have a copy of Cordelia's Mina Loy book somewhere." He stood up and walked over to one of the many bookshelves that lined the room. Mina looked at Octavian again and he smiled. She had never before been so grateful for her name.

"Pop, I'm going to walk Mina out, okay?" Octavian said.

Cyrus, still scanning the bookcase, looked up and smiled. "Okay. How about you ask Mina to come over sometime soon, maybe for dinner, sometime when you two don't have to skip school?" And he raised his eyebrows at Octavian.

"Yes," Mina said. "I'd like that."

You Must Learn

MINA DIDN'T SKIP SCHOOL again, but she did start leaving early from her last period study hall to meet Octavian at U. City High before going to work. They sat in her Volvo in the parking lot behind the bank and listened to music and kissed until the windows were fogged and their breath became heavy. Or they went to Mina's, where they would close the door and listen to music, lying naked on her bed while they smoked weed. Or they went to Octavian's, where they listened to music sitting upright on his floor, with the door open. For weeks they went back and forth about whether or not they should tell anyone at Rahsaan's that things had changed.

On a Saturday morning while they lay in her bed before they both had to go into work, Mina ran her finger down the side of Octavian's bare arm. "It feels weird," she said, "to keep acting like I don't know what you look like naked."

Octavian rolled over and faced her. "I know. I'm just worried Bones'll start tripping," he said. "Change the schedule so we can't work together or something."

163

That afternoon was slow in the store and Mina walked over to where Octavian stood behind the counter. She was wearing a Jungle Brothers T-shirt over a short-striped dress. She had on tights and cowboy boots.

"You look cute today," Octavian whispered.

"Thanks," she said. "It felt like a good day to wear a dress."

He was about to say that he knew how much cuter she looked without the dress, when Ivy came up to the counter.

"Yo, Tave," he said, "your girl just walked in." They looked into the R&B section where Ivy pointed, and saw a small, light-skinned girl. She was also wearing a dress. Hers was aqua, knitted and tight against her curves.

"That's Keisha Putnam," Mina said.

"You know Keisha?" Octavian asked.

Mina nodded. Keisha was captain of the Clayton cheerleading squad and the president of the Black Student Caucus. At the beginning of the school year, Clarissa had convinced Mina to come with her to a BSC meeting, pointing out that Mina was friends with everyone in the club. Everyone except Keisha, who didn't acknowledge Mina at first and, when she did, simply asked, "What are you doing here, again?"

Mina looked at Octavian and said, "You know Keisha?"

"Does he know her?" Ivy said, still watching her. "Tave's been trying to get with her forever."

Mina felt her whole heart fill her throat and she swallowed. She looked at Octavian. His ears were bright red and his hands were shaking. Fred called to Ivy to help a customer in the hip hop section and, as Ivy passed Keisha, she looked up and smiled. That's when she noticed Octavian and put down the CD she was holding. Mina watched Keisha's hips swing wide, the same way she knew her own hips did, when she walked toward Octavian.

"Octavian Munroe, where have you been hiding?" Keisha sing-songed.

"Hey, Keisha," Octavian said.

"How you been?" she asked when she got to the counter.

"I'm cool," he said. "You know Mina, right? Don't y'all go to school together?"

Keisha looked at Mina as if to ask again what she was doing there. "We do," she said and gave Mina a tightly sealed smile.

Mina mumbled awkwardly and then made an excuse about organizing the dollar cassettes. For the longest ten minutes of her life, she tried to look busy. She was far enough away that she couldn't hear them. Though, at one point, Keisha's laugh filled the store and Mina looked up and saw Octavian's smile.

After Keisha left, Octavian tracked Mina down in the employee bathroom. "You've been avoiding me," he said.

"No," she said without looking at him. "I'm acting like you. Like there's nothing going on between us."

"I don't like Keisha."

"I don't see why not," Mina said. "She's super cute."

"And she's a cheerleader who likes Keith Sweat," he said and tried to smile at her.

"I like Keith Sweat."

"Mina," he said and took her hand.

"What?"

"How about we don't keep it a secret anymore? How about we let people know we're together."

Mina looked at him. She knew right then that she loved him. She knew she shouldn't, that it was too soon, but she did. She wanted more than anything to tell that to everyone she knew. She wrapped her arms around his neck and kissed him. They were still kissing when Fred came to the back and cleared his throat.

"Alright now, that's enough," Fred said. "Back to work."

A week before Thanksgiving, on a day when their after-school kissing had progressed to bare skin and unzipped jeans, Octavian arrived late to work, the taste of Mina still in his mouth. Brendon met him at the door, his *It Takes a Nation of Millions* T-shirt stretched tight across his wide body. Around his neck hung thick wooden beads of red, black, and green and a leather piece in the shape of Africa. On his head he wore a white crocheted kufi.

"Damn, B," Octavian said. "You're serious about the man today."

"I'm serious about the man every day, and you're late."

"Yeah, I know," Octavian said. The store was empty except for some Dead Head kids in the Reggae section and Mr. Nance in his constant brown leather cap, who stood in the back fingering a record. He caught Octavian's eye and nodded.

"Afternoon, Mr. Nance," Octavian said. "Find anything good?"

"Maybe," he said. "Just maybe."

Octavian scanned through the records on his hold shelf behind the counter and felt Brendon at his back. He was about to turn around and say something when Mr. Nance walked up and handed Brendon *Jazzical Moods Volume 2.*

Brendon turned the record over tenderly in his hands. "This come in on your watch?" he asked Octavian.

"Yeah. Came in with a big collection I bought off the estate dealer."

"Musta been before you started getting lost with the devil," Brendon said, still not looking at Octavian.

Mr. Nance's confused milky eyes moved from Octavian to Brendon.

"What is your problem today, B?" Octavian said.

Brendon rang up Mr. Nance. "I'm not the one with the problem," he said to Octavian. "You're the one walking around with that ofay on your arm like you done forgot who you are." Brendon handed Mr. Nance his bag, and Mr. Nance nodded, tipped his cap a little, opened his coat, and placed the bag up against his chest. He buttoned the coat over it before walking out.

"Oh, now Mina's an ofay?" Octavian said. "Was she an ofay when y'all were up in here discussing French poetry or whatever other bullshit you two talk about? Or when y'all went to that book signing together last month?"

"I was just hanging with her," Brendon said. "We're friends. You're out here taking it to another level and you know we can't afford to do that shit. At least I thought you did."

"Are you serious?" Octavian said.

"As a heart attack."

An old white lady approached the counter and asked if one of them could help her find her favorite recording of Bach's *Art of the Fugue*. Octavian glanced at Brendon, who set his jaw and trudged away from the counter. Octavian found the Emerson String Quartet recording the woman was looking for and led her back to the DJ booth. He put a pair of massive headphones carefully over her fine white hair. He watched as she listened and her eyes filled with tears. She squeezed Octavian's hand inside her puckered fingers.

"Yes, yes," she said loudly. "This is it!"

At closing, a couple of skinheads with Nine Inch Nails T-shirts, black-painted fingernails, and spikes through their ears sauntered into the store and hovered around the used cassettes. One had an SS tattoo on his neck and the other had a swastika patch on his blue jean vest. Over the speakers Hendrix sang about his house burning a hellfire red, and Octavian saw Freddy and Bones exchange a glance across the store.

"Hey there, boys," Bones said as he approached them.

The one with the SS tattoo gave Bones a look and both moved away from the cassettes down the Hip Hop/Rap aisle, but Bones followed them.

"You know, I think y'all is in the wrong section of the store," he said. "As a matter of fact, I think you in the wrong store altogether."

"What are you talking about?" said the kid with the swastika.

Bones leaned a little into a shelf and said, "I don't sell my records to racist punks like you."

"It's a free country," the kid with the SS tattoo mumbled.

"Well then, I guess I'm free to kick you out of my store," Bones said.

SS tattoo grabbed his friend and said, "Fuck this. Let's go."

They took off for the front door and Bones yelled after them, "And stay your KKK asses the fuck out."

Octavian watched them go and then looked over at Brendon, who stood behind the counter staring at Octavian. "You got more to say to me, B? 'Cause I wish you'd stop eyeing me down like you trying to meet me after school or some shit."

"I'm worried about you, Tave," he said.

The store was empty now other than Bones organizing the poster section in the back.

"What are you so worried about me for? Please, enlighten a brother," Octavian said.

"I don't see no brother. Just another sellout," Brendon said and walked out from behind the counter. "Do I need to take your ass back downtown to the Old Courthouse so you can see, again, the exact spot where her ancestors enslaved and sold yours?"

"Brendon, Mina's ancestors weren't anywhere near downtown St. Louis during slavery and I am not fucking Dred Scott."

"That's where you are wrong, Octavian," Brendon said. "We are all Dred Scott. And how do you know her ancestors weren't near there?"

"Her mom's family is from Russia. Last time I checked, that's pretty fucking far from downtown."

"And her daddy?"

"Okay, you got me, I don't know who her daddy is, but Jesus Christ, neither does she."

Brendon took off his glasses, which had become clouded. His sad eyes met Octavian's and he said, "I thought you understood. This is not about you or me. This is about our people. About black folks. Mina is white. I thought you loved being black."

Octavian stopped short. He tried to laugh it off. "You have got to be kidding me. What kind of shit is that? I do love being black, and I don't think I should have to be up in here saying that to you of all people."

But Brendon didn't laugh or smile. "Let me give you something to help you remember the difference," he said. He went behind the counter, and when he came back, he dropped something in Octavian's hands.

Octavian looked down at the worn copy of *The White Man Talk* that he had loaned to Brendon a year ago. He turned the soft blue book over to see his mother's face staring back at him. Her eyes in the black-and-white photo seemed to ask whomever held the book in their hands to please understand. Octavian felt the rage move out from under the rocks and stones inside him.

"Fuck you, Brendon," he said. He turned and walked out of the store, holding the book in his hands like a prayer.

Out on the street, Octavian wiped his tear-filled eyes. His beeper buzzed in his pocket. He took it out. Code 007. Mina was at Clarissa's house. He put the beeper back in his pocket and walked east. Octavian was glad the night hadn't gotten too cold and he walked without really thinking. But as soon as he crossed Skinker and walked past Church's Fried Chicken, he began to pay attention. The difference in the darkness between University City and St. Louis City was instantly palpable. Octavian wondered whether they used cheaper streetlights in the city, or maybe no one cared to fix them when they broke. The emptiness around him was spared only by the shadows he saw out of the corner of his eyes. He knew he should go home, or stop at a pay phone and call Mina, meet her over at Clarissa's house. But he didn't. His mother's book of poems in the back pocket of his jeans pushed him to keep walking.

Francis had not come around since the night at Cicero's. And right then, Octavian needed him because he needed his mother and the only way he could really remember his mother's face was to look at his brother's. Francis had the same narrow bridge to his nose, the same upward slant to his eyes when he smiled. Octavian thought about what would happen if he could introduce his mother to Mina. Would she feel the way he felt? That she was different somehow? Or would she feel like Brendon and remind him that there was no difference?

Octavian was farther down Delmar than he'd been in a long time. He stopped in front of the crack house where he'd often found his brother. From the outside, it was no different from the other run-down buildings on the block. The only thing identifiable about it was that it had a tower with a broken window.

Once upon a time, this had been the rich part of St. Louis. Octavian always imagined, long ago, how a young girl might have sat in that tower, gazing down at the dignified boulevard dreaming of a different life. Never would she dream that one day her house would be ripped apart by desperate thieves and sold bit by bit. First the chandeliers and the crystal doorknobs and then the brass sconces. Next the crown molding, the stained glass, the carved mahogany banister, the lead-glass windows, the claw-foot tub. Finally, the bricks of the walls, smashed in and removed, sold to a building company in Chicago that remodeled gentrified kitchens. Eventually, the crooked tower with the broken window was the only thing that remained of the rich man's home it once was.

Inside, the air was thin and Octavian retched at the smell of vomit, human shit, and urine. His beeper went off. 007. Mina was worried, he could tell. Across the room he was sure he saw Francis, but when he got closer, he was face-to-face with an old woman whose great height must have been stunning back in the day. She looked at Octavian out of one good eye and opened her arms wide.

"C'mere, baby," she said.

Octavian's heart seized. For a brief moment, he thought he might collapse right into the woman's outstretched arms. But instead, his heart took off on a familiar breath-stealing dash. *Not here, not now*, Octavian thought as he pushed his way through the smoke-filled darkness, taking blind, careless steps over piles of people.

Someone yelled at him to watch the fuck out. Octavian's chest tightened further. He choked on his own attempts to gather the polluted air into his lungs, but it was useless. He was going to have to sit down, right there in the crack house, and wait for the attack to pass. He tried to conjure Mina's voice over the ringing in his ears as she sat on his bed a few days before, muttering the lyrics to "You Must Learn" under her breath while she flipped through the giant college directory Cyrus had brought home.

"Here, Tave," Cyrus had said. "Time to get started."

It's calm yet wild the style that I speak,
Just filled with facts and you will never get weak, in the heart.

Weak in the heart, that's what he was, Octavian thought. He wished he could reach in and hold it still for a moment, soothe its wild beating. He was sure that one day soon it was going to run itself down and stop, but he did not want it to be when he was in the crack house with a book of his mother's poems in his back pocket.

In fact you'll start to illuminate, knowledge to others in a song.

In his slippery confusion, Octavian couldn't tell who spoke to him. Was it KRS or Mina? Or was it Brendon? His mom? Whoever it was, it kept him moving in the direction where he thought he remembered the door.

Let me demonstrate the force of knowledge,
Knowledge reigned supreme,
The ignorant is ripped to smithereens.

He pushed his way out and fell down the broken front steps. On the empty, cold sidewalk he took giant, grateful breaths. His beeper went off again. 007.

Octavian crept, bewildered, to the curb. He took his mother's book out of his back pocket and looked at her photograph. It trembled in his hands. He heard Brendon's voice and wondered what he would do if Cordelia was alive and told him to leave Mina alone. He stood up from the curb and wiped his hands on his jeans. Slowly he began walking west. He wished there was a way making the right decision could feel like something other than empty cold space. He stopped when he got to a pay phone, dropped a quarter into the slot, and dialed Clarissa's number.

Mina answered. "Hey," she said. "You okay? I came by the store and Freddy said you broke out."

Octavian felt his courage dissolve at the sound of her worried voice, and he cleared his throat. "Yeah, I'm alright," he said. "It's been quite a night."

"Where you at?" she asked.

"Down on Delmar and Goodfellow."

"What are you doing way down there?"

"Looking for Frankie."

"You find him?"

"Not yet."

The quarter dropped to the bottom of the pay phone signaling he only had a few seconds to add more money before the phone cut off.

"Um, Min, I'm going to keep on looking. I need to find Frankie. I'll call you when I get—" There was a click and the phone went dead. Octavian reached into his pocket. He had more quarters, but he didn't call back.

Rebel Without A Pause

OCTAVIAN DIDN'T CALL HER back the next day either, or the day after that. On Thanksgiving, he went with Cyrus to another professor's house, and, needing to walk away from the conversation at the table, he excused himself and wandered into the den. He started to pick up the phone, but then changed his mind. He let the battery on his beeper die and told his father he didn't want to talk to anyone when the phone rang at home. The following morning, he called in sick to work.

"Tave, you know this is one of the busiest shopping days of the year. You sure your ass is sick?" Bones said.

"For real, Bones, I am. You don't even want to know. It's gross."

"Aight, aight," Bones said. "I don't want to know." There was a pause.

"Something else?" Octavian asked, trying to make his voice sound strained.

"Mina's looking for you."

"And?"

"I was just letting you know."

"Okay."

There was another pause and Bones said, "Hope you're better by tomorrow. Fishbone gonna do an in-store before their show."

Octavian sat up in bed and cursed under his breath. "I forgot to get tickets to the show. You still got some, right?"

Bones chuckled. "Nah, man. You ass out. Mina took the last two."

Octavian could hear him adding numbers on his antiquated calculator.

"You sure you're still sick?" Bones said.

"Yeah. Going to puke now."

"Umm-hmmm."

Octavian spent the day in bed even though he wasn't sick. It had been four days since he collapsed in front of the crack house, four days since he talked to Mina. In the scarce times Octavian found himself involved with girls, either they'd stopped calling him or he'd stopped calling them and it only took a few days until he stopped thinking about them altogether. But it wasn't working with Mina. Every day meant more and more things he wanted to talk to her about. And it didn't help that Frankie wasn't there to give him bad advice. There was still no sign of him, not even on Thanksgiving, which drove Cyrus to distraction, and even made Octavian consider worrying.

Whenever Octavian needed to talk about something, he went to Brendon, or Ivy. He sure as hell wasn't going to talk to Brendon now, so at the end of the night, when he knew Ivy would be closing Rahsaan's by himself, Octavian got out of bed and got dressed, knocked softly on his father's door.

"Come in," Cyrus said. There were papers piled around Cyrus, but Octavian could tell by the gravel in his voice that he'd fallen asleep.

"I'm going down to Rahsaan's for a minute," Octavian said.

Cyrus nodded. "When was the last time you saw Francis?"

"A couple of weeks ago. Over at Cicero's starting shit."

"It's not like Francis not to come home around the holidays," Cyrus said.

"I know," Octavian said. "I went looking for him a couple of nights ago, but I couldn't find him."

Cyrus nodded and Octavian knew he wanted him to say more, but he wasn't up to one of their empty conversations about Francis. *Have you seen him? Yeah, I saw him. Nah, I ain't seen him in a week, a month, two months. It's been that long? Guess we better find him.* Instead he kissed his father on the forehead and walked out of the apartment.

Ivy drove a 1984 Ford LTD station wagon named Lucinda. She had one working window and a glove compartment held shut with duct tape. Both the speedometer and the gas gauge were broken so Ivy stayed getting pulled over and running out of gas. Her plush brown interior was pockmarked with countless cigarette burns and, even though she was a station wagon, there was only room for one passenger because the whole back of the car was filled with subwoofers and speakers. Well before Ivy and Lucinda came into view, the haunting sound of a Public Enemy track could be heard through the neighborhood. And when they rolled up, the whole ground shook.

Octavian got in the car and Ivy pressed play on his CD player. "Yo, you heard that new *2Pacalypse Now* shit just came out from that Digital Underground kid?" Ivy said.

Octavian nodded. "It's dope."

"Shol is. Still, no matter how much new shit comes out, all I ever want to listen to is Public Enemy," Ivy said and laughed. "Where we going?"

"I don't know," Octavian said. "To the park, I guess."

The night was abruptly warm the way St. Louis could turn around and be in late fall. They drove into Forest Park where a line of cars parked at the waterfall. Ivy started to slow down.

"Waterfall lookin' like summertime and shit," Ivy said. "Errybody's up in here tonight."

Evan and Brendon stood leaning against Evan's mom's car, and Octavian saw Clarissa getting out of Mina's Volvo. "Keep driving," he said.

"What for?" Ivy asked.

"Keep on," Octavian said. "Drive up to the Pavilion or something."

The World's Fair Pavilion was at the top of Government Hill in Forest Park. During the day, it was a place for business lunches, weddings, and corporate events. And sometimes, at night, before the cops came, it was a place for getting drunk. Mostly, it was a place to take a date—the elegance of the open-air columns, the red roof, the light of the fountain at the bottom of the hill, gave it added romance and meaning.

"It's straight dead up here," Ivy said and jammed the car into park.

"Good."

"You alright, Tave? What's up?"

Octavian sighed and leaned his head back. "I'm not trying to deal with Brendon's punk ass," he said.

Ivy reached under his seat and pulled out a forty of Olde English 800. He held it up and started rapping Eazy E, and handed Octavian the bottle.

Octavian took a drink and spit it out. "Shit, Ivy, Eazy said he'd take it in a forty, quart, or a can, but he didn't say he'd take it warm."

"So?" Ivy said and grabbed back the bottle. "C'mon, let's get out."

They walked around to the picnic tables and sat down. The city spread out below them in a carpet of twinkling lights. Octavian could see that some of the families in the big houses on Lindell Boulevard already had their Christmas trees up.

Ivy took another drink and passed the bottle to Octavian. "Is it Frankie?"

Wasn't it always Frankie? Had he ever had a problem that he couldn't follow back, like a lifeline, to Francis? But no, this time it wasn't Frankie. And yet Octavian's head hurt because, in reality, it was Francis's advice he wanted, not Ivy's.

"It's Mina," Octavian finally said.

"Mina? Mina Rose?"

"Yeah."

"Y'all been kickin' it?" Ivy said and gave Octavian a slight shove.

"You could say that."

"What's the problem?" Ivy asked. He lit a cigarette and took a drag, then handed it to Octavian.

"I think I like her a lot," Octavian said, taking the cigarette.

Ivy smiled. "'Course you do. She's mad chill. Crazy cute too."

"You know, I've known her since fifth grade?"

"That's right. She did go to Delmar Harvard before they moved out to Clayton," Ivy said. He took the cigarette back and passed the now half-empty bottle back to Octavian. "That shit's cool. I don't know no girls from back in the day that I can even kinda stand. What's the problem, you think she don't like you or something?"

"No, she likes me," Octavian said and took a sip. This time the bland warmth of the alcohol made the cloud of confusion he'd walked around in since he last went looking for Francis start to dissipate.

"So?"

"So, she's white," Octavian said. It was the first time he'd let the words come out of his mouth. He looked at Ivy when he said it. Ivy, with his transparent white skin and blue veins that crisscrossed at his temples. "No offense."

Ivy laughed. "I'm not offended," he said. "Shit, I live with Brendon. I gotta hear about how white I am every day. And Francis is my best friend. To be honest, I agree with both of them most of the time." Ivy looked at Octavian. "Problem is, none of that shit matters if you fall in love."

"I'm not in love."

"If you say so."

"You know what my real thing is?"

"What's that?"

"My mom."

"What, you think Mrs. Munroe would trip off you being with Mina because she's white?"

"That's the problem," Octavian said. "I can't ask her."

"No," Ivy said. "You can't."

The cigarette and the forty were gone and Ivy was quiet. Below them the cars wound through the labyrinth of the park's quiet streets, from the Art Museum to the Zoo to the History Museum to the skating rink.

"Listen," Ivy said. "I know it's not the same, and I don't know if it means anything, but your mom loved me."

Octavian laughed a little remembering the times when Ivy would spend days and nights over at their house—especially when Ivy's own mother disappeared on a bender for weeks on end. They always joked with Ivy that Cordelia loved him so much because he could never get enough of her food.

"She did love you," Octavian said. "Loved to feed you anyway."

"For real though, Tave, you laugh, but you don't know what that meant to me back then. Seeing as my moms called a good dinner some Frosted Flakes and shit—especially if it had milk in it. And I won't never forget the time me and Frankie got in that fight and he busted up my lip. I mean we used to fight a lot, but that time, ooh, your mama was so mad at him. Didn't matter that I'd given Francis a black eye, she was through with him for hurting me."

"That's because you were probably fifty pounds to Francis's one hundred," Octavian said. "Still don't know how you even managed to get that punch in."

"I remember when she was cleaning me up, she said something that made me laugh and I busted my lip open even more and that made both of us laugh harder. I was little, but she made me feel big, you know? I needed that back then."

Octavian nodded and looked away. He didn't care if Ivy saw him crying—shit, Ivy'd seen him cry many times. But he was sick of the feeling of tears in his eyes—the burning that came with them and the salty pressure in his throat. Would there ever be a time when he learned to hold them back? When they were no longer so quick to materialize?

"You know," Ivy said, "your mom's heart was bigger than anyone's I ever met. And I don't know, man. I mean, I think she'd probably prefer it if you were with a black girl, but at the same time, I don't think she'd be mad at you for liking Mina. Mina's a good girl and she's smart and nice and pretty. I think your mom would want you to be with a person like that, regardless." Ivy gave Octavian a soft whack on the back of the head and said, "It might take a minute, and she might give you some hell at first, but I bet she'd like her, Tave. For real."

If Not Now . . .

EARLY THE NEXT MORNING, the sun slanted through Rahsaan's
front window. The store was empty aside from Mina and
Fred, and Tracy Chapman's voice, which wrapped Octavian in
questions the minute he walked in. Mina looked up, but she
turned back to the records she was shelving as if Octavian was
simply just another customer. Fred gave Octavian a wave and disappeared into the back of the store.

Octavian pulled his intention in close like an overcoat as he
walked over to Mina. "I'm sorry I didn't call you," he said.

Mina pretended not to hear him.

"I was sick," he said.

"For five days? You sure don't look like someone who's been
sick that long." She still wouldn't look at him.

So he said, "Bones told me you bought the last two tickets to
the Fishbone concert?"

He should have said something different. Maybe something
about how she made him feel or how he couldn't stop thinking
about her. Or he could have told her all he wanted was to lay in
her bed smelling the Nag Champa coming up from a shrine to

Buddha in the living room. That he wanted to listen to her mix tapes, to sit in her window and smoke cigarettes. But he couldn't think of any of those things when he saw the angry tendons of her neck as she clenched her teeth against him.

She dropped the albums back into the box with a bang and looked at him. Her gray eyes had taken on the appearance of steel. Her nostrils flared and her cheeks sucked in. "Fuck you, Octavian," she said.

"I know," he said. "I fucked up."

He could tell she hadn't expected him to say this, but she didn't soften. She shook her head and said, "Listen, Tave, let's just let it go, okay? I thought it was something more, but now I know it was just a thing. We smoked some weed, talked about music, and you hit it a few times, and now it's done. I understand. I didn't before, but I do now."

"Hold up," he said. "I'm not saying what I want to say."

"Don't worry about it, Tave," she said shoving the box closed. "I'm not listening anyway." She walked to the back and disappeared into the stockroom.

Octavian heard her moving things around, but he didn't follow or call to her. Instead, he stood in the empty store encased in the beams of scattering dust. He bet Francis never felt like this. And if he did, he knew exactly what to do about it. Octavian tried to remember when it was that he last let himself love Francis and couldn't. Maybe this time when Francis came back, he would try.

Octavian heard the sharp sound of Mina dropping something and she cursed. He went behind the DJ booth and changed the record. He lowered the needle on Prince's "Something in the Water" and the speakers filled with a rapid-fire snare. He thought she'd come out. That she'd fight him some more so they could make up, but she didn't. Octavian let the song play and walked out the front door.

Octavian went home from Rahsaan's and lay on his bed, listening to The Smiths. He felt sure that Morrissey's sad claim that heaven

181

knew he was miserable would make him forget about Mina. As he considered the peach-colored twilight coming through the slats in the blinds, Octavian heard Francis in the kitchen.

Cyrus had made a rule. Francis had to be sober for a month before Cyrus would let him move back home. How Cyrus was going to know this, Octavian was never sure, because lies cascaded out of Francis's mouth like a waterfall, like it was so full of them he could no longer hold them back. But not once since Cyrus made the rule had Francis lied. Instead, he didn't come home—at least not to stay. Octavian knew Francis snuck in and took clothes sometimes, came to eat food, but not when Cyrus was there. As if Francis respected the rule or something. He stayed fucked up and he stayed away.

Octavian wondered at the fact that Francis was there so close to when Cyrus would be getting home. He thought about how he'd wanted to love his brother earlier and if he should go in to the kitchen, too. If Octavian were out there and talking shit with Francis when his dad walked in, Octavian knew there would be relief in his father's eyes as he closed the door behind him and put down his attaché. But without Octavian in there, it was open to interpretation. Cyrus could see Francis in the kitchen, no way thirty days clean, and tell him to get out. Or he could be glad, because rule or no rule, Francis in the kitchen meant Francis wasn't locked up, or dying, or already dead.

Octavian rubbed his eyes, as if even they were tired from thinking about Francis, and tried to think about Mina instead. About her mouth that tasted like honey—the kind that was gold and thick and you had to scoop it out of the jar with a spoon.

Francis knocked on the door while opening it and walked in. Usually Octavian asked why the fuck he even bothered to knock, but today he simply watched as Francis set a plate with a sandwich on Octavian's bedside table, and then sat down at the desk where even Octavian hadn't fit since he was twelve, and began to eat.

"You know Pop don't let me eat in here anymore," Octavian said.

"If you hadn't been so nasty, keeping dirty plates up under your bed for months 'til they was covered with hairy little gray monsters, you wouldn't have this problem."

Octavian turned away from the sandwich and his brother. "Still," he said.

"Still nothing. Hurry up and eat that before he gets home."

Octavian started to argue, but he was hungry, and no one could hook up a sandwich like Francis, so he took a bite.

"Tave," Francis said.

Octavian chewed slowly. He knew what was coming. Another one of Francis's bullshit apologies.

But Francis didn't say sorry. Instead, he said, "You wanna come with me to see Fishbone tonight?"

Octavian swallowed, and in his head he cursed Francis and his uncanny ability to make things right. Sometimes Francis would come in late at night with a joint and a VHS copy of *Coming to America*, or he'd tell Cyrus that the puke at the foot of the back staircase was his and not Octavian's. Or it was a sandwich and Fishbone tickets. And every time, those balled strings of anger that Octavian was determined to hold on to would unravel and roll away down the hall. Later, Octavian kicked himself for falling for it like a girl with a bad crush. Deep down, he wondered if he would always be waiting for Francis to show up and be the Francis he loved, the one who snuck him out the back door so he could go see Prince.

The hard sound of their father's key in the front door made Francis stand up. Carefully, he wiped his mouth before he walked over to Octavian and kissed him on the forehead. He ran a long finger over the pink sliver scar on Octavian's cheek and said, "I know. I'm an asshole."

"Yeah," Octavian said. "You are."

The front door opened, and they heard Cyrus sigh softly as he took off his shoes.

Francis opened the window by the fire escape. "You going to meet me at Mississippi Nights or what?"

"I ain't meeting you nowhere."

Francis pushed his legs through and began to quietly make his way down.

Octavian waited a second and then rolled over toward the still-open window. "Hey, Frankie," he whispered. "What time?"

Francis's footsteps stopped. "Nine thirty."

Cyrus knocked on Octavian's door. "Tave," he said. "You home?"

Octavian closed the window and grabbed Francis's plate. He shoved it and his own under the bed. "Yeah," he said. "Come in."

Mina exhaled weed smoke and turned when he called her name, but he could tell by the way her smile fell off her face that she wasn't expecting to see him. She stood next to Clarissa, who was nearly six feet tall with her afro puffs and platform shoes. Ivy, who was already heavily drunk even though the show hadn't started yet, gave Octavian a pound.

Out of the corner of his eye, Octavian saw Mina mouth something to Clarissa and disappear into the crowd. Octavian followed behind her and reached boldly through the chaos to catch her hand. She snatched it away and gave him a look.

"What, Tave?" she said.

"I'm sorry," he said.

"Yeah, you are," she said and pushed her way back into the crowd. She'd woven her way up by the bathrooms before he stopped her again. "Jesus, what do you want, Octavian?"

Octavian leaned back against the tatters of posters plastered on the wall. He pushed a combat boot through the grime on the floor and said, "Damn, Mina girl."

"Damn, what?"

"If you knew me, you'd know. I don't really know how to explain it, but with you . . . I don't know. Something's different."

"I do know you, Octavian. And you can stop running game, okay? You don't like me. Not really. And it's cool."

Octavian's face twisted a little and he took a long breath and spoke fast. "Listen," he said. "You know me, but here's what you don't know. I am always pretending. I pretend shit doesn't bother me so my dad doesn't worry, I pretend to be happy when I'm not, I pretend to not care about Francis. But not with you. For some reason, maybe it's because of what happened between us when we were little, I don't pretend with you. And you don't know how good that feels or how much it scares the shit out of me."

Mina kept her eyes on the still-empty stage. Octavian could tell she wasn't buying it. She wanted to, but she wasn't.

Octavian reached for her hand again, but she moved away. "I didn't call you," he said, "because I thought that would make it go away."

"According to what you said, you've felt that way for a long time."

Octavian smiled. "Okay," he said, "that part was game. But this, this is for real."

Mina couldn't help but laugh and when she did, he pulled her to him, pressed his forehead against hers. "If you knew what I had to do in order to get in here," he said, "you'd know how serious I am right now."

The lights dimmed. Angelo walked shirtless onto the stage and the room around them erupted. Mina leaned closer to Octavian so he could hear her. "Yeah, how did you get in anyway? I thought the show was sold out," she said.

Octavian nodded toward the bar. Mina turned, and Francis gave her a careless smile, saluted her with two fingers.

"He got tickets?"

"Frankie doesn't need tickets," Octavian said.

"Right," she said.

Her crooked-tooth smile pulled hard at his insides and he took her hand and brought it gently behind his back. He cupped his other hand under her jaw and kissed her.

Self-Portrait in Three Colors

I T WAS JUST THE beginning of December, but Cyrus came home from the library with his head down, guarding his face from the cold, and his arms full of books. He walked up the back staircase thinking about the final exam he was going to give the next week, and found Francis at the back door, the box containing Jackson's pearl-handled letter opener tucked inside his jacket.

"Where the hell do you think you're going with that?" Cyrus asked.

Francis pulled the box to his chest. "I'm going to show it to a friend of mine," he said. "He does appraisals. I thought—"

"Give it to me," Cyrus said and he backed Francis into the kitchen, pressing at him with his armload of books. Inside, he put the books down on the table and said again, "Give it to me." He could hear the rage tremble in his voice.

Francis handed him the box and Cyrus opened it. There the letter opener lay unharmed on its bed of dark-green velvet. Cyrus snapped it shut and Francis jumped.

"Get out of here," Cyrus said, barely able to make his words into a whisper.

"That's cool," Francis said and, as he moved around Cyrus, he gave him a shove—a small one, but unmistakably a shove, and under his breath he said something along the lines of, "Fuck you, old man."

Cyrus turned quickly to face him. "Don't come back, Francis," he said. He put the letter opener down next to the books. "Don't come back even if you're clean."

Francis, who was already four steps toward the back door, came back and stood towering over Cyrus. "Here's the thing, Pop," he said. "I can't be clean. I love getting high too damn much. Always have. No threats you make are going to change that."

"If your mother was alive," Cyrus started to say, but Francis only laughed.

"But she's not, is she? And you think you're the only one that wishes she was still here? You don't know how much I want her back. And you definitely don't understand that the only time I don't feel the pain of not having her is when I'm high. So no matter how much you sit wishing into your glass of port wine that she'll come back, she won't, and no matter how much you wish I would stop, that's not happening either."

Cyrus felt himself crumbling, and he grabbed ahold of the table.

"Fuck this," Francis said and he pushed out the back door and ran down the stairs.

"You can look for your stuff out on the street," Cyrus yelled after him. "I'm putting it out tonight so you better come get it quick before your other crackhead friends show up and take it."

But Cyrus didn't put it out. Francis's clothes were still folded neatly, right where he left them.

A week later, Cyrus sat next to Octavian in the St. Louis County Courthouse and wondered if there was anything he could have done to save them from the angry, disappointed look on the judge's face when she asked Francis to explain why he tried to rob the plaintiff as he entered his house.

Francis kept his head down and said quietly, "Because I needed to get high, ma'am."

The plaintiff, a tall, thin black man in a pinstriped suit named George Davidson, whispered something to his lawyer before standing up and asking if he could make a request. The judge took her glaring eyes from Francis and agreed.

"I'd like to ask that Mr. Munroe not be sent to jail, your honor," he said.

Cyrus held his breath.

"I have a niece and, well, she's addicted to drugs. I cannot even fathom the pain that my sister goes through. They tried a lot of things, but nothing seemed to work until last year, through their church, they got her into a treatment program and she seems to be making it. I realize this is a little out of order, but I'm wondering, since I was the one Mr. Munroe tried to rob, if I could request that you sentence him to a treatment center instead of a prison?"

Francis leaned over to his lawyer and said, "Is this cat for real?"

Cyrus grabbed hold of Octavian's hand.

The judge's fierceness folded into worry as she turned back to Francis. "Mr. Munroe," she said, "you know that you and I have been here before. And both of those times you asked me for a second chance. So, technically, this would be the third time you got a second chance."

Francis hung his exhausted head. "Yes, ma'am."

Octavian leaned into Cyrus and said, "I'm late for work. You want me to call Bones so I can stay?"

"No," Cyrus said. "I'll see this one through."

Octavian rubbed his father's shoulder and said, "This could be good, Pop. I don't think Frankie would handle prison well." He stood up and looked long at the back of his brother's head before he walked out of the courtroom. His footsteps echoed and Francis turned to watch as Octavian pushed out of the swinging doors.

Cyrus studied his son. Francis didn't look good. His skin was ashy and dirty. He had an angry cut above his ear that was crusted and yellow. His nails were bitten to the quick and the cuticles, which he now chewed on, were bloody. Cyrus could no longer philosophize it away as Octavian had once accused him of doing. If he didn't do something real, something other than think on it, Francis was going to die. Francis would never agree to go to treatment on his own, but the judge could make it so he had no choice. In the back of his mind, Cyrus felt himself return to hope—that elusive emotion he'd spent less and less time with lately. Maybe in treatment they could get Francis to hit the mat hard with those demons of his, lock them up in a good full-nelson.

"Mr. Munroe," the judge said, "I want to be quite clear. This is your last chance. If I find you in front of my bench again, I will send you to jail. Do you understand?"

Francis seemed to take a moment to think, or maybe only to sigh, before he nodded and said again, "Yes, ma'am."

Cyrus used his own felt-tip pen to sign the papers that said he would deliver Francis to St. Augustine's Treatment Center in O'Fallon, Illinois, the following Wednesday. He and Francis drove home in silence. When they got to the apartment, Francis stopped before walking up the stairs and asked Cyrus if he wanted him to stay someplace else.

Cyrus didn't tell Francis that he had no intention of letting him out of his sight until Wednesday. But he did open the door wider and said, "Why don't you go on in and take a shower? I'll make you something to eat. After that, we can talk about what happens next."

Francis nodded and ducked inside. Cyrus could hear him in his bedroom, opening drawers and closets. He wondered if Francis was surprised to find that his clothes were still there. Cyrus heard the shower turn on and he went into the kitchen. He placed a Charles Mingus CD in the player and pulled out the foil-covered plates of leftover food he'd cooked that weekend.

Cooking on Saturday was the way things had been done in Cordelia's house growing up and, when she was alive, Saturdays had been magical. Cordelia in her bright red-and-orange apron, flour

189

coating her fingers as she made cornbread and catfish. Cyrus's specialties were collard greens and braised pork chops, mashed potatoes and barbeque. Octavian's task had been to play his mother's favorite records—Luther Vandross, Minnie Ripperton, Sam Cooke. Francis was in charge of the table, meticulously ironing the tablecloth and polishing each piece of silverware until he saw his own reflection bent sideways in the spoons.

After Cordelia died, Cyrus thought about giving up the cooking. But then, when Saturdays came, he got down the mixing bowls, the cast-iron pans. He pulled out the boxes of macaroni and began to grate the cheese, and when he did, he felt her over his shoulder, shaking her head because she preferred to slice the cheese thinly, because he never did cut the garlic right. Now, nearly ten years after she died, Cyrus still cooked with Cordelia on Saturdays. He still put on Luther and could hear her singing along, begging to hold someone tight, if only for one night, as he soaked the black-eyed peas and measured the cornmeal.

Cyrus put a plate down at the small kitchen table and motioned for Francis to sit. Francis gathered his long body into the chair and delicately placed the cloth napkin across his lap. He picked up the fried catfish and gingerly put it on a slice of white bread followed by some onion and two slices of pickle. But when Francis reached for the hot sauce, his shaking hand knocked it over. Cyrus took the bottle and poured the hot sauce for him.

Once Francis had some food down, his hands stopped trembling and he picked up the glass of cider and emptied it. Cyrus could see more of Francis's golden-brown color begin to come out from under the gray pall, more light in the hazel eyes that watched Cyrus clear his plate and run it under the hot water.

"I know that you're not my real father," Francis said.

For a moment, Cyrus thought that he'd simply heard the dark words in his own head. That the running of the tap water and the humming of the refrigerator were playing tricks on him, but he turned and saw those same hazel eyes penetrating him with the truth, and Cyrus knew Francis had spoken the words aloud. He steadied himself against the counter and hid his own shaking hands in the blue-and-white plaid dishtowel. He sat down carefully, because now Cyrus was a body of flesh exposed, his heart open and raw. "When did she tell you?"

"You remember how, at the end, she started talking? Saying crazy stuff and telling those stories?"

"I do," Cyrus said.

"It was then," Francis said. "On the day you caught me drinking over at Ivy's."

"I remember that."

"That night she told me. Told me I should know about my real father because he died of a heroin overdose. She said that, you know, liking to get high and drink and all could be hereditary. Said I needed to be more careful or my messing around could bring me real problems one day."

"Why have you not said something to me before?" Cyrus asked.

"She said I shouldn't. Said it would hurt you and that you had been and would be the best father to me. Better than my dad would have been if he lived. She said, and I'll never forget this, that any man can shoot cum out his dick, but not every man has the strength to be a father. Even less have what it takes to be a father to another man's child. I'd never heard her talk like that, you know? Anyway. I guess she thought it was the right thing to do." Francis paused and pressed his fingers into his temples and closed his eyes. "Still, I wish she hadn't told me."

"Why's that?" Cyrus struggled to say.

"I think she told me to warn me away from drinking and drugs, but for me it was more like she gave me an excuse. From then on, I could always tell myself that it was in my blood. Shit, I even told myself I was supposed to die that way. I don't know if it would have happened anyway, me getting strung out and all, if she hadn't told me, but I guess there's no reason trying to figure that out now. I went ahead and followed right in my father's footsteps."

"I'm your father," Cyrus said. The words came out filled with anger even though he hadn't meant them to.

Francis looked up.

"I'm your father," Cyrus said again, more softly. "You are my son."

Francis sat back in his chair and said, "But let's be honest. It's different with Octavian than it is with me, and you know it. Thing is, when she told me, I wasn't even that surprised. I always felt like you loved him better, and after she told me, at least I knew why."

"Does Octavian know?" The words came out fast. Cyrus knew it was the wrong thing to say, but he'd said it anyway. He had to know.

Francis let his eyes rest on Cyrus again and said, "Nah, I never told him. If she had wanted him to know, then she would have told him herself."

"Francis," Cyrus began.

Francis held up his hand to stop him from saying anything else. His open palm was just like Cordelia's, the brown lines sharp, deep spirals. "It's okay, Cyrus," he said.

Cyrus swallowed the taste of humiliation on his tongue and folded his own hands in his lap. "Please don't call me that."

"It's okay, Pop," Francis said and stood up. He stretched his long arms as if he'd just put down something heavy. "And don't worry," he said. "I won't tell Octavian." He walked out of the kitchen and into his bedroom, closing the door carefully behind him.

Cyrus sat alone in the kitchen and remembered how he once felt it was his calling to raise Francis. Francis who was so prone to viciousness and impulsive tenderness. He'd wanted to raise him the way he had been raised by Jackson. But Cyrus soon realized that hours of reading were out of the question seeing that Francis could never sit for longer than two minutes. Their time was spent instead at Cardinals games and on fishing trips down the Merrimack River—where, miraculously, the child sat silently in the front of the boat with a preacher's patience, waiting for a bite.

Cyrus remembered that when Cordelia got pregnant with Octavian, Cyrus was as ecstatic for Francis as he was for himself. They decided to take Francis to brunch at the Wash U Faculty Club to tell him the news. They had agreed that Cordelia should be the one to tell him, but as soon as their food was served, Cyrus blurted it out.

Francis held his fork over his plate, the maple syrup dripping slowly off the suspended bite of Belgian waffle, and said, "But why?"

Cyrus explained how the only thing he'd ever wanted was a brother or sister. Now Francis would never feel the loneliness he felt as a child.

"I'm not lonely," four-year-old Francis said matter-of-factly. "I don't need anyone."

When they brought Octavian home, Francis gave his baby brother a glance and said, "His eyes sure are big," and went back to reorganizing his matchbox cars. It became obvious to both parents that what Francis declared that day had been true. He didn't need anyone.

Cyrus, on the other hand, had never needed anything the way he needed Octavian. Cyrus was consumed wholly by his infant son's tight-gripping hands, his soft, downy earlobes, the smell of his milk breath. And it wasn't until Cordelia shook Cyrus and said, "Remember, you have two sons," that Cyrus came out of it to find Francis taller, his chest and arms more like a young boy's than a toddler's. Cyrus took Francis by the back of the neck and pulled him into an embrace. He pressed his face into Francis's gold curls and smelled the hair lotion Cordelia rubbed into his scalp. That day he made another vow. He vowed that he would do everything he could so that Francis would never know how much more he loved his own blood than the one he'd sworn to love.

Back in the kitchen, the refrigerator started in on its hum again. Apparently, Cyrus had spent years convincing himself that he had convinced Francis. He felt an odd sense of relief that it was over. Like he, too, had put down something heavy. But then he picked it back up. Those years were gone but, as far as Francis was concerned, Cyrus was simply a liar.

Cyrus walked to the closed bedroom door. He would apologize to the boy, tell him how hard he tried, tell him that he loved him. God knew he loved him. It may have been different with Octavian, and easier, yes. But there was no doubt that he loved Francis. He knocked on the door, but there was no answer. He knocked again, and his old friend fear reared its withered head and told him that Francis wouldn't be there when he opened the door. That the window he'd snuck out of so many times would be open and he would be gone. But when Cyrus opened it, he saw Francis asleep, knees curled to his chin, hands folded under his cheek. *Same way he's always slept,* thought Cyrus, remembering a much smaller body with the same furrowed brow, the same weighted breaths.

For the Love of You
(Part 1 & 2)

THE NIGHT BEFORE FRANCIS left for rehab, he came into the bedroom where Mina and Octavian lay on Octavian's bed watching TV and closed the door behind him.

"Pop doesn't let me—" Octavian began.

"I know, you can't have girls over with the door closed," Francis said. "But he's not gonna worry about nothing happening if I'm in here too. Scoot over." Francis climbed in next to Octavian and draped a long leg over them both. "Plus, *The Wiz* is on," he said. He changed the channel and Nipsy Russell sang about what he would do if he could feel. The heavy, relaxed weight of the brothers beside Mina told her that nights like this used to happen more often, and that they were endangered now, their habitat nearly gone.

"Hey, Frankie," Octavian said, "remember how Mama cried when I brought home *Thriller*?"

"I forgot about that. Why'd she cry again?"

"Because of his nose. You know Mama loved big ole noses and Michael had gone and chopped his off."

"That's right. She wouldn't even let you listen to the record."

"Yeah, until she heard 'Human Nature' on the radio and then she wouldn't turn it off," Octavian said. "Nearly drove Pop crazy."

"Shit, think of what she'd say if she saw him now."

Mina felt the bed shake as Francis laughed his deep laugh, and next to her Octavian's body softened.

Francis's face peered over Octavian's chest at Mina. "Hey, Mina girl," Francis said. "Why you so quiet over there?"

"I'm just listening to y'all," Mina said.

"Tave told you how we share?"

"Don't listen to him, Mina," Octavian said.

"No, for real, Mina. Me and Tave share, don't we, Tave?" and he rubbed his leg up and down across both of them.

"Frankie," Octavian said, "your ass will be sleeping with Pop in about thirty seconds you keep that shit up."

"Damn, Tave, you sound serious."

"I am, Francis. Stop fucking around."

Francis turned to Mina again. "You hear this, Mina? He ain't going to share you with me. He must really like you for real." Francis reached across Octavian and patted Mina on the head like a little sister.

"That's enough," Octavian said, and lifted Francis's hand off Mina's head.

Francis sat up on his elbow. "Hey, Mina girl," he said again.

"Yeah?"

"You know he really likes you, don't you?"

"I think so," she said.

"Y'all," Octavian broke in, "I'm right here."

"Listen, Mina, I know right now my brother just about can't stand me."

"Frankie," Octavian said.

"Shut up, Tave, I'm talking. Like I was saying, he's through with me and I understand. And even if he doesn't think so, I love Octavian. To be honest, I don't really love no one *but* Octavian. I never have. I've tried to love other people, but it's too damn hard, you know what I'm saying? Especially after Mama died, I just

couldn't. But Tave? I've tried *not* to love him and there is no way.
I mean, I love him in a way you can't understand. Shit, I love him
in a way I can't understand. Okay?"

"Okay," Mina said. Next to her, Octavian lay perfectly still.

"I'm saying this because you better not hurt him, you hear me?"
Francis's angled face, which hovered over Octavian's chest, really
was as beautiful as everyone said, but it was also so full of pain.

"I hear you," she said.

"No, you don't. He's sensitive. He understands things, he feels
shit. Feels it bad sometimes."

This Mina knew. She nodded.

"What are you talking about?" Octavian said. "I'm hard."

But Francis ignored him. "So, you better be for real, you hear?
Don't be up in here lying and carrying on and messing with his
head the way how y'all women do."

"I won't, Francis," she said.

"You promise me?"

"Frankie," Octavian said.

"I promise," Mina said.

"I'll come back from the dead and get you if I have to."

"Frankie," Octavian said.

"Yeah?"

"You're not going nowhere."

"I know," Francis said and lay back down. "But still."

Once Francis was away at rehab, a quiet relief moved through the
apartment. Cyrus sang songs under his breath and felt ease in the
space between his eyes. He bought a copy of *Madhur Jaffrey's Indian Cooking* and three paper bags full of spices that he lined up
on the counter and carefully labeled. He went on a date with a
visiting professor and had a good time, but he cried on the drive
home from her house because the only woman he ever wanted
he'd already had and she was already dead.

With Francis gone, Octavian's panic attacks went underground again. He met a kid named Curtis at a pottery class who

told him they could rent a whole floor of an empty downtown warehouse for $100 a month, and asked if Octavian wanted to share the rent. It was a filthy cement-floored room and its floor-to-ceiling windows rattled as they let in the wind, and the lead paint chipped from the walls, but they loved it. They called it the loft, and Octavian began to stretch canvases ten feet long and seven feet tall. He covered them with images of screaming black babies in the middle of dollar bills or used them to rebuild craps games with shadows and shoes. Mina was supposed to be working on her college applications, but instead she watched him paint and put on their favorite albums: *Exile on Main Street, Sunday at the Village Vanguard, Ghetto Music: The Blueprint of Hip Hop, The Specials.*

Octavian and Mina spent every day of Christmas break together. They smoked weed at the Botanical Gardens and admired themselves in the silver pools of the Japanese garden, where the plump lips of giant orange carp forced ripples on the surface. They spent the day sneaking into movies at the Esquire. They took late night drives to White Castle and ate burgers, which slipped out of the cardboard containers as they drove home. More than that, they made love and made more love—to jazz, to old soul songs, to classic rock. They tasted the lyrics to Bunny Wailer songs on each other's tongues and slow-danced to the Isley Brothers. They saw nothing but their own reflections in the other's face and got on everyone else's nerves.

One night after hanging out at Rahsaan's, Octavian drank more than he should and asked Mina to drive him down to Eat-Rite before they went home. They'd been in the tiny box-shaped diner on the corner of Chouteau and S. 7th Street a hundred times in many combinations—as a whole group, sometimes Octavian, Clarissa, and Mina, sometimes Mina with Ivy and Octavian, but they had never gone in there just the two of them.

Inside, there were a few customers sitting around the worn countertop that circled the steaming kitchen—most of them in the same shape as Octavian or worse. Gray-haired Maggie, who was always tired, always cranky, didn't even look up when they sat down. But a few seats down, a man stared at them.

Octavian noticed him right away and tried to get his eyes to focus on the menu that hung on the wall over the kitchen. He reminded himself that this was why he didn't get drunk. It made him forget that going to the South Side alone with his white girl-friend at 2:00 a.m. was a bad idea. The man stood up and walked unsteadily toward them. His stomach was so big it pulled up on his American flag T-shirt and revealed a strip of chafed dry skin and the rim of his dishwater gray briefs.

"Hey," he said to Mina. "Girl."

Mina looked away from the menu and at the man. Octavian could tell she was confused. "Are you talking to me?" she said.

"Yeah," he said. "Are you okay?"

Mina looked at Octavian and back at the man. "I'm okay, are you okay?"

"Well, I'm a little concerned, to be honest," he said. "Want to make sure this one over here isn't bothering you or nothing." While he talked, he pointed a meaty finger at Octavian.

Octavian bit the inside of his cheek, but before Mina could respond, Maggie leaned across the counter. "Leon," she said. "Either sit down and eat your goddamn slinger before it gets cold or get the hell outta here."

The man took a step back and looked Octavian up and down. "You sure you're alright?" he said again to Mina.

"Leon," Maggie said. "You got about five seconds to leave my customers alone."

On New Year's Day, Mina lay on the futon on the floor of the loft, and looked out the window at the putty-colored winter sky.

Octavian stood on a ladder and laid thick coat upon coat of paint on the canvas and without turning around he said, "What?"

"You written your college essays yet?"

"Who said I'm going to college?"

Mina leaned up on her elbow and said, "You. And your dad."

"I think I might live here in the loft for a year and paint instead," Octavian said.

Mina sat up and wrapped the thin blanket they'd bought from the dollar store on Locust around her. She scooted to the edge of the futon and lit a cigarette. She took a long drag and scratched at the dry skin of her bare feet.

"C'mon, Tave, you know how it is. You said yourself that you didn't want to be one of those people that never got out of St. Louis."

"What's wrong with St. Louis?" he asked and laughed.

"I'm serious," Mina said. "What about art school? You said once you wanted to go to art school." Mina walked over and put her face into the curve of his back. "I'm going to New York. There's so many different kinds of schools in New York. What if we went to New York, together?"

Octavian didn't say anything, but she could tell that he had heard her, that he was thinking about what she said.

"We'll see," he said.

Caution

ST. LOUIS WINTER DIDN'T hang around for long. It pulled itself together and moved on around Valentine's Day, leaving behind purple and white crocus heads that pushed through the dark squares of earth around the gingko saplings lining Octavian's street.

It was on one of those early warm days in March that a pale-skinned white girl Mina had never seen before walked into Rahsaan's, put a baby into Ivy's arms, and said, "This here's yours."

Ivy and Mina were stationed in the T-shirt and poster shop toward the back of the store, and Ivy looked at Mina before he looked at the girl.

"What the hell do you mean, mine, Tammy?"

Tammy had dyed blonde hair, acne scars on her face, and the beginnings of a sleeve of tattoos on her left arm. She reminded Mina of Ivy's mom.

"Remember that night last summer?" she said.

"I remember it was one time," Ivy said.

"I told you you were the first," Tammy said. "You were also the only."

"And you going to tell me you haven't been with no one else?"

Tammy stared at Ivy with big, confused eyes and shook her head.

Bones had come lumbering to the back and Ivy turned to him, still holding the sleeping infant in his arms. "This bitch says this baby is mine."

"Hey now," Bones said. "Ain't no need to call this young lady anything other than a young lady."

"I'm sorry, Bones," Ivy said. "But I just can't believe this shit."

Bones turned to Tammy and said, "Honey, would you mind going on across to Brandts and getting yourself a coffee or something? We need to talk." Bones reached into his wallet and gave Tammy some money.

At this point, both Brendon and Octavian had made their way to the back of the store and were peering over Ivy's shoulder, trying to get a look at the baby and at Tammy.

Tammy nodded gratefully and moved to take the baby from Ivy.

Bones stopped her. "You can leave that baby girl right where she is," he said. "We'll look after her for you. I bet you could use a break now, couldn't you?"

Tammy nodded and slipped quickly out of the store.

"Tave," Bones said. "Go on up there and lock the front door."

Ivy looked down at the little child in his arms, who had an up-turned nose and light brown hair, and burst into tears.

"Jesus Christ," he said. "Jesus Christ, Bones, what the fuck?"

Bones took off his baseball hat and smoothed down his hair before he looked at Ivy very seriously. "Could that be your baby, Ivy?"

Ivy choked on a sob and said, "I guess so. I mean, like I said, I did sleep with her, but only once."

"It don't take more than once," Bones said.

Brendon, who now stood between Mina and Octavian, licked his lips and looked thoroughly confused. "I thought you didn't like white girls, Ivy."

Ivy laughed a little through his tears. "I guess sometimes I do."

"Well, you better get good at liking them," Brendon said. "Looks like you about to start raising one."

Carefully, Brendon took the baby from Ivy's arms and held her close. His eyes behind his glasses filled with tears.

"You suck, Ivy," he said. "Now I gotta go and be this little girl's uncle. Gotta make sure she's not afraid of black men, gotta keep her off the damn stripper pole."

Tammy knocked on the front door and Bones let her in. She walked to the back of the store and her big saucer eyes got bigger when she saw Brendon holding the baby.

"You afraid of black men, Tammy?" Brendon said.

Tammy shook her head but took two steps backward anyway.

"Brendon," Octavian said.

"What?"

"Give Ivy back his baby."

Brendon placed the child against Ivy's thin chest.

Bones said, "Tammy, can you tell her daddy what he's supposed to call his baby girl?"

Tammy smiled. "Sunshine, her name is Sunshine."

"Of course it is," Bones said. "Makes all the sense in the world."

The image of Ivy holding his daughter followed Octavian home from work. Ivy would probably never leave St. Louis now that he had a child, he thought. Octavian wondered if Ivy would wind up like Fat Andy or Steven Jones—guys who'd once wanted to leave St. Louis and never did. Now they hung around high school parties and tried to disguise their thinning hair, and, even though they were only twenty-five, their waists already pressed hard against their jeans.

Octavian opened the door and saw a large envelope, with the Cooper Union logo on the return address, sitting on the floor by the mail slot. He stared at it. He knew rejection letters came in small, thin envelopes, containing only the boilerplate reasons you weren't wanted. Mina had received one from every school in New York she'd applied to except Barnard. Octavian, on the other hand, had been accepted at Howard, Morehouse, the Art Institute of Chicago, and Parsons in New York. Octavian left the envelope unopened on the kitchen table and went to his room.

Francis was still away. After doing a month in rehab, he had gone to a sober halfway house in St. Charles and they'd only talked on the phone. Octavian hadn't told him about being accepted to schools. Any time he thought about going, he would feel his long-dormant heart start to flip-flop. And after the last acceptance letter came in, he told Cyrus that he planned to defer. Cyrus agreed, on the condition that if Octavian got into Cooper Union, he would go. Octavian had shook on it, convinced he'd never get accepted. Even though the letter sat in the other room, Octavian could still feel the weight of it. He tried not to think about it and pulled out his new Bob Marley box set.

Cyrus called to Octavian the moment he walked into the kitchen. Octavian went slowly from his bedroom. He wasn't sure what he wanted from his father. Maybe resignation that now Octavian would have to leave, or an attempt at feigned uncertainty that maybe Octavian didn't get in. But Cyrus did neither. He immediately sent Octavian for Jackson's letter opener and poured them both a glass of scotch.

"You don't have to make a ceremony out of it, Pop," Octavian said.

"Why not?"

Octavian caught a little of his father's excitement and said, "Go on then. Open the dang thing."

Cyrus drew the letter opener across the seal and carefully removed the contents. He adjusted his glasses and picked up the housing brochure that fell. "Your mother," Cyrus said and stopped to swallow. "This is what she wanted."

Octavian nodded. The tears in his father's eyes threw the moment into fast relief.

"You know this is the most prestigious art school in the country? And between their scholarship plan and my professorship benefit, we won't have to pay anything. Which means no loans, no debt."

"I understand that."

"And you won't defer?"

"That's what I said."

"So you'll go?"

"Do you want me to? I mean, do you think it'd be a good idea?"

Cyrus removed his glasses and wiped his damp eyes with a handkerchief. "Of course it's a good idea. What are you going to do instead?" He laughed. "Stay here? With me and Francis? No." He shook his head with utter seriousness. "No way. Not after you've achieved this. I won't let you."

"Okay, Pop, damn." Octavian took the papers and tried to fit them back into the envelope. "I thought this was supposed to be a happy occasion."

"It is, boy," he said. "It sure enough is." Cyrus raised his glass. "Congratulations. You have done your mother and me proud."

"To Mama," Octavian said, and raised his glass.

"To you," Cyrus said.

How I Could Just Kill a Man

MINA EYED THE CLOCK at the far end of Rahsaan's. She replayed the conversation she and Octavian had earlier, when he said that he'd come by. She tried to remember whether he'd said he might come by or definitely would come by. She wasn't supposed to work that night, but Brendon hadn't shown up for his shift and no one had heard from him. She had been busy when Octavian called her back and he sounded mad because she'd paged him twice and then couldn't talk.

"What's up with your boy? Thought he was coming through," Ivy said.

Mina shrugged. "I guess something came up," she said. "You think Brendon's okay?"

"Yeah," Ivy said. "He probably got hung up over at his mom's house and forgot to call."

Clarissa walked toward the front of the store and, as she got closer, Mina saw Ivy's eyes lock on her. Clarissa saw it, too, and she laughed. Not her big loud-girl laugh, but a softer, easier one. Mina was about to say something, but the front door swung open and

Brendon stormed in. He was covered in sweat and his shirt was torn. His glasses sat crooked on his face and he had scratches on his forearms.

"Brendon, are you okay?" Mina asked, coming out from behind the counter.

He didn't answer her but kept walking to the back of the store.

Clarissa looked at Fred, who locked the front door. They went to the back, followed by Ivy. Brendon was in the employee bathroom washing his arms.

"B," Clarissa said, "what happened?"

Brendon looked at her through his broken glasses and said, "I got fucking jumped."

"Who jumped you?" said Fred.

"The cops," Brendon said.

"What do you mean the cops jumped you?" Mina said.

Brendon looked at her out of the corner of his eyes and said, "I thought you listened to enough hip-hop to know the cops are the biggest gang out here."

Mina looked down at the floor. She didn't know what to say.

Freddy put a hand on Brendon's shoulder and said, "What happened, Brendon?"

"I was on my way here and these two City cops, they decided I fit the description of some guy who robbed Church's fucking Fried Chicken last night. They threw me up against the wall and broke my glasses, dropped my ass on the ground and cuffed me. Then they put me in the back of the cop car, where I've been for the last two fucking hours."

"Jesus," Mina said.

"That is messed the fuck up," said Ivy.

"Did they take you in?" asked Fred.

"Nah, they didn't take me in. Want to know why? Because after they got me in the car, they checked the description I supposedly fit and that kid was one hundred and fifty pounds. One hundred and fifty fucking pounds. I weigh at least two bucks thirty. And you know what those motherfuckers did for the next two hours while

I sat in the car with my hands cuffed behind my back? They argued about whether or not they could make it stick. Finally, they realized that it wasn't possible, even though, believe me, they wanted it to be, and they let me go."

"And that was it?" said Clarissa.

"That was it. They uncuffed me and told me to get going before they found something they could charge me with."

"Wow," Mina said.

"*Wow*," Brendon mocked her. He shook his head.

Mina took a step back. Recently, Brendon had been cold to her and she didn't know why. They used to be friends. When they worked together, they drove everyone crazy playing Odetta, Joan Armatrading, and Phoebe Snow. One day Brendon had even shown up and given Mina a copy of *The Ravishing of Lol Stein* by Maguerite Duras. But for a while now, Mina had felt like Brendon didn't even want to acknowledge that she existed.

"They messed with the wrong brother, though," Brendon said. "I tell you that."

"What are you going to do?" Clarissa asked.

"Ima call a lawyer, that's what I'm going to do."

"My mother is a lawyer," Mina said, stepping closer again. "Do you want me to call her? I bet she wouldn't even charge you. She hates the cops."

Brendon looked at Mina, then looked away. "I'll get my own lawyer, thanks."

"Okay," Mina said. "I was just trying to help."

"Yeah, I know," said Brendon. "I know about you out here trying to help us poor black folks, but I don't need your help."

Mina closed her mouth and turned. She walked back into the empty store. Her face was hot and tears burned her eyes. She hated herself for not knowing what to say. She hated that she sounded like a white girl. "Maybe that's because that's who you are," she mumbled, her voice tight in her throat.

Clarissa came out and Mina wiped her eyes and tried to look like she was busy closing out the register.

"Ivy's driving Brendon home," Clarissa said. "Can you give me a ride to Soulard? I'm staying over at my dad's tonight."

"Sure," Mina said. Octavian still hadn't come and he hadn't called either. He wasn't going to show up now.

Highway 40 was nearly empty as they drove downtown. Something about the way it wove through the city, under overpasses where the world got dark, and up alongside old worn-down factories, where the streetlights shone as bright as daylight, always made Mina feel better.

Clarissa fumbled with the pile of tapes in the back. "This is mine," she said pressing a tape into Mina's player. She turned up the tinny speakers and they both sang along with Diana Ross's honeying promise that, someday, we'll be together.

Soulard was dark at night. Especially down by Clarissa's dad's, where no one really lived. In the daytime, the neighborhood was loud with semi-trucks and strong, cursing men loading and unloading warehouses. At nighttime though, those old buildings filled with shadows and ghostly sounds that moved through empty rooms and out of broken windows.

Mina pulled in front of Douglas's house and Clarissa looked up at the one pale light coming from the hallway on the top floor.

"You don't have to go right home, do you?" Clarissa said. "I'm not trying to go in there yet."

Mina shook her head. She knew Clarissa didn't like being in Douglas's apartment by herself. She worried that someone would come try to rob the place and no one would be around to hear her if she screamed. Mina lit a cigarette and rolled down the window. The thick, sour smell of the brewery filled the car.

"It's funny," Mina said. "I can't stand that smell at first and then, after a few minutes, I don't even notice it anymore."

Clarissa lay her seat back and wrinkled her nose. "I hate it," she said. "Smells like feet." She dug in the tapes again and pulled out Cypress Hill.

"What's up with you and Ivy?" Mina said. "I saw how he was looking at you tonight."

Clarissa put the tape on and smiled. "You have to admit. He's type cute."

"I guess," Mina said. "For a white boy."

Clarissa turned to face Mina. "Did you really just say 'for a white boy'? Since when do you say shit like that?"

Mina shrugged. "I've never known you to look twice, no matter how cute a white boy is."

"I haven't. But now I am." Clarissa took the cigarette from Mina and took a drag. "Maybe you and Tave are inspiring me to, I don't know, give someone different a chance." She exhaled a long stream of smoke and then pouted a little. "And we have fun," she said. "He cracks me up."

Mina clenched her jaw at the mention of Octavian. She remembered now. He definitely said he would show. But he hadn't. "Why do you say that me and Tave are inspiring you to look for someone different? I've never been with a white boy."

"I know, but have you seen the light-skinned fat booties Tave has dated? I mean, I know there haven't been many, but you certainly are different for him."

Mina thought about Keisha Putnam and wished she could light another cigarette without Clarissa telling her that she smoked too much.

"I'm serious. Y'all have made me think differently," Clarissa said. "What if Ivy is the love of my life and I wasn't even trying to look at him because he's white?"

"The love of your life? I don't think so. Plus you know he's got a kid now."

"Do you think Tave's the love of your life?"

"That's not the point," Mina said.

"You do, don't you? See?"

"Yeah, but like you said, I'm probably not the love of his."

Clarissa reached over and rubbed Mina's knee. "I never said that, Min. I said you were a different choice. And he certainly didn't stay with those other girls that long. So maybe you are, who knows?"

"I know I'm not," Mina said. "I'm not black."

"Yeah, well, there is that," said Clarissa.

Mina lit another cigarette, but Clarissa didn't say anything.

B-Real and Sen Dog rapped about putting a hole in someone's head and Mina listened to the bass line sample of Jimmy McGriff's "The Bird" that had been playing in Octavian's loft the last time they were there. Mina wondered if she'd ever hear a single song again without thinking about Octavian.

Clarissa looked back up at the empty night sky around her father's apartment and said, "Interracial relationships are hard, though. I've watched my dad try that shit a few times and it never works out. Not because the women aren't nice or pretty or anything. It just seems like there's a whole lot of stuff they don't understand, or my dad doesn't understand, or something."

"Do you think I understand?"

Clarissa smiled at her. "It's not that you don't want to," she said. "But there's shit you *can't* understand. I know you don't want to think it's true, but you're not black."

"I know I'm not black," Mina said.

"Do you?" Clarissa laughed.

"Yes," Mina said, but she didn't laugh.

"Don't get me wrong, you're crazy down, Mina, but you'll never know what the world looks like through eyes that aren't white, just like I won't know what the world looks like through eyes that aren't black. And I know you don't want to think it's that different, but it is."

Mina's stomach tightened and she nodded.

Clarissa pulled her seat back up and snapped down the visor to look in the mirror. She had recently dyed the ends of her curls blonde, and they hung around her face, brought out her round eyes with the thick lashes.

Mina watched as Clarissa twisted a curl around one of her long fingers. She pulled down her own visor and quickly shut it. She closed her eyes and imagined a life without having to wonder if things with Octavian would be different if her hair curled instead of fell hard and straight.

"I guess I do forget," Mina said. "Most of the time, I just think things would be so much easier if I wasn't white."

"The only reason you say that is because you *are* white," Clarissa said, and Mina could tell she was pissed. She'd said the wrong thing again.

"You know that shit that happened to Brendon tonight?" Clarissa said. "That will never happen to you. It could happen to me, but it will never happen to you. And offering your mother's help, as nice as that is, doesn't change anything." Clarissa closed her visor and turned to Mina. "Listen," she said, "the world looks at you, says *white*, says *girl*, and then it moves on. But the world looks at me, my mother, my brothers, Octavian, Brendon—even Evan— says *black* and then adds a whole bunch of shit on at the end. About our morals, our motives. It hates us, wonders whether it's safe around us. And if you act like that's not real, if you act like that's ever an easier way to live, then you are full of shit and nowhere near as down as you think you are."

Mina felt her eyes fill with tears again. She focused on trying to find another tape on the floor. "I wish things were different," she said.

"Well," Clarissa said, "so do I."

They were quiet for a few minutes before Mina asked, "What about Ivy? Do you think he would understand this?"

Clarissa shrugged and laughed. "I guess, if he were the love of my life, I'd have to make sure he did," she said. "And as much as this matters, it's not all that matters, you know what I mean?"

It was Mina's turn to look out at the thick night sky. "I think so," she said.

Can You Stand the Rain

S PRING IN ST. LOUIS was Octavian's favorite time of the year, even if it didn't last long before summer kicked it out the door. He loved being able to smell the fresh-cut lawns and hear songs blasted out of car windows.

The windows in Mina's kitchen were open wide as they sat at the table and Mina shuffled the cards. He liked the way her strong hands made a classic bridge, cards neatly falling one on top of the other. He liked the way she looked, too. She wore a skintight T-shirt under her giant Dickie overalls, and the chunky turquoise bracelet he'd given her for her birthday slid up and down her arm as she dealt. She'd hennaed her hair again, a dark auburn color that deepened the gray of her eyes. She glanced up and caught him looking at her and blushed.

"Why don't you put on some music or something instead of sitting there staring at me," she said.

"Oh, I can't look at you now?"

"Not like that."

"Why not?"

"Because I know what you're thinking and Kanta is gonna walk through that door any minute."

"Then we should be out," Octavian said. He wasn't a fan of Kanta.

"Okay, but let me beat you at this game real quick."

"Like that's going to happen," Octavian said. He got up and put the Black Sheep CD into Kanta's new player, which sat on the kitchen counter.

Nearly a week had passed since Octavian and Cyrus had clinked Waterford glasses across the kitchen table, but Octavian still hadn't said anything to Mina about getting accepted into Cooper Union. He knew Mina would see it as fate, as their futures intertwined in some universal karmic plan. And when she lay soft in his arms singing Dinah Washington songs, the two of them living in New York City sounded like the best plan ever. But, when his clothes were on and his back was turned, he thought twice and worried. He worried because Mina didn't. She thought all they had to do was get out of St. Louis and get to New York City, where the two of them together would somehow break down racial barriers with her new perspective on their old-as-God interracial relationship.

Octavian had planned to tell her about Cooper. Over and over he'd planned it. But every time he started to, the words caught in his throat. Now, looking at her, bobbing her head and dealing the cards, while over the speakers Dres offered him the choice to get with this or that, he thought that maybe she was right. They could go to New York. He didn't really think that they could change the world, but at least things would be different than they were here.

"Mina," he said.

"What's up, baby?" she said, looking at her cards.

Octavian opened his mouth to tell her, but right then Kanta walked in. Her sway spoke of a dinner party where she'd had plenty to drink. She pulled out the chair between them and sat down hard. Octavian immediately began to gather the cards off the table.

"Octavian," Kanta said, "I want your opinion on something."

Octavian glanced at the front door. "Okay."

"I got into an argument with this idiot tonight at dinner because I think that black people, African Americans, should leave the dorky, uncool professions—like science and medicine—to the boring white people. And that they should stick to doing the cool things, the things they're good at, like drumming and dancing. I'm right, right?"

Octavian looked at Mina. "Time for me to go."

"Kanta," Mina said in barely a whisper, "you need to stop talking right now."

"Why?"

"Because you have no fucking idea what you're saying."

"Sure I do." Kanta laughed. "Tell her, Octavian. I'm right, aren't I? You know. You're not out there trying to be white, trying to be a nerd, trying to be smart. You're an artist. You're expressive. Black people are so much better at that than white people are. They're just so much cooler. Tell her, Octavian."

But Octavian had already pulled on his sweatshirt and was beginning to walk out of the kitchen. He stopped and turned around.

"Actually, Kanta," he said, "your daughter is right. You don't know what the fuck you're talking about." He looked at Mina. "I'll be out front."

From the porch he heard yelling, doors slamming. The sound of stomping up the stairs. Mina came out onto the porch, her face drawn up. "I'm sorry," she said and lit a cigarette.

"It must suck to have a mother who is a *racist bitch*." Octavian yelled the last part, hoping Kanta would hear. Mina handed the cigarette to him, but he waved it away and walked over to the other side of the porch. The air vibrated with cicadas and Octavian wished they would slow down their erratic rhythm, or at least bring it together, so that his heart knew where the beat began.

"I got accepted to Cooper," he said.

"What?" Mina rushed to the other side of the porch and tried to hug him, like none of what happened with her mother had actually happened. Gently, he pushed her away.

"When did you find out?" she said.

He had planned to lie. To say that he'd found out that very day, but his mouth was a honeycomb of anger. "I got the letter last week."

The electric charge that had bolted Mina across the porch blew like a fuse and she went dark. "You've known for a week and you haven't told me until now?"

"Shit," Octavian said. "I didn't know I had to report to you at a certain time. Forgive me. I thought this was my life."

"Oh, c'mon, Tave, you know we've been waiting to hear from Cooper. It's all we talk about."

"No," he said. "It's all you talk about."

Most of the time, Octavian appreciated the way Mina let the drama between them dissipate like fog, but other times, like right then, he wanted her to wild out, to get up in his face, to call him names, maybe even call him the one word he knew she never would. The one he knew her mother must say—at least inside her own head—when Octavian walked through the door.

Mina waved her hands across the air between them as if to erase what she didn't understand. Around him the open windows of her neighbors made Octavian uneasy. It was Clayton, after all. A black boy and a white girl arguing could mean an easy phone call to the cops. Maybe it was better that she stayed quiet.

Mina flicked her cigarette across the front lawn. "Fuck you, Tave," she said and turned and went inside.

Octavian stood there for a moment and then started to walk away from the house. It would only take about an hour to walk home and he knew it would really piss Mina off if he left without saying anything. She didn't even ask why he might not want to go, he thought. She didn't even think about what it would mean for him to pick up and leave Cyrus, to leave Francis. He felt the vice grip tightening on his heart and stopped at the end of her front walk. The two times that he had walked home from Mina's house, it was the afternoon and he still got stopped by the cops and asked where he was going. Both times he was told to hurry up and get his ass back into U. City before they found a reason to take him in.

In the back of his mind he heard Brendon. *See, you shouldn't even be over that way, not at this time of the night, with this crazy white lady talking about how we shouldn't be doctors, and you dependent on her daughter to get you home safely? What kind of shit is that?*

Around him, the lights of Mina's neighbors shone down like eyes of accusers. Octavian knew he'd have to make a choice soon. Standing alone in a Clayton neighborhood in the dark was even more dangerous than walking home.

I don't have time for this shit, he thought. He turned and walked back to the house. He lifted the giant iron door knocker and let it drop. Mina opened the door quick, like she'd been standing right there.

"I need you to drive me home," he said.

"Oh, you don't need to tell me about getting into the one school you know I want you to get into for a week, but now you need me to drive you home?"

"Mina," Octavian said quietly. "I need to go home."

"And?" she said, her gray eyes burning. "Your legs hurt or something?"

"No, but in case you hadn't noticed, I am black and you live in Clayton."

"What the hell does that mean, in case I hadn't noticed? I know you're fucking black."

"Oh, and that's a problem?"

"No, it's not a problem, Tave," Mina said.

"Next thing I know you going to be like your mother in there talking about how we should stick to shucking and fucking jiving and not strive to be anything else, right?"

Octavian felt the dark, watchful neighborhood pressing against

one side of him and the bright foyer, with Kanta upstairs and Mina
saying all kinds of shit, pressing against the other. He cursed.
Brendon was right. He shouldn't even be over this way with nowhere to turn.

"I can't believe you," she said.

"Believe it or don't," he said. "Just take me fucking home because the longer we stand here arguing, either your white neighbors or your white mother is going to call the white fucking cops
and I'll be going to jail."

They drove in silence, even though it was Saturday night and
the underground hip-hop show was on KDHX. Octavian wondered if she noticed when they passed two different cop cars on
Hanley Road, but he didn't say anything. In front of his building,
Mina jammed the car in park and lit a cigarette. He knew she
wanted to talk, but he didn't. He slammed the door and didn't
look back.

The apartment was silent. Cyrus slept, Francis was still away,
and his mother was dead. Octavian wanted to revel in the peace
of solitude, but he couldn't shake the angry squall in his stomach.
He went in his room and wished Francis were there. Wished they
could stay up late talking shit and watching *Trading Places* or *Weird
Science*. He started to take out his comic books, but the sight of the
Dark Knight made him think about Mina during the climbing
tunnel days and he shoved the box back into the drawer. He
pulled out his record crates, but he felt like he could smell her
fingertips on his records, so he turned off the lights and switched
on the TV. When James Earl Jones came on dressed as the disturb-
ing, ominous Thulsa Doom chopping off the head of Conan the
Barbarian's mother, Octavian laughed out loud.

"Damn, Mina girl," he said. "What the hell part of my life hav-
en't you infiltrated?"

He changed the channel to BET, but videos were no better.
Prince serenaded the thick-browed twins in "Diamonds and
Pearls" and Octavian thought about how, if he was with Mina, with
her legs wound up around his, she would crack jokes about how

the video made no kind of sense. When a New Edition video came on and Octavian's pager buzzed on the night table, Octavian picked up the telephone, said, "Fucking Johnny Gil. He'll make a punk outta anyone," and dialed her number.

"Tave," she said.

"What?"

"I'm sorry."

"For what?" he said. He could hear her listening to the new Cure album she'd bought the day before.

"For not saying what I wanted to say, for saying what I didn't mean to say. I was mad, but I shouldn't have forgotten about the whole walking home thing. That's not cool."

"No," he said. "It's not."

"And Kanta."

"Yeah."

"I can't believe she said those things."

"I can," he said.

"Why didn't you tell me earlier about Cooper?"

"Because I'm not sure."

"You said you would be sure if you got into Cooper."

"Yeah, 'cause I didn't think I'd get in."

"But you did."

"But I did."

He could hear her creaky old bed as she got up and opened her window. He could see her sitting in there, wearing a long T-shirt and panties. "You smoke too much," he said.

"I know," she said. "Why aren't you sure?"

He took a deep breath and said, "Because of Francis."

"Francis?"

"I need to know he's going to be okay. I don't want to leave Pop here to deal with Francis by himself."

"But your father wants you to go."

"Okay, listen," Octavian said. "I'm going to try to explain something to you that I've never explained to anyone before."

"I'm listening."

"There's no way for me to separate myself from my brother and no way to separate Francis from, I don't know, being Francis. Do you understand?"

"I think so," Mina said.

"I know it sounds crazy, but before I can even know what I, Octavian, want, I have to be sure that Francis is going to be alright first."

"I understand," she said.

"How?"

Mina took a deep breath. "Because that's how I feel about you sometimes."

Slow Down

SUMMER IN ST. LOUIS started in May and dragged a needle across the soundtrack record of Octavian and Mina's love montage to a screeching halt. It was nearly impossible to be in love when it was so hot it made you angry.

The front door of Rahsaan's opened and closed every few minutes and scooped clouds of boiled, damp air into the store, so it didn't matter that the old AC cranked in the back so loud you couldn't hear music over it. Still, it was the summer to bump Mary J. Blige's *What's the 411?* and Eric B. & Rakim's *Don't Sweat the Technique.* In Mina's car, Gang Star's *Daily Operation* stayed on and Brendon kept Brand Nubian and Poor Righteous Teachers playing in heavy rotation.

They rushed out into intermittent rainstorms seeking relief, but the water was already lukewarm by the time it hit the ground. The trees ached as they stretched big, dark-green leaves in every direction but were only able to offer large swaths of meaningless shade. Night took forever to arrive, the light lingering still when the metal gate in front of Rahsaan's slammed shut at ten. And the heat did not abate with the sunset. In fact, it hung harder over the city and itched like a wooly electric blanket.

They rode in air-conditioned cars, blowing smoke out of barely cracked windows. They congregated in the Pavilion or at the Waterfall and drank sweaty beers and smoked weed until at last the heat became one of them, another person to entertain. They searched for house parties that someone had heard about in Kirkwood, the Central West End, downtown in a loft.

Sometimes when they got there, the party was already busted and people were scattered in the streets, making plans of where to go next. Sometimes the party would be going on and they'd roll in, three, six, ten deep hoping for air-conditioning and cold beer, or a back patio and a good stereo system. Nights ended in fistfights in the Steak 'n Shake parking lot, in the park behind Flynn Park School, at the Galleria.

Francis came home at the beginning of June. The six months he'd been gone left him with a line of seriousness between his eyes. A line that did not go away when he smiled, or when he stood with Cyrus and watched Mina and then Octavian graduate from high school. And it was still there as they told Francis their plans for moving to New York City.

Soon he had a new girlfriend, a mixed girl with freckles named Deena, who he met at AA. Francis and Deena sat in Cyrus's kitchen smoking cigarettes and drinking endless cups of coffee until they pushed their chairs back from the table and went to a meeting.

The day the air conditioner at Rahsaan's broke, Bones nearly fainted and went home early. Ivy, who always drank more in summer, handed Octavian a beer right at noon. Octavian took the beer because Brendon had already called him a sellout twice and reminded him that the blacker the berry the sweeter the juice. Octavian was drunk by the time he got to a party at Brian Finklestein's giant home in the Central West End.

Mina had been blowing up his beeper all night with 007s. He didn't really feel like talking to her, but when someone put on that damn Pearl Jam song that she hated, Octavian wished she were there to talk shit with, and he went to find the phone. Brian's parents' sprawling black-and-white kitchen looked as if a meal had never been prepared there. There was no sign of grease on the stove, no stray cloves of garlic hidden under the kitchen cabinets. There was, however, Keisha Putnam standing right by the phone, biting her bottom lip.

She slid a manicured hand around Octavian's waist when he walked over. "I heard you got into Morehouse?" she said.

"I did."

"I'm going to Spelman in the fall."

Octavian didn't pick up the phone. Instead he cleared his throat. "I think I'm going to go to New York," he said. "To art school."

"That's too bad," she said without letting go. "I was hoping you and me could spend some time together."

Octavian never told Mina this, but his freshman year of high school, Octavian had summoned every bit of shy-boy courage that he had and asked Keisha to the homecoming dance. Without even thinking about it, she'd said no. And when his boy Jason had asked her what was up, Keisha told him she'd never go anywhere with Octavian with his bad skin and his strange style. Not to mention his wide-ass nose. "But," she'd said, "his brother, Frankie, now he's fine. He can take me anywhere he wants."

Octavian looked down at Keisha. She was soft and brown and looked like Janet Jackson with her baseball cap and tight pink T-shirt. He let her push up on him and he was thinking about what might happen if he bent down to kiss her, when he heard a voice say, "Tave."

Octavian turned and Keisha quickly moved out from behind him. "Oh, hey, Frankie," Keisha said.

Octavian was about to ask Francis what the fuck he was doing there, when from the corner of his eye, he saw Keisha's eyes locked on Francis. She bit her bottom lip way deeper than she had when she'd seen Octavian.

"I'm out," Octavian said.

Francis followed Octavian onto the street and yelled, "Tave. Hold up."

Octavian stopped. "What are you doing here, Frankie?"

"Mina called me. Said she's been trying to reach you. Her car's broke and she asked me to come get her. Thought I'd come through and grab you first. Good thing I found you, too. Keisha Putnam?" Francis shook his head. "Nah, man, you do not want to do that."

"Back in the day, you would have told me I could never get a girl like Keisha," Octavian said.

Francis unlocked the passenger side of Deena's busted-up Civic hatchback and opened the door for Octavian before he walked around to the other side and got in. "C'mon," he said.

Octavian stood on the sidewalk. "I can't believe you are out here getting righteous and shit," he said. "Like you saved me from a crackhouse, or from getting the shit kicked out of me again."

"Let me tell you something," Francis said. "Deena's cool and all. But if I had a girlfriend like Mina . . ." He stopped talking. "Can you get in the car?"

Octavian sat down reluctantly. "If you had a girlfriend like Mina, then what?"

"I probably wouldn't ever have needed to get fucked up, that's what."

"You're full of shit. You can have any girl you want. You're Francis Munroe."

"That's where you're wrong, Brother. Sure, I've had some of the prettiest girls in St. Louis—the black ones and the white ones, the mixed ones, too. But I ain't never had a girl who loved me the way Mina loves you. Don't fuck it up, Tave." Francis put his seat belt on and checked the mirrors.

Octavian hadn't seen this version of Francis since right after their mother died. The one that merged carefully onto Forest Park Parkway and drove in the slow lane. Francis didn't seem to notice anything and turned up the volume on the classic rock station. He didn't know the words, but he sang along with Bowie anyway about how all they had was five years.

Octavian felt a cold shiver go down his back even though it was eighty degrees and the AC in Deena's car sucked. "You listening to music again, Frankie?" he said.

Francis smiled. "Yeah, man. It's one of the many gifts of sobriety," he said. "I can actually listen to songs, even sing along and not start crying 'cause I miss Mama so much."

When the song ended, Octavian said to his own reflection in the window, "Do you remember how, right before she died, she started saying militant shit?"

Francis was quiet for a moment. Sometimes they had reminisced about what their mother was like when she was alive, but they never talked about what it was like when she was dying.

"I remember," Francis said.

"I just don't know if Mama would be okay with me and Mina being together because she's white."

They were stopped on Clayton Road where the streetlights shone bright enough that Octavian saw a shadow cross Francis's face.

"I wouldn't worry too much about it," Francis said. "Mama said a lot of things right before she died. Who knows how much of that shit was true."

"Why? What did she say to you?"

Francis turned into Mina's neighborhood and pulled into her driveway. "Shit she shouldn't have," he said.

Mina jumped off the porch and into the back seat of the Civic. "Guess what, you guys?" she said.

"What?" Francis said as he reversed out of her driveway.

"I quit smoking."

Octavian, who had looked away when she got in the car, turned around. "Say what?" he said.

"Yup," she said, smiling with her crooked teeth. "That's why I've been paging you. I haven't had a single cigarette today."

Francis turned the car onto Wydown and Octavian felt the same deep tug in his abdomen that was always there when Mina smiled at him. She was cute like that, all proud of herself in her *Dark Side of the Moon* tank top, her cutoff shorts, and the oxblood Doc Martens boots he'd convinced her to buy at Ziezo's. He was about to reach back and smooth down one of her eyebrows, rough up her crazy red hair that she had been trying so hard to make curly lately, when the back of the car filled with blue-and-white lights.

Francis's eyes went wide in the rearview mirror.

"Fuck," Octavian said. He turned to face forward and pressed his hands into his knees.

"Are we getting pulled over?" Mina asked.

"Don't say anything," Octavian said to Mina without looking back. "Don't say a goddamn thing and don't turn around. And *don't* tell them you're my girlfriend."

Before the first cop even got out of his car, another car pulled up in front of them and another until they were surrounded by the erratic flashing combination of blue and red and white lights. Octavian wiped his hands on his shorts.

"You alright, Tave?" Mina said.

He didn't answer.

It was silent in the car. Francis sat with his hands on the steering wheel, his license and car keys in his lap. A flashlight shone through the window and into their faces, one at a time. It stopped on Mina in the back seat. "Everyone out," a voice ordered.

For a moment, things seemed to be okay. Francis spoke to one police officer and explained that he was sober, that it was his girlfriend's car. Octavian answered the other in the way his father taught him to—eyes down and with soft words. But he felt the weakness in his knees and in his fingers and he hated himself, hated the weakness. He felt his heart begin to race and he tried to think of a KRS song, but he couldn't. He knew he was going to have to sit down, either that or he was going to fall down. He wished he could think of a song, wished he could hear Mina's voice.

Mina was sequestered away from both of them behind a female officer with acne and thick, rounded shoulders. When Mina moved to try to hear what the cops were saying to Octavian and Francis, the lady cop grabbed ahold of Mina's wrist.

"You stay right there," she said. She looked Mina up and down and popped her gum. "What are you doing with these two anyway?" she said. "That one there has a record, you know. Your father know you're riding around with him?"

"I don't have a father," Mina said.

"Well, that about explains things, doesn't it?" she said.

Mina was about to answer, but another cop walked over to Octavian and said something she couldn't hear and in the next moment, Octavian was on the ground.

"What the fuck?" Francis said and moved to go to Octavian. But in the space of a breath, the cop had Francis turned around with his hands cuffed behind his back, and was shoving him into the back of the car.

Mina jumped, but the lady cop pushed back. "I don't think so," she said.

Two cops were over Octavian now. One had his knee in Octavian's back, the other was wrapping up his feet and wrists, pushing his face into the concrete.

"That's what I thought," the cop said, loud enough that Mina didn't have to strain to hear. "Just exactly what I thought when I seen you. I thought, this little shit looks like he *wants* to go to jail tonight."

They dragged Octavian to his feet and shoved him into the back of the car next to Francis.

"What you want me to do with this one?" the lady cop yelled, holding Mina's arm in the air like she was the winner of a prizefight.

The cop who had been standing over Octavian looked Mina up and down. "That's the girl that lives up there on Polo Drive," he said. "She's always got black kids up in her house. Take her home and tell her parents they better watch their girl unless they want a bunch of mixed-up grandkids running around."

Kanta opened the front door after many hard slams on the knocker. The cop began explaining that she was bringing Mina home for violation of curfew, but Kanta pulled her bathrobe around her body and changed her face into that of an attorney. "Violation of whose curfew? I thought I was the mother, I thought I set the curfew." Kanta looked at Mina. "Who was driving?"

"Francis," Mina said. "Octavian was in the front seat. We weren't doing anything wrong."

Kanta looked at the cop and said, "Tell me something, Officer. Do you like being a racist piece of shit?"

Mina stared at Kanta.

"Ma'am," the cop said, "I don't think there's any call for that kind of talk."

"Give me my fucking daughter," Kanta said grabbing Mina by the arm harder than the cop had. "Tell your superiors they messed with the wrong mother. They'll be hearing from my office in the morning."

Cyrus arrived at the Clayton police station fully dressed even though it was close to midnight. Octavian knew he had made sure to put on a pressed shirt, maybe even taken the time to buff out his shoes before he left. Not to make his sons wait, but so that there was no question what kind of father he was once he looked the policemen in the eyes.

Octavian and Francis were cuffed to chairs on either side of the room, and when Cyrus saw them, he narrowed his gaze at Francis and then looked away. Cyrus held his hat in his hand, as the officer unlocked the handcuffs, and quietly said thank you before he walked out the door.

Deena had already come to get her car, arriving with tears staining her freckled cheeks. She tried to wait until they let Francis go, but Francis told her to go on. They needed to wait for their father.

"Pop," Francis said when they got to Cyrus's car and he unlocked the door.

"I don't want to hear it," Cyrus said.

Octavian saw the way Cyrus turned away from the pleading look on his brother's face and he said, "Pop. It wasn't Frankie's fault. We were just driving."

Cyrus dropped his head for a moment and then looked at both of them. "How many times do I have to tell you, if you are black and male, it's always your fault?"

"Yeah, but, Pop," Octavian said, but Francis stopped him.

"He's right, Tave," he said. "I should know better." Francis got into the back seat. Cyrus waited for Octavian to get in before he quietly sat down and closed the car door.

Home Is Where the Hatred Is

WHAT NO ONE UNDERSTOOD, Francis thought, what no one ever understood, was how much sobriety hurt. Not emotional, make-you-want-to-cry hurt, but actually hurt. Your bones, your muscles, your head. It hurt to take air in and out of your lungs. It hurt your heart to beat. Everyone else, they went on about their day—heart beating, lungs breathing—and they didn't even notice. *But not me*, Francis thought. *I gotta feel every fucking thing.*

Walking hurt, and eating, and taking a shit. When he was using, he kept it at bay, made it so he never felt it fully. A shot of vodka could hold back the violent sound of the rush of blood through the veins. A hit off a joint could turn the firing of synapses in his brain down to a low simmer. A line of coke, well, that could crank everything up so high, even pain felt good. And a shot in the vein? That was the ultimate quieting, the purity of silence. That's what heroin washed through him. It made the shivering, the watering eyes, the itch under the fingernails that he could never reach, disappear.

Sobriety shouted in his ears and woke him in the night to sheets soaked in sweat, T-shirt and boxer shorts drenched, salt in his mouth and eyes. At treatment they told him to give it up to God, to count twelve steps, to amend and pray. But he worried that God would not be able to hear his prayers over the yelling in his head.

Francis walked, he meditated, he made love, he was celibate. He bought gifts for his father, he listened to his brother's records, and read his mother's poems. He walked some more, danced, ate only vegetables for days, tried to pray. Sometimes he would look up from his walking and find himself down on Goodfellow, right around the corner from an easy silence, and he'd turn quickly, nearly rushing into traffic, to put distance between himself and the relief that was so close at hand.

And then sometimes, sometimes, there would be moments. Moments when peace broke through the pain like gold bars of sunlight streaming through holes in the clouds. And then Francis wondered if, somewhere on the other side of the noise and the pain, there might be a moment when he didn't feel like he was running for his life. And just the brief possibility of even a little less pain calmed him long enough to make it another day.

Inner City Blues
(Make Me Wanna Holler)

MINA HAD BEEN DOING their laundry in the cellar, three floors below the loft. Something they determined was desperately necessary after spending days forgiving each other's mistakes. They were excited about a future away from St. Louis, from St. Louis cops, that would begin in a few weeks when they packed Kanta's Volvo and left for New York City.

Mina had walked by four times before she realized that what she thought was a pile of cellar detritus of rags, wood, and tools was actually a body of bones, hands, and feet, a face with eyes gone wide, skin already cold and hard. She dropped the basket of clothes and ran. The undershirts and towels spread across the dirty floor like a trail of luminescence through a dark pond. A trail that led toward the shell that had once held Francis.

She ran. Through tunnel vision she went up the concrete steps to the loft where Marvin Gaye hollered through the speakers and Octavian stood high on a ladder before an immense canvas. Mina held him there for a breath. There was cerulean paint in his hair. He held a small paintbrush between his fingertips. He sang, threw up both his hands.

Mina walked to the record player through what felt like an ocean of mercury, and lifted the needle. The paintbrush fell from Octavian's hand. Maybe he saw it on her face, maybe he felt it, had felt it for days, or maybe it was just what he always said.

"Is it Frankie?"

After that, the edges dropped off. Down in the cellar, Octavian cradled his brother's body in his lap, wiped his tears away with blue-painted hands. Cyrus came and unwrapped Octavian from Francis, and covered his terrified eyes with one of Octavian's clean Rahsaan's T-shirts from the floor. Octavian shadowboxed the emptiness around him, pushed away Mina's trembling outstretched hands, and disappeared.

Mina lost track. There were sirens and the static of police radios delivering distant voices. Cyrus cried silently. His head in his hands. Ivy appeared and he clutched at fistfuls of Brendon's shirt, and sobbed. Clarissa was there, too. She wrapped her arms around Mina's shoulders and did not let go as she walked her up the cellar stairs, as they sat in the back of Evan's car and drove home. And then there was Kanta, laying Mina down and pulling up the sheet, pulling down the shades.

In the forced darkness of the room, Mina prayed for sleep, but when it came she dreamt of Octavian sitting on the cellar floor, holding Francis's crumpled body—and her unable to climb down the stairs.

Lilac Wine

OCTAVIAN MET MINA'S EYES only once to tell her that he would not be going to New York with her. It was five days before they were meant to leave and three weeks after they'd put Francis in the ground and still Octavian couldn't see Mina, without remembering the way she looked when she took the needle off the Marvin Gaye record and said, "Frankie's dead. He's downstairs in the cellar, and I think he's dead."

They sat in her car, parked behind Rahsaan's where Mina had waited, chain smoking, until he got off work.

"Then I'll stay here with you," she said.

"No, you need to go," Octavian said.

"Tave, you need to go too," she said. "I understand if you don't want to be with me anymore, or if you don't want to come to New York, but you shouldn't stay here. He's gone now. You don't have to stay."

Octavian gritted his teeth against the advice that everyone wanted to give him and said, "I'm not leaving. So just stop."

Octavian had gone back to focusing on details—the smell of the old leather in the Volvo, the deep indigo sound of Nina Simone's voice coming through the speakers, the grateful quiet of his heart that now decided to rest. Mina stared at his profile and he felt the questions she wanted to ask. But he did not have the energy to make words that could explain. Francis was gone. Mina needed to go too.

Quietly, she leaned over and kissed his cheek and he let her wind her fingers in his for a moment before he carefully moved his hand away.

"I love you, Tave," she said. "I've loved you since we were little. I'll never not love you. I'll wait."

"I don't want you to wait," he said. "You've got to let me go."

She attempted to say no, but there were tears in the way and so she just shook her head.

Octavian tried to look at her, but he still couldn't, not even now when he knew it would be a long time before he saw her again. He opened the car door and, from in the back of his gray mind, he knew he should do something kind, say something to acknowledge the ending, and so he clumsily touched her shoulder and said, "Be safe, Mina." He rushed from the car, appreciative for every step he put between them.

On the morning that she left, Mina prayed that Octavian would be on the porch with his duffel bag, but when she opened the door, there were only the empty bricks, the torn jute of the welcome mat.

The early morning sunlight was bright and already hot. Mina squinted down the street in case he was still on his way up the hill.

"C'mon," Kanta said and started the car. "He's not coming."

They drove toward the sunrise down an empty Highway 40. Mina watched the city pass by, like a silent movie of her life going backwards. She longed for the vision she had originally created of this moment. The one where she felt the release of the angry town as it receded in the distance while she and Octavian argued over whose mix tape they would listen to first.

Kanta cleared her throat and said, "I might as well tell you now, although I'm sure I'm not the only one who imagined this drive a little differently. I'm selling the house in Clayton and moving to New Jersey."

Mina turned her body to face her mother and said, "What the fuck are you talking about?"

"Hey, watch your mouth. It's not my fault this mess happened. Last thing I heard, you were out of St. Louis and never looking back, so I decided it made more sense for me to be closer to where you are," Kanta said. "I took a job at a firm in Hoboken, right across the water. And I got an offer—a good offer—on the house last week. I'm taking you to New York and coming right back here to pack everything up."

Mina knew any attempt she made to beg her mother to stop the car and turn around would be ignored. She pressed her face against the window. She wanted to open the door and fling her body out onto the highway, let the impact of the speeding asphalt peel back her skin. They passed Forest Park, Busch Stadium, and the elegant Arch. None of it seemed sad to see her go.

Tonight's Da Night

WITHOUT FRANCIS TO THINK about or Mina to see, minutes lasted for days, sunlight seemed to never abate, and midnight took forever. For months Octavian found himself face-to-face with Francis's ghost on every street corner and in every room of his house. Only when he was at Rahsaan's could Octavian tell himself that Francis had simply disappeared again, that he'd turn up in a few weeks full of promises and apologies like always. But when he was at Rahsaan's, there was no Mina.

Bones was worried and asked whether Octavian was painting.

Octavian shook his head. "I can't yet," he said, and Bones nodded.

"Well, it's been near four months now, and Brendon said you still ain't hangin' with your friends."

Octavian shrugged. "I'm working too much," he said and tried to smile at Bones.

"You called Mina?"

"Bones, will you get the fuck out of my business?"

"Alright, alright. But I need you to tell me if I can help you."

"I'll tell you," Octavian said and when Bones gave him the side eye, Octavian said, "I promise."

What he didn't tell Bones was that he didn't even really sleep. He lay in the bed in his loft and listened to the new Redman album on repeat.

It was on one of those nights, just after Christmas when a soft snow silently dusted the city, that Evan came, banging at the door of the loft like the cops, and screamed, "Tave, I know your ass is in there so open the goddamn door."

Ivy had told him that, a week before, Evan came in late to work for the fifth day in a row so high on coke that Bones fired him on the spot. Since then, Evan had been paging Octavian all day every day and Octavian hadn't called back. Octavian knew he should pretend not to be home, knew nothing good could come from letting him in, but he got up anyway and opened the door.

Evan fell into the room followed by two girls Octavian had never seen before. They sat down at the table—a board on top of record crates—and Evan busted out a mirror and a bag of coke.

"What are you doing, Evan?" Octavian said.

"Cocaine," Evan answered and the girls laughed.

Evan pointed the rolled-up bill at Octavian and said, "Here. Frankie ain't around to tell you you can't no more, remember? I think it's your turn to have a little fun."

The cocaine in his veins felt like a miracle. In one moment, Octavian became Francis, and at the same time, he was released from his brother's shadow. At first, his heart went wild, screamed, *Tave, what the fuck?* But then he grew wings, soared over the snow-covered streets of downtown, over the Loop and past his lonely apartment building where his suffering father sat in his chair pretending to read. After that, Octavian's heartbeat was unrestricted, finally free, and he laughed out loud and screamed into the lights, *I feel you, Frankie, I fucking feel you, Brother!*

Evan grabbed him by the shoulders and they jumped into a cab, going where, Octavian didn't care. The only thing he worried about now was whether or not there was going to be enough cocaine, because he was certain that there could never, ever be enough.

For the next two weeks, Octavian missed work, or showed up late and wouldn't take off his sunglasses. When he tried to sell Fred his rare Linval Thompson record, Fred looked at him and said, "What are you doing, Octavian?"

"What do you mean? I'm trying to sell this record."

"Cocaine is a helluva drug, isn't it?" Fred said and pushed the record back across the counter. "I'm going to let you think about this one for a little while."

After Francis died, Cyrus heard Octavian say he wasn't going to college, and he saw him come and go amidst words about work, and Cyrus let him. Cyrus sat in his study at home, his office at work, and rode across the waves of grief that woke him with an accusation of failure and then let him bask in a blissful sense of relief. Eventually, when he couldn't stand either, he immersed himself in work, in his beloved philosophers, who shuffled like old men through his mind. And at first, when Bones walked through the door of his office, and said, "Professor, you alright in there?" Cyrus didn't know who he was.

"Jimmy?" Cyrus said.

"My apologies for coming here and all," Bones said. "But we need to talk."

Cyrus listened to Bones awhile before he began to understand what he was saying. "Are you telling me that Octavian has been doing cocaine?"

Bones balled up his shirt and said, "Doing a lot of it, I'm afraid."

Cyrus leapt from the chair where he had been sitting for so many hours that it no longer held a sturdy shape and began to pace the room. He stopped to focus on Bones's face, his blue eyes, his pale, puffy skin.

Cyrus sat back down and said, "I need to get him out of here. His mother loved the ocean. I should take him to the ocean."

"That's a great idea," Bones said. "Get him away from St. Louis. Seems like he's haunted, like he's trying like hell to outrun himself."

Without warning, a sob rose up inside Cyrus and flew out of his mouth. He tried to stop it, but once it was out, it seemed as if an entire lifetime of unshed tears decided now was their time. He turned away from Bones, embarrassed at the power with which the choking cries shook his body.

Bones got up and slowly maneuvered around the stacks of books until he stood next to Cyrus. He put his heavy arm across Cyrus's narrow, trembling shoulders and said, "C'mon now, Professor. It's gonna be alright, you'll see. Ol' Bones's got you. You let it out, now. Ain't no sense in keeping it in no way."

From somewhere inside his sorrow, Cyrus heard Bones's soft, soothing voice and his kind words, and at that moment, he saw Octavian and Francis plain as day, sitting in the kitchen, laughing. And it was Octavian who said, "Take it easy now, baby-pa."

And Francis who said, "Jus' let Ol' Bonesy hold you a minute, now, you gonna be jus' fine."

From the same place where the sob had come moments before, Cyrus began to laugh. Soon he was coughing on the tears and choking on the tangled-up laughter. Bones, who surely had no idea why Cyrus was laughing, started laughing too. He laughed so hard he had to sit on the floor next to Cyrus's chair, and when he did, he knocked over a stack of books on the way down, sending them both back into hysterics.

Cyrus took his handkerchief out of his pocket and wiped his eyes, found a box of tissues and handed it to Bones. When the laughter subsided, Cyrus stood and helped pull Bones off of the floor.

"C'mon, Jimmy," he said. "Let's go get my son."

For a week, Cyrus and Octavian sat on the shore of the beach in Trinidad with their feet buried in the heavy, wet sand and let the salt of the air penetrate into the place where they remembered one another.

On the last night of their stay, Octavian put his hand on his father's shoulder and said, "Thank you, Pop."

"I'm sorry I got lost in my own sadness," Cyrus said. "I forgot I still needed to be a father."

They sat at a bamboo bar lit softly by candles and tiki torches. In front of them were the cold fruity drinks that they had tried to resist at first, but gave into after a few days, as the surroundings seemed to offer them little choice. Octavian twirled the orange paper umbrella between his fingers.

"I'm sorry, too," Octavian said. "About the drugs. I don't know what I was thinking." Behind them, the sweet green waves pulled at the shore. Octavian thought that maybe he should stay in Trinidad. Maybe call up Mina, see if she wanted to come down and stay too.

Cyrus looked closely at Octavian and said, "I think that maybe Francis was so much a part of both of us that we didn't recognize ourselves once he was gone. We didn't have anything to talk about anymore."

A half-moon had risen slowly. Around it glowed a peaceful halo and Octavian tried to picture Francis with wings. He bet they'd be giant and groomed to perfection, and that they'd glisten when he turned toward the sun.

"It was the one thing I swore I'd never let happen," Octavian said.

"Hey now," Cyrus said slowly. "You couldn't have stopped Francis. Neither of us could. Shit, it's not like we didn't try, but there was no way we ever really did anything but hold him up."

Octavian started to tell him about his panic attacks, to ask his father to explain why they went away whenever someone he loved died. But instead he said, "All I know is I'm not ready to talk about Francis, or Mama, and I don't know if I'll ever be. Not really."

"Okay," Cyrus said.

Octavian nodded. "But it's not because I don't miss them," he said. "Because I do. I miss them so much."

"You're supposed to, Tave," Cyrus said. "They're gone."

The tension around his father's eyes had lessened and his skin was sun-bronzed. Octavian thought about his endless kindness, his constant ability to be soft when he needed to be and strong at the same time. Octavian decided that Cyrus probably already had a set of wings of his own, hiding somewhere underneath his starched button-down shirt.

Before I Let Go

AT FIRST, MINA WROTE Octavian letters. She told him about her classes. How she'd registered for a course called *Rap Music and Culture in Contemporary America*. She wrote to tell him that every morning she bought a Snapple Iced Tea at the deli, and every afternoon she bought a nickel bag of weed in the park. She told him how she'd seen Biz Markie dancing in the crowd at Giant Step and Eric B. making a call at a pay phone around the corner from her dorm. She wrote to tell him that for five dollars she could go to this tiny club up above a store on Bond Street and see Stretch Armstrong spin on Thursday nights. She bought him Ron G mix tapes and asked him if he liked the Wu-Tang album, the Nas album, the new Tribe, the new De La, because that's all anyone played in New York. Her letters were full of love and sorrow and stories. She wrote to ask if she should come home for Christmas break, for summer.

Octavian never responded to a single one.

Early in 1995, midway through her junior year at Barnard, Mina sat in a diner on the corner of 110th and Broadway with red-plastic seats and a ten-page menu and let the tears silently roll down her cheeks. Her sweet, soft-spoken roommate, Ursula, held her hand under the table.

"I think I've waited enough, don't you?" she said.

Ursula nodded and took a delicate sip of her Diet Pepsi.

"You know, this whole time I thought he was going to show up one day? That my phone would ring and it would be him?"

Ursula nodded again. "I know what we should do," she said. "Let's go to Soul Kitchen."

Soul Kitchen was no longer the small underground party it was when Mina first moved to New York, which meant that Mina and Ursula were underdressed. But Mina didn't care because she could still count on Frankie Inglese to play songs that made her want to dance. And as she danced she thought about, if Octavian could see her, he would see how she'd learned how to wind her hips to dance-hall reggae and how she still knew the words to his favorite songs. And he would wish he'd come to find her earlier, before she, like Frankie Beverly and Maze, let go.

But it wasn't Octavian watching, it was Rubio who leaned on the bar and saw loneliness in Mina's heavy, drunken eyes. And when she left the dance floor, he stood ready with a tall glass of water and a place to sit down.

If Mina had known anything, she'd have known that *rubio* meant blonde. But she didn't and he wasn't. His real name was Fernando. Fernando Figueroa, and he had been born with a head of thick, ash-colored hair that earned him the nickname. Even though it was a curling dark-brown by the time he was a month old, a month was all it took.

What caught Mina's attention, other than Rubio's strong hands as he pulled out her chair and counted bills out from a thick roll of money to pay for her drinks, was when Rubio told her he grew up in Patterson Projects in the South Bronx.

"As in, *Patterson and Millbrook Projects, Cassanova all over, ya couldn't stop it?*" she sang.

Rubio laughed. "Yo," he said, "you're from where?"

Every night, Rubio arrived promptly at seven at Mina's dorm to take her out to eat. Whatever she wanted, he told her. Voraciously she ate. Steak at The Palm, Indian food on 100th and Broadway, Ethiopian food on Amsterdam, falafel downtown at Mamoun's. Quickly, she filled out her jeans as he let her choose whatever she wanted and never let her pay. His attention filled her fuller than any of the plates of food she consumed. She talked to him about her classes, about her professors, and Rubio nodded and sometimes looked interested and sometimes looked away. That was when Mina would ask him to tell her again about the Bronx and about the block parties and break dance battles, the time he met MC Lyte in the elevator of his building, and Rubio would always smile and tell her again.

One Saturday afternoon, when they were sitting at an outside table at Sidewalk Cafe eating French fries, Mina asked Rubio where he worked.

He scoffed. "Work? I don't work."

"So how do you have all this money?" she said.

Rubio lit a cigarette. "Where do you think I get it?"

Mina felt a tingling in her jaw, like she'd said something wrong. "I thought you had a really good job."

"I guess you could call it a good job," Rubio said. "But it's definitely not no nine-to-five."

Mina looked away. She could feel Rubio studying her. "You don't sell drugs, do you?" she said.

Rubio shrugged and exhaled. "Sometimes," he said.

Mina could now taste the old grease that the fries had been cooked in and put down the one she held in her hand. "That's not cool."

Across the table, all the muscles in Rubio's face tightened and he flicked the cigarette into the street. "I thought you were this down-ass white girl," he said. "I thought you listened to hip hop and all that."

"What is that supposed to mean?"

"Well, all that shit you've been listening to, they're not just songs to me. Remember, I'm from the Bronx. I'm not no fake-ass cat from Missouri."

Mina ignored the voice inside her head that yelled at her to leave. To get up and walk as fast as she could to an uptown train. "Are you telling me that you're a drug dealer?"

"No, no," he said. "Sometimes I sell some weed, but mostly I just hustle shit with my boy Orlando."

The voice in Mina's head was yelling so loud that Mina couldn't think of anything to say.

"You're gonna stop fucking with me now, aren't you?" His face was etched with worry. "I knew this was too good to be true." He sat back in his chair and began to nervously straighten the silverware. "Listen, if it's the drugs that you don't like, I'll stop. For real. It's just weed, and only sometimes."

Mina reached across the table and took his hand. "No," she said. "No, it's cool. I understand."

After that, Rubio began to show up earlier in the day, saying he couldn't wait until dinnertime, even if it was simply to meet Mina outside one class and walk her to the next. When Ursula raised her eyebrows after Mina turned her down again to go get dim sum, Mina pretended not to notice and paged Rubio instead. He always called her right back. She didn't even have to put in 911.

One night over raviolis in Brooklyn, Rubio asked Mina what she was.

"What do you mean?" Mina asked. "I'm white."

"Yeah, but, from where?"

Mina didn't know. "In St. Louis, you're either white or you're black," she said.

"Well, you're from somewhere," Rubio said.

The next day, Mina called Kanta.

"You're Jewish," she said.

"And?"

"And celestial. Why do you want to know?"

"This guy I met, he asked me."

"I hope he's not Jewish," Kanta said.

"No, he's Puerto Rican."

"Oh, for Christ's sake," Kanta said. "Out of the frying pan and into the fire you go."

The next day, Rubio and Mina walked west along the park on 59th Street toward Columbus Circle and Rubio nodded when she told him what Kanta said.

"That's why you like sauerkraut on your hot dogs," he said.

"You like sauerkraut too," Mina pointed out.

"Yeah, 'cause I'm trying to be white," Rubio said and laughed. He passed her the blunt he kept cupped in the palm of his hand.

Mina took a hit. "Let me ask you something," she said. "Doesn't it bother you that I'm white? I mean, don't you feel like you should be with Puerto Rican girls? Or, I don't know, not a white girl?"

"For what?" Rubio said and stopped walking. "I've been wanting to be with a white girl for a long time, and I ain't never met a white girl like you."

Mina was unprepared for what it felt like to have it not matter that she was white. She was unprepared for the way the part of her that she kept ashamed and folded up inside, like a note passed in class—the part where the candle of love and hope for Octavian still burned—unfolded.

"I'm telling you," he said. "You're the one. You're the one I've been waiting for."

Mina thought about what it was like to wait for someone for so long. It made her wonder what it would feel like to be the one someone was waiting for, instead of the one who was still just waiting.

As if Rubio knew the shaky ground on which Mina now stood, he wrapped his strong arms around her. Slowly, he bent down and kissed her and her mouth filled with the cold taste of Newports, her nose with the tang of his Nautica cologne.

Behind them, a jittering, garbage-bag-clad crackhead careened down the sidewalk and yelled that Jehovah was coming. They stopped kissing and watched him pass.

Mina said, "My girlfriend Clarissa has a cousin they called Porkie because he was so fat, and when he became a crackhead and got super skinny, they still called him Porkie."

Rubio chuckled and pulled Mina close to him again. "My next-door neighbor in the projects was a girl called Chuletta. That means pork chop in Spanish."

They laughed and their laughter made it feel a little like love.

That summer, Mina moved into Rubio's apartment in Woodhaven, Queens. It was really a single, ill-lit basement room with a kitchenette and faux-wood-paneled walls. On the first day she was alone there, Mina stood up on the couch to look out the tiny windows and only saw one set of feet pass by. She felt a strain of fear that she was making the wrong decision and sat down. She couldn't call Clarissa. Clarissa would tell her the same thing the voice in her head was still telling her, *Yes, you definitely made the wrong decision, get out of there now.* Plus, these days, whenever Rubio found out she'd talked to Clarissa, he got mad, told her that if she loved her friends in St. Louis so much, she should go back there. Mina watched cable until Rubio came home and found her crying from an acute state of boredom and fear. Rubio told her not to worry, he would take care of her. Then he looked away.

The apartment was an hour-long commute on the J train to Mina's internship at a publishing company in the Village. The trip was shorter if she took the A train, but then she had to change trains in the East New York subway station. And in the East New York station, Mina learned that that story she'd always told herself about how comfortable she was being the only white face in the crowd was untrue.

East New York was a place of everyday life, filled with people who moved in and around each other to get to where they needed to go. Families on their way to visit friends pulled children to the side, to let old women shuffling home from a long day of work pass by. Young couples walked fast, holding hands, on their way out to dinner. Boys and fathers walked together, aunts pulled at dawdling nieces. People rushed in different directions. Others had no reason to rush.

In every other situation where Mina was the only white person, she was also always with friends: Makeba, Clarissa, Octavian, Ursula. But, alone in East New York, Mina was no different from the fat blonde lady behind the token booth, or the cop that stood with his back against the iron gates. There, she became aware of how her eyes blinked, how her teeth set. She experienced the pink-mottled length of her arms and wondered if her gait gave something away. She felt as if every set of eyes was on her but, other than the Dominican girls with tight ponytails and tight jeans, who seemed to burst out laughing when she passed by, no one else even noticed Mina. Mina scolded herself for not being able to act like she did in Grand Central Station, but her feet fumbled underneath her and she tried not to fall.

Little by little, things with Rubio began to change. He no longer dug what he said he loved about her. Why did she still wear those baggy jeans? And her oxblood Doc Martens? She needed to dead them shits. And damn, how long *did* it take white girls' hair to grow? People on the train probably thought she was some kind of lesbo or something. And could she do a little more to clean up around the place? I know it's not your white mother's fancy three-story house in St. Louis, but damn.

Mina shed it like an unwanted skin. Put on the gold bamboo earrings and the dark-brown lipstick and went out to Jamaica Avenue to buy Timberland boots. As she laced them up, she pressed the mute button on the voice inside her head, and let herself believe that everyone thought she was Puerto Rican.

But when Mina asked Rubio to take her to the South Bronx, he laughed. "I can't take you to the Bronx," he said.

"Why not?"

"Because you're white."

"So?" Mina said and swallowed down, feeling the familiar knot in her stomach that she'd forgotten still existed.

"So something might jump off. Don't forget, the Bronx ain't St. Louis." He took a drag off his cigarette and gave Mina a cold smile. "It ain't even East New York."

Mina blamed the way things were changing on the fact that she didn't know how to make rice. If she could figure out how to make rice, she was sure things would go back to the way they used to be. The first time she tried, she followed the instructions on the back of a box of Uncle Ben's the way Kanta did. Rubio dropped the entire plate in the trash and told her that Uncle Ben's was black rice—didn't she see the old black man on the box? He was Puerto Rican and therefore ate Puerto Rican rice.

The next day, Rubio came home from FoodTown with a giant bag of Canilla rice and told her, "Don't forget to wash it."

"Wash it?"

"Three times," he said and left.

Mina washed the rice and used the special pot that Rubio bought, but it still came out burned on the bottom or stuck together in a massive clump or it crunched with every bite. Rubio asked her what the hell good was a college education when she couldn't even make rice, and Mina burst into tears. Rubio muttered something and left.

Mina took the heavy bag of rice back out and slammed it on the counter. The directions didn't say anything about washing at all, but there were directions in Spanish on the other side, and Mina thought perhaps those directions included a step about washing. She poured a cup of rice into a bowl and covered it with cold water. As she pressed the hard grains against her palm, her eyes filled with tears. The water in the bowl turned a murky, milky white, and Mina thought about packing her stuff and walking the four blocks to the J train. She drained the bowl and filled it a second time.

Mina thought about calling Bones. He would help her, tell her to come home, and he'd probably give her a job, but for what? So she could watch Octavian come into Rahsaan's with other girls?

Back when she and Clarissa still talked, Clarissa told her about how Octavian was doing a lot of drugs after she left, but then he started getting better and was painting again. Mina was sure he had a new girlfriend by now. Mina dumped out the water that was less murky this time and filled the bowl again. She thought about going to Kanta, just across the Hudson. But Mina would rather figure out how to make the fucking rice.

An hour after she'd thrown another inedible batch of rice in the trash, Rubio returned with a girl with a long black ponytail and big boobs.

"This is Chuletta," Rubio said. "She's going to teach you how to cook."

Mina didn't know whether to be furious or relieved.

Rubio pulled Mina to him by her belt loop and brushed his lips across hers. "I love you, *Blanquita*," he said and walked back up the stairs and out the door.

She told Mina to call her Chula—which, at this point, Mina knew meant cute, and which suited her much better than anything resembling a pork chop. In the fluorescent light of the kitchen, Mina saw a razor-thin scar that started at the corner of Chula's right eye and ended at the corner of her mouth. It pulled her face into a pretty, perpetual smirk. Chula saw Mina staring at her and her smile turned kind.

"Damn. *No te preocupes, Mamita*," she said. "It's only rice."

This Broken Heart

WHEN OCTAVIAN GOT HOME from Trinidad, he quit working at Rahsaan's and began bartending at Blueberry Hill where the money was so good he didn't have to work so much and he could spend more time painting. He was part of a group show at a gallery in the Art Lofts and sold three pieces—one of them to Brendon, who had gone back to school to get his MBA. The gallery owner told him he was wasting his time in St. Louis.

"You should be in a bigger city," she said. "You're too talented for this town."

There were two places Octavian should be, she said—either New York City or Chicago. Mina was in New York—or at least he thought she still was, and even though her letters had stopped coming the year before, he decided he should probably go to see her. Tell her what happened since she left. See if maybe she still loved him. But when he asked around, nobody knew where she was.

"What do you mean you haven't heard from her in over a year?" Octavian asked Bones. "And Evan doesn't know and neither does Ivy."

Bones stopped stacking CDs and said, "You tried Clarissa?"

Octavian nodded. "She said they kinda fell out. That Mina stopped returning her calls after she went to live with some Cuban guy. Now the number she had for her is cut off."

Bones nodded. "I paged her a while ago, but she never called me back."

"Pager? You mean like a beeper?"

"Umm-hmm."

"Why didn't you tell me Mina had a beeper?"

Bones gave Octavian a look.

"Well, what the hell does she need a beeper for?"

"I'll give you the number if you want. Not sure if it'll work, but you could try."

Octavian turned over the new OutKast album and read the back. "I'm going to New York anyway," he said. "Whether I get to see her or not."

Bones nodded. "Well, if you do, hug her tight for me."

Octavian waited until he got to Brendon's cousin Peaches' apartment in Brooklyn, where he was staying, to page her. He used code 007 and the phone rang right away.

His voice trembled in his throat when he picked up the phone and said, "Hey. It's me."

On the other end, a man's voice said, "Al?"

"Al? No, this is Octavian."

"Octavian? Who the fuck is Octavian?"

In the background he thought he heard a girl's voice say, "Octavian?" There was a click and the line went dead.

Octavian stared at the phone and tried to convince himself that the voice in the background wasn't Mina's. It was probably someone else's number now, or maybe he dialed it wrong and should try again. The horn-filled bass line of Jay-Z's "Friend or Foe" boomed out of a passing car and Octavian decided to take a walk first. Go to the bodega and get a beer, sit and drink it on the stoop like a real New Yorker. Then the phone rang again.

Most likely it was a call for Peaches, he thought. Or maybe it was Peaches herself calling to see how Octavian was doing. He picked it up.

"Octavian?"

"Peaches?"

"Who the fuck is Peaches?"

"Mina?"

"Octavian."

He took a long slow breath. "Hey, Mina girl."

He heard her light a cigarette.

"I'm here," he said.

"Here like in New York?"

"Yes," Octavian said. He felt loose at the edges and looked out the barred windows. "I came to see you," he said.

She laughed a little. "You're pretty fucking late."

Hearing her voice made things feel urgent, necessary. He had wanted to play it cool, but instead he said, "Can I see you?"

"Tonight?"

"Yeah, tonight."

"Not tonight." She said it like she was looking over her shoulder.

"Tomorrow?"

"I have to work."

"What time do you get off?" He hated that she was making him do this, but he wasn't going home without seeing her.

"We'll see," she said.

Octavian waited on the corner of Eldridge and Houston. Old men with withered faces, dark pointed stares, and tight-drawn mouths rushed past him. Exhausted women with covered heads, children, and pulley baskets of groceries moved by slowly. There were lots of girls who could have been Mina, but there was no Mina. Octavian gave up and went into the bar alone.

It was a lounge with big soft couches and low tables. He'd found it the night before as he walked through the streets of the

Lower East Side and he knew Mina would like it there. When she called from work to tell him she could meet him, he asked her if she knew where it was.

"You mean Sapphire Lounge?" she said.

"Is that what it's called? There was no sign."

"Yeah," she said. "I ain't been there in forever."

Behind the turntables, a good-looking kid, with hair cut close to his scalp and fierce cheekbones that reminded Octavian of Francis, played Donald Byrd's "Rock Creek Park." Octavian ordered a whiskey and soda.

Behind him, he heard a voice say, "Tave."

He would have been able to recognize her voice in a crowded room, but he didn't turn right away. He let his name, as she said it, hang in the smoky soul-filled air. When he turned around, only one girl stood behind him, but she didn't look like Mina. She had a long brown ponytail and she wore thick gold hoops, tight jeans, and brand-new Nikes. Only when he looked closely and saw her dark-gray eyes was he sure.

Octavian pulled her to him and hoped that, even though she looked like someone else, she'd still feel the same, still smell like Mina. She didn't. She smelled candy-sweet and she stiffened in his arms and waited to be let go. When he looked at her again, he felt himself smile, but she had already turned to the bartender.

"Ay yo," she said. "Can I get a Heineken?"

The song changed to Roy Ayers's "Searchin'" and they sat silently on one of the low sofas.

Octavian finally said, "Hey, Mina girl."

"What up?" she said, keeping her eyes on her brown-painted nails.

"You stopped biting them," Octavian said.

"Nah, these ain't mine. Got 'em from the Koreans. They're acrylics."

"You got fake nails?" Octavian tried again to get her to look at him.

"What's wrong with that?"

"Nothing. They look really real."

Mina took a sip of her beer and glanced at him out of the corner of her eye. He smiled and she quickly looked away. She took a pack of Newports out of her jacket pocket and lit one. She offered the pack to Octavian and he took one, but didn't light it.

"You know, Frankie used to call these genocide cigarettes," he said.

"I know."

At the mention of Francis, Octavian felt a crack in the ice around her and she met his eyes for longer than a beat before quickly turning her gaze toward the dance floor, where two white girls were pretending to grind on each other and laughing.

"Yo, G," she said. "This place has gotten wack."

Octavian laughed and said, "Did you just call me G?" He waited for her to laugh too, but she sucked on her Newport and didn't even smile. For a moment, Octavian wished he were with the girls laughing on the dance floor. Anything, he thought, would be better than this.

The DJ put on Funkadelic's "This Broken Heart" and Octavian laughed a little. "Remember how we used to sing this at the top of our lungs?"

She shrugged. "Not really," she said.

Octavian could tell she was lying. "I heard you have a boyfriend."

"I told you I wasn't gonna wait no more," she said. "In my last letter, I told you."

The sharp menthol smoke of the Newport in his lungs was cold, and he felt like George Clinton, like no other heart could love her like his broken heart could.

"Are you happy?" Octavian asked.

He thought he saw her swallow a little before she said, "He's mad cool. He's from Puerto Rico—or, well, his parents are. He grew up in the Bronx, in Patterson Projects." She paused and Octavian could tell she wanted him to be impressed, but he only felt sad.

"Did you meet him at school?" Octavian asked.

"Barnard is an all-girls school," she said. "I met him at a club."

"What does he do?"

"What does he do?" she mimicked him, and now she laughed. She took a long sip of her beer. "He hustles shit. He works sometimes, but mostly him and his boy get stuff off a backs of trucks—big shit like appliances—not no *Goodfellas* cigarette shit. And he makes mad money selling boosted cable boxes. Sometimes he moves weight, but that's just sometimes."

"Mina," Octavian said.

"What?"

"Are you for real? I mean, I don't know, I keep waiting for you to bust out laughing and tell me this is a joke. But you're serious, aren't you?"

She looked directly into his face and said, "Why are you here, Octavian?"

Octavian took a deep breath and said, "Because I miss you. Because I finally understood what you said when you left. I can't stay in St. Louis, and the first place I thought to go was here. To you. To where we made those plans."

"That was a long time ago. Things have changed."

"I can see that," he said. They watched the girls stumble together into the bathroom. "Why did you come, then? You obviously don't want to see me. You didn't have to come here."

"Because I'm not you, how about that?" she said. "Because I don't just not come. That's what you do."

"Mina, I never told you I was going to come. I told you to move on, to let me go."

"Oh, and that shit is easy, right? To just let somebody go. How is that working out for you? You let Frankie go yet?"

Octavian didn't answer. It was his turn to look away.

"I'm sorry," she said. "That wasn't cool."

"No, you're right. I shouldn't have shown up here expecting things to be the same. I guess I just didn't expect them to be so different."

Mina's voice locked in her throat. It would be so easy, she thought, to rip out the ponytail that was so tight it made her scalp ache. To sing the lyrics to the Earth Wind & Fire's "Fantasy" that the DJ put on. But instead, she took another sip of her beer and heard Rubio's voice as he stepped into her reflection in the mirror while she got ready to go meet Octavian.

"Where you think you're going?"

She had almost made it out the door, even had her North Face on. She didn't look at herself or Rubio in the mirror, but at her hands as they pulled her hair back. Hair that never shone in the light the way Chula's did. Hair that tangled by the end of the night. White-girl hair. She felt her legs tremble a little as she walked around him and grabbed her lighter, her pack of Newports, the ones Frankie used to call genocide cigarettes.

"I'm going to see Chula at work," she lied. She never lied to Rubio—mostly because she never did anything she had to lie about. But this was Octavian and that meant lying. Because maybe if she was able to do that, the voice inside her head told her, she might be able to do something else.

She looked up. Octavian was pulling on his coat. He had paid for the drinks. "It was good to see you," he said. His voice shook.

"Wait," she said and stood up.

Octavian stopped and said, "It was bad for a while, Mina, I mean after you left. I got caught up in some stupid shit and when I came out of it, all I could do was paint. It took me a long time to get through it, but when I did, the first thing I wanted was to see you, to be with you, but like you said, I'm too late." He reached in and wrapped her quickly in his arms.

"Octavian," she said when he let her go. But he turned his back and walked out the door.

Mina grabbed her coat and chased him to the corner of Houston, where he held his hand up as the cabs sped by. She stood close to him, and that's when he noticed what was so different about her face. She no longer had those thick and wild eyebrows that he loved to smooth down with his thumb. Instead, they were waxed into thin lines of exclamation.

"I don't know what I was thinking coming here," he said as cab after cab passed by. "Actually, I do know what I was thinking. The only real part of myself I've got left are my memories from when we were together. I guess I thought you would still feel the same, but you don't and I don't blame you. Really, I don't. It's my fault. I understand."

He felt the familiar pounding, the racing of his heart, but this time he knew her voice wouldn't soothe him, not after the way it had burned in his ears all night.

"Can you help me get a cab?" he said. "You know how it is for a black man in Manhattan."

She grabbed a hold of his wrist. "Tave," she said.

"Do me a favor," he said and pulled his arm away, "and hail me a fucking cab, okay? Don't make this worse than it is."

She started to protest, tried to grab his arm again, but he pulled it aside and a cab slowed down and stopped.

"Tave," she said again. "You think you understand, but you don't."

He opened the door and got in. "I don't want to understand," he said. "You used to be beautiful. You used to be free. I'd rather remember you the way you were. I don't need to know who you are now."

2014

CYRUS THOUGHT IT UNFAIR that his own skin should pucker, dry, and age, while the skin of his wife would always be smooth, the pores open, the moisture captured. That she had left him to raise their sons alone—to bury one and try to heal the other—was not as hard to bear as the fact that she had not stayed with him to endure old age.

Many times during the eternal whirlwind that was single father-hood, he wished she were there to advise him, to celebrate with him, to console him, but now that he was alone, a glass of port wine in his palm, he wanted nothing more than to look into her tired eyes, to see the ways that the years would have honed her beauty, made her old, wise, and refined. It was as if he felt her absence more now than he did when she first left.

Left. She didn't leave. She died.

And Francis died and he, too, soon would die, but not before he told Octavian everything. About the fact that Francis was not Cyrus's biological son, about why he chose to lie about it for so long, about how it got harder and not easier to be without Cordelia.

Cyrus thought of the Yeats poem, the one that started, *When you are old and grey and full of sleep*. He could not remember the next line and he got up from the table and went to the bookshelf, but instead, Cordelia's book of Mina Loy poems caught his eye, and he took it off the shelf.

Cyrus opened the book to a page that had been turned down, releasing the intimate smell of whispers of a book that hasn't been opened for years. He wondered if some forensic scientist would be able to find Cordelia's fingerprint where she'd pressed the little triangle into the top of the page so that she could revisit that particular poem another time. He closed his eyes and touched his own thumb and forefinger on the fold and hoped for a moment to feel her fingertips between his.

When he opened his eyes and saw the title of the poem on the marked page, he laughed a little out loud. Slowly, he walked over to the table and sat down, took a sip of his port, and cleared his throat.

"An Old Woman," he read aloud. The lonely shadows that lived in the corners of the apartment seemed to creep forward to listen, and Cyrus adjusted his glasses and read on. When he finished, there was a soft knock on his front door and he wondered if he had read so loud that he disturbed someone. He didn't get up right away; instead he hoped that whoever it was would hear that he was no longer reading and go on. Even in his apparent loneliness, there was a sweetness to isolation that he preferred over entertaining strangers, especially at an hour when he'd already finished his glass of port. But the knock came again, so he closed the book, stood up, and straightened his collar, his cuffs, and walked to the door.

Through the fish-eye peephole, Marcia Cohen stood with her arms crossed in front of her, her mouth drawn into a thin, straight line.

"Shit," Cyrus said to himself. "I know she's not coming here to complain about me making noise."

He opened the door. "Good evening, Ms. Cohen."

She dropped her arms and then folded them again. "Good evening, Mr.—I mean, I'm sorry, Dr.—Munroe."

"It's okay," he said. "You can call me Cyrus. We're neighbors, after all. Would you like to come in?"

She shrugged like her knocking on his door had been his idea and stepped carefully inside. He closed the door behind her and invited her to the table.

"I was having a glass of port," he said, "and reading a little poetry. Usually, I don't allow myself more than one glass, but if you'd join me, I think it'd be okay if I have another."

"Port? What's that?"

"It's a dessert wine from Portugal. I haven't had dessert, but I still enjoy having a glass after dinner."

Marcia sat down at the table and dropped her hands into her lap. She looked around the room and hesitated. "Okay," she said.

He poured her a glass and refilled his own before he sat down and said, "Is there something I can do for you?"

"I just wanted to say, you see, well, my son, Adam. He's, well, you know Bones, right?"

"You mean Jimmy, from Rahsaan's?"

"Is that his real name? I've only ever heard Adam call him Bones."

"Yes, I know him."

"Right," she said. "Bones, Jimmy, he thought you might be able to help me. You see, my son, Adam, well, as you know, we haven't been getting along; and the other morning—I'm surprised you didn't hear us—we got into a horrible argument and he packed a bag and left." She said it in one breath and tilted her small head at Cyrus.

Cyrus had heard the whole thing. Their argument had pulled him out of yet another dream where he was searching for his wife by following the smell of her Vaseline Intensive Care lotion, the one in the tall yellow bottle, down a long corridor in Harvard's Memorial Hall, but he didn't feel inclined to share this with Marcia Cohen. He invited her to go on.

"Well, I went to see Bones to find out what was going on with Adam. He told me I should talk to you. Somehow Bones knows we're neighbors, and he said that you raised two of your own sons and that you might have some good advice for me about Adam."

Cyrus was certain now that his wife was talking to him, but what Cordelia was trying to tell him he wasn't exactly certain. Still, he was pretty sure it had something to do with making necessary amends while there was time.

Across the table, the timid woman sat glancing furtively about his apartment and Cyrus found it interesting that Bones, who knew both his sons, considered him to be in a position to give advice about raising boys. Maybe that's because he didn't know how long Cyrus had told his own lies.

"I can't tell you what to do, Ms. Cohen," he said. "I can only tell you where I went wrong."

"I guess that's a good place to start," she said.

Cyrus drank a sip of his port and she did the same.

"I didn't tell them the truth," he said.

Marcia Cohen nodded and took another sip of her wine. "I have also told lies," she said. "You think if I tell Adam the truth about the lies I've told, things will be better?"

"It can't help but change things, can it? And if you feel that anything is better than what it is now, then I guess different is going to be better, right?"

"I guess so," she said.

"Believe me," Cyrus said, "it is advice I must take myself."

Marcia Cohen quickly drained her glass and said, "Can I ask you one more thing?"

"I don't see why not."

"That stuff going on over in Ferguson, you know, that's on the news?" She stopped there and waited.

"What about it?" Cyrus asked.

"Is it true?"

"What part?"

"That the cop shot that boy, even though he didn't do anything wrong, even though he had his hands up?"

"You mean Michael Brown."

"Yes, and that now there are riot police spraying tear gas on innocent people?"

Cyrus leaned forward in his chair and cupped his port glass between his two palms. "What makes you think I know the answer to that?"

"Because . . . I don't know," she paused.

"It's okay for you to say that you think I know the answer to that because I'm black," Cyrus said.

"It is?"

"You thought it, right?"

She nodded.

"Let me ask you something, Ms. Cohen. What do you think would happen if we actually asked the questions we wanted to ask? What do you think would happen if then we actually listened to the answers?" Cyrus sat back in his chair and said, "Talk about things being different."

"Do you think you could take me there?" she said. "I mean, to Ferguson?"

"Why?" he said.

"I want to see."

"It's not a reality show, Ms. Cohen."

"If I can't call you Dr. Munroe, then you have to call me Marcia," she said. "And I said that wrong. I don't want to see, I want to help."

Cyrus was tired. Tired and ready for Ms. Marcia Cohen to go home. Still, if this woman wanted to help, she should help, and Cyrus was grateful for a reason to get up from the table. He took a piece of paper and a pen from the shelf by the phone and wrote down Evelyn Morris's name and the address of the church.

"This is a woman who is doing good things in Ferguson," he said and handed Marcia the piece of paper. "If you want to help, start with her. She'll be happy to put you where you're best needed."

Marcia Cohen looked into her glass as if wishing it were full again. Then she blinked her eyes at Cyrus and said, "But can't you take me there? Introduce me and everything?"

Cyrus shook his head. "I'm afraid I'll be too busy getting ready for my son's visit."

"Then I can't go," she said.

"I thought you wanted to help."

"I did. I do. But I can't go over there alone, you know that."

"I don't know that, Ms. Cohen. If you want to help, this is where you can go to help. There are many other . . . volunteers there. You'd be surprised. What do you need me for?"

"To . . . I don't know. Protect me?"

Cyrus laughed. "Ms. Cohen," he said, "I am nearly eighty years old. What exactly do you think I am going to be able to protect you from?"

Her smile was tight. "I don't know," she said.

Cyrus took her glass from the table and walked into the kitchen. He stood for a moment in front of the sink and asked himself why in the world he was holding back. Why did he let her feelings matter more than his? He walked back into the room and over to the front door, which he opened.

"If you think I can protect you from blackness with my blackness, Ms. Cohen," he said, "you're wrong. It is old men like me who need protecting from people like you. I think it is time for you to go on home now."

Marcia Cohen stood up. "I'm sorry," she stammered. "I don't know what I said."

"I know," said Cyrus opening the door wider. "And therein lies the bigger issue."

At the door, she offered him her limp hand, but he didn't shake it. "Good luck with your boy," he said.

She walked out and Cyrus closed the door behind her. The scrap of paper with Evelyn's address sat on the table. Marcia Cohen had left it behind. Out loud he said to the room, "I understand, Cordi, I understand. From now on, I will revel in my loneliness. I will rejoice in the silence of being an old man whose wife is long gone, whose children are dead and far away. And I will tell the boy. I will tell Octavian the truth."

Cyrus changed his clothes and got into bed. As he turned off the light on his bedside table, he thought that maybe if Octavian did come home for the closing of Rahsaan's, before that, before the party, they could sit down, have a drink, and he could tell him. When he asked himself why he'd never told Octavian this story, even now that he was grown, Cyrus knew it was because he didn't want to remind his son, to remind himself, what the cancer did to Cordelia. How it stole away during the night everything that they loved. How it made it so that the anger that grew in her eyes was the final thing to go.

The mournful light from the alleyway reflected the ebony polish of his Harvard chair, the sharpened pencils in the first clay cup Octavian made in grade school, the silver frames on his desk with photographs of his family at Hampton Beach, on the Screaming Eagle at Six Flags, Octavian graduating from high school, his smile sad and unsure.

> > >

THAT THERE WAS ONLY one bathroom in Mina's apartment was more of a metaphor for single motherhood than anything. A second bathroom would have been a luxury and, by definition, there was nothing luxurious about being a single mother. For a year after their father left, Chloe and Riley would not let Mina out of their sight—including when she went to the bathroom. And so they sat wide eyed as she removed and inserted a tampon and then tried to close the lid before they were able to peer over and see the bowl full of blood. The night she got food poisoning, when the girls were barely five and three, they sat in the bathtub and watched in horror as Mina retched into the toilet.

Mina craved privacy like a fix. A moment of quiet and release without being watched, without hearing the rustle of footsteps outside the door, the quiet rap, the call: "Mom, are you in there?"

"Of course I'm in here, don't you see that the door is closed?"

"I have to pee."

She was convinced that like Pavlov's dogs they heard the door close, the water turn on, and immediately rose from where they were sitting and decided there was something in the bathroom they needed urgently. The nail polish remover, a Q-Tip, to use the toilet right away. At one point, there was a lock on the door. But when she was seven years old, Riley went through a phase of violent tantrums and locked herself in and destroyed every breakable item, poured the shampoos down the drain, and emerged with fingers cut and bloody and Vaseline in her hair. Mina removed the lock.

The coming of female adolescence gave the bathroom yet another meaning. It became the place where they could hold her captive and tell her about the problems they were having, and most importantly, the ways in which she had failed them. That day it was Chloe who needed her attention as Mina tried to find a way to shave her legs and bikini line.

"I'm not going to school tomorrow," Chloe said. "In fact, I'm not going back to that school ever."

Mina didn't want to lower herself to the level of a thirteen-year-old girl, but it was hard. Chloe's side-eye glances away from the phone to her naked aging body didn't help.

Mina let her eyes roll toward the ceiling before she said, "Chloe, you know the rules. You go to school unless you're sick."

"I need a mental-health day."

Mina gave up on her bikini line. It didn't matter anyway. No one saw her vagina anymore except her teenage daughters. She considered letting her pubic hair grow like Kanta—that would scare them away from her body. Then they'd give her privacy.

"I don't believe in mental-health days," Mina said. "If I let y'all start taking mental-health days, no one would ever go to school. I don't take mental-health days."

"Yeah, well, maybe you should," Chloe said. She smeared a towel around the mirror so she could look at herself. Her pale skin had reddened in the steaming bathroom and her straight hair started to frizz. Mina hoped that would be enough to get her to leave.

Mina turned off the water and wrapped herself in the only towel that hung damp in the bathroom. The rest, she was sure, were on the floor of Riley's bedroom. "Is there anything else I can help you with, Chlo?"

Her younger girl did the one-shoulder shrug that said she was sad, that said there was something on her mind. Something she needed Mina to know. Mina took a deep breath and wondered how she could move this conversation out of the tiny steam-filled space to somewhere she could bob and weave the darts her child had stored up in the back pocket of her jeans, ready to be thrown.

"You know she's terrible to me," Chloe said.

"I thought you said this was about school."

"Well, it's not," Chloe said. "It's about my bitch sister." Chloe pursed her lips at her reflection, widened her eyes like she did when she took a picture of herself on her phone.

"Chloe, you're too pretty to talk like that. It doesn't suit you."

"Don't try to change the subject, Mom," she said. "We're talking about Riley."

Mina felt the heat of anger crawl up the back of her damp neck and she yanked her sweatshirt over her head with a jerk, pulling out one of her hoop earrings. Mina refastened the earring and wrapped her hair up in the towel.

"You're not taking me down this rabbit hole with you, Chloe," she said. "I love you and your sister, but whatever you are going to accuse her of doing, you're going to do the exact same thing to her next week. Until both of you are willing to cut this shit out, it will be this way and I, for one, am all set."

"You say that, but you always take her side, always." She choked on her sob and her eyes filled with big, sad tears. She sat down on the toilet seat and covered her face with her hands.

Mina stood there, looking at the thin back of her young child as it heaved, the agony so heavy the room seemed to sag underneath it.

"Chloe," she said.

"It's true," Chloe said. "You love her more than me and I know why. I've always known why. I've just never said it out loud to you."

Mina knew she shouldn't succumb, but the sound of the pain pulled her down so that she crouched next to the toilet, rested a hand on the arm of her girl.

Chloe moved out from under her mother's touch. "Why don't you just admit it?"

"Admit what?"

Chloe looked into Mina's eyes and said, "Admit that you love her more than me." She was no longer hunched over, no longer sobbing. Now she was lifted by her anger, her clarity. "You love her because she's got brown skin like you wish you had. But I look like you, like a white person, and you hate white people, you hate yourself, you hate me."

Mina felt the waiting, the expectation that she say something to contradict her daughter, to tell Chloe that she was ridiculous. But there was a hollow place in Mina where her voice had been and she was overcome with an exhaustion that made her joints soften and her bones ache. She pushed by Chloe without saying a word and went into her bedroom where the lock on the door still worked.

Mina sat down on her bed. She wished her own misunderstanding of herself hadn't manifested in her daughter thinking she hated her because of the skin they shared. She knew she should talk to Chloe, try to make it better for both of them, but she wasn't sure if she could. She didn't know what to say. She wasn't sure she had the energy to manage the life she had created.

On the dresser, her phone buzzed and she unwrapped the towel from her hair before she picked it up. Octavian's name on the screen pulled her heart up from where it had sunk to the bottom of her stomach and brought it right to her throat.

HEY, the text said, THERE YOU ARE.

the 2000s:

A MIX TAPE

YOU DON'T KNOW—BOB ANDY

MY FRIEND—JIMI HENDRIX

SHOOK ONES PART II—MOBB DEEP

BAG LADY (RADIO EDIT)—ERYKAH BADU

You Don't Know

CHICAGO WASN'T NEW YORK CITY, but it wasn't St. Louis either. In Chicago, no one had ever heard of Francis Munroe. In Chicago, Octavian wasn't anyone's little brother. He hadn't started out intending to lie about Francis. But then he met a girl he liked. Tanya, whose family came from Lebanon. She had dark hair and long eyelashes and always smelled like almond soap. One night Octavian got drunk and told her about Francis, and then immediately had a panic attack so strong that Tanya had to take him to the emergency room. Before releasing him, the doctor told Octavian he probably shouldn't drink so much, should definitely get some therapy, and offered to prescribe some meds. The next day Tanya called to say that, though she liked Octavian a lot, it was a little more than she could handle right now.

Octavian made it through one therapy session and then decided to cut back on the whiskey and not to tell anyone about Francis ever again.

The first person Octavian told he was an only child was a girl named Rachel, who he met in a graphic design class he enrolled in at the Art Institute. Rachel came from a wealthy family of

Northside Jewish lawyers. She was good at design and had thick brown hair and, Octavian learned after their first date, the largest breasts he'd ever seen. She was smart and paid for everything and so Octavian tolerated her terrible taste in music and the fact that she thought Stouffer's made good macaroni and cheese. Until the day he realized that they'd been sleeping together for three months and she had never washed her sheets. After that he went home, put on Public Enemy, and stopped answering her phone calls.

The next girl Octavian lied to was Sheila. She was Cape Verdean, from Rhode Island, and never asked Octavian much about his family. He wasn't sure whether that was because she sensed his hesitancy or because she didn't actually care. She eventually left him to go home and marry her ex-boyfriend.

By the time Ramonda walked into Pan Asia where Octavian was working two years later, the Octavian Munroe who shook her hand had the only-child story down pat. Ramonda had long legs and skin that reminded Octavian of the chestnuts he used to stuff in his pockets as he walked home from school. She wore her copper-colored curls cut short to her head, and her smile was a wide half-moon. When they were introduced, she grasped his hand in her slender fingers, and for the rest of the day, her bright eyes danced at him when she caught him unable to look away.

Octavian didn't see her breasts on their first date, but he did learn that she, too, was in fact an only child. They fell in love hard and fast, and by the end of the summer, Ramonda had moved into Octavian's apartment. She was a graduate student at the University of Chicago, getting her PhD in Ethnomusicology, and she added her Bob Andy albums and rare South African pressed recordings of Hugh Masekela, and her John Lomax folk recordings from the 1940s, to Octavian's collection. She knew how to play the piano and the guitar, and she went to cello class on Thursday nights.

She inspired Octavian to paint again, to learn to play the trumpet. And it was her idea for him to sign up for an accelerated course to get his teaching certificate. Ramonda filled their home with beautiful things—fichus plants that she whispered to softly, scented candles in the shape of red pears, paintings of women with baskets on their heads from Dominica, where her grandmother still lived.

Octavian felt like the sorrow he had lived through until he was with her was worth it if she was the reward. The only problem was Francis. Even dead, Francis was still the problem. Octavian knew he had to tell Ramonda about him, knew that every day that passed was another day he was lying to her, but each morning that he rolled over and saw her arm thrown over her head like she was desperately trying to make a point, he was filled with such unbridled gratitude that she was there and such a stomach-clenching fear that she would go that he couldn't do it.

Then, one afternoon in April, Octavian came home and Ramonda said, "Someone named Ivy called. Asked that you call him, said it was urgent."

"Ivy?"

"That's what he said. Sounded sort of like a white boy."

"That's my boy from St. Louis," Octavian said. "He is sort of like a white boy. He said it was urgent?"

"I didn't know you had white friends in St. Louis," she said.

Octavian already held the receiver in his hand and he stopped dialing to look at her. "Why wouldn't I?"

Ramonda shrugged.

"You never had any white friends?"

"Not really," she said and turned back to the book in her lap. "It's not a big deal, is it?"

Octavian shook his head and finished dialing the number. Ivy's mother was dead, that much Octavian got through his inconsolable weeping. Other than that, he could only make out Ivy's repeated request that he come home for the funeral. "I know you don't like to come home, but I can't do it without you, Tave," he said. "If your brother were here, I wouldn't ask, but you know, he's gone too."

Octavian hung up the phone and said to Ramonda, "I have to go home."

"Home?"

"I mean to St. Louis."

"You told me you were never going back there."

"Ivy's mom died. He wants me to come to her funeral."

Ramonda closed her book and got up from the couch. She walked into the kitchen. "Some guy named Ivy you've never talked about needs you to come to his mother's funeral?"

Octavian followed her. "I'm sure I talked about Ivy to you before. He's one of my best friends, he was definitely my . . ."

Ramonda pulled a box of guava juice out of the fridge. "Your what?"

The words *my brother's best friend* stuck in Octavian's mouth like a clot of blood. He would have to tell her. He knew this. But not now. He would tell her when he came back.

"I'll come with you," she said, taking a glass from the cupboard.

"You don't have to do that, baby," Octavian said.

She put a loving hand on Octavian's arm. "If it's that important, I want to."

My Friend

A S SOON AS OCTAVIAN walked Ramonda into Rahsaan's, he wished he had brought her there sooner. Not only did her eyes light up as she began to search through the vinyl, but Brendon—who still helped out Bones on the weekends—took one look at her and nearly fell on the floor. Both he and Bones made fools of themselves following Ramonda around, dashing off to seek out rare recordings she was looking for, smiling up in her face when she clapped after Bones found a mint condition Smart Nkansah & His Super Sweet Talks album she'd never heard of.

Octavian managed to pull them both aside and asked them not to bring up Francis, giving them the excuse he'd given Cyrus the night before about her having bad experiences with friends and drugs and said, as matter-of-factly as possible, that it was simply something they didn't discuss.

Bones gave Octavian a look, but Brendon said, "Whatever, man. Do what you have to do to hold on to that one. She is F-I-N-E."

Before the funeral, Octavian tried to run the same lines on Ivy, but Ivy's lens of devastation was so thick he couldn't even see his way through more than a few words of conversation before disintegrating again, so Octavian gave up.

They stayed for two nights, and on the last night, Octavian and Ramonda lay in the same bed where Octavian and Mina had once lain with Francis and made jokes about Michael Jackson. They listened to Jimi Hendrix, and Octavian's heart filled with sadness. He longed for Francis in a way he hadn't since before he died. He wanted him there, with them right then, teasing Octavian about how in love he was.

"I'm hungry," Ramonda said and rolled over on her side so her long body was closer to his. "You all, excuse me, *y'all* got anything good to eat in this town or what? And don't tell me about that damn Imo's Pizza. I had some of that last night at Ivy's house after the funeral and it was nasty."

"You're crazy," Octavian said. "Imo's is the shit."

"The shit is right," she said. "And I don't mean that in a nice way."

"How about toasted raviolis?" Octavian said. "I bet you've never had those before."

Ramonda scrunched up her nose and said, "That does sound kinda good. Do we have to drive somewhere far to get them?"

"Nope," Octavian said and sat up. "We can walk right to Blueberry Hill. And I can beat you at darts while we're there."

They walked hand in hand down toward Delmar, and Octavian felt St. Louis tugging hard at his heart. Made him wonder if maybe they couldn't come back more often. He pushed open the heavy door of Blueberry Hill and there sat Bones, Brendon, and Ivy in their favorite straight-backed booth right in the front. When they saw him, they yelled his name in unison.

Ramonda smiled her half-moon smile and said, "Damn, babe, you're like Norm from *Cheers*."

Quickly, they shifted around to make room and Brendon stood up to offer his seat to Ramonda. A voice from behind Octavian said, "You got room in there for me, too, big B?"

Octavian turned and saw a heavy-eyed Evan—who, for a moment, didn't recognize Octavian. But then he said, "Oh shit, Tave, is that you?"

Octavian took in Evan—his ragged shirt, his aging skin. "Hey, man," he said and smiled.

Evan grabbed Octavian by the back of the neck and hugged him, pounding his fists gently into Octavian's back.

They sat. Evan acknowledged Ramonda with a nod and Octavian felt her stiffen next to him.

"Ay yo, Ivy man," Evan slurred, "I know your mom's died and all, but how 'bout we celebrate this motherfucker Tave finally gracing us with his presence?"

Ivy, who was lucid now that his mother was in the ground and he had enough beers in him, raised his bottle and said, "To Tave."

Octavian looked at Ramonda. She was smiling again and she raised her glass of water and lemon to him and winked.

Bones went to the jukebox and soon the restaurant was filled with the funky sound of KC and the Sunshine band singing "I Get Lifted." Octavian thought about Mina and wondered if Bones remembered how much she loved that song. Drinks and toasted raviolis, fried mushrooms and hot wings arrived, and within moments Evan and Ivy began reminiscing about old times. Octavian shot Bones a look, but he shrugged. No one had briefed Evan or Ivy that the topic of Francis was off limits, and it didn't take long for it to circle back around.

"Yo, Tave, remember that night when your brother put fifty bucks' worth of quarters in the jukebox and we were up in here, jukebox DJ'ing all night?" Evan said.

"Hell yeah," Ivy laughed. "What about that time Tave had to go rescue him from where he was hiding in the closet of that older woman he was kickin' it with, after her husband came home?"

"I remember that," Brendon said. "Tave had to knock on the door talking about how he was raising money for the football team or some shit. Meanwhile, I was back there trying to help Frankie's uncoordinated ass climb out a window."

Octavian didn't look at Ramonda. He knew he should have gotten up, should have said goodnight and walked home with Ramonda's hand in his. Then he could have laid his broken soul bare. But in that hard-backed booth, with Chuck Berry looking down from where he stood outlined in neon on the wall, Octavian felt Frankie's smile arch over him and he wanted to sit in its warmth for a few minutes more. He ordered another drink, and let Ramonda's fried ravioli lay cold and untouched in the plastic basket with the red-and-white plaid paper.

For the entire train ride back to Chicago, Octavian talked. He told her everything about Francis, about looking for him in Eastgate, about Prince, about how Francis died. Ramonda stared out the smudged window at the dirty backs of Illinois towns and said nothing. When they got home, she locked herself in the bathroom, turned on the shower, and wept. An hour later, she came out. Octavian reached for her, but she gently pressed his arms away and tried to meet his eyes.

"I hope you know," she said, "that I would never lie like that to you."

"I know," he said. "I'm sorry."

She lifted her wet eyes and Octavian felt something inside him crumble. "I wish I could have met him."

Neither of them mentioned it again and Octavian went back to thinking he was the luckiest man alive. That was until he came home from work one night at the end of summer to find her on the couch, her lovely head in her hands. Octavian thought of death right away. Her grandmother in Dominica maybe, her uncle in Detroit. Cyrus.

"No," she said. "No one has died."

"Then what is it?"

"I got the Fulbright," she said.

"The scholarship? That's great, baby. Why do you look like the world has come to an end?"

She shifted her legs underneath her and dropped her hands. "Because it means we have to say goodbye and I wasn't ready for that to happen. Not yet." She stared down at her lap.

Octavian felt his heart race as it had been doing more since they got back from St. Louis. "I don't understand."

Ramonda gave him an exasperated look. "Octavian, I am going to Zimbabwe for two years."

"So?" he said. "I can wait for two years. I'll visit you. Shit, I'll even go with you."

Without looking up, she said, "I don't want you to come with me and I don't want you to wait."

The words were loud in their now dark space and Octavian barely heard what she said next.

"Tave, you know how I am. I need to devote myself to my work, entirely. I need to become a resident. I can't do that with my American boyfriend in tow."

"Wait a second," Octavian said, shaking his head against his own thoughts. "When you applied, we agreed that if you got it, we would work something out."

A shadow moved across Ramonda's face. "That was before."

"Before what?"

"Before . . . before, I don't know. Before I found out that you are this whole other person you neglected to tell me about." She looked away. "I'm sorry," she said. "I tried to let it go. Really I did, but I just can't."

"Ramonda," Octavian said, but she shook her head.

"Octavian, it has been three months since we got home and you still don't ever talk about Francis. It's like he never existed and yet I can see now how he haunts you. Maybe you're okay with living with a ghost, but I'm not."

Octavian felt his insides drop into a reservoir of confusion. He sat down on the edge of the couch. He wished he could find the words to explain something, but he wasn't even sure what he wanted her to understand. One look at Ramonda and he knew it was pointless. She was going, no matter what he said.

"When do you leave?" he asked.

Ramonda sat back into the couch. "Next week. I need to go back to Connecticut first and get my recording equipment from my mother's."

Octavian stood up and walked over to the window. He looked down at the wide, dark-green summer leaves of the giant old oak tree that grew behind their building. He never did tell Ramonda about his heart. In the beginning, it hadn't mattered because he was sure she'd cured him, and now that it beat wildly in his chest, there was no use in explaining. It would be just another thing he neglected to tell her, another lie. He turned away and walked into the bedroom, leaving the door cracked open in case she changed her mind.

She didn't. In the morning, Octavian found her asleep on the couch with her books spread across the floor beneath her. He crouched down close to her face and memorized her chin, her soft eyelashes, the curve of her nose. He slid one of his hands under hers and felt the dry creases of her knuckles, the cool metal of her rings. Finally, he stood up and went into the kitchen where he wrote down the address where she should leave her keys.

Shook Ones
Part II

ON SEPTEMBER II, 2001, Mina clutched two-year old Riley and newborn Chloe against her as she sat in front of the television in their apartment in the Bronx, and watched the Twin Towers crumble over and over again. Gone were her remaining romantic notions about being a hustler's wife. In reality, she was nothing more than the unfortunate neighborhood white woman who pushed her baby's stroller up and down 245th Street with her snarl-headed toddler in tow. Since Riley's birth, Mina had begun to pressure Rubio to find what she called a real job, but he refused. For hours at night she sat alone, holding their baby and wondering what would happen if he'd got arrested, or worse.

A month after the towers went down, Rubio announced that she was right. It was time to call it quits. They were going to move to Boston so he could open a bar with his boy Angel. Mina agreed without question. She'd never been to Boston, but she'd go anywhere if it meant he was going to stop hustling and be legal. Plus, she was tired of New York.

A week before they were supposed to leave, Rubio came home with a cell phone for Mina, and Mina's friend Marisol, who lived downstairs, taught Mina how to text.

"You ain't never checked Rubio's text messages?" Marisol asked.

Mina shook her head.

Marisol rolled her eyes. "You better do that before you up and move out to fucking Boston."

While Riley watched Sesame Street, Mina checked Rubio's phone and learned all there was to know about Katie. A white girl. Irish. From New Jersey. They were madly in love.

If Mina were Marisol, she'd call up Katie and threaten to scratch her eyeballs out or blow up her car, and if she were Chula, who now lived around the block from Mina, she might actually do it. But Mina could only put the phone back in its spot next to the television and pick up Chloe, who'd begun to fuss. She pulled out her already withered twenty-seven-year-old breast and placed her less-sore nipple into the baby's mouth. Outside the window, the 4 Train rumbled along elevated tracks through the hazy concrete sky. The idea of spending another day in that sad apartment was worse than the unknown of going to Boston. Mina convinced herself that if Rubio wanted to move, Katie must not be anything serious and she pushed Katie's name out of her mind.

In Boston, with Rubio snoring on the couch, boxes still unpacked, Mina couldn't shake a nagging feeling. She locked herself in the bathroom with Rubio's phone and found out that when Rubio said he wanted to stop hustling, to move to Boston and open a bar, what he meant was that having a girlfriend *and* a wife would be simpler if they lived in different states.

The next night, after she put the girls to bed, Mina sat down next to Rubio at the folding table they had set up in their new, empty kitchen and told him that she knew about Katie.

Rubio nodded and pushed himself back from the table, but didn't say anything.

"Why?" Mina asked.

Rubio looked at her the way he used to when he sat across the table from her at the Palm and watched her eat the rib eye he convinced her to get.

"Because she loves me," he said.

"Do you love her?"

Rubio shook his head. "I love you," he said. "Since the moment I laid eyes on you in that club. But you've never been in love with me. Not really."

Mina started to protest, but Rubio held up his hand to stop her. "Sure, you love where I come from and the stories I have to tell about the real shit I've seen—shit that you've only heard about in songs. But you've never actually been in love with *me*. Katie, she's in love with me. Not because I'm Puerto Rican and from the South Bronx, or because she thinks it makes her down to be with someone like me. She's not like you."

"She's white," Mina said.

Rubio shook his head and laughed a little. "Yeah," he said leaning toward Mina, "but she doesn't think that being with a black guy, or a Puerto Rican guy, or listening to Mobb Deep, means she's not white no more." Rubio sat back again and lit a cigarette.

Mina stood up and walked over to the sink. He was right. But he was no better than she was. He wasn't anymore in love with Mina than she was with him. They'd both fallen in love with the ideas of who they thought the other one was, not the real person. With her back still to him, she said, "Maybe we should get a divorce."

"Divorce?" he said.

The air in the room went thin and sharp and Mina turned around. She saw the flare of his nostrils, the clench of his jaw. Quickly, he stood up and hurled his order of *carne guisada* across the room. He screamed, "You want a fucking divorce?"

"Rubio," she said, trying to keep her voice calm.

"Here I am telling you I love you and you talking about a divorce? How about this, instead of a divorce, I just burn the whole fucking house down with us in it?" Rubio picked up his chair and held it over his head, but before he could swing it, Mina ran into the bathroom and locked the door. She thought he would surely pick the lock, or even break it down, but instead she heard nothing until the front door slammed and he drove away.

The next morning, Rubio was still gone. Mina knocked on the door of Mama Nora, the Dominican woman who lived in the duplex next door and, in her best halting Spanish, Mina asked her if she could watch Chloe for a few hours. Mama Nora happily agreed.

Mina drove Riley to her new preschool and explained that Daddy hadn't meant those things he'd said after Mina thought Riley was asleep, but the sharpness of her three-year-old's eyes in the rearview mirror told her she didn't believe her. Mina took Riley into preschool and smiled at the softhearted teachers before she got in her car and cried. Then she swallowed the tears, the guilt, the wounds on her pride, and called Kanta. Mina told her what she was able to say without crying.

"And don't say, 'I told you so,'" Mina said. "Because I know you did."

Kanta sighed, but she didn't say "I told you so." Instead she gave her a list of instructions. The same ones she gave to her clients. Mina went through the motions with little hope. She made phone calls, found the library, wrote a resume, emailed the addresses that the woman with the nasal voice from the Barnard Office of Career Services sent her. Three days later, Rubio appeared in the living room with a bouquet of flowers and new dolls for the girls. Riley promptly threw hers on the floor and broke it, and Chloe burst into tears.

"I'm getting a job," Mina said that night while Rubio lay in the bedroom watching TV like the word *divorce* had never been said, like there wasn't a beef-stew stain on the wall in the kitchen.

"Who's going to take care of my kids?"

"Riley's going to preschool and Mama Nora said she'd watch Chloe."

"Good," Rubio said. "Maybe she can cook me some real dinner, too."

The following weekend, he was gone again. This time he left without slamming the door. And so it went for months. Mina took a temp job as the receptionist at a small children's book publishing company and breathed much easier on the weekends. When he was gone, she took her kids to the playground and got takeout Indian food.

After a year, Mina's temporary job became permanent. She was skilled at faxing and fielding phone calls and so when she answered the phone one morning and a familiar voice asked to speak with Mina Rose, not Mina Figueroa, the pencil in her hand immediately stopped twirling.

"This is Mina Rose," she said.

"Hey, girl. Damn, I've been trying to find you forever."

"Clarissa, is that you?" Mina said. "How did you find me? Where are you?"

"Believe it or not, I'm at Rahsaan's right now," she said. "I came into town and was visiting Bones. I told him I'm heading out to Boston next week and he said we had to call you."

The other line rang and Mina put Clarissa on hold. When she switched back, it wasn't Clarissa's voice she heard, but Bones's.

"Is that my Mina girl?"

Mina's eyes filled with tears at the sound of his thick voice and she quickly reached for the box of Kleenex that sat squarely between her pile of Post-It notes and the framed photo of the girls taken in the portrait studio of JC Penney right before they left the Bronx.

"Hey, Bones," she said and cleared her throat. "How'd you know I was in Boston?"

"Dang, girl, don't you know who I am? I stay keepin' tabs on you, even if you don't want me to. How you been? Don't tell me you're no Red Sox fan."

What could she say? That she had a cheating husband, an angry toddler, and a baby who spent more time with the old lady next door than she did with her? So she said, "Don't worry, Bones. I'll never be a Red Sox fan."

"Well, Ima put your girl back on. She over here trippin', because I knew you was in Boston and she didn't. Ima call you again, okay? You got a real phone number or should I call you at work?"

Mina gave Bones her cell phone number and wondered if, since Bones knew how to find her, he also knew how to find Octavian.

"Love you, girl," he said.

"Love you, too, Bones."

Clarissa was coming to Boston. Next week, she said. Going to a conference at MIT.

"Jesus, that sounds really grown-up," Mina said.

"You're the one with two babies. I'd say that's grown-up," Clarissa said and laughed. "And you better believe Auntie Clarissa is going to spoil the shit out of them."

"Will you be here over the weekend?"

"I can be, why?"

"Weekends are better."

Bag Lady
(Radio Edit)

CLARISSA'S LARGE FRAME IN Mina's doorway was more powerful than she remembered. She folded Mina into a hug, and when Mina felt the soft flesh of Clarissa's arms, smelled the deep familiar smell of her Nivea cream, and heard the low echo of her laugh in her chest, Mina didn't want to be a mother anymore. She didn't want to make it work with Rubio anymore. She simply wanted to let her spine collapse into a pile so that she wouldn't ever have to stand up again.

Riley's voice shook her. "Mom," she said, "what's going on?" Mina let go and waited for her structure to implode, but it didn't.

Clarissa let out a squeal and Riley's little body disappeared into that same smothering hug and came out smiling.

For the next hour, Clarissa sat on the floor listening to Erykah Badu and played with Riley. And when Chloe woke up, Clarissa pulled the baby onto her wide lap and turned pages in a board book and wiped the drool from Chloe's chin with the back of her sleeve without missing a beat in their memory game. Mina watched her and thought she had been like that once. Down on the floor, immersed in Riley's imaginary world of cheerleaders and dragons and dolphins who sang. That was before Chloe. No wonder Riley was always so ready to push her little sister out of the way.

"You want some tea, Riss? Coffee?"

Without taking her eyes off the game, she said, "Coffee would be awesome. I'm exhausted. I've talked more today than I did for a week at that conference. I do not know how you do this every single day."

Mina went into the kitchen, where the yellow paint peeled off the walls, and boiled water in a saucepan. She took the coffee sock out of the drawer and the bag of Cafe Bustelo from the cabinet. At one point she thought making her coffee like the old Puerto Rican ladies made her less of a white girl. But now, she couldn't remember why the coffee sock would have changed that. It was just another one of those things she'd collected for so long—the coffee sock, the lyrics to "My Philosophy," the memorized Audre Lorde poems, the recipe for *arroz con gandules*—all of which were now lost somewhere beneath the toys.

Clarissa sat down at the kitchen table. Mina turned and tried to smile, but she failed so she sat down instead.

"Shit, girl," Clarissa said reaching over to take Mina's hand. "Is it that bad?"

"Worse," Mina said. The truth tasted like chalk on her tongue. "Where's he at?"

"With his girlfriend in New Jersey. He'll be back tomorrow."

"What, are y'all like divorced parents or some shit? You have him for the week, she's got him on the weekends?"

Mina nearly spit out her coffee, the laugh came out of her so fast and unannounced. Then the two of them laughed the way they did when they were kids. Laughed so hard their bodies shook and tears streamed from their eyes.

When they finally stopped, Clarissa said, "Mina, what the fuck are you doing?"

The lines between Mina's eyes pulled tight. "I don't know," she said.

"What do you mean you don't know? You know you deserve better than this."

"Do I? I knew what I was doing, so isn't this exactly what I deserve?"

The foreign sound of her mother's laughter had brought Riley to the door.

Before Mina could tell her to go on, Clarissa said, "Baby girl, can you go in there and get Candy Land set up? Auntie'll be right in to play with you."

Riley considered her mother carefully before she nodded.

"Listen, if this is what you want," Clarissa said, "you got to tell me. Because if it is, I won't say shit. Some women like this kind of arrangement, and if that's who you are, then . . ."

"This isn't what I want," Mina said quickly. "I don't really care about me, but I don't want my girls to grow up thinking this is what marriage is supposed to be." Mina wrapped her hands around the coffee mug and looked into the living room where her girls were now fighting over blocks. From the television set, Barney gave them directions to clean up, which they ignored.

"How'd you even wind up with him in the first place?" Clarissa said. "I mean, I never pictured you with a guy that treated you bad, for real."

"In the beginning he treated me better than anyone ever has. But then slowly, he started to fuck with me, you know? And I kept thinking that if I just did this or that or changed the way I dressed or looked, things would go back to being the way they used to be. By the time I realized they never would, I was so deep in it, I didn't know how to get out. And then I got pregnant. I wasn't going to marry him at first, but then I felt like I should. For the baby and all."

Clarissa nodded and Mina took a long, deep breath.

"And since I didn't want Riley to grow up an only child the way I did, I had Chloe. Funny thing is, all they do is fight."

Mina felt the hot tears in her eyes and Clarissa took her hand again. "This isn't you, Mina," she said.

"I don't know, Riss," Mina said. "I have no idea who I am anymore. I forgot how to be the Mina I was a long time ago. Now I'm pretty sure she's gone."

Clarissa reached over and wiped away Mina's tears with the back of her hand. "She's not gone, I just saw her. When you laughed so hard like that, it was like we were back at Rahsaan's laughing at some stupid shit Bones said."

"Auntie," Riley called from the living room. "Do you want to be blue or red?"

Clarissa stood up and said, "Girl, I'm from the North Side of St. Louis. I definitely cannot be red." She threw up a crip sign and Mina laughed.

"See," Clarissa said. "There you are again."

Mina stood up and took their cups to the sink. She turned on the water. Outside the dirty window, the neighbor's German shepherd, who made it impossible for her children to play in the patch of backyard, paced the chain-link fence. Slowly Mina rinsed the sock clean of coffee grounds and placed it upside down next to the sink to dry.

2014

THE WAY FROM BONES'S one-story shoebox house in Dogtown to Rahsaan's was simple and familiar, like the scent of a loved one. Often on the drive, Bones would let his mind wander, and look up and already be in Rahsaan's parking lot next to Fred's truck. But on this morning, Bones made an effort to think about what he passed. It was too early even for the teachers, the janitors, the sleepless secretaries to be on the road. The rounded edges of the hills across the golf course of Forest Park glowed gold with the sunrise, and Skinker Boulevard spread wide in an empty, elegant expanse. Bones took a deep breath.

"God, I love this town," he said.

He stopped at the light on the corner where Talayna's Pizza used to be. Talayna's opened up just about the same time as Rahsaan's, and, back in the day, Bones used to pick up a pie at least three times a week. He never thought it would close. Now it was a coffee shop with Wi-Fi and wood tables made to look like trees.

Bones pulled into the back lot of Rahsaan's so early that Fred wasn't even there yet. He chuckled as he unlocked the door. He could probably count on one hand the times he'd beat Fred to work.

The darkness of the back of his store was like his own face. He didn't need lights to see the wiry hair of his eyebrows, the heavy flesh of his cheeks, the stiffness of his beard. Likewise, he knew there was a rack of 45s to the left of the door, a long row of tapes to the right. Behind those were the boxes of rolled-up posters stacked like matchsticks. Still, something felt strange and made him flick the switch flooding the storeroom with light. In the corner, he saw a blue sleeping bag and inside it a sleeping body, neither of which were part of the original design.

Whoever had trespassed so willfully on his storeroom floor was unmoved by the bright lights and continued to sleep peacefully. When Bones got closer, he saw dark eye shadow smeared and stuck in the creases of his closed eyelids, painted mouth slack, a small circle of drool on his pillow. Adam. With his home pillow, Bones thought. Pillowcase with flowers on it and shit. Sleeping bag straight from sleep-away camp. Bones knew the boy should be getting up, getting ready for school. According to his mother, and his boyfriend Marcus who also worked at Rahsaan's, Adam hadn't been home in days.

"Hey," Bones said and gave Adam's shoulder a nudge. "Hey, wake up."

Adam groaned at first, then his eyes flew wide.

"Time for school," Bones said.

Adam sat up nervously. "Hey, Bones."

"Umm-hmm. Now that I found you, you know you gotta go home," Bones said.

"Can't," Adam said.

"What you can't do is keep on sleeping on my floor and making folks who love you worry."

"She worries anyway."

"Shouldn't she?"

Adam slid his thin, bare legs out of the sleeping bag and picked up a pair of black leggings that were next to his pillow. That's when Bones saw it. His Walther pistol. It had been underneath the leggings.

"What the fuck are you doin' with my gun?" Bones said.

Adam didn't answer.

Bones rushed over and grabbed the gun. "What're you doin' with my gun, Adam? Plannin' some crazy-ass white-boy school shooting?"

"God, no," Adam said.

"What then? Going to kill yourself or somethin'?"

In the quiet of the storeroom, Bones heard Adam swallow back a sob, saw his skinny shoulders start to shake. Bones's mind was muddled.

"Alright, alright," he said. "You don't gotta go to school. You can stay here one more day, but then you gotta go home."

Adam kept his face turned toward the wall and Bones remembered that commercial he'd seen. The one where celebrities told young gay kids that things get better, and so he said, "It won't always be this way. Take it from me, I know. You'll be grown before you know it, be able to make your own decisions, do your own thing."

Adam turned around. Tears ran with his makeup down his pale cheeks. "I'm not crying because kids bully me at school, or because my mom doesn't know I'm gay, Bones," he said. "Shit, I've been dealing with that my whole life. I'm crying because you're closing the goddamn store."

"You tryna kill yourself over Rahsaan's?"

Adam took a deep, frustrated breath. "Bones, Rahsaan's is the only place I can go where it doesn't matter if I am straight, gay, boy, girl, black, white. And this is St. Louis. That shit matters everywhere. Especially at my shitty, white, all-boys private school."

"I know that's right," Bones said.

"No, you don't, Bones. You know how that kid got killed in Ferguson?"

Bones nodded.

"At my school, they call him the n-word, except they actually say it, and they say he deserved to be killed. They say that they hope other n-words get killed too. And I sit there, I sit there and I think about Mr. Nance, and I think about Marcus, who I love more than anything in this world, and I say nothing." He was sobbing now, the words barely making it out beyond his throat.

"Slow down, Adam," Bones said. "Take a breath."

Adam blinked hard and swallowed. "And now, you're taking Rahsaan's away, making it about money, making it about you. It has never been about you, Bones. Rahsaan's is about us. Don't you fucking know that by now?"

Bones waited until the echoes of Adam's yelling stopped bouncing around the room. He swallowed down the bile that rose in his throat. "Rahsaan's stopped being that place a long time ago," he said.

"No, it didn't." Adam stood up and walked around the room, his thin feet barely touching the cold cement floor. "If you weren't so busy feeling sorry for yourself in your office, you'd know."

"Adam, can you stop pacing?" Bones said. "And put on some shoes? There's broken shit in here."

Adam stopped and stared at Bones. "You think this is a joke, don't you?"

"I don't think it's a joke," Bones said calmly. "I just think you have no idea what you're talking about."

Adam was still staring at Bones. "Okay, how about this. If I promise not to do what I planned with that gun of yours, if I even promise to go back home, just like this—bad makeup and all, will you work the register for the whole day, like you say you used to? Watch who comes in the door. It won't only be Mr. Nance, it'll be Suzie, the girl from the Chinese grocery down at the end of Delmar who loves Coldplay even though her parents punish her for listening to any kind of American music."

"Coldplay is British," Bones said.

Adam ignored him and said, "Daron, from City Hall up the street, he's gay but has been married to the same woman for thirty years. Daron loves '70s funk and soul. And Jenny, who goes to Fontbonne and has pink hair and a face full of piercings. We can't

keep a Cure record in here for longer than a day because of her."
He stopped and took a deep breath. "If you promise me you'll
work the register, so you can see that things aren't as bad as you
think they are, then I'll go home right now."

Now it was Bones's turn to look away. He knew it wouldn't matter. In front at the register or behind the closed door of his office,
nothing was going to change the bottom line. But he gave the boy
a crooked half-smile.

"You got yourself a deal."

A wide grin filled Adam's face and he thrust his small hand out
to Bones. But Bones stood up and walked past the extended hand,
gathered the boy up in a hug.

"Go on home," he said. "Go and see your mama."

Adam nodded and walked slowly toward the back door. When
he got there, he stopped and said, "She may send me right back—
you know, when she sees me like this."

"Well, you'll know where to find me. Right behind the register."

Adam wiped his eyes one more time and closed the door
quickly behind him.

Bones sat back on the stool and turned the Walther over in his
hands. He pictured Adam sprinting down Melville, his tiny black-
legginged legs a blur beneath him, running up those steps to his
mama and whatever she may think about him without his yarmulke,
makeup smeared on his face, dirt under his fingernails from sleeping on the hard cement floor of the Rahsaan's Records storeroom.

He thought about what Adam said and wished it actually mattered. But he knew little Jenny from Fontbonne was not going to
get him out of debt buying up his Cure records.

The back door creaked open again and Bones looked up to see
Fred. "Hey there, Dr. Long," Bones said.

"Morning, Jim," Fred said. "Everything alright?"

Bones saw how he must look—sitting alone in the storeroom
with a gun in his lap, and he started to laugh, but then he started
to cry. He held up his hand to Fred in hopes it might hold back
the sobs that shook his whole body, but it was no use.

Fred stayed frozen at the door and said, "Jimmy, take a deep breath and calm down now. It's not that bad."

But Bones's sobbing wouldn't allow for any type of breathing except the kind that choked him.

Fred walked slowly toward him and said, "How about you put the fucking gun on the floor, then, okay? You are not going out like this. Not with me watching anyway."

Bones gingerly lowered the gun to the floor and sat back up. He held his hands up in the air and managed to say, "I wasn't going to shoot myself, Fred."

Fred picked up the gun and put it on the table. "Why the fuck are you sitting in here with it then?" he said.

"God, it's too much," Bones said, wiping his eyes. "I can't explain, there's just too damn much." Bones leaned his head back. He had stopped crying, but his chest continued to heave. "Freddy, man, what's going to be left when Rahsaan's is gone? I mean, do you think anyone will remember? Will it even matter that it was here to begin with?"

Fred dragged another stool over so that the two of them sat face-to-face in the middle of the room. "I was going to wait, Jimmy," he said, "but I guess now's as good a time as any for me to say what I've got to say."

Bones got up and wiped his eyes, blew his nose in a paper towel, and sat back down on the stool. "Okay," he said, "lay it on me. Can't get any worse than shit is right now."

Fred hooked his feet on the rungs of the stool so that his long legs were folded into triangles and said, "I've been stealing from you, Bones."

"What?"

"For twenty years, I've been stealing from you. All in all, I've got about $250,000."

Bones got up and walked to the other side of the room to put distance between himself and Fred. Then he walked back. "Are you telling me that you stole a quarter of a million dollars from me? How is that possible? I've never even made that kinda money."

"Well, I didn't actually steal money," Fred said slowly. "I stole records. You know, rare shit that sellers brought in, collections belonging to grandparents and dead uncles. Those estate-sale boxes that get dropped at the door full of albums? I took 'em from you, Bones. Took 'em and sold 'em on the Internet for a whole lotta money to buyers in England, New York, and Japan. Mostly in Japan."

"What the hell are you talkin' about, the Internet? What do you mean, Japan?"

"Japanese cats, they love jazz, Bones," said Fred. "And, believe it or not, old fucking hip hop. And they'll pay more than you'd ever dream for good vinyl."

Bones felt like there was a cold, ice-blue fluid revolving in a slow circle through his veins. "How could you do me like that, Fred?" he asked.

Fred cleared his throat and said, "Bones, do you realize you haven't given me a raise in fifteen years? My ass could make more money working across the street at Starbucks, except no one's gonna hire me 'cause I'm too old. I've been working for you for forty years, Bones. I've been here so long, I can't work anywhere else. How could I do you like that? Gimme a fucking break, Jim." Fred scratched his forehead and looked at Bones. "I bet you don't even know what it is I do here," he said. "*I* place the orders. *I* do the fucking payroll. You don't do shit but stand around and be Bones. The fact that you didn't go under twenty years ago is because of me. So I fucking stole records. Records you wouldn't have even known what they were worth if I had shown 'em to you. Records that probably would still be on the shelf right now. I stole 'em and sold 'em. And now, I got a whole hell of a lot of money."

"Jesus H. Christ," Bones said, "I'm going to have a fucking heart attack. I'm serious."

"No, you're not, you goddamn drama queen," said Fred. "You're not going to have a heart attack, and you're not going to close the store, either. You're going to sell it to me."

"Sell it to you?"

"Well, sixty percent of it. We're going to be partners."

Bones stared hard at Fred and said, "You think you know a person, work with 'em for decades, and then come to find out they stealing your shit, right out from under your nose."

"Did you hear a fucking word I said, Bonesie? You don't have to close Rahsaan's."

"I don't understand how you could do it, Fred. I just don't get it."

Fred looked up at the ceiling as if he needed help from God. He placed his hands on Bones's big shoulders. "Bones," he said, "I don't have kids, I don't have a wife. Shit, I don't even have a mother anymore. I got Rahsaan's, my measly damn near minimum wage, and a quarter of a million fucking dollars. I'm going to pay off your goddamn debt, you're going to make me a partner. You still get to walk around in here and be big man, be Bones, *and* I'm going to make this place profitable. Like it used to be. Like it's supposed to be. Do you hear what I'm saying to you?"

Bones was quiet for a moment. "This has been one hell of a morning," he said. "You have no idea."

Fred took his hands from Bones's shoulders and dropped them to his sides.

"You mean to tell me, Freddy," Bones said, "that you made a quarter million dollars selling vinyl on the Internet?"

"I did."

Bones looked around the familiar storeroom that now seemed as if it were a brand-new place. "To Japanese cats?"

"Japanese cats."

"They dig jazz like that?"

"They do. And Big Daddy Kane."

>>>

A TEXT CAME THROUGH late at night and lit up Octavian's ceiling in Apple-blue light. Octavian rolled over and picked up his phone.

Mina Rose. After days of texting, it still did something to him to see her name. Their texts had been measured and careful, allowing for significant spans of time between them. Life going on implied.

WHERE DO YOU LIVE?

She was in Boston.

YOU'RE IN MAINE?

I GO TO BOSTON SOMETIMES. I WONDER IF WE EVER PASSED EACH OTHER ON THE STREET AND DIDN'T KNOW IT.

I THINK WE WOULD KNOW, DON'T YOU?

YEAH.

Octavian thought about how he could get into his car and see her in three hours. Something about that made his heart race differently. She was still real.

She had daughters, two of them.

He taught art. To troubled kids.

She went on his website and bought three mugs. One sky blue and white, one black with a deep turquoise interior, one dark gray. WE DRINK MORE COFFEE THAN WE SHOULD, she wrote.

HOW OLD?

FIFTEEN AND THIRTEEN.

HOW OLD WERE WE?

WHEN?

WHEN WE GOT TOGETHER?

NOT TOO FAR FROM FIFTEEN.

IS SHE LIKE US?

He tasted the honesty of his thoughts on his tongue as if he'd actually said the word *us* out loud.

SHE HIDES IN HER ROOM, LISTENS TO MUSIC AND READS COMIC BOOKS . . . JUST LIKE US.

WHAT ARE YOU LISTENING TO RIGHT NOW?

ODETTA. YOU?

ABOUT TO PUT ON THIS NEW PHAROAHE MONCH.

Soon, Octavian was taking his phone out during class to tell her about his students. Like when Brian, a kid with such severe OCD that he wore a new pair of white gloves every day, learned to throw pots. How he wrapped his pristine fingers around the clay and laughed.

She sent a picture of the cover of a children's book that the company she worked for had published because she thought he'd like the cover art. But he didn't look at the cover. He zoomed in on the blur of her fingers holding the sides. Her nails were no longer fake, but they weren't bitten down either. It was all he'd seen of her since Houston Street and he stared as if he might somehow be able to make out the rest of her.

Then there was the text that came through late at night that said that Bones was no longer closing the store and she asked if he would still go home. Outside the window next to his bed, the dark leaves that covered up the stars until the wind pushed them aside were beginning to fall. He liked the way his heart felt and liked her words on the phone screen, her address on his Ship To list.

I'M STILL GOING HOME, he wrote.

ME TOO.

Octavian lay in the dark and tried to picture Mina. Was her hair starting to gray like his? He was wondering if he should ask her when she wrote: REMEMBER THAT NIGHT AT SAPPHIRE LOUNGE, HOW YOU TOLD ME THAT THE ONLY REAL PART OF YOURSELF YOU HAD LEFT WERE YOUR MEMORIES WITH ME? I COULDN'T ADMIT IT THEN, BUT THAT'S THE WAY IT'S BEEN FOR ME SINCE I LEFT STL. IS THAT CRAZY? BECAUSE THAT WAS MORE THAN TWENTY YEARS AGO.

Octavian read the text three times and found himself wondering about her eyebrows. He wrote: NOT AS CRAZY AS THE FACT THAT EVEN THOUGH WE HAVEN'T TALKED THIS WHOLE TIME, YOU ARE STILL THE ONLY PERSON ON EARTH WHO ACTUALLY KNOWS ME.

HAS IT ALWAYS BEEN LIKE THIS WITH US, TAVE?

EVER SINCE THE 5TH GRADE.

Octavian pressed the send button and put the phone on the bedside table. He lay back down and watched the stars appear and disappear through the leaves before he curled himself around his heart and smiled. He was excited to go home.

> > >

THE STREETS OF FERGUSON were quiet. Octavian saw no signs of reporters or crowds, no signs of riot police or young boys with pants slung low. The voice of the GPS guided him past the somewhat new-looking one-story buildings, which were attached by a single long roof. Octavian wondered why urban planners didn't at least try to vary the color of paint from one front door to the next, why they didn't switch up the way the porches were set. Instead, the homes looked like they belonged on the planet Camazotz, from *A Wrinkle in Time,* where the people were programmed to think with the same external brain, and the children who bounced the ball differently from the others were sent away.

But, he thought, low-income housing was always angry and thoughtless. The grass around it was rough and brown, the attempts at spaces where folks could meet and talk were hard and broken. The walls showed early signs of tags and graffiti, and though many would blame those who lived there for defacing the property, they never felt the insult of living within cinder-block walls or the flat-out *fuck you* in the color of green paint in the hallway.

The night before, Cyrus sat Octavian down, poured both of them scotch in those same Waterford glasses that they'd used when Octavian got into Cooper Union, and began a long story, one that Octavian could tell he'd been planning for quite some time. One that included a woman from social services and his mother wearing an Ethiopian cross and a sundress. All of this to tell Octavian that he was not Francis's biological father.

He looked at Octavian with wet eyes and said, "Are you angry with me, Son?"

"No," Octavian said. "I'm not angry."

And he wasn't. In a way, Octavian was relieved. It took some of the shine off Cyrus's angel wings, but that allowed Octavian to believe that maybe he could, one day, be a man like his father. One who told lies and also one who told the truth.

"Is there anything else you want to know?" Cyrus asked.

Octavian shook his head. He thought about this version of his mother's history. The one that included her falling in love with a soldier who became a heroin addict who died in a white lady's bathtub, a needle stuck in his thigh, but he didn't need to know more. What Octavian needed was to hold his wounded brother, but he couldn't. And since he couldn't, he stood up and went to where he, thankfully, could still hold his trembling father.

Octavian pulled into the parking lot of the Ferguson Community Center and got out of the car. He stood for a moment watching people come and go, carrying in tables, carrying out signs. A group of young girls in sneakers and jeans, hair natural and pulled back, took boxes out of a van. A cluster of young men with serious expressions talked in low voices outside the front door.

Inside was as busy as outside. A group sat at a table making signs and others were counting and organizing water bottles. Beyoncé's "Flawless" played from someone's phone attached to a speaker. Across the room, Octavian saw Brendon giving directions to a man setting up camera equipment. His face lit up when he saw Octavian. He walked over and gave him a long hug.

"Man, is it good to see you," he said.

"You, too, B," Octavian said, looking at his old friend. "You look good. You're thin."

"Shit, I ain't thin, but I sure ain't what I used to be. Diabetes got me, man."

"Damn, I'm sorry. I didn't know."

"How would you? Your ass ain't been back in how long?"

Octavian couldn't remember.

"Yeah, well, the diabetes sucks, but it made me lose some weight. I got kids, man, I can't die. At least not yet." Brendon took out his phone and showed Octavian pictures of his children. Pride spread across his face.

"Wow," Octavian said. "Three boys?"

"Yeah, man. My house is crazy," he said and laughed.

303

An older woman with a lanyard around her neck and a shirt that read *Hands Up Don't Shoot* came over to ask Brendon something.

When Brendon turned back to Octavian, he said, "Can you sit for a second?"

"If you've got time, I know I do," Octavian said.

Brendon led him into a side room, where the walls were decorated with kids' drawings of jack-o-lanterns and witches cut out of construction paper.

"This is amazing, man," Octavian said.

"It's the revolution," Brendon said. "The shit is finally here." He laughed again.

It felt good to be with Brendon. To hear his easy laugh, see his big hands. "And you're right here in the middle of it," Octavian said.

"You goddamn right. Looks like we could have about a thousand people marching downtown on Saturday."

"Cyrus told me," Octavian said. "We'll be there."

"How's he doing?"

"He's exactly the same. Older, but the same. Thank God."

"You coming to Bones's I'm-closing-the-store-not-closing-the-store party?" Brendon asked.

"I wouldn't miss it either way."

"I'm so glad he's not closing Rahsaan's," Brendon said. "His ass woulda driven me crazy. Bones with no store?" Brendon looked at Octavian. "You know he woulda been up in my shit every day talkin' about, 'Hey, Bren, what you doin' today, baby pa? Wanna come smoke some reefer, listen to some blues?'"

Octavian laughed.

"And," Brendon said, "we lose places like Rahsaan's, we can't possibly win the war. You know what I'm saying?"

Octavian nodded. "Who else is coming to this party?" he asked.

"Ivy, of course. You know he works with me now? He's downtown organizing today, but he'll be there. And his daughter, remember Sunshine? She just graduated college. She's helping, too."

"Evan?"

"Ain't no one heard from Evan in a minute, but you never know where he'll turn up. And Mina. She's coming." Brendon stopped and raised an eyebrow at Octavian. "Have you talked to her?"

Before Octavian could answer, a young white man with a beard and a bun came to the door.

"Mr. Graves," he said, "can I bother you for a second?"

"Sure," Brendon said and got up. "Be right back, Tave."

Octavian was grateful for a moment to think about how to talk to Brendon about Mina. When Brendon came back, Octavian said, "We've been talking, Mina and I, I mean."

"Good."

"That's good?"

"I tell you what, man. I'm not sorry for what I said back then, because I believed it, but I will say that I understand now why you love her the way you do."

"I don't know that love, in the present tense, is the right term," Octavian said.

"Yes, it is. Because I love her. Not the way you do, but you know what I'm saying. What I didn't understand back then was that we were different. I was different, Mina was different."

"What do you mean?"

"Tell me something," Brendon said. "Outside of Rahsaan's, you ever met anyone else like me? Like Ivy? Like Mina? Like you? Like fucking Bones?"

Octavian thought for a minute and said, "Not really. I never had friends like y'all—black or white. It always seemed like I had to explain one side to the other."

"Exactly," Brendon said. "And that's why Bones can't close the store. Music is the one thing that can bring people together. It's what got all of us to know each other like we did."

Octavian nodded. "That's true."

"And it's what saved us, you know? I still think things started to go really bad for Francis, not when your mother died, but because he stopped being able to listen to music."

Octavian wished that, after more than twenty years, the wounds didn't still feel so fresh.

"Man, none of us knew how good we had it," Brendon went on. "I mean the way we hung out and everything. Wasn't until later, when everyone kinda went their separate ways and I started doing more work in the community, that I realized how rare it was that we knew each other like that. Shit, Ivy spent more nights at my house than his own. And now he talks to my mother more than I do. I can't tell you how many white folks tell me that I'm the only black person they've ever had a conversation with—they don't even talk to the people who work for them." Brendon leaned back in his chair. "And that's a lot of black people who've never even heard 'Hi, how are you' from a white person. You know how far a hill that is to climb when you're talking about bringing folks together?" He shook his head. "Shit, imagine Ivy never having had a conversation with a black person? Ivy don't barely know how to talk to white people. And Bones? And me? I couldn't come in here and do what I do if I hadn't come up going over to Evan's mother's house for Greek Easter and shit. I tell you, we were given a gift and we—including Mina, and me, and you—we didn't even know it."

"I never thought about it that way," Octavian said. "But you're right."

"I'll tell you what though, Tave," Brendon said, rubbing the back of his graying head. "Trying to get people to understand each other, to see themselves the way others see them and then actually put that shit to the side so that they can just talk? It's hard. Like, sometimes it feels impossible. And these are the people that *want* to talk, are here *to* talk to each other. Never mind everyone out there—black and white, who could care less about ever talking to the other. And how in the hell am I supposed to do that?"

"I don't know the answer to that," Octavian said. "But I do know that I've had more conversations with white folks about racism since Michael Brown got killed than I've had in my lifetime. And I live in Maine."

"Well, that's good to hear," Brendon said.

Octavian could see his friend's sad eyes through his thick glasses and he felt the weight of the world he'd abandoned for Brendon to carry on his own.

"I'm sorry, B," Octavian said. "I talked a lot of shit back in the day. I know I haven't been much help."

"Please," Brendon said. "Teaching art to kids? That's, like, the most revolutionary thing you can do. What sucks is, no matter how much I work, or you work, or Ivy works, no matter how many people take to the streets, won't none of it bring back Michael Brown. No matter how many hoodies we wear, ain't none of us actually Trayvon Martin. Those young men are still gone. And there will be more. Before this comes to an end, if it ever comes to an end, there will be so many more. I talked a good game about the revolution, but real talk, this is not easy."

Outside the door, the group of young girls laughed and drew on poster board with colored markers. Octavian nodded and thought about what Mina used to always say: "Nothing important ever is."

>>>

MINA AND HER DAUGHTERS arrived in St. Louis and went directly to Rahsaan's, where Bones clutched them to his chest and crooned. Then Mina handed each girl twenty dollars and didn't say a word when Chloe used hers to buy a Taylor Swift poster.

That evening, standing in front of Cyrus's apartment building, Mina remembered that there were forty-two steps from the sidewalk to the front door. Octavian once told her that when he was little, he counted them every day when he came home from school.

"I got superstitious when my mom got sick," he said. "And since she loved Jackie Robinson, and his number was forty-two, I used to count the steps every time I went up or down. Thought something bad would happen if I didn't. Even though she's gone, I still do it."

They had been standing in front of the building and he'd taken her hand. "Count them," he said.

Now Mina stood at the bottom. Above her, the yellow lamplight shone down from the second-story window. Octavian was in there. Octavian. Octavian *and* Cyrus. But not Francis. Mina felt the distance she had put between herself and that sorrow for more than twenty years as she put her foot on the first step. She counted: one.

At the front door of the building, she pushed the bell for apartment five. Her same finger, the same bell. How could it feel like it always did when so much had changed?

Octavian came down in bits. She saw his shoes first, then his legs, and then he was there, on the other side of the door. Big, wide eyes. Octavian smile. He opened the door and immediately she was gathered in his arms.

She took a breath. "Tave," she said.

"Hey," he said and pressed his forehead into hers. "Hey, Mina girl."

ACKNOWLEDGMENTS >>>

First and foremost, I would like to acknowledge Lezley McSpadden, Michael Brown, Sr., and all of Michael Brown, Jr.'s family and friends. This is a fictional story, but Michael Brown, Jr. was a very real and treasured person. I hope I have honored his memory by including him here.

To the amazing people of Amberjack Publishing: Dayna Anderson, thank you for believing in this story from its infancy and welcoming it back as an awkward teenager. Cassandra Farrin, you are the ultimate dream editor. I feel so fortunate to have been able to work with you and even more fortunate to know you're in the world. Cherrita Lee, thank you for being so supportive at every turn. Reema Zaman, you are an incredible beacon of light who is changing the world one heart at a time. I hope someday to have the words to express how much your immediate sisterhood means to me.

To my beautiful family: Pop, I cannot wait to put a copy of this book in your hands. Everything I love about reading and writing comes from you. Thank you for always being a kind and loving father. To my mom, thank you for all of your beams, for reading everything I write, and for being whatever I need, whenever I need it. To my brothers and sister, thanks for loving and accepting me in the way only siblings can. Abigail Ortiz, thank you for holding and loving me as we continuously come to terms with all the painful and joyous truths. John Ortiz, thank you for the best dang book title ever. Dan and Carol Goodenough, thank you for teaching me the value of boundaries and unconditional love. To Sine Berhanu, I owe much of who I am to the mother you've always been to me. Ma and Jack, thank you for your continued guidance and your constant love. And to Roland Paul Everett, we miss you every day. We wish we could hear your laugh and see your dimpled smile as you enjoy your wonderful nieces. You remain loved and cherished, always.

To my incredible sister friends: Saaba Lutzeler, you were with me as I wrote every page of this book. May I always have the honor of being the Thea to your Saab. To Jennifer Tseng, thank you for the milky tea, for making me laugh and always believing in the writer in me. Jessica Roddy, I feel so lucky to call myself loved by you. Thank you for the pizza, the cursing, and the raising of daughters. Pilar Gizzi, thank you for always seeing me the way I wanted to see myself. And Tasha Green, thanks for bringing babies into the world with me when we were babies, and for always, always being there.

To the brilliant writers and creators who have shown me so much love: Pam & Harry Belafonte, Hanif Abdurraqib, T Kira Madden, Alison C. Rollins, Leesa Cross-Smith, Bret Anthony Johnston, Naomi Jackson, Marcus Moore, and Alonzo Lee. And the journals that took a chance on my work: *Disclaimer Magazine, Slush Pile Magazine, The New Engagement Journal,* and *Anti-Heroin Chic.*

To my St. Louis folks: Tom Ray, thank you for selling me my first record and for creating and maintaining the amazing space that is Vintage Vinyl. And to all my friends—there are too many of you to name—thank you for every shared song, drink, and laugh. I am still my best self when I'm with you.

To my Island people: Emily Cavanagh and Sarah Smith, thank you for the near decade of writing community. Your support has been integral to the creation of this book. To everyone at the Martha's Vineyard Public Charter School, teaching alongside you is among the greatest gifts I've been given. To Shannon Rynd-Ray, thank you for your photographic brilliance and the sharing of raising our girls. To Ann Smith, Justen Ahren, and the entire Featherstone/Noepe family, thank you for believing in me and for working with me to continue to create a space for writing and writers.

Finally, to my powerful, extraordinary daughters, Isabella, Delilah, and Zora. Please know that belonging to you is the most important thing in my life. I could never have done this if you didn't love and support me the way you do. I hope I make you as proud as you make me.

And, of course, to Chi. This book wouldn't exist without your love. Thank you for knowing me and letting me know you. Thank you for the dinners, late night stories, games of dominoes, and love songs. Most of all, thank you for still being the boy in the basement to my girl in the attic. I have always been, and forever will be, yours.

MATHEA MORAIS grew up in St. Louis, Missouri. She has a degree in Literature from NYU and worked in music journalism for many years. Her work has appeared in *Trace Urban Magazine, The New Engagement, Slush Pile Magazine, Arts & Ideas,* and *Anti-Heroin Chic.* She is the Director of the Noepe Center for Literary Arts on Martha's Vineyard and has taught creative writing to children and young adults for over fifteen years. She lives with her husband, her three daughters, and, of course, a beloved dog.